# DANGEROUSLY CHARMING

## DEBORAH BLAKE

BERKLEY SENSATION
New York

BERKLEY SENSATION
Published by Berkley
An imprint of Penguin Random House LLC
375 Hudson Street, New York, New York 10014

ISBN: 9781101987162

First Edition: October 2016

Printed in the United States of America
1   3   5   7   9   10   8   6   4   2

Cover art by Tony Mauro
Cover design by Sarah Oberrender
Book design by Kristin del Rosario

*To Leis,*
*who believed in me*

# ACKNOWLEDGMENTS

All books are difficult to write, in one way or another. This one took it to a whole new level, and probably wouldn't have made it to print at all if it hadn't been for the gallant efforts and stalwart help of a few people. My beloved and brilliant agent, Elaine Spencer, and my first editor, Leis Pedersen, were instrumental in pointing out (as gently as possible) where I had gone horribly wrong, and then helping me to figure out a way out of the hole I'd dug for myself and my characters. Bethany, my current editor, came onboard mid-book and finished the digging. Numerous first readers, including the indispensible Judy Levine, guided me through the ensuing quagmires. But my biggest thanks go to the heroic efforts of Sierra Newburn (researcher and brainstormer extraordinaire and my go-to lady for all things fairy tale and riddle related) and Kari Blackmoore, who read the manuscript at the last possible minute at the highest possible speed and helped me figure out the rest of the answers. Without Sierra and Kari, this book would undoubtedly never have seen the light of Day. (See what I did there?) My gratitude is beyond measure.

# CHAPTER 1

**MIKHAIL** Day was rather enjoying the sound of the rain on the metal roof as he read by the warmth of the crackling red-and-orange fire. Rain was one of the things he liked about this side of the doorway; it never rained in the Otherworld, although there was always plenty of moisture to balance the heat of eternal sunless summers.

He'd always taken pleasure in the time he spent in the Otherworld, that enchanted land where the paranormal folks had gone to live permanently after retreating from the encroachment of Humans. But after six months spent there healing from the horrific wounds he and his fellow Riders had suffered at the hands of the deranged former Baba Yaga Brenna, he'd grown tired of the perfect weather and the pitying looks and had retreated to the anonymity and imperfection of the mundane world.

The Queen's generous parting gift of a sack full of gold coins (almost certainly not the kind that disappeared the day after you used them) had purchased him a year's rent in this rustic cabin deep in the woods of the Adirondack Mountains. Built to provide an austere but comfortable writing space for an author who'd then discovered he couldn't create amid that much quiet, the cabin was miles from the nearest road and as private as Day could wish. The coins had bought him plenty of supplies, but most of all, they'd gotten him what he truly wanted: nobody else around.

Much had changed in his life in the last year. Brenna had stolen more than his immortality with her torture; she'd stolen his abiding self-confidence, and his identity as a Rider. He couldn't bear to be around his brothers, his fellow Riders, who had lost all that and more because of his error in judgment. Mikhail had no idea what he was going to do with the rest of his now-limited life, with the exception of one vow: he was *never, ever* going to help a damsel in distress again. The last time had cost him too much.

A piece of wood snapped and sparked in the fireplace just as thunder crashed overhead. May in the Adirondacks could be chilly and volatile, but it was still better than being out in the world. Mikhail gave a small sigh of satisfaction as he turned the page of his book, an amusing mystery he'd picked up in his travels that took place in the imaginary town of Caerphilly, Virginia, a setting as far removed from witches and faeries and magical mayhem as was Humanly possible, and where all the murders happened to people he didn't care about.

*Let the rain fall and the wind blow*, he thought, taking a sip from a glass of deep red merlot. He might not know what he was going to do with the rest of his life, but for now, doing nothing was just fine with him.

**JENNA** Quinlan stared down at the inert mass that a few minutes before had been her beloved if ancient Dodge Colt and said a rude word. Then said a couple more, just in case the gods hadn't heard her the first time.

Not that they seemed to have been listening lately. It hadn't been a good few weeks.

First there had been the shocking, impossible news from her doctor. Then the fight with her now-ex-boyfriend, followed rapidly by being fired by her now-ex-boss.

She'd gone into work a couple of days after her talk with Stu to find her belongings in a box on the top of her desk and Mitchell standing next to it with his arms crossed and a miserable expression on his face.

"Sorry, Jenna," was all he'd said. "Stu and me, we go way back. And his father's company sends us a lot of business." He'd handed her a pathetic severance check and the box with her Hello Kitty coffee mug perched on top, and that had been that. It wasn't as though she'd loved the job; being a personal assistant wasn't as glamorous as it sounded. But after the first two blows, the third one practically knocked her off her feet.

She'd spent days calling around town looking for work, only to find that Stu's influence had preceded her there in every instance. Then she started feeling as though she was being watched.

It was subtle, at first. A glimpse of the same unfamiliar face at the store, an anonymous figure lurking in the shadows across the street from her apartment. One day she came home to find scratches around the edges of her locks and signs that someone had been inside, rifling through her belongings. She had no idea what on earth anyone thought they were going to find, but she suspected Stu's less-than-delicate hand there too.

Jenna hoped it was Stu. The alternative was a lot more frightening.

In the middle of the night, she'd woken up with the memory of her grandmother's voice ringing in her ears. "When it happens," the older woman had said, holding on to Jenna's hand with surprising strength for someone with one foot in the grave, "and it will, don't stay in the cities. *She* can find you in the city. Too many eyes and whispering tongues that no one can see. Run to the woods, far away from everything

and everyone you ever knew. Run, girl, run as far and as fast
as you can."

**THE** next morning, Jenna had taken what little money she
had in savings, grabbed the go bag she always kept on hand
more from paranoia than any true belief that she'd ever need
to use it, and taken off toward upstate New York. There was
a cabin deep in the woods there that belonged to a distant
cousin. Jenna's grandmother had inherited it long ago, and
passed it on to Jenna when she died. Jenna had never even
been to the place. But under the current circumstances, that
was a good thing, since no one would think to look for her
there . . . assuming she could actually find it. In theory, all
Jenna had to do was follow the handwritten map the cousin
had given her grandmother, hike in with her bag of supplies
(including her grandmother's journals, which contained everything the older woman had known or guessed or re-
searched), and hole up until she could figure out the answers
she needed.

Her world might have been rocked on its axis, but Jenna
Quinlan wasn't just going to curl up in a corner and give in to
fate. She was going to run and hide, yes, but only so she could
fight another day. Of course, that plan would have worked better
if her transmission hadn't seized on this back road in the middle
of nowhere. One minute she'd been driving along, watching
the rampant green underbrush for errant deer and other unexpected hazards, and the next, her poor car had given one last
agonized *thunk grind whine* and then slid lightly into a gully
on the side of the road, its steering completely frozen and the
engine as dead as the life she'd left behind.

Jenna banged her head gently against the steering wheel a
few times, but not surprisingly, that neither fixed the car nor
improved her general attitude. Wind whispered in through the
open driver's-side window, bringing with it the luxuriant scents
of late spring in the mountains, barely touched by the intrusive

burnt-rubber aroma of technology self-destructing. Birds flew by, singing their coquettish flirtations in alternating keys. Jenna had never felt so alone in her life.

And yet she wasn't truly alone, was she? Not anymore. And that fact meant she didn't have the luxury of sitting in her car and crying, as much as she might feel like it. Doing nothing was no longer an option.

**"THERE'S** no mistake, Ms. Quinlan. You're eight weeks pregnant. These things happen," the doctor had said, not unsympathetically. She supposed he'd used those words with other bewildered and slightly indignant twenty-nine-year-old women, all of whom said much the same things as she had.

"But I am so careful," Jenna had protested anyway, knowing there was no point but needing to say it out loud. "I'm on the pill, and I use condoms, *and* I watch the calendar. Plus my current boyfriend has a vasectomy, for God's sake! It's not possible."

The doctor leaned back on his stool, his golf tan dark against the pristine white of his coat. Brown hair starting to go gray at the sideburns added to the professional air he projected. Jenna had never seen him before she'd gone into the clinic that day, so she had no idea if he was as competent as he seemed. It didn't matter, since the test results couldn't be argued away.

"No form of birth control is one hundred percent effective," he said, looking at the clock on the wall and not at her. "Vasectomies do fail, although not often. Yes, the odds were against it, but as I said, these things do happen." He finally met her eyes and gave her a tentative smile. "I understand that you hadn't intended to get pregnant, but at your age, you might want to consider that it will only become more difficult to do so later on, should you decide you want to have children. Perhaps you could look at this as a miracle, rather than a disaster?"

Jenna had swallowed down bitter irony and just shaken her head instead. The doctor could utter any platitudes he liked, but she knew what really lay at the heart of this so-called miracle: curses simply couldn't be thwarted.

And as curses went, this one was a doozy.

She sat in the car for a moment or two more, remembering that day when everything changed. Then she squared her shoulders, grabbed her duffel bag out of the trunk, slung her purse across her chest, and set off. According to the map, she couldn't be more than ten or twelve miles away from the cabin. A manageable hike in decent weather.

When the rain started falling an hour later, she almost laughed.


**AT** first, Day mistook the pounding on the door for a part of the storm. After all, there was no reason for him to expect visitors, not out here in the middle of nowhere. But when he finally got up to answer the persistent knocks, he got the sinking feeling that the storm had come to him.

A bedraggled woman stood on his doorstep in the pouring rain, and his first impulse was to slam the door in her face.

But she had clearly come as far as she could; her pale face was twisted in pain, and she shivered convulsively beneath a denim jacket that was as soaking wet as the rest of her. Long black strands of hair hung down in twisted ribbons like seaweed in the vanishing daylight, reminding him of a sea creature he'd once dated briefly in his more adventurous youth.

Mostly, though, it was her eyes that captured and held him: a strange shade of icy blue, large and wide and luminous with trepidation, surrounded by long dark lashes decorated by tiny droplets of rain. A duffel bag dragged in the mud behind her and an incongruously cheerful Hello Kitty purse was slung over one drooping shoulder.

He couldn't send her back out into the storm. But that didn't mean he had to be nice about it; Mikhail Day, the charming Rider, was dead and gone. He was someone completely different now, and happy to be so.

"Lost?" he asked briskly, his own voice sounding strange in his ears after months of silence.

The woman blinked water out of her eyes. "Not at all," she said. "This is the Holiday Inn, right?"

"Very funny." Mikhail reluctantly held the door open a little wider. "No holidays here. No inn either. But I suppose you can come in until the storm passes."

The woman looked justifiably unimpressed by his less-than-gracious welcome, but she walked through the door anyway, parking her duffel bag on the mat next to it along with her soggy sneakers, and gazing around with a mixture of caution and curiosity.

Day knew what she saw: a simple one-room cabin built with clean lines and simple elegance, but no frills. The large double-sided fireplace heated the kitchen space on one side and the bigger living area on the other, its warmth barely reaching to the neatly made double bed in the loft space overhead. Almost everything was crafted out of wood, the floors and ceiling, walls and cabinets. The only color came from the royal blue comforter on the bed and the subtler blues and greens of the couch and recliner. All of it had come with the cabin when he rented it; only a few treasured keepsakes belonged to him, arrayed atop the fireplace mantle, or tucked away out of sight in a small ebony chest.

"Um, are you here by yourself?" the woman asked. One hand hovered over a pocket of her purse, and he wondered idly if she had some kind of weapon in there. Not that he cared.

Day sighed. "Not anymore. Look, you're perfectly safe here, if that's what you're worried about. Why don't you take off your jacket and hang it over the kitchen chair nearest the fire so it can dry. I'll go fetch you a towel." He looked at her again. "Or two."

She did as he suggested, limping noticeably as she crossed the floor to reach the other section of the room. After she placed her jacket on the chair, she turned to stand in front of the fire, holding her hands out gratefully to the warmth.

"Did you hurt yourself?" Day asked, not bothering to try and sound like he cared.

The woman nodded, spattering rainwater over the polished wood floor. "I was doing okay, but then a couple of miles back I slipped on some wet leaves and twisted my ankle. It's swelling up pretty nicely, or I would have kept going. I'm sorry to bother you. I'll wrap it in something and warm up a little, and then I'll be on my way again."

*Right.* Day might not be charming anymore, but even he wasn't going to send a woman out into the pouring rain as night fell. For one thing, he rather liked the bears that lived in the neighborhood, and he'd prefer not to give them a temptation they might regret later.

"We'll see" was all he said, tossing her the towels and letting her use them to dry her long hair and the worst of the wetness on her clothes. Finally he relented and fetched a pair of loose linen pants with a drawstring waist and a long-sleeved cotton shirt—both of them a dark green, not white. Never white. Not anymore.

"You're dripping all over my floors," he said briskly. "Put these on and we'll dry yours by the fire. It won't take long."

She hesitated for a minute then took the clothing, waiting for him to turn his back before dropping what she was wearing to the ground with a sodden *plop*.

Day's mouth quirked up when he turned around again. She was slim and tall for a Human woman, probably five nine or so. But he was six three, with broad shoulders and long arms; his clothing made her look like an adorable, slightly damp child.

No, not adorable. Just silly. At least that's what he told himself. Either way, it was hard not to laugh. Fortunately, his unwelcome guest clearly had a good sense of humor, and grinned back at him as if she could tell how ridiculous she looked.

"I have clothes in my bag," she said. "Unfortunately, I'm

pretty sure they're almost as wet as the ones I was wearing. So thanks for lending me these."

"Better that than to have you ruin my floors," he said. "Do you want to tell me what you're doing up here in the middle of the woods?" He gazed at her milky white skin, dark hair, and wide eyes. "If you're looking for the seven dwarfs, they live in the next forest over."

"Thanks, but I prefer my men on the tall side." She looked up at him, as if reconsidering her words. "And, you know, friendly."

"That doesn't answer my question."

"I know," she said brightly. "Got any tea?"

Day rolled his eyes but put the kettle on top of the stove anyway. "How about a name?"

"Sure," the woman said. "Steve."

Day glared at her, his blond brows drawn together. "Very funny," he said. "I meant, what is your name? Or should I just call you Snow White?"

The woman's teeth chattered together, and she moved closer to the fire. "I'll tell you what: if you give me that cup of tea, you can call me anything you want."

Day poured the hot water into a pot filled with tea leaves and let them steep for a few minutes before letting the dark, aromatic liquid slide into a mug. Then he held it up in the air, just a tantalizing couple of inches out of reach.

"Jenna," she said. "Jenna Quinlan. And you?"

He handed her the mug, smirking a little. "Mikhail Day. Nice to meet you, Jenna Quinlan."

"Uh-huh," she said, not believing it. "Did you say Michael?"

"Sure," Mikhail said. *New life, new name. Why not?* "Michael Day. You can call me Mick."

As Jenna sat drinking her tea, her chair pulled as close to the fire as she could get without actually being inside it, Mikhail rooted around in one of the kitchen cabinets to find his first aid kit. What with one thing and another, he and the other Riders tended to get a bit banged up as they traveled around assisting the Baba Yagas. Banged up, blown up, and occasionally stabbed just a little. Especially huge Alexei, who liked fighting and drinking almost as much as Mikhail liked women (and fighting) and Gregori liked philosophy (and fighting).

He suppressed a sigh as he pulled out the supplies he'd need to wrap Jenna's ankle. Even with their supernaturally fast healing, they'd often had to resort to the bandages and salves that Barbara, the herbalist among the Baba Yagas, had supplied them with. Now that he wasn't immortal, Day had no idea if his powers of rapid healing remained or not. But it probably didn't matter, since the Riders were Riders no more and the Baba Yagas would have to manage without them from now on.

Jenna's eyes widened at his muttered cursing. "Is it that bad?" she asked.

Mikhail shook his head. "Sorry, no, I was thinking of something else." He turned his attention to the slim ankle and shapely foot he held in his hands. Other than the obvious swelling and redness, there didn't seem to be anything wrong with her ankle. Or the rest of her, not that he was looking.

"It doesn't seem to be broken," he said. "Just a bad sprain. I'll wrap it for you; that ought to help. But you're not going to be able to put much weight on it for the next couple of days."

Her porcelain complexion turned even paler at his pronouncement. But she sat up straight in the wooden chair, her chin raised defiantly. "I'll be fine," she said. "I'm tougher than I look."

*That might be*, Mikhail thought, as he glanced from her duffel bag to her mud-caked sneakers to her lightweight jacket, all dripping wetly onto his floors. *But you're sure not equipped for a long hike through the woods. Who or what are you running away from?*

Then he reminded himself sharply that such things weren't his business anymore. Hopefully, she was as tough as she said, since she was going to get no help from him beyond a bandage and a place to warm up for a night. He was out of the rescuing business for good. Truth was, the way things ended up when he tried to help, she'd probably be better off with the bears.

**JENNA** tried not to wince as Mick wound the bandage tightly around her injured ankle. His large hands were gentle but professional, his expression grim and his eyes shuttered as he focused on his task. He clearly knew what he was doing, but just as obviously would rather not be tending to her at all. She didn't know whether to be embarrassed, indignant, or alarmed, so she vacillated among all three.

With his attention turned elsewhere, she had a minute to take a good look at her reluctant host. When she'd stumbled in from the storm, all she'd taken in was a general impression of intimidating size and blond hair. Now that she had time to absorb more details, she discovered that the hair was long and straight, hanging loose past his shoulders like a fall of liquid sunlight. His eyes, what she could see of them, were the blue of a crystalline lake, with slightly bushy eyebrows above. His position, kneeling at her feet, made his shoulders look even broader than she'd thought at first glance, and strong, muscular forearms dusted with light hairs were revealed by the rolled-up sleeves of his simple blue cotton shirt.

In truth, Jenna thought Michael Day was the handsomest man she'd ever seen. Too bad he was also the rudest.

Still, she reminded her rapidly beating heart, she wasn't exactly in the market for a guy anyway. Not only had she just gotten out of a relationship, but she was on the run from a faery curse. And twelve weeks pregnant, of course. That would probably have kept her from being interested even if it weren't for the other issues and Mick's clear lack of any social graces whatsoever.

Whatever. She wasn't sure if he was shy or just a

woman-hater, but he had a dry roof over his head, and hopefully some food, since she hadn't eaten since the questionable
diner breakfast she'd bolted down—and barely held on to—
that morning. If it had been just her, she might have kept
going, ankle or no ankle, but she had someone else depending
on her now. She'd just have to hope he was simply a grumpy
hermit and not an axe murderer. She had Mace in her bag and
had been taking kickboxing for years, but somehow she didn't
think this guy would be stopped by anything short of a
grenade.

Part of her wished she could just hobble back to her car and
keep going within its familiar confines. The realistic part knew
that even if she had money for a new transmission, which she
didn't, and even if it made sense to put one in a car that was
worth at best five hundred dollars if you included the duct tape,
she didn't dare run the risk of attracting attention by calling
in a tow truck and a mechanic. Or have the time to waste while
she waited for them to dig up parts for a car that hadn't been
made in over a decade.

No, her only option now was to hunker down with her
reluctant host until the rain stopped and she could put enough
weight on the twisted ankle to go find her cousin's cabin. If
she couldn't run, she'd limp as fast as she could. Jenna put
one hand protectively over her stomach. She might not have
gotten pregnant intentionally, knowing as she did what it
would mean if such a thing happened. But now that it had,
she wanted to keep this child safe more than anything in the
world. Whatever it took, no one was getting her baby.

# CHAPTER 2

**DAY** wasn't really asleep—not with some strange woman in his cabin, invading his hard-won solitary space. Mostly he was just lying in bed trying *not to remember*, when a small whimper from the couch below brought everything slamming back with the power of a runaway freight train, carrying him along helplessly into a dark tunnel of despair.

The tiny sound faded away without being followed by another; probably the woman having a bad dream about whatever it was that had set her on the run. But it was too late for Day. That small noise brought back echoes of others, and they brought along smells and sights and feelings he'd spent many long months trying to leave behind him.

He knew that was never going to happen.

Even now, the flashback grew in strength until cave walls seemed to form around him, replacing warm and sturdy wood with dank and dripping rock, redolent with the odor of pain and fear and the acrid, caustic mix that had churned and bubbled in Brenna's iron cauldron.

The smell had been horrific, worming its way into his nostrils so that he'd still been catching stray whiffs long after they'd finally escaped from the cave where he and his brother Riders had been held captive. The stink of their own filth had been the worst of all, coated as it was with the copper tang of blood, shed and re-shed for the monstrous potion the former Baba Yaga had labored over at such a great cost to him and his friends, all in an effort to attain an impossible eternal life.

But the sound of Jenna's whimper had mostly triggered his memories of lying in the muck, hopeless and helpless as he listened to Gregori and Alexei try to suppress their moans of pain. Pain that he had caused. Pain that none of them would ever be able to forget, no matter how much their bodies healed outwardly. He'd only ever had a fraction of what most people would consider to be a family—his brother Riders, and the Baba Yagas. And he'd let them all down.

Shudders racked his body as the memories poured over him once again, a tsunami against which there was no way to swim to safety. Safety was an illusion, as much as the cave walls that seemed to surround him. When the torture continued in your own mind, there was no place to run, no place to hide. All he could do was endure, and wait for the blessed light of morning.

**WHEN** Jenna woke up early the next morning, it took a minute before she could figure out where she was. Rain still streamed down the windows and intermittent lightning flashes through a skylight overhead showed her the shadowy insides of a peaceful cabin, silent other than the rumbling of thunder outside and an almost musical snoring coming from the bed up in the loft.

The couch she was lying on was reasonably comfortable and the soft woven blanket covering her was warm, but the pressure on her bladder was too strong to allow her to lie there and enjoy them. She swung her legs over and put her feet on the floor, but when she went to stand up, her ankle wouldn't hold her weight and she fell face-first onto the braided throw rug with a *thud* and a muffled "*Shit.*"

Two large bare feet appeared in front of her nose. "Problem?" an amused bass voice asked.

"Not at all," Jenna said to the rug. "I was just communing with the floor. It's a spiritual thing. I try and do it every morning."

"Uh-huh." Mick scooped her up as if she weighed about as much as the blanket. "I assume you have to use the outhouse?" He started walking toward the door before she could protest, not that she really had a lot of choice. For one thing, the guy was huge. For another, she really had to pee. Being pregnant came with all sorts of unexpected annoyances.

She'd managed to shuffle outside by herself last night, although her host had insisted on lending her a strong right arm to lean on and carrying a lantern to light her way. But this morning the ankle seemed worse instead of better, so she forced herself to endure the indignity of being carried out to the tidy little wooden shed, although thankfully she was able to get in and out on her own, hopping on one foot. The leather coat he'd tossed over her shoulders covered her like a tarp.

"I still can't believe you have an outhouse," she said indignantly after she was done and Mick had taken his turn, then carried her back into the cabin and plopped her down at the kitchen table. "The rest of this place is so nice."

Mick shrugged, his broad back turned to her as he coaxed the fire back into life from embers of last night's logs. It might be May, but here in the woods the mornings were still brisk.

"You're lucky there's a pump to bring running water into the house," he said calmly. "Most cabins around here don't even have that. Besides, it beats sleeping in the woods."

She couldn't argue with that. A sudden sinking feeling told her that the temporary refuge she was heading toward wasn't likely to be as comfortable as she'd originally assumed.

Nor was she in any position to argue when he insisted on

making breakfast. After all, she couldn't exactly make it herself, and despite her somewhat unsettled stomach, she was starving. These days she was either starving or so nauseous she couldn't even look at food. She felt like a yo-yo.

At least her own clothes were dry, so after they ate she was able to change back into something that fit. Mostly. She tugged surreptitiously at the waistband on her pants and wished she'd had time to do some shopping before she'd left the last large city behind her. It was early days yet, but she could see the handwriting on the wall. Maybe she'd be able to convince Mick to lend her his drawstring pants when she moved on.

Speaking of which, she tried again to put weight on her bad leg, leaning against the couch this time so she didn't end up on the floor.

"The more you stress it, the longer it will take to heal," Mick said from behind the book he was reading while she changed clothes, his eyes still on the page. Jenna didn't know how he always seemed to know where she was and what she was doing, and it annoyed her to no end.

"How long do you think it will take before I can walk on it?" she asked, trying not to sound like a cranky child. "I can't just stay here forever."

"I'm that bad to be around, eh?" he said, one bushy eyebrow raised. But she thought she caught a glimpse of something that looked like hurt in his eyes.

"Don't worry, I'll be happy to see the back of you too," Mick added. "Give it another day or two, the storm will pass, and I'll carve you a walking stick and shove you out the door. Now shut up, will you? I'm trying to read."

Or maybe not.

Her host was certainly a marked contrast to Stu, her former boyfriend. Stu was polished and civilized, always polite even when he was being critical of her clothes or car or apartment, none of which ever quite measured up to his standards. Of course, as one of *the* Wadsworths, his standards were rather lofty. She'd never been quite sure what he saw in a quiet PA from a dubious family; they certainly didn't run in the same social circles, and would never have met if Stu hadn't played racquetball three times a week with Jenna's boss.

Unlike Mick's towering height and heart-stopping good looks, Stu was more generically attractive, with brown hair that flopped endearingly over one brow, and eyes that twinkled when he smiled. He could be quite charming, when he bothered to be.

Not a bad guy exactly, Jenna often thought. Just a bit spoiled and self-involved and used to getting things his way. On the other hand, he didn't have much in the way of morals or backbone and was a lot more interested in having fun than contributing to society in any useful way.

Jenna kept trying to convince herself that she was in love with him, since on paper he was the perfect guy, but really, they didn't have much in common. They'd been going out for about a year, and it had started to look like things might get serious, which gave Jenna a funny feeling in her stomach that she'd tried to tell herself was hope.

After all, what woman in her right mind wouldn't want a wealthy, good-looking, pleasant man? And for her, of course, the fact that he'd had a vasectomy and had no interest in children had seemed like a gift from the gods.

Funny about the gods and their gifts, wasn't it?

Now, sitting in a cabin in the woods, trying not to stare at the grumpy blue-eyed wonder studiously ignoring her from across the room, Jenna scanned her emotions for even a modicum of heartache over losing Stu. Like poking at a loose tooth with your tongue, waiting for it to hurt but unable to resist the action anyway, she waited to feel a pang of regret.

All she could find was a sliver of *what if* that didn't bear much resemblance to the prospect of whatever a life shared with Stu would have brought. She'd spent most of her adult existence seeking a way to create a family to replace the one she'd lost, knowing it couldn't be done. Maybe a real relationship was nothing but a fairy tale she told herself, alone in the dark late at night, hugging her arms around herself for an illusion of comfort. If so, she would probably never have found what she was looking for in Stu, no matter how much she'd tried to convince herself otherwise.

Still, she thought, patting her stomach, it wasn't as though he hadn't given her something, even if that parting gift was likely to threaten her heart, her sanity, and maybe even her life.


**THE** next day, the swelling in her ankle was noticeably less and Jenna was able to make her way to the outhouse and back with the promised walking stick, which Mick had carved the evening before as they sat by the fire. Jenna was impressed by his skill and unanticipated artistic ability; she'd expected a simple staff but instead had been presented with a piece of wood almost as tall as she was, carved with detailed fanciful creatures like dragons and tiny sprites and other things she couldn't even identify.

The rain had finally stopped and the daylight hours were warm and pleasant enough to only warrant having the fireplace going at night. She figured that she could soon be back on her way. She was almost, but not quite, sorry.

Despite their occasional moments of détente, Mick was mostly sullen and withdrawn, simply ignoring her presence whenever possible. She still tensed whenever he moved too fast, and she kept the Mace in her pocket at all times. Just because he'd taken care of her didn't mean he couldn't still turn out to be a crazy murdering rapist instead of just a cranky hermit. He clearly couldn't wait to have his solitude back. Which was okay with her—she had a mission to accomplish, and she wasn't getting anywhere sitting on his couch and watching the most gorgeous man in the world read a Donna Andrews mystery.

Today she was determined to make herself useful, so she'd started preparing lunch while Mick was outside chopping wood. Jenna stood for a moment at the window over the sink, still leaning most of her weight on the counter while she gazed out at his strong, manly form, clad in only a pair of jeans and some work boots. The movement of his muscles under his skin as he swung the axe was almost graceful enough to be a dance, and the breeze through the open window brought with it the sharp scent of freshly split wood, and just a hint of tangy sweat.

She took a deep whiff, enjoying the aroma. Which turned out to be a mistake as the outside smells mixed uncomfortably with the tuna salad she'd just put together for their sandwiches. She'd barely been tolerating the canned fish by trying not to breathe too deeply, and now her stomach rebelled, roiling like the ocean during a squall. She just managed to stagger lopsidedly to the doorway before losing the remains of her breakfast all over the ground.

Surprisingly gentle hands held back her hair until she was done and then handed her a pristine white cloth to wipe her mouth with. Day brought her back inside and set her down on the couch—mercifully far from the aggressively smelly tuna—and brought her a glass of water. Then he pulled a chair up and sat in front of her.

"How long have you been sick?" he asked. He glanced over his shoulder at the kitchen, brows pulled together. "I hope I didn't give you food poisoning. I feel fine, but that doesn't mean much, since I have a pretty tough constitution. Do you think it was the eggs I made for breakfast? They seemed okay to me."

Jenna sighed. She'd hoped to be gone before there was any need to have this conversation again. It hadn't gone well the last time, and that was with someone who supposedly knew and loved her. On the bright side, since Mick clearly didn't like her much or want her around, hopefully he'd just shrug and send her on her merry way.

"It's not food poisoning," she said, wadding his handkerchief up in a ball between her hands. "And I'm not sick."

"Of course you're sick," he said, a trifle impatiently. "You just threw up all over my front steps."

"Yeah, well, sorry about that. I'll try not to do it again."

"That would be good," Mick said. "But that wasn't my point. You're obviously ill. Maybe I should take you down into the nearest town to see a doctor. I have to warn you, though, it is quite a haul, and my transportation is pretty basic. It may be kind of a rough ride if you're not feeling well."

Jenna's stomach gave another heave, but this one was due more to panic than to morning sickness. "NO," she said more sharply than she'd intended to. "I can't go into town. It isn't necessary anyway. I'm not sick. I'm pregnant."


*YOU* have got *to be kidding me,* Day thought. "No," he said. "Hell no."

Jenna blinked at him. "You're telling me I'm not pregnant? Because I'm pretty sure I am."

"Oh, I believe you," Day said bitterly. "I was just talking to the universe."

"Uh-huh. And do you do that a lot?"

"Only when provoked," he said.

Jenna looked a little concerned, one hand sliding into her pocket and her eyes going to the door and back as if trying to figure out if she could make it outside if it turned out he was a madman. "I don't know what kind of a reaction I expected," she said. "But this isn't exactly it. I don't know whether to be insulted or alarmed that you consider the fact that I'm pregnant to be a personal affront from the universe. After all, I'm the one who is pregnant."

"And you showed up on my doorstep," Day said. "In the middle of nowhere."

"Well, it was the middle of nowhere," Jenna pointed out in a reasonable tone. "Yours was the only doorstep there was. I didn't do it on purpose."

"Which?" he asked. "Show up on my doorstep or wind up pregnant?"

She blinked those big, icy blue eyes at him again. "Both, actually."

"Well, that was careless of you," Day said, knowing that he sounded rude and cold and not knowing how to stop. It felt like the gods were taunting him: taking away his ability to help those he was supposed to, and then mocking his vow to stay away from damsels in distress by having one arrive literally at his door. After everything that had happened, he didn't think it was too much to ask to just be left alone. He didn't want anything to do with this woman or her problems. Clearly she'd brought them on herself, and she could solve them herself.

"Careless?" Jenna repeated. "It was careless of me?" She made a choking noise that surprised him by turning into laughter. Gales of laughter, followed by more laughter, so that every time she came close to stopping she'd look at him and say, "*careless*," and then be off again. Eventually, she subsided into hiccups, wiping her eyes with the back of one hand.

"Sorry," she said, biting her lip. "But honestly, that is the least appropriate word to apply to me. I used every form of birth control known to man, plus the guy I was dating had a vasectomy. I was anything but careless. Not that it is any of your business."

"Oh." Day didn't quite know how to respond to that. "Then how did you end up pregnant?" he asked.

Jenna looked down at the now-twisted lump of cloth in her hands, dark lashes hiding her eyes. "You wouldn't believe me if I told you."

"Try me."

She raised her head and stared at him defiantly. "Fine, then. No amount of birth control worked because I'm under a curse."

*A curse. Of course there would be a curse.* Day got up

from his chair, walked over to the door, opened it, and stepped outside to yell at the sky, "What part of *NO* did you not understand?!"

Then he went back to his seat and said in a calm voice, "So, what kind of curse? Evil witch? Offended faery? Enchanted object?"

Jenna's jaw dropped and she tried to speak a couple of times before words actually came out. "Uh, offended faery. You . . . you believe me?"

Day sighed. "I do."

"But why?" Clearly she'd been braced for ridicule or skepticism; it seemed she didn't know how to handle his easy acceptance of her circumstances. "Why would you?"

He shrugged. "Let's just say that I have some familiarity with the veracity of certain fairy tales." As in, he'd spent most of his life as part of a particular Russian one. The Riders had always been associated with the Baba Yagas, and the stories about them had been around for a very, very long time. Some of the stories were even true, more or less.

"So you believe me when I say I'm cursed," Jenna said in a small voice, and then surprised him by bursting into tears as copious and unexpected as her laughter had been a few minutes before.

Day patted his pockets desperately for a handkerchief before remembering that he'd already given her the one he'd been carrying. He loped across the room to pull another one from a drawer and then handed it to her. He couldn't stand the sight of a woman crying; it made him want to punch or stab whatever or whomever had caused it. Which might be a little difficult in this case.

"Sorry, sorry," she said, snuffling in a way that shouldn't have been adorable and yet somehow was. "Hormones are evil. Just ignore me. I'm okay, really."

"You don't seem okay," Day said doubtfully. "I didn't mean to upset you." Well, maybe he had, but not to the point of *crying*, for goodness' sake.

"I'm not upset," Jenna said. "The opposite. I've been carrying this damned curse around my whole life, and since my mom and grandmother died I haven't had anyone I could talk to about it. The couple of times I tried telling people I considered friends, they either laughed at me or thought I was crazy. I eventually learned not to tell anyone. I feel . . . lighter somehow, having someone else who knows."

"That's great. But I can't help you," Day said briskly. "I believe you, but that doesn't make it my problem."

Jenna scowled at him. "Did I ask you to help? I don't think I did. I just said I was glad you believed me, that's all. God, you're an even bigger jerk than my ex-boyfriend, and that takes some doing."

It was nice to know he'd accomplished *something* today, anyway. "I'm going to go chop some more wood," he said, getting up and heading for the door. "Don't worry about lunch. I'll finish making it when I'm done."

And then, like the big, strong hero he was, he bolted for the outside as if the devil was behind him, carrying a pitchfork with Day's name on it in blazing letters.

# CHAPTER 3

**JENNA** felt like she was on a roller coaster, and not just because of her out-of-control hormones. She stared blankly at the doorway, through which she could see Mick chopping wood as if he had a personal grudge against each log. The man clearly had baggage. And not only didn't like women, but hated the idea of babies too. Swell.

She sighed and got up to hobble across the room to her duffel bag, now only a tiny bit damp after sitting next to the fireplace for a couple of nights. Her clothes were completely dry, so she packed them all, folding each piece as carefully and methodically as if it were a puzzle piece that had to be slotted precisely into its own designated space.

If only her life could be arranged as neatly. And the puzzle that would save her baby could be solved by simply rearranging things. The truth was, she had no idea where to start, other than with the riddle that held the secret to breaking the curse, and her grandmother's journals, which contained the other woman's lifetime of searching—and failing—to find the answer.

Of all the women in Jenna's family, her grandmother had come the closest to solving the riddle. But even she had been forced to give up a child in her turn, as did her daughter, Jenna's mother, after her. Jenna was determined to escape their fate, even if it meant spending the next six months finding some way to survive in the woods while she went over the riddle and the journals until the answer somehow became clear to her.

A gigantic yawn escaped from her lips as she set the bag down behind the couch. The book on pregnancy she'd bought before she left town had said that women in their first trimester were often tired, but it hadn't prepared her to be wide-awake one moment and ready to nod off the next.

Mick walked in from outside just in time to catch her in another yawn.

"Not my usual effect on women," he said, smiling at her. It seemed as though taking his tensions out on poor innocent pieces of wood had helped his mood.

Either way, she was relieved. Jenna got that he had come out here to be by himself and then she'd shown up and thrown herself on his mercy, strained ankle and all. He'd made it pretty clear he was just counting the minutes until he could have his privacy back, but for both their sakes, it would be easier if the little time they had left together wasn't spent with him being grumpy and bent out of shape.

"I was just packing up my stuff," she said. "I figure if I rest my ankle for another couple of hours, I'll be able to leave this afternoon."

Mick nodded. "You're probably right. As long as the place you're heading to isn't too far from here. Did you ever figure out where it was?" He asked the question idly as he went into the kitchen to finish making the lunch she'd failed at so miserably.

Jenna yawned again. "I'm pretty sure it is a couple of miles farther down this road. If you can call this deer track you live on a road."

"Does your hiding out in the forest have something to do with this curse of yours?" he asked, plopping a plate of sandwiches on the table. Jenna noticed he'd exchanged the tuna for peanut butter and jam on whole grain instead, for which she was grateful. She thought, not for the first time, that Mick was a strange mix of consideration and kindness and what seemed like deliberate coldness and cruelty.

"It does," Jenna said. "There is a riddle that can break the curse. My grandmother tried her whole life to find the answer, but like all the women in our family before her, she failed. I've got all her notes and I'm hoping that if I can buy myself some time, I can figure out the answer." She tried nibbling her sandwich, but she couldn't keep her eyes open. "Sorry," she said, yawning again. "I think I might take a nap and then eat my lunch later, if you don't mind."

"I don't care one way or the other," he said, devouring most of a sandwich in a single bite. "Go ahead and use my bed in the loft if you like. It's a lot more comfortable than the couch."

There he went again. Rude in one sentence, thoughtful the next. If pregnancy was a roller coaster, being around Michael Day was like a trip through the house of mirrors. It was hard to say which man was real and which wasn't. Either way, she was happy to take him up on his offer.

**JENNA** wasn't sure how long she'd been asleep when the sound of knocking woke her up. For a minute she thought Mick was out chopping wood again, but then she heard him mutter, "Seriously? Is there a neon WELCOME sign outside my house that I don't know about?" from underneath her as he stomped to the door in his bare feet.

Jenna was debating whether or not to get up and go downstairs when she heard a musical voice say, "Mikhail Day! What are *you* doing here?" She froze, flattening herself to the bed. As far as she knew, she'd never heard the voice before, but something about it sent cold chills down her spine.

"I live here, Zilya," Mick said, sounding about as happy to see this new visitor as he had been to see Jenna that first night. "But I might ask you the same thing. You're a long way from home. And as I recall, the wilderness isn't exactly your style."

The woman he called Zilya let out a chiming laugh that sounded like bells. "Dear me, no. I much prefer civilization, if you can call anything on this side of the doorway civilized. I suppose Paris is quite nice, all things considered."

"Then perhaps you should go there," Mick said rudely. "I'm not entertaining these days."

Upstairs, Jenna stuffed the edge of the pillow into her mouth to keep from crying out. She might not know the voice, but the name had been etched into her brain since she was old enough to be told the stories. Zilya was the name of the faery who had cursed her family and stolen her older brother. What were the odds that there were two women with that name? And *why* did it seem as though Mick knew her?

Panic sent waves of adrenaline flooding through her system, making her heart beat fast and her legs want to run, run, run. Instead, she pressed herself even deeper into the soft bed and prayed that her temporary savior wouldn't turn out to be in league with the one person in the world she feared the most.

**MIKHAIL** stifled a sigh. He supposed the Queen had sent someone to check up on him, although why she'd chosen Zilya, he couldn't imagine. They knew each other, of course. The royal court was small enough, and all those who came and went lived long enough that sooner or later you got to know everyone, at least superficially.

Day had even flirted with the faery at the occasional ball or festive event, but she was a little too sharp edged for his tastes. He went more for cuddly blondes. Or passionate redheads. Or agreeable brunettes. In truth, his conquests were many and his women eclectic, over the centuries. But Zilya had never appealed to him.

Not that she wasn't attractive enough; all the faery people tended to be tall and beautiful and graceful. She had short silver hair that curled around her head like an undeserved halo, bright inquisitive eyes like a crow, and always wore clothes that flowed around her model-thin form as if they were wafting on an unseen breeze. Beautiful, but too cold to be called pretty. An unlikely choice for a nursemaid or whatever else it was the Queen had in mind.

"It is kind of you to stop by," Day said, still standing in the doorway and pointedly not welcoming her in. "But you can return to the Otherworld and inform the Queen that I am quite well and have no need of any assistance. Or company."

Zilya shook her head, making the silver curls bounce. "My dear White Rider, I have no idea what you are talking about. The Queen did not send me."

Mikhail thought about correcting her; he was no Rider, not anymore. But he decided not to waste his breath. "If the Queen didn't send you," he asked instead, "then what are you doing here?"

"Ah," Zilya said. "I've misplaced something, and I was looking for it. Some*one*, in point of fact."

"Here?" Mikhail glanced around at the endless woods that surrounded his cabin. "Really. Here." He had a bad feeling in the pit of his stomach, but he kept his face impassive. Centuries of practice helped with such things.

"Well, clearly I was misled," the faery said waspishly. "Magic. So unreliable." She sighed, sounding put out. "There is something that is owed to me by a Human. You know how it is. I seem to have lost track of it. Her."

"How careless of you," Day said. From the cabin behind him, he thought he heard a choking noise. He ignored it. "Whatever made you think you'd find it here?"

"I was tracking the Human using some hairs I stole from a comb I found in her apartment," Zilya admitted. "But clearly they were not her hairs. Or something else went wrong with the spell. I cannot imagine what; it has always worked for me before."

She peered past Day at the simple, unadorned interior of the cabin. "The Human world is so *plain* and so predictably ordinary. I cannot imagine why you would choose to stay here when the Queen invited you to live out the rest of your life in pampered indulgence in the Otherworld."

Day shrugged. "The court was too crowded for me. I prefer it here, where I can be by myself."

Zilya missed his pointed comment, or perhaps, chose to ignore it. Faeries tended to be insensitive at the best of times, and Zilya was even less empathetic than usual for her race.

"But, Day, your life is so short now. Would it not make more sense to come home and be comfortable?"

"I am comfortable enough here, Zilya, although I appreciate your thoughtfulness," he said with sarcasm that also sailed over her fluffy silver head. "Perhaps you had best be off, to find whatever it is you've misplaced, since you clearly won't find it here."

Zilya pouted prettily. "That *is* annoying. But I have time." She smiled up at him, a coy glitter in her dark raven eyes. "Since I'm here already, perhaps we could pass a few hours together. You might find it amusing."

"I might not," Mikhail said, not moving from his stance blocking the door. "I came here to be alone." The fact that he wasn't didn't make the statement itself any less true. "I suggest you go back where you came from. There is nothing for you here."

**PART** of Jenna unclenched as it became clear that Mick wasn't going to turn her over to the faery. The sensible part, which said, *Hide, keep your head down, keep your baby safe.* But whether it was pregnancy hormones or the sheer hatred that had burned in her soul for years, ever since she'd learned who Zilya was and what she'd done to Jenna's family, a howling voice rose up and drowned out anything that resembled rational thought.

Before she even realized she was in motion, Jenna's feet had moved her down the steep stairs to the loft and over the floor, her ankle barely slowing her down as she flew across the room, propelled by decades of rage and fear.

"You *bitch*!" she shrieked, edging past Mick and shoving Zilya so hard the silver-haired woman fell on her ass and slid across the rain-slick yard. "How dare you use your stupid curse to put me in this condition and then follow me to steal my baby?"

Jenna grabbed the first weapon she could find, a long piece of wood lying by the door, and swung it at the faëry, who just barely ducked out of the way. "Haven't you done enough damage already? You've taken the firstborn children from women in every generation of my family, stolen them away from the parents who loved them. My father drank himself to death when I was eight because of you!" Swing. "My mother had a heart attack when I was fourteen!" Swing. Zilya dodged, slipping on the mud, and Jenna went after her again. "The doctor said it was a fluke, but I know what really killed her—a broken heart, caused by *you*!"

Another swing and then a massive hand closed around the end of the stick, just past Jenna's fingers, and twisted it out of her grip. "Jenna," Mick said. "Stop it. That's not going to solve anything."

Zilya stood up, her apple green tunic and billowy emerald-hued wide-legged pants streaked with brown mud and her black eyes flashing. Fury contorted her lovely face as she raised both hands up in front of her, sparks sizzling from dark green nails.

"No, indeed, it will not," she hissed through clenched teeth. "How dare *you*, you puny Human strumpet? How dare you lay hands upon my person? Do you not know with whom you are dealing? I am one of the Fair Folk, as far above your ilk as the moon is above the dirt under my feet. I claim your child because it is my *right*, and nothing you can do will stop that from happening, just as nothing will stop me from making you suffer in the process for the impertinence of your attack upon my person."

Jenna stood frozen in place, hands stretched protectively over her belly as she watched the magic streak from the ends of Zilya's fingers, knowing that the faery was right and there was nothing she could do. Just as her grandmother could do nothing, and her mother could do nothing. Why had she thought her willingness to fight would make her story's ending any different?

# CHAPTER 4

**DAY** didn't stop to think—not about his vow to stay away from women in trouble, not about the fact that he was no longer immortal, and quite likely as vulnerable to Zilya's magic as the Human she had launched it toward. He just moved, stepping in front of Jenna right before the sparkling silver lights could hit her, a noise like a growl slipping out past bared teeth.

Instead, the magical energy impacted against his broad chest and then simply . . . fizzled, and disappeared. He didn't know which of them was more surprised, him or Zilya. From behind him, Jenna gave a tiny squeak, one hand reaching up to grab his shoulder.

*Well. That was interesting. Completely unexpected, somewhat puzzling, but definitely interesting.* He reminded himself to give the incident more thought later, when he wasn't caught between a stunned and frustrated faery and a furious Human woman trying to defend her unborn child.

Zilya drew herself up and gave Day a wintry look. "That

shouldn't have happened," she said, sounding equally baffled and put out. "You should be writhing on the ground in agony. And what was with the glowing eyes?"

"Sorry to disappoint you," he said. "But then that's life: full of unexpected disappointments." He should know. And what the hell did she mean about his eyes glowing? Must have been something to do with the magic or maybe a trick of the light.

Jenna stepped out from behind him, eyeing the faery with wary caution. "What did she do? Are you okay?"

"I'm fine," he said shortly, still fairly amazed that it was true. He nodded his head toward Zilya. "What *did* you do? Or at least, what was that blast supposed to accomplish, before it hit me instead of its intended target? Surely you weren't trying to kill her; that would defeat your purpose, wouldn't it?"

He stayed alert for any more attacks, ready to step in front of Jenna again if necessary. But for now the faery seemed to have given up on magic, although her fists were clenched at her sides and the furious look in her eyes gave him no illusions that she would simply walk away.

"Of course I was not going to kill the stupid girl," Zilya snapped. "I was just going to place my mark on her unborn child, so there was no chance of her slithering out from under the curse. Not that she could anyway, but still, no point in taking chances, is there? I may have added a tiny extra twist to show her what happens to people who attack faeries."

She scowled at Day. "Now that you're not immortal anymore, it should have worked on you too." She didn't look as though she would have been sorry if it had. "You shouldn't have interfered. This is none of your business, White Rider. Now stand aside and let me get on with it."

Day could feel Jenna tense beside him, and he smothered a sigh as all his good intentions slid away. He was going to have a very pointed conversation with the universe later.

"I'm sorry, Zilya, but I can't do that." He crossed his arms. "How about you just give up this curse thing instead and go get a different hobby. Maybe take up needlepoint. You'd like it; you get to jab a piece of cloth repeatedly with a sharp, pointy object."

The faery ground her teeth. "This is not a hobby, Mikhail Day, nor is it your place to tell me what to do. The Queen has given me leave to continue; you have no right to stand in my way."

"The Queen of England knows about my curse?" Jenna said in a loud whisper. "I don't understand."

Zilya rolled her eyes. "The Queen of the Otherworld, you ninny. Did your ancestors teach you nothing?"

"They taught me right from wrong, which is clearly more than yours taught you," Jenna said, chin held high. If things hadn't been so serious, Day might have laughed. Or possibly applauded. The woman might be in way over her head, but she had spunk, he'd give her that.

Jenna turned to Day. "My grandmother told me about the land of Faerie; is that the same as this Otherworld? Granny never said anything about a Queen."

"The High Queen rules over all of the Otherworld and its denizens whether they reside on that side of the doorway or this," Day explained. "She is very beautiful, very powerful, and somewhat . . . unpredictable."

The faerie snorted. "That is putting it mildly. But I assure you, she knows of this curse and has not forbidden my continued actions. If you will not hand this Human over to me, I insist we go before Her Majesty. She can tell you herself."

She glared at Day. "You might have been one of her favorites once, but you no longer have any standing in Her court. Do not think that she will allow you to interfere. You are nothing now. A failure who let down the Baba Yagas and the Queen, and dragged his brothers down with him. She will not listen to you. Best to simply give me the girl and walk away. Then you can get back to what life is left to you, in whatever peace you can find." She gave him what she probably thought was a sympathetic smile, although it bore less resemblance to such a thing than a shark bore to a guppy.

Day drew in a deep breath through his nose, trying not to give in to the waves of anger and despair that threatened to overwhelm him. "No," he said. "I will not."

Jenna started to speak, and he shook his head. "There is no point in arguing with her. She has the right to demand that we present our quarrel to the Queen. And since this concerns you most of all, we're all going."

Her eyes widened. "I'm going to the land of Faerie to meet the Queen?" She stared at him. "Wait—you know the Queen of Faerie? And what's that thing she called you, a White Rider?"

"The Otherworld," Day corrected automatically, "and it is a job title. One that no longer applies." And didn't add out loud, *And let's hope that Zilya is wrong about the Queen being on her side in this, or you may be sorry you ever went.*


**JENNA** wasn't sure how they were supposed to get to this mythical Otherworld; she only knew it was next to impossible to find a doorway that led from here to there. Her grandmother had been the only one in her family to ever make her way there, although it had been before Jenna was born and the older woman rarely spoke of it. But Jenna knew her grandmother had searched for years and finally stumbled upon an opening somewhere in Ireland. They'd gone back to try and find it again after Jenna turned eighteen, but the place had been empty and useless, nothing more than a mossy green hill like hundreds of others they saw on their trip.

Zilya had apparently arrived on a gorgeous dappled gray mare, who trotted out of the woods at the faery's whistle. Mick shook his head and went to fetch their own ride, which turned out to be a shining white Yamaha motorcycle with gleaming chrome and fringed white saddlebags.

"Um, we're going to the Otherworld on a motorcycle?"

Jenna asked. This hadn't been in any of the fairy tales she'd ever read.

Mick patted the bike as if it were alive. "Don't worry," he said. "You'll be perfectly safe on my bike. She could go to the moon and back without so much as loosening a lug nut." He paused and gave Zilya a worried look. "I assume you plan to take the fast route?"

The faery shrugged, leaping onto her horse's back effortlessly. "Of course. What other way is there?"

"Is there a problem?" Jenna asked. *Other than the obvious one.*

"Probably not," Mick said. "Almost certainly not." He didn't sound as confident as Jenna would have liked. "Zilya's horse and my motorcycle are both magical. They have the ability to move faster than should be possible in this world, as if they could pleat up the miles and simply skip the inconsequential ones. I can't really explain it any better than that. The thing is, it isn't usually done with Humans on board. Certainly not pregnant Humans. I'm not completely sure what effect it will have on you. Probably none, but I can't be positive."

*Oh, great.* "Will it hurt my baby?"

Zilya let out a great gusty sigh. "Would I allow it if I thought the child would be endangered? It is *mine*, after all. Get on Day's steed and let us be on our way." She wrinkled her pert nose. "You would think that people who have such limited lifetimes would be in more of a hurry."

**THE** journey was mostly a blur to Jenna, but it definitely seemed to go by quickly. Mostly she just concentrated on holding on to Mick, her arms wrapped around his slim waist, head pillowed against his broad back as the wind whistled in her ears and the miles flew past. She could smell the musky scent of the black leather jacket he wore, and the hot tar and dust of the road, sensing more than seeing the ripple of his muscles underneath her arms as he leaned into the curves.

Finally they eased to a halt under a stand of huge pine trees overlooking a large body of water.

"Did that last sign say 'Saranac Lake'?" Jenna asked, still feeling as though the world was spinning her around like a chunk of ice in a blender. She slid off the bike, barely able to stand. "That should have been about an hour's drive from where your cabin is, and I would have sworn the trip only took fifteen minutes."

Mick's handsome face swam in and out of her vision, concern written across his features. "Are you okay?"

"Fine," she said, and then bolted on wobbly legs behind the nearest tree where she lost everything she'd eaten for the last week. At least that's what it felt like. Eventually she staggered back out to where Mick was standing waiting for her patiently.

"I take it back," Jenna said. "Definitely not fine. Can we take the slow route when we go back, pretty please?"

Day nodded grimly. "Absolutely. I'm sorry, Jenna. I wouldn't have taken the risk, but I didn't want to let Zilya get too much of a head start on us, talking to the Queen." He glanced around, and pointed toward a break in the bushes that might have been some kind of animal trail. A wisp of light green tunic could just be seen at the edge of the path, along with the swish of a horse's tail. "Speaking of which, she's already headed toward the doorway. If you can walk, we should get going."

"I can walk," Jenna said. She pulled herself up straight and they started moving. "Do you think she made us travel this way on purpose, knowing it would make me sick?"

"Anything is possible," he said. "Faeries are notoriously devious. But most likely she just didn't care one way or the other, as long as she was sure it would make you uncomfortable and not truly ill."

He stopped, and Jenna stopped with him.

"What?" she said.

"We're at the doorway," Mick said, pointing at what looked

to her like a small waterfall cascading musically over a serrated stone cliff. "I hope you don't mind being wet for a minute."

Before she could ask him what he meant, he'd pulled her into the waterfall itself. The sensation of brisk, freezing cold water shocked her briefly, and then she was warm and dry again, standing inside a cavern that glowed with an unearthly light. The ceiling was a scant two feet over her head, and the figure standing in front of them was so tall, the tip of his helmet almost touched the granite roof.

Jenna blinked, her eyes adjusting to the dimness inside the rock walls. Then blinked again, just to be sure, but the huge man still wore shining black armor, and held a silver sword as if he knew how to use it. Strange runes seemed to shiver in the stone wall behind him, appearing and disappearing when she tried to make them out.

"Mikhail Day," the guard said in a deep voice that echoed through the cavern. "You are free to pass through any portal to the other side, but who is this who travels with you, and what is her business in the Otherworld?"

"Didn't Zilya tell him we were coming?" Jenna whispered, resisting the impulse to hide behind Mick.

"There is a ritual to these things," Mick whispered back. "Faeries tend to be very ceremonial and stick to tradition. Think of it like crossing the border into Canada and being asked if you have anything to declare."

"I declare I'd like to go home," Jenna muttered, but she stood next to him and gazed calmly at the guard as though she did this every day and twice on Tuesdays.

"My companion, Jenna, is here to visit the Queen at court," Mick said in a formal tone. "At the behest of the faery Zilya and with my consent. I will vouch for her behavior while in our world, and guarantee her return to her own world when the time comes."

The guard nodded and moved closer to Jenna, allowing her to see the details of his pointed ears and yellow slitted eyes. "Very well," the soldier said. "Put out your arm, if you please, miss."

Jenna glanced at Mick, who nodded his head, so she held her right arm out in front of her. It was barely shaking at all.

The guard put what looked like a chunky lapis lazuli bangle around her wrist, clicking it shut with a decisive snap. The stone began to glow with a gentle warmth, throbbing in harmony with Jenna's heartbeat. She found it strangely comforting, although she couldn't have said why.

"The bracelet will keep you safe from the sometimes erratic effects the Otherworld's shifting time can have on Humans," Mick explained. "If you had been traveling with a Baba Yaga, or even me, back in better days, you wouldn't need it, since our ability to travel back and forth between the worlds would carry over to any who traveled with us. The bracelet's charm will make sure you come out at more or less the same time you came in, give or take a few hours."

"Oh," Jenna said, swallowing hard. "So I don't have to worry about becoming another Rip Van Winkle or Tam Lin. That's good. And, um, Baba Yaga? Do you mean the witch from the Russian fairy tales? Why would I be traveling with one of them?"

Mick snorted. "They come and go to the Otherworld quite a bit; I know because I used to work with them. It's a long story."

"Them? I thought the Baba Yaga was one woman," she said. "Wait—the Baba Yaga is *real*? And you worked with her? Them?" That certainly explained a lot, like why he wasn't fazed by talk of curses, and why he knew about faery and all the rest. There was clearly a lot more to the man than he'd let on.

"You have been granted entrance to the Otherworld, Human," the guard said. "You may pass." He gestured into the darkness that lay past this section of the cavern. "Do not leave the side of your escort. Do not eat or drink anything while in the Otherworld, unless you have been expressly bidden to do so. Do not stray from the path. You have been warned." He turned his back on them and went to stand at his post, motionless.

"Do not pass go. Do not collect two hundred dollars," Jenna muttered. "This was way more fun in my imagination."

Next to her, Mick gave a snort. "Don't worry," he said. "It gets more impressive from here out."

After a short stroll through an eerie mist, which echoed with the sound of high-pitched laughter from some source Jenna couldn't see, they came out into a meadow filled with exotic wildflowers and tall purple grasses. As Mick led the way down a faint path, they passed dainty miniature gossamer-winged horses nibbling on fuchsia-spotted yellow mushrooms and a tall weeping willow tree with branches that moved gently in a nonexistent breeze. For a while they followed a deep, narrow river, and Mick called out a greeting to a woman sitting on a large rock combing her long green hair and singing what sounded like a Beatles tune.

"Is that, uh . . ." Jenna didn't know how to phrase the question. "A mermaid?"

Mick's lips curved into a breathtaking smile. Jenna thought he should do it more often. Or, considering the effect it had on her heart rate, maybe not. "Not a mermaid. No tail, see?" The former Rider started humming the same song under his breath, probably without realizing it. "Merilinda is a Rusalka. They're water creatures from Russian mythology. Mostly they're pretty nice as long as they're kept away from the temptation of drowning children or luring Human men into a watery marriage." He frowned. "Mind you, there's always one bad apple."

Jenna swallowed hard. "Oh. Well, I guess it's good she lives on this side of the doorway, then."

"Creatures like the Rusalkas are one of the reasons the Queen decreed that all paranormal creatures had to move here permanently," Mick explained. "Once the Human population became larger and more sophisticated, it was harder and harder to hide those among the magical folk who look different or wouldn't follow the rules. Only those who couldn't leave—like the mermaids you mentioned—were allowed to stay behind. No oceans for them here, you see."

"Ah," Jenna said. "And how did she learn 'Hey Jude'? Don't tell me they have satellite radio here."

"Hardly." Mick snorted. "No technology works on this side of the doorway. I suspect the Baba Yaga named Beka, actually. She plays the guitar now and then, and she sometimes entertains the court when she visits. Her musical tastes are pretty much stuck in the sixties, as far as I can tell."

He pointed up ahead. "Speaking of the court, we're getting close, so I should probably give you a few pointers."

Jenna couldn't believe she was going to meet an actual faery queen. Suddenly her jeans and blue cotton blouse didn't seem very suitable. "Do I have to curtsy, or something?" *How do you curtsy in jeans, anyway?*

"If you're not comfortable with that, a small bow will do," Mick said, tugging his own black leather jacket and dark jeans into order. "The main thing is always to be polite and respectful, and don't speak to Their Majesties unless they ask you to. In fact, it would probably be best if you let me do most of the talking."

"Happily," Jenna said, wishing she'd had a chance to comb her hair before they'd left.

As the castle grew nearer, its magnificence distracted Jenna from her growing case of nerves. It was built out of some kind of glittering gray stone that managed to look both strong and yet ethereally delicate at the same time. Colorful pennants flew from pointed towers that seemed to reach for the sky, which was an even turquoise blue with no sign of clouds or sun. The temperature was perfect, like the best summer day of childhood.

"Is there really no sun here? It's so warm and bright. My grandmother raised me on fairy tales—she always thought that maybe the answer to the riddle might be found somewhere in one of them—but I never thought that I'd find myself in the middle of one. It's amazing."

"That's the enchanted nature of the Otherworld," Mick said with a shrug. "It usually feels like midday here, unless the Queen is in the mood for evening, in which case it gets darker." He pointed overhead. "The moons are always out, though, day or night."

"Moons, plural?" Jenna tilted her head back. "Oh my." Three glowing white moons hung in the sky, one of them full, the other two crescents that curved in opposite directions. "Is it my imagination, or is the one on the right hanging a little crooked?"

Mick grimaced. "The Queen got a tad upset. It's better not to mention it."

Jenna resolved not to speak at all, if she could get away with it. Yeesh.

As they drew closer to the castle, they started to see groups of people clustered together, chatting and playing croquet, or eating elaborate picnics while sprawled on colorful woven blankets. Mick nodded to a few folks as they passed by, but didn't stop to speak to anyone. Instead, he steered them toward one particular gathering, where the picnic was taking place underneath a gauzy tent that looked like something out of the Arabian Nights.

As they approached, Jenna could see two figures seated on ornately carved wooden chairs that managed to be both informal and regal at the same time. Around them, uniformly beautiful men and women sat or reclined as they dined on colorful tidbits of unidentifiable origin. Jenna would have thought they were all models or movie stars if it hadn't been for the occasional glimpse of a pointed ear or a scaly tail peeking out from under a flamboyant swirl of cape.

Loveliest of them all by far was the Queen.

The ruler of the Otherworld was dressed in flowing lavender silks with a simple crown of spun gold and amethysts that matched her stunning purple eyes and an ornate necklace ending in diamond and amethyst droplets. Her shining white hair was braided and coiled into an intricate mass on top of her head, making her seem even taller than she already was. An upright posture and air of power made her crown an unnecessary adornment; no one looking at her could doubt that she was the Queen.

Next to her, her consort the King had a more subtle but equally impressive presence. He wore a doublet and hose of dove gray velvet, with amethyst buttons that matched the Queen's jewelry. His raven black hair was pulled back into a long tail, and his neatly pointed beard gave him an aura of slightly wicked sexiness.

When Mick and Jenna entered the space under the diaphanous canopy, Zilya already stood in front of the royals' chairs, but she had the air of someone who had been told to wait until the rest of the group arrived before the meeting could get started. Nearby courtiers pretended not to notice her, and a scowl marred her otherwise lovely face.

The Queen set down her teacup made of porcelain so thin it was nearly transparent and sat up even straighter.

"Mikhail, this is a pleasant surprise," she said. She gave their attire a disapproving glance. "The faery Zilya informed Us you would be arriving soon. We are pleased that you have returned to Our realm at last, no matter what the reason."

Mick bowed low, nudging Jenna to remind her to do the same—which she managed to pull off without actually falling over.

"I apologize for our informal attire, Your Majesties," Mick said. "Zilya insisted on our immediate attendance. I meant no disrespect."

The Queen waved one languid hand. "Yes, yes, White Rider. We are always happy to see you, no matter what your garb. So, may We assume this pressing matter has something to do with your companion?"

Jenna realized that this was her cue and bowed again, trying frantically to remember everything she had ever heard about the proper way to address royalty.

"Greetings, Your Majesties," she said. "My name is Jenna Quinlan. It is a very great honor to meet you, and I thank you for allowing me into your august presence. Your kingdom is even more beautiful than I had imagined."

The King and Queen exchanged glances, seemingly mollified by her good manners.

"This is your first visit to Our lands?" the Queen asked.

Mick responded for her. "Jenna has never been here before, but her grandmother Flora once visited your court, twenty-five years or so ago."

The Queen pursed perfect pink lips. "Time means little here, as you know, and while we rarely have Human guests, those few we entertain do tend to blend in together after a while."

"You might remember this one," Mick said. "She managed to make her way here on her own, without the assistance of an intermediary such as myself. And she came to speak to you and your consort about Zilya and a curse."

"Ah yes," the Queen said, making a subtle moue of distaste. "We do remember her; she was very brave and quite determined. Alas, We were unable to assist her in her quest, despite her worthy cause. If you have brought her grandchild here on the same mission, then you will meet with the same lack of success, since the curse, although ill-advised, was quite within the bounds set for such things at the time."

"See!" Zilya said triumphantly, taking a cautious step forward. "It is as I said. The Queen has given her permission. Jenna has lost her battle before it even began."

The Queen set down her cup with the faintest of clicks and frowned at all three of them. "We are surprised that this issue has been brought before Us again. We may not be happy about it, but rules are rules."

A few courtiers looked torn between watching the unfolding drama and edging away from any possible fallout should the Queen lose her temper.

Mick bowed again, shooting Jenna a reassuring look as he did so. "Of course, Your Majesty. No one would be so foolish as to question your earlier ruling. We are here to ask you for a completely different boon, should you be so gracious as to hear us out."

Mollified, the Queen put her hand over that of her consort where it rested on the arm of his chair, and nodded. "Very well, We are listening. What is your request?"

Jenna glanced at Mick, hoping that she was getting her lines right. They'd hardly had any time to discuss the idea he'd come up as they'd walked to court. "As you may remember, Majesty, Zilya put a curse on my family line that allows the faery to steal away the firstborn child of a woman in every generation."

"Indeed." The Queen narrowed her eyes. "It was that kind of behavior that necessitated Our people's permanent retreat to this side of the doorway. I was not well pleased at the time and I am not pleased now, but it happened in an era before such things were forbidden."

She gazed at Jenna with something remarkably like pity. "We rue that it took Us so long to enact such a law. We might have saved your foremothers great grief had We acted sooner, and for this you have Our profound regrets."

Jenna had the feeling, from the expressions on the nobles surrounding her, that the Queen didn't often say she was wrong or offer an apology. "Thank you, Your Majesty. I appreciate you saying so," she said, hoping she was getting it right. "I understand that things were different back then."

"And so they were," the Queen agreed. "What is it you wish Us to do now, pray tell?"

Mick bowed again. "The matter has become somewhat urgent, Your Majesty. Zilya has brought us here because despite Jenna's best attempts to prevent it, it would appear that she is pregnant."

There was an audible gasp from those in attendance. Faery children were few and growing fewer, according to what Mick had told Jenna as they walked through the Otherworld, and so babies were a rare and valuable thing.

Zilya looked unbearably smug.

The Queen rose from her chair and beckoned Jenna to come nearer. "How far along are you, my dear?"

"About three months, Your Majesty. I'm not really showing yet."

A tiny smile flickered around the edges of the Queen's rosebud lips as she gazed intently at Jenna's belly, one hand hovering about an inch away. "May I?"

Jenna knew it was too early for the baby to be kicking; she hadn't even felt it move yet, and that would happen long before anyone could feel it from the outside. But who was she to deny the Queen of the Otherworld? "Of course," she said.

The Queen stood for a moment with her hand on Jenna's stomach and then stepped back, almost regretfully. "Congratulations, my dear. Your daughter is healthy and growing well."

"I'm having a girl?" Jenna's breath caught in her throat. "How can you tell?"

A peel of laughter like chimes echoed through the tent. "You are in my land now, child. I can sense most anything within the borders of my kingdom, should I choose to pay attention to it."

"A girl," Jenna repeated, folding her hands protectively over her belly. "I'm having a girl." Although she tried to stop it, tears filled her eyes, and the Queen shook her head regretfully and returned to her seat.

"Your Majesties," Mick said in a formal tone, as if reminding them of why they were all there. "Zilya is already aware of the pregnancy and has made an effort to seek Jenna out in order to lay her magical claim on the baby. We have come here to ask that you forbid Zilya to do so until after the child is born."

Zilya hissed, but said nothing as yet, clearly biding her time.

"What difference can that make, White Rider?" the King asked, leaning forward in his chair. "Either way, Jenna will still have to give the baby up when the time comes."

"Ah, but you see, Sire, I believe that Jenna may be the one

to finally solve the riddle her many-times-great-grandmother was given, and break this curse once and for all. But for this she needs time, which Your Majesties alone can give her."

The Queen arched one white eyebrow, clearly intrigued. "You truly believe this, Mikhail?"

"I do," he said firmly. "I have every faith in Jenna's cleverness and determination."

Jenna felt a glow that had nothing to do with being pregnant, and she gave Mick a watery smile. The Queen and King exchanged looks and whispered for a moment behind the Queen's upraised lace fan, their light and dark heads bent together as they pondered.

"I protest, Your Majesty!" Zilya said, her voice shrill yet somehow still musical. "This girl I have not met in person before today, but her family and I have a long history, which I am looking forward to continuing." She gave a smile that strayed dangerously close to a smirk. "I would assume you have no problem with that, Highness, since you agreed to my rights in this matter many years ago."

"Never assume anything, Zilya," the Queen said, her voice so cold that frost crept over the surface of her teacup, making lacy white patterns that crackled in the warm pseudo-summer air. "You have taken many an infant from this woman's family, and you seek to claim the child she carries within her now, do you not?"

Zilya held her narrow chin up high. "I do, Your Majesty. It is my right."

The Queen pursed her lips but didn't argue. "When this woman's grandmother came to seek Our aid some years ago, that much was established, it is true. But We are curious as to the origins of this curse. Explain them to Us."

Zilya looked startled. "You didn't ask me about that the last time, Your Majesty."

The King simply said, "We are asking you now, Zilya. Answer the question, if you please. I am quite certain you would not like your Queen to have to ask you twice."

The faery bobbed another quick curtsy. "Of course not, Sire. As to the beginning of it all, well, there was this man."

"Of course there was," the Queen said, with what on any lesser person might have been called an eye roll. "Was he one of Our ilk, this man?"

"No, Your Majesty, he was a Human. But he was mine, and then Rose, this woman's many-times-great-grandmother, stole him."

"And young Jenna's ancestor, she somehow tricked or beguiled this man into choosing her over you?" the Queen asked.

Zilya pouted. "She must have. Why else would a man choose a mere Human over me?"

"Why indeed?" the King muttered.

The Queen tapped one slim finger against her lips. "So, this curse was cast on a woman who is many and many years dead, because of a man who is also many and many years dead, is that what you are saying?"

"Yes, but—"

"The girl Jenna has asked of Us this boon: that you be forbidden to claim her unborn child until after it leaves her womb, thus allowing her the remaining days of her pregnancy to solve the riddle you set her ancestor. Under the circumstances, this seems a reasonable request, and We will grant it. Therefore, Zilya—"

"Your Majesty! That's not fair! That child belongs to me! You have to give me a second chance."

The King rose so swiftly from his chair, Jenna barely saw him move. "Do you dare to interrupt My beloved, your Queen? You forget yourself, Zilya." The faery turned pale; clearly the King was a power in his own right, to be taken no less seriously in spite of the more benign manner he usually displayed.

The Queen's amethyst gaze turned even colder. "You were given your second chance centuries ago, Zilya, when you flirted with My consort and I did not banish you from this kingdom forever. Perhaps it would be best if you did not ask for any favors beyond that one."

Out of the corner of her eye, Jenna saw Mick's lips curve. Why did she suspect that he already knew that Zilya wasn't the Queen's favorite person?

"My apologies, Sire, Your Highness," Zilya said. "I was merely taken by surprise by your decision, since you had previously said that my curse was legitimately cast and you would not interfere." She gave a belated curtsy, gracefully bending her knee and waving one arm out in front of her body.

"Nor will We, should the Human fail in her attempt," the Queen said coolly. "If that is the case, you will have the child anyway. You need only wait. For now, you are forbidden to approach the girl until the babe has left the womb. Should she still be unable to produce the solution to your riddle, you may collect the infant one fortnight after it is born. Is that clear?"

"What's a fortnight?" Jenna whispered to Mick, almost giddy with relief now that the Queen had ruled in her favor.

"Two weeks," he whispered back. "That means Zilya will be entitled to take your baby two weeks after it is born, if you fail."

"I understand, Your Majesty," Zilya said with an expression that made it look as though she had bitten into something bitter and not to her liking.

"Very well," the Queen said, waving her fan at the faery. "Then you may leave Us."

Zilya curtsied politely and made her way out of the tent. As she passed Jenna, she hissed, "Don't get to attached to that creature growing inside you. I *will* have it from you in the end."

"Over my dead body," Jenna hissed back.

"If you insist," Zilya said, and swept out into the day.

After she was gone, Mick and Jenna expressed their gratitude to the Queen, who accepted their thanks with a graceful nod of the head.

She looked a bit wistful, if such a thing was possible. "My dear Jenna, might We request a boon of you in return?"

Jenna swallowed hard. She couldn't imagine what the Queen would ask for: seven years of servitude, or some other impossible task? "Your Majesty?" she said.

"If you succeed in breaking the curse, perhaps you would bring the child to visit Us when it is born? We should like to see her."

Jenna could only nod. "I would be happy to, Your Majesty."

The Queen gave her a wintry smile, and then she gazed intently at Mick. "We are well aware of your long relationship with the Baba Yagas, but no Baba Yaga may act in her professional capacity to help this girl achieve her goal. That would be against the rules."

Mick looked thoughtful. "Yes, Your Majesty."

"If," the Queen added, "for instance, you were to go visit the one called Barbara, she would be unable to assist you in any official way. Is that quite clear?"

Mick returned the Queen's look squarely. "Very clear, Your Majesty. I am sure Jenna agrees that you have been most gracious and generous." Jenna nodded in agreement.

Neither of them said anything until they were most of the way down the path, followed at a discreet distance by an official who would reclaim Jenna's bracelet when she left. Jenna's feelings were such a volatile mixture of triumph and fear and just plain stunned amazement that she, Jenna Quinlan, had just met the Queen of the Otherworld, she barely knew what to say anyway.

Finally, though, Mick said, "You were very lucky that the Queen doesn't like Zilya. I suspect that made her more willing to grant your request than she might have been otherwise."

"I'm grateful to you for bringing me to see her," Jenna said.

"But?" Mick raised one blond eyebrow.

"Well, I just wish I knew what to do next," Jenna said, feeling a little discouraged despite how well things had gone. "I still don't really know where to start."

To her surprise, Mick let out a sharp laugh. "Ah, but you weren't paying attention. The Queen already suggested our course of action."

"She did?"

"Of course. She told us to visit Barbara Yager, one of the Baba Yagas."

"But I thought she said this Baba person couldn't help. She was quite specific about it." Jenna felt like she was missing something.

Mick gave her a wicked grin that made her heart skip a beat and cheered her up despite her dire situation. "Exactly. The Queen is a wise and wily woman. She warned me that the Baba Yaga can't act in any magical way to help you, which is definitely a shame, because that might have been my next move. But doesn't mean she can't give you advice or suggestions as one woman to another. The Baba Yaga can't solve the problem *for* you, but the Queen purposely pointed out that there was no reason Barbara couldn't give you the benefit of her wisdom and experience."

Jenna stared at her. "That's *sneaky.*"

"Welcome to dealing with the fae," Mick said. "They don't lie, but they can make words dance around so cleverly, you'll think you just agreed to one thing when it turns out you've done exactly the opposite. That's why you never make a deal with a faery if you can help it."

"You know, all the old stories said that, but I always figured they'd exaggerated."

"Hardly," Mick said.

They walked for another minute and then Jenna said hesitantly, "The stories mostly said that the Baba Yaga was a scary, evil witch. Was that an exaggeration too?"

Mick chuckled. "You can decide for yourself. You're going to meet one in about five minutes."

# CHAPTER 5

**MIKHAIL** stole a glance at Jenna out of the corner of his eye and saw her take a deep breath and brace herself for the worst. He bit his lip so he wouldn't laugh. He had to admit—if only in a kind of internal whisper—that even though he hadn't wanted to get involved, he was sort of enjoying himself. He'd definitely gotten a kick out of watching Jenna stand up to Zilya, even if the poor girl really was way out of her league.

Not that he wouldn't be happy once he'd handed her over to Barbara and returned to the peace and solitude of his cabin. But for a couple of days it had been nice to think about somebody else's problems instead of his own. Not to mention actively doing something instead of sitting around and replaying scenes from Brenna and the Cave of Torture in his head, over and over. He still didn't want to ride to anyone's rescue anymore, but helping Jenna with her issues was a hell of a lot more entertaining than obsessing about his own.

They'd come directly from the Otherworld, using the doorway that came out into Barbara's Airstream trailer, currently parked next to a red barn that sat out behind a yellow farm-house with a tin roof. Luckily, the Riders could always come and go freely through any of the Baba Yaga's magical passageways, and apparently that hadn't changed despite the fact that technically, none of them were Riders any longer.

Day had enjoyed watching Jenna's reaction as they walked out of the eerie mist, through a narrow cupboard door, and into the small but luxurious interior of the Airstream.

"Wow," Jenna said. "This is amazing. I've been in a couple of RVs, but I've *never* seen anything like this."

"You think this is impressive," Day said. "You should have seen it when it was a wooden hut on giant chicken legs. Still, I'll admit this is a lot more comfortable."

It certainly looked comfortable. The furniture was covered in rich jewel-toned brocades and velvets, with silk accents. Instead of the conventional boring carpet, there was a luxurious antique Persian rug decorated in flowers and tiny creatures so detailed they looked like they could get up and crawl around. The compact kitchen was crafted out of some kind of glossy wood, and there were herbs everywhere—dried herbs in jars, herbal tinctures in small cobalt blue bottles, fresh herbs hanging from hooks in the ceiling and scenting the air with their delicate woodsy aromas.

"Your friend Barbara really lives in this and travels around the country?" Jenna asked, gazing around with wide eyes, probably wondering where the owner was.

"She did," he said, patting the couch affectionately as they walked to the door. It didn't do to ignore the Airstream; it had a personality and magic all its own, and was capable of making an unwanted visitor very uncomfortable. Luckily, it had always had a soft spot for the Riders, Day in particular, so it probably wouldn't even bother to sound the alarm. Which was just as well, since he didn't want Barbara running out here, shiny silver sword in hand, and scaring the crap out of an already nervous Jenna.

"She lives in the house now, and just uses the trailer for

Baba Yaga business," he explained as they walked up the driveway and arrived at the front of the house.

"Go ahead," he said to Jenna, who stood there, one hand hovering over the door, clearly intimidated by the idea of who or what might answer. "I'll just be over here to the side." He was curious as to how these two strong women would react to each other, plus, just maybe, he needed one more minute before he talked to Barbara for the first time in almost a year.

Jenna finally started to lower her hand, only to have the door open before her knuckles could touch the wood, as if by magic.

A woman stood there, wearing black jeans and a long-sleeved black tee shirt with a picture of a dragon on it. The caption underneath read DO NOT MEDDLE WITH THE AFFAIRS OF DRAGONS, FOR YOU ARE CRUNCHY AND GOOD WITH KETCHUP.

The woman was strikingly beautiful in a way that no one would ever mistake for merely pretty, with a cloud of long dark hair, piercing amber eyes, and a slightly hawkish nose. There was a scowl on her oval-shaped face and a huge white pit bull at her feet.

"What?" she asked, with the air of someone who might agree with the sentiments of the dragon on her shirt.

"Um, I'm sorry to bother you so early, but I'm looking for Barbara Yager?" Jenna smiled at the dog. "Your dog is very handsome, by the way. Would he mind if I petted him?"

The expression on the woman's face became a fraction less severe. "He'd probably love it. His name is Chudo-Yudo, by the way. But I have to tell you that if you're trying to sell me something while I'm attempting to get a small child ready for school, I will probably let the dog bite you."

A tall, attractive man with dark blond hair appeared in the doorway behind her. "Honey, how many times do I have to tell you that you can't threaten to sic the dog on perfectly innocent strangers?" He grinned at Jenna, looking decidedly friendlier than his companion. "I apologize for my wife. I'm afraid we're still trying to get her house-trained. The dog, on the other hand, is perfectly harmless."

"Unless you're trying to sell something," the woman muttered. "Or hand out religious pamphlets."

"I wouldn't think of it," Jenna said. "I don't even want to borrow a cup of sugar. The Queen sent me and Mick to see the Baba Yaga. Is she home?"

The woman exchanged shocked glances with her husband and then stood on her tiptoes to look over Jenna's shoulder. Even the dog perked up, sticking his black nose in the air and snuffling.

"Mick? Do you mean Mikhail Day? Where is he?" she asked eagerly, amber eyes glowing. "Did he bring you?"

Day stepped forward out of the shadow of the house. "Hello, Baba. Hello, Liam. You're looking well."

Barbara narrowed her eyes at him. "What was this, some kind of test?" She punched him on the arm, not all that gently. "It's about time you came to visit."

"Wait. What?" Jenna stared at Barbara. "She's the Baba Yaga? The cranky old wicked witch?" She slapped her hand over her mouth, a minute too late. *Oops.* Day tried not to snicker.

Barbara sighed, and Liam pulled her close for a brief hug before letting her go. "She's only a little wicked," he said to Jenna. "And way less cranky than she used to be. Would you like to come in?"

Barbara hesitated for one long moment and then stepped out of the way. "Yes, do come in. You obviously know who I am. This is my husband, Liam."

She led the way into a cheerful kitchen with slightly worn wide-plank floors, cream-colored walls, and gray-blue cabinets. The sun was shining in past blue-and-cream-striped curtains, highlighting the dark-haired girl sitting at a long, rectangular wooden table. The child, who looked about six or seven, was perched on a high stool so she could reach the table, her pixie-cut hair, pointed chin, and sharp cheekbones making her look like a tiny urchin. A gigantic pile of pancakes sat in front of her on a glossy blue pottery plate. At the sight of Day, her whole face lit up.

"Mikhail! You came! Barbara said you would, but that we might have to wait for hell to freeze over first. Did it?"

As soon as she spotted Jenna, the girl set her fork on her plate, hopped down from the stool, and marched over to shake Jenna's hand briskly. "Good morning," the urchin said politely. "Welcome to our home. My name is Babs. I live with Barbara and Liam now. I am eating breakfast. The pancakes are excellent. Would you like some?"

Jenna bit her lip, trying not to laugh. Mick smothered a grin.

"We're working on manners," Liam explained, wiping at a smear of syrup on the small girl's face. "Babs was adopted from somewhat unusual circumstances, and she's still trying to figure out how things work here." He smiled kindly at the child. "Very well done, sweetie. Why don't you go finish your pancakes before the bus gets here."

"Do I have to go to school?" Babs asked, big brown eyes looking at Jenna plaintively. "We have a guest. She looks interesting. I think I might learn more if I stayed home than if I went to school." She turned to Jenna. "I already learned my alphabet and numbers. Barbara says I am too smart for my own good, but I think being smart is excellent."

"I think so too," Jenna said. "But I will probably still be here when you get home. Your, uh, Barbara and I have a lot to talk about."

"Excellent," Babs said, and sat back down at the table.

"That's her word for the week," Barbara said, mouthing *thank you* as she finished packing a lunch box sitting on the counter. Two fresh plates of pancakes suddenly appeared at the table, a cup of coffee steaming next to each one. "Sit down. You might as well have some breakfast since you're here." It wasn't gracious, but Day figured that since the old Barbara wouldn't have even thought to feed guests, it still showed a certain improvement in her attitude. Clearly marriage to Liam agreed with his old friend.

A honking sound came from the road, and Liam scooped

up Babs, her lunch, and a sheriff's hat, somehow juggling them all long enough to give Barbara an extended and surprisingly passionate kiss. "That's my cue," he said. "I'll be heading out to work after I take Babs up to the bus." He hesitated, looking from Day to Barbara and back again. "Unless you need me to stay?"

Barbara cocked an eyebrow. "I'm sure that Mikhail wouldn't come all this way and not have dinner with us. *Would you*, *Day*?" The hint of a threat colored her words and Day nodded, although in fact he'd had no intention of staying any longer than it would take to drop Jenna off and explain her situation.

"Great," Liam said, plopping his hat on his head. "I'll call you later and see if you want me to bring home anything for dinner."

The kitchen seemed quiet and empty after the tall man and the chatty child left, and it was clear Jenna didn't quite know what to say to Barbara now that they were alone with her. After all this time, Day wasn't sure either.

The other woman solved the problem by sitting down at the table with a cup of coffee and gesturing Jenna to take the seat opposite her. "Go ahead and eat. A ride on the back of a motorcycle can work up quite an appetite. I have one, so I know that from long experience. If you'd rather not have coffee, I have a variety of herbal teas, too."

"We didn't come by motorcycle," Day said, trying to eat without talking with his mouth full. But it was tough, since the pancakes were light and fluffy, topped with real maple syrup and a pat of fresh butter. "We came straight from court. I took the liberty of bringing Jenna through the doorway in the Airstream, since it was a lot faster than going back to my place, then riding here. I hope you don't mind. My bike is still outside of Saranac Lake at the gate there, so I'm going to need to use the door again on my way back."

The white dog, which had been sitting quietly at Barbara's feet, let out a loud *woof*. Barbara raised her eyebrows. "I agree, Chudo-Yudo," she said to the dog. "It sounds urgent. Especially

if whatever it was actually got you to go back to court again."
Of course, to Jenna it sounded like barking, but after all these
years, Day understood him perfectly.

"Um, you talk to the dog?" Jenna asked.

"He talked to me first," Barbara said with a straight face.
"It would be rude not to answer. And he's actually a dragon.
He's just disguised as a dog because the neighbors might
notice a ten-foot dragon in the backyard, and it is challenging
enough to fit in as a Human as it is."

Jenna glanced helplessly at Day and he shrugged. "You're
the one who grew up on fairy tales. I don't know why you
find any of this so surprising."

Barbara gave Jenna a tiny smile, taking pity on the woman.
"I'm sorry. We're teasing you, just a little. I suspect Liam
would say we were doing it to avoid dealing with our uncomfortable emotions. He's full of nonsense like that."

"Which doesn't make it any less true," Chudo-Yudo said,
reaching one large paw up to snag a pancake off of the table.
"Are you going to ask them why they're here, or should I? It
clearly isn't just a social visit, not after they came directly
from the Otherworld."

"The Queen suggested that there was no point in turning
to you," Day explained.

"Did she?" Barbara said, looking thoughtful. "How very
interesting. I suppose that must mean you have a problem she
thinks falls under my particular area of expertise, but for some
reason she doesn't want to authorize my involvement. Care
to tell me what it is?"

Jenna put her fork down with a thud. "My family was
cursed by a faery. And if you can't help me, she's going to
steal my baby."


BARBARA looked around the room. The woman had come
into the house with a purse and a small backpack, which were
still leaning against the wall in the front hallway, but she

didn't see a baby anywhere. Despite her time with Babs, she wasn't very good with children, but you'd think that she would have noticed something like that.

Chudo-Yudo gave a snort, tiny wisps of smoke dissipating into the air. "It's still inside her, silly. Can't you smell the hormones?"

Barbara sniffed, but all she could smell was maple syrup and dark, rich coffee with a hint of blue roses. Still, when she focused on Jenna's energy, she could clearly make out the tiny separate but attached aura of a growing Human life. Well, didn't that just complicate things. She didn't know what the hell Day thought he was up to, but she was going to give him a swift kick the next time she got him alone. Assuming she did, of course. He'd been avoiding her and her two Baba Yaga sisters since they'd rescued him from Brenna ten months ago. And now he'd clearly only turned up so that he could dump whatever problem this was on her. They'd see about that.

"So, you're pregnant," Barbara said to Jenna. She had a sudden, unsettling thought. "Wait, it isn't Mikhail's, is it? I mean, I thought he couldn't, that is, we don't know anymore, but—"

"Oh no." Jenna's cheeks turned quite pink in her normally pale face. "I only met Mick a few days ago. My car broke down and I twisted my ankle while I was walking through the woods in a storm. I showed up at his cabin and he took me in until I could walk again. I wasn't going to say anything about the curse, but when I had a bout of morning sickness, somehow I ended up telling him the whole story." She blushed again. "He's very easy to talk to. You know, when he isn't being horribly rude."

"Horribly rude? Day? You're joking." But Barbara could tell by looking at the other woman that she wasn't. She knew that his experiences in Brenna's cave and the loss of his immortality had changed her friend, but she was surprisingly dismayed to hear that he had come so far from the man she knew, who couldn't have been rude to a woman if you held a gun to his head.

Day stared ahead stoically, not commenting.

"Well, I was in his home when he clearly wanted to be alone," Jenna said with a shrug that didn't quite cover the hurt. "You can't really blame him."

Barbara could, actually, but that was an issue for another time.

"Why don't you tell me about this faery curse," she said. "And we'll see if there is anything I can do. But I have to warn you, such things are complicated."

"Complicated?" Jenna said. "What do you mean?"

Barbara sighed, tapping the side of her coffee cup with one blunt-cut nail. "Faeries. Curses. Fairy tales. They're a pain in the ass, frankly." At her feet, Chudo-Yudo *woof*ed in agreement. "There are all sorts of rules and traditions that have to be followed. Sometimes they work in your favor; sometimes they don't. And when they don't, they *really* don't."

"The Queen already told us that she couldn't help me," Jenna said. "And that you couldn't either."

"Oh?" Barbara stared at Mikhail, not at Jenna. "Then why are you here?"

"The Queen very clearly pointed out that you would not be allowed to do anything in your capacity as Baba Yaga," Day clarified.

"Ah," Barbara said. Things were becoming clearer.

"And the faery involved, Zilya, has already made one attempt to seal her claim on Jenna's baby."

"Huh. As I said, fairy tales, very annoying."

Jenna blinked at her. "But, uh, aren't you a fairy tale? I mean, the Baba Yaga is a fairy tale, right?"

Barbara gave her guest a sharp-edged grin. "Yep. And sometimes I'm a pain in the ass too. Let's just hope in this case, I can be a helpful one."

"I could use all the help I can get," Jenna admitted ruefully. "But I'm not sure where to start."

"The beginning is always a good place, I find," Barbara said, only a trifle sharply. "Why don't you start there and just go on. Tell it as though it were a story, if that makes it easier."

Jenna nodded. "Okay, then." She took a deep breath. "Once upon a time in a land far, far away, my many, many-times-great-grandmother Rose lived in a small village in the middle of Europe. She was nothing much to look at, so I've been told, but sweet and generous of spirit, and hardworking. From the time she was young, she'd been best friends with the son of the local blacksmith, and it was widely accepted that they would marry as soon as they were old enough.

"Then a mysterious woman appeared in the woods near the village. She was very beautiful, with shining hair and fine clothes. The young blacksmith, who was only seventeen, was flattered by her interest and spent many a fine afternoon in her company when he should have been working, or helping Rose with her chores."

"Aha," Barbara said. "Enter the faery, stage left."

"Something like that," Jenna said. "The story passed down through the family says that her loveliness and charm, even when she was glamoured to appear as a Human noblewoman, entranced the blacksmith, John, and they dallied together for a time.

"But John was an honorable man, and already engaged to his childhood sweetheart, Rose, a plain but decent girl who lived in his village. Although he was intrigued and flattered by Zilya's attentions, he eventually chose Rose over her. Zilya was furious, and couldn't understand how some plump and homely Human girl could 'steal' the man she wanted. Although, of course, Rose loved him with all her heart, and Zilya was incapable of such an emotion.

"When Rose became pregnant on their wedding night, Zilya flew into a rage and cursed the girl and her entire line, swearing to steal a child in each generation as payment for the man who was stolen from her. Rose, who knew her lore of the fae folk, demanded a way to free herself from the curse, and Zilya gave her an impossible riddle. Alas, no one in Rose's line has ever been able to decipher the riddle, and so the curse continued into the present day."

Jenna sighed. "And that brings us to me. I was so determined that the curse would end with me, since I am the last of my line. But as you can see"—she patted her barely visible belly—"I underestimated the power of the curse. Now my only chance is to figure out the riddle and beat Zilya before she can take my baby too."

"No one in your family was ever able to make any sense of it?" Barbara asked. "I know it was designed to be tricky— they always are—but there are rules to these things, and one of the rules is that the riddle has to provide an answer for the one who is clever enough to unravel it."

"My grandmother is the only one who even got close," Jenna said. "She devoured every fairy tale she could get her hands on. I remember her reading most of them to me when I was growing up. She told me that her research eventually led her to the land of the faeries, and she was finally able to make her way there with great difficulty when she was in her fifties, right after my mom got pregnant. But the Queen had to rule in Zilya's favor, apparently, because the curse predated her ban against such things."

As Barbara listened to Jenna tell the story of her great-great-whatever-grandmother's misadventures, her heart sank. She really liked the girl and she wanted to be of assistance, but it clearly wasn't going to be that simple. Faeries, bah.

"You can't help her, can you, Baba?" Chudo-Yudo said, his massive head sagging onto his equally large front paws.

Barbara shook her head. Frustration bubbled up like a mishandled potion. Helping worthy seekers on their quests was usually one of her least favorite parts of the job, but she would have made an exception in this case. After all, the woman liked her dragon-dog. And Day brought her. Barbara *really* hated the idea of letting Day down, especially after everything he'd been through.

"So, what do you think?" Jenna asked eagerly, her icy blue eyes wide and filled with hope.

"Zilya, huh?" Barbara said. "I'm not really familiar with her, although I can ask a few friends at court if they know anything about her." She got up to get a chocolate chip oatmeal cookie. Yes, she'd just eaten pancakes, but cookies helped her think. She offered one to Jenna, who nibbled on it absentmindedly.

"But here's the big problem," she went on. "Remember how I said there were all kinds of rules about these things?"

"Sure," Jenna said. "Like how my many-great-grandmother was able to force Zilya to give her a riddle that would enable her to undo the curse, if only she could figure it out. Because there was a rule that said Zilya had to. Mick and I talked about that while we were walking here."

*Mick, eh?* Barbara raised an eyebrow. There was more going on here than met the eye, or she wasn't the scariest witch in town.

She tapped her finger on the table. "Exactly. Only that's the problem. Normally, if someone came to me with Ye Olde Evil Curse, I'd be able to jump in with both booted feet because the person who cast the curse in the first place didn't play fair. But since your great-grand was clever enough to insist on the riddle, tradition was satisfied. My hands are tied. You have to solve this one yourself, I'm afraid."

"Oh. I see." Long black lashes blinked back tears, but Jenna held her head up high. "Thanks for listening, anyway."

*Dammit.* She really liked this girl. She had spunk. And she'd talked Babs into going to school without a fight. That bought her something right there.

"Hang on a minute," Barbara said, holding up one hand. The fact that it happened to be the one holding the cookie only took away from the drama of the gesture a little. "I didn't say I wouldn't try to help, just that I couldn't do anything in my official position as Baba Yaga. But you already knew that. If the Queen sent you to me, even obliquely, she must have thought I could do *something.*"

Under the table, Chudo-Yudo made a coughing noise that sounded a lot like *"Softie."*

"Is your dog okay?" Jenna asked, bending down and looking at him with concern. "It sounds like he might be choking."

"Not yet," Barbara said with a growl. "But if he keeps up the wisecracks, it might become a distinct possibility."

Chudo-Yudo chuckled and moved over to lay his huge head on Jenna's foot, generously allowing her to scratch his favorite spot under his chin in case it made her feel better.

Barbara drummed her fingers on the table, thinking so hard that some spindly geraniums in a ceramic pot on the windowsill grew three inches and turned from red to pink. "There has to be something . . . You said that no one in your family has ever been able to figure out this riddle?"

"No. My grandmother thought that there was something in it that indicated part of the answer might lie in the faerylands—sorry, the Otherworld. But she didn't get any further than that."

"Huh," Barbara said, thoughtfully chewing on her cookie and scattering crumbs all over the table. "This riddle, can you recite it for me? The Queen must know it; she knows almost everything her people are involved in. Maybe she thought I could come up with a clue that could help you unravel it." She smiled at Mikhail. "And my friend here was always great at riddles. Between us, perhaps we can see something you didn't. I'm guessing that's what the Queen had in mind, although it is always hard to tell with her. She's about as easy to read as a muddy lake in a snowstorm."

"Um, wouldn't that be cheating?" Jenna asked, a hesitant smile flitting over her face.

"Not if you do the solving yourself," Barbara said. "I can't actually tell you the answers, even if I could figure them out. But maybe I can at least find you a place to start and a hint or two. And there is nothing to stop Day from helping you solve it."

He choked on a pancake and pushed his plate away.

*Ha.* As if she was going to fall for the old "unload my problem on you and run away" routine. The Queen might be subtle and devious, but Day was as clear as glass. *Nice try, old friend, but I'm onto you,* Barbara thought smugly.

"That would be great," Jenna said. "To be honest, I'm completely stuck. I've been going over and over it since I was a kid and my mother first taught it to me, but it all just seems like nonsense."

"All good riddles do," Barbara said. "That's what makes them riddles. But the classic fairy-tale curse riddle usually comes in three parts. The first part tells you what you did, the second part spells out what's going to happen to you because of it, and then the rest of the riddle contains the solution to breaking the curse. So that's what you really want to focus on."

She refilled their coffee cups and got them each another cookie, plus one for Chudo-Yudo so he'd stop giving her that pitiful look. "Okay, I'm ready. Let's hear it."

Jenna took a deep breath and recited the riddle, her voice a mixture of resignation, desperation, and a persistent, lingering layer of hope.

> *"I chose a man and he chose me*
> *You should have simply let it be*
> *I chose a man and he chose you*
> *Now this choice you both shall rue*
> *You stole mine so I'll steal yours*
> *Each mother's child that she adores*
> *From every generation born*
> *The first new child she will mourn*
> *This curse unbroken now shall be*
> *Down into eternity*
> *Unless you find the pathway through*
> *And solve the riddle with this clue*
> *A rose's cry at rock enchanted*
> *The sun's bright ray where none is slanted*
> *A magic key to a gift divine*
> *True love must merge when stars align"*

"Well, well, well," Barbara said. "Isn't that interesting?"

Chudo-Yudo picked his head up. "What am I missing?"

Barbara ignored him, although she'd happily explain it later, when the other two weren't there.

"Did you get something from that?" Day asked. "Already?"

"Maybe," Barbara said, not wanting to sound too encouraging. From the look on Mick's face, she succeeded. Barbara knew she would have to play this very carefully, or risk having the situation backfire and become worse instead of better. But if she was right, the solution to the riddle might solve two problems at once. And as far as she was concerned, she was willing to bend more than a few rules and, if necessary, twist a few arms, to make that second one happen.

"The riddle clearly follows the traditional format. The first stanza explains why the curse was cast—in short, because some bad-tempered faery thought your great-great stole her man. Who wasn't hers in the first place and who she would have lost interest in sooner or later anyway. But never mind that. The *why* is rarely fair, unless you happened to be stupid enough to steal some enchanted item from the witch it belongs to." That had happened once or twice, and in her experience it never ended well for the other party.

She went on. "The second stanza spells out what the curse entails, of course."

Jenna held one hand protectively over her belly. "Yes, that part is crystal clear, unfortunately. And the section after that just tells me I have to solve the riddle to lift the curse, and something about a 'pathway through' that my grandmother thought meant that the solution lay in the Otherworld. The true riddle is that last stanza, and that's the part no one has ever been able to decipher. I don't even know where to start."

"I suggest starting in the land where the sun's rays are never slanted," Barbara said with a grin. "With the sun's bright ray." She lifted her mug in Day's direction. "Have you met my friend the White Rider, sometimes known as my 'Bright Day'?"

# CHAPTER 6

**DAY** snorted coffee out through his nose.

"What? What?" He grabbed a napkin and wiped his face, then waved it like a white flag. "No way, Barbara. You are *not* going to tell me that I am in the goddamn riddle." He glared at Barbara, which had about as much effect as it usually did. Which is to say, none whatsoever. This was SO not going the way he'd planned it.

Barbara shrugged, not bothering to try and hide the hint of a smile that hovered around the edge of her lips. "I wasn't telling you. I was telling Jenna. You just happen to be sitting at the table."

"That line does *not* refer to me."

"Really?" Barbara said. "You don't think 'The sun's bright ray where none is slanted' refers to the Baba Yagas' Bright Day, who comes from the Otherworld, where there is no true sun? It seems like rather a good fit to me."

"It could refer to Gregori Sun," Mikhail said, knowing he sounded a little like a child wanting to put the blame for a broken vase on someone, anyone, else. "After all, it says 'sun' right in the phrase."

Barbara just stared at him.

"Okay, fine! Day threw up his hands. "It has to refer to someone from the Otherworld, and it does sound like it could mean me. But it could mean something entirely different. That's all I'm saying." He subsided back into his seat and picked up his coffee again, glowering equally at Barbara and Jenna (but not at Chudo-Yudo, since, after all, he was depressed but not suicidal).

"I don't understand," Jenna said, glancing from Barbara to Day and back again. "How can Mick be part of the solution to a riddle that was created hundreds of years ago?"

"That's the funny thing about curses and riddles," Barbara said. "And why fairy tales are such a pain in the butt." Chudo-Yudo snorted in agreement, almost setting the edge of Barbara's pants on fire. "Once such things are set in motion, not even the people involved have any control over them."

Day took pity on Jenna, who looked even more confused than ever. "Think of it like this: once someone casts a curse—in this case, Zilya—destiny kind of takes over. I suppose that's the only way it could truly be fair, with no room for cheating."

"Which, let's face it, Zilya would have done, if she could have," Barbara added.

"So Zilya cast the curse, but once your many-great-grandmother invoked the riddle clause, whatever riddle Zilya made up on the spot didn't actually come from her. She would have opened her mouth and recited it, but without any conscious power over how it came out. Then both she and your family were stuck with the results. The universe maintains the balance. Think of it as another unseen law, like gravity. Nobody really knows why it works the way it does; the universe is just designed that way."

Jenna wrinkled her nose in a way that Day found absurdly endearing. "Well, okay, I kind of get that. I mean, it goes along with a lot of the fairy tales I've read. But that still doesn't explain how Mick could be in a riddle that was given to my great-great-great-great-whatever-grandmother all those years ago, does it?"

Day and Barbara exchanged glances, and the witch raised one eyebrow in question. Day shook his head at her and sighed.

"There are a few possibilities," he said, putting off the moment of truth. "Maybe you really are meant to be the one who solves the riddle."

"Or maybe any of your relatives could have met him, somewhere along the line," Barbara said flatly. "Mikhail is, or rather he was, the White Rider, companion to the Baba Yagas. He has been around for thousands of years."

Jenna's eyes got round and her jaw dropped. She stared at Day. "So when Zilya said something about you not being immortal anymore, she wasn't making some kind of snide comment? You really are immortal?"

"Not now," Day said, and pushed his chair away from the table with a scraping noise that made Chudo-Yudo put his huge paws over his ears. "And I still don't believe I am any kind of solution to this riddle. I'm not any kind of solution to anything, as Barbara well knows."

He winced inwardly at how unpleasant he sounded, but he couldn't just sit there and have the rest of this conversation. Not with Jenna. Not with Barbara. Not with anyone.

"I'm sure Barbara can come up with some ideas on the rest of the riddle," he said abruptly, heading for the door. "Since she was clever enough to figure out this bit. I need to get some air." He figured he'd duck back into the Airstream and be gone before either of them realized he'd left.

"Just be back in time for dinner," Barbara said. And added in a deceptively sweet tone, "By the way, I've locked the trailer from here, so if you're planning on returning to your hideout in the woods, you've got a long walk ahead of you."

Day grunted and slammed the door behind him. Hard.

* * *

**DAY** stared at the trees behind Barbara's barn blindly, not seeing sturdy oaken wood and tall pines. Instead, his sight was filled with the memory of his fellow Riders' limp bodies, dragged into magical cages when they followed him into Brenna's trap. A trap that never would have worked if she hadn't played on his well-known weakness for rescuing helpless women.

Vision after vision played out in his mind, as they had so many times before. Alexei and Gregori, tortured until they passed out or screamed in agony. Alexei's hands burned red and oozing from his attempt to distract Brenna, Gregori bleeding from a dozen stab wounds as he did the same. The look on their faces when the Queen pronounced the three of them immortal no more.

He doubted they'd ever forgive him for that. It didn't matter; he'd never forgive himself. Brenna might have been the one who stole away their futures, but it wouldn't have happened if it hadn't been for Mikhail.

Mikhail had no idea where his brothers were now. Out seeking their new lives and their new paths, like him, probably. He didn't even know which side of the doorway they were on. He hadn't spoken to either of them before he'd left the Otherworld, and they'd barely spoken to one another while they were still there and healing. Everyone insisted they weren't angry, merely recovering, as he was. But how could they not be angry? He was so furious with himself, sometimes the heat of it threatened to burn him up from the inside like the fires Brenna set to fuel her rank potion.

His cabin in the midst of the woods was the closest he'd come to peace, of a sort. Not forgiveness, never that, nor excuses for the harm he'd allowed to befall his beloved comrades. But at least until today he'd stopped seeing their bruised and battered faces, except in his nightmares.

Now this. Jenna had no idea what she was asking. He

wanted to help her, really he did. She was sweet, and no one deserved to have their baby stolen away just because a faery had suffered a fit of pique centuries before and Jenna's entire family had suffered the consequences. But he just couldn't. Not after what happened. Never again. She would have to find her help elsewhere.

Day blinked rapidly, coming back to find himself kneeling on the grassy earth, white-knuckled hands clenched on his thighs, so tight he could barely loosen them again. He dragged in a ragged breath, suddenly tired beyond measure.

He staggered to his feet, not sure if it had been hours or only minutes since he'd sunk into the fugue state he thought he'd left behind him in the Otherworld along with the two men he loved best in all the world. Apparently he wasn't quite as healed as he'd thought. Clearly he needed more time on his own to regain his equilibrium. A lot more time. Maybe as many years as he had left in a life now measured in decades instead of centuries.

No matter. He knew himself well enough to admit that he would never be able to find the peace he sought if he simply abandoned Jenna. But with any luck, by the time he'd taken a long walk and pulled himself back together again, Barbara would have solved the entire thing and figured out a way past whatever barriers would prevent her from telling Jenna what to do.

And then he could just go home and . . . well, do whatever he was going to do with the rest of his life. As soon as he could decide what that was.

**"IS** he all right?" Jenna asked Barbara softly. The look on Mick's face before he'd stormed out just about broke her heart. She could tell he'd been terribly wounded by something in his past, but she had no idea what to do or say to help. And was a little afraid to ask what had happened to him. She really wanted to know, but it was none of her business. Not to mention that Barbara didn't seem like the type to gossip about her friends.

"It kind of seems like being involved in my mess is bringing up some bad memories and making things worse. Maybe I should go." Although where she'd go if she left, she wasn't sure.

"Not a chance," the other woman said, glaring down her slightly long nose. "You and Mikhail were brought together for a reason. I know it, you know it, and deep down, he knows it too. Baba Yagas don't believe in coincidence, and neither do Riders. He just needs a little time to adjust to the idea that his time for hiding out is done."

**"I'M** not hiding out," Mick protested a few hours later, when he returned from wherever he'd disappeared to. "I just need some space to figure out who I am now. Hell, *what* I am now, since I'm not a Rider anymore." He took a sip of the tea Barbara had forced on him. He would rather have had vodka.

"Ding!" Barbara said cheerfully. "Time's up. Life calling on line two."

"I knew I would regret the day when Liam introduced you to television," Mick muttered under his breath. "So, what have you been talking about since I've been gone? Have you come up with any more answers?"

"Not exactly," Jenna told him, shaking her head ruefully. "We went over all of my grandmother's notebooks, but we didn't spot anything helpful." She gestured at the leather-bound books spread all across the table, next to her empty knapsack.

"We also talked about how the fact that Jenna showed up on the doorstep of the only person for miles around who actually had years of experience with faeries and the Otherworld was too convenient to be a coincidence," Barbara added, giving Mick a pointed stare. "I told her you would agree."

Mick sighed. "Yeah, there's really no escaping that one. Sometimes fate is a relentless bitch." There was a bitter tone in his voice.

Jenna gazed at him across the table. "I'm sorry. I really didn't mean to drag you into my troubles." Not that she wasn't grateful that his long walk seemed to have brought about a change of heart.

"No, I'm sorry," Mick said. "I don't mean to be so ungracious about this. It's not your fault." He gazed at her over his mug, his eyes a startlingly bright blue. "I don't know if I believe in destiny, exactly, since that would imply that we don't have the freedom to choose our actions, and I think we do. But I have seen enough in my very long life that I've come to believe that there are times when some power—call it the gods, the universe, whatever you please—decides to take a hand in events. Maybe this curse has gone on too long, and the universe feels a need to right the imbalance. Maybe your baby is going to grow up to be someone special and the gods want him or her to stay on this side of the doorway." He shrugged. "Either way, I'm clearly a part of this whether or not I want to be. We'll just have to make the best of it."

Jenna held back a sigh. It wasn't exactly an enthusiastic endorsement, but she supposed it was the best she was going to get. At least he was willing to help, no matter how reluctantly.

"What do we do next, then?" she asked.

Barbara pulled a laptop out from underneath the cupboard. "Now we search the World Wide Web," she said. "There has got to be a clue out there somewhere, and by golly, we are going to find it. Preferably before dinner. I'm a terrible cook when I'm rushed, and I'm not all that great when I'm not."

# CHAPTER 7

**STUART** Wilmington Wadsworth III, Stu to his friends, very carefully swung his golf club and tapped his ball a little too much to the left so it went into the rough.

"Bad luck," said his father, Stuart Wilmington Wadsworth II, as he sank a putt into the eighteenth hole. "That's just like you, isn't it? So close, but no follow-through." He leaned down to pocket the ball.

Stu glanced at their caddies, who were studiously ignoring the conversation as usual. "I suppose you're right, Father. I guess this means I owe you a drink at the clubhouse." He tapped his ball in, added up his just-lousy-enough score, handed his club to his caddy, Miguel, and climbed into the golf cart.

His father heaved himself up into the driver's seat. The two were clearly identifiable as family, although the elder Wadsworth was forty pounds heavier and what little was left of his hair was more gray than the brown it had started out. But they both had straight patrician noses, strong chins, and an air of prosperity. When Stu looked at his father, it felt as though he could see a mirror into his future. It wasn't a comfortable sensation, although that was only one of the many reasons he saw his father as little as possible.

The fact that the guy was a merciless, mercenary, inflexible son of a bitch might also have something to do with it.

As they rode down the fairway toward the clubhouse and that promised drink, they returned to the conversation they'd been having when Stu threw the game. He'd hoped that gloating over his triumph would distract his father from the topic, but apparently Stu wasn't going to win there either.

"To be honest," Stuart Senior said, his jowls jiggling as they bounced onto the path to the clubhouse, "I don't know why you stayed with her as long as you did. She was a nice enough girl, I suppose, but she wasn't good enough for you. I always thought she was after your money."

Stu sighed. Jenna was a lot of things, but greedy wasn't one of them. At least, he hadn't thought so. Before. Ironically, he'd mostly dated her to make his father happy, since his playboy ways had gotten him into such trouble, and she'd seemed like a stabilizing influence.

"You think everyone is after our money, Father. Jenna didn't ask me for anything. She just stood there and lied to my face. Tried to tell me that the baby was mine, when she knew damn well I'd had a vasectomy when Julie and I were at the end of our marriage."

Senior grunted. "And don't think I've ever forgiven you for that particular piece of stupidity either. I can't believe you threw away any chance of my having a grandchild from my eldest son just so you could thwart a woman you ended up divorcing two months later." He scowled at Stu, barely taking his eyes off the road. "You're an idiot. You've always been an idiot. I can't believe you're my son."

"Sometime I find it hard to believe, too, Father," Stu said. He occasionally had fantasies about being the secret love child of his mother and the gardener. Or a plumber. Anyone other than the man sitting next to him. Of course, if that were true, he'd be broke, and he wouldn't like that much either.

"So what are you going to do about the situation?" Senior asked, finally getting to the meat of the issue. Stu knew his father hadn't asked him to play golf just for the joy of his company.

"There's nothing *to* do," Stu said. "I already told her that I knew the baby couldn't possibly be mine and that there was no way I was going to marry her and raise some other man's bastard. It was bad enough she fooled around on me, but trying to lie her way out of it was ridiculous. So I told her we were through, made sure that Mitchell understood that it wasn't in his best interests to keep her on as his personal assistant, and then wiped my hands of the entire mess." He didn't mention how stunned he'd been by her betrayal, as unexpected as it was unfair. He'd actually been faithful to her, probably the first time in his life he'd ever bothered, including during his previous marriage. And this was how she repaid him.

"Are you completely certain the baby isn't yours?" his father asked, sounding both annoyed and marginally hopeful. "After all, vasectomies do fail occasionally."

"That's what Jenna said," Stu groused. "You know as well as I do that the odds are astronomical. It's a lot more likely she thought she could have both me and some piece of fun on the side."

"What's sauce for the goose is sauce for the gander, eh?" his father said in a smug tone. He prided himself on never straying from his marriage vows, even after he and Stu's mother moved into separate bedrooms. Stu didn't figure it was much of a hardship, since as far as he could tell the old man was a lot more interested in money than he was in women anyway.

"Still, you should at least get her to take a blood test. After all, there were astronomical odds against my grandfather striking oil the first time he sank a well, and yet here we are.

The Wadsworths are all about beating the odds. And taking advantage of every opportunity when it comes along. Get the girl to take a test, just in case."

*Shit.* "It's too late, Father. She's gone. Good riddance, I say."

The golf cart screeched to a halt, startling a nearby flock of geese that had been dozing on a water hazard.

"What do you mean, she's gone?" His father turned around now and gave him the full force of the Wadsworth Senior basilisk glare.

Stu shrugged. "Gone. She's got no job and no prospects of one. I made sure of that. I hired a PI to check up on her." Well, less to check on her than to find out who the hell she'd been sleeping with. Then the incompetent ass had failed to find so much as a clue. "It looks like she's cleared off. There's no sign of her. Like I said, good riddance."

He thought actual steam was going to come out of his father's slightly sunburned ears. "Oh my God! What did I do to deserve such a moron for a son?" Senior threw his hands up in the air. "Situations like this have to be controlled. You can't just let the woman disappear into thin air. Who the hell knows what mischief she is up to?" His face turned reddish-purple, and for a minute Stu hoped the man would actually have a heart attack.

"You've always been a loose cannon, boy, bringing embarrassment to the family with drugs and partying and inappropriate women and bad business deals, but this is the last straw. Don't you realize what's at stake here? What if the child *is* yours? Then Jenna could go after your inheritance, what's left of it, plus try to get her hands on a chunk of the family money. Even if the child isn't yours, we need to be able to prove it."

Senior shook his head. "Your brother Clive would never have let things get so out of hand. I've had it with you, Stuart. Go find the girl and get her to agree to a prenatal DNA test. I'm not waiting nine months to find out just how screwed we are. If that baby is a Wadsworth, it needs to be under our control from day one. If it's not, we want to make sure your woman doesn't go around telling everyone it is."

Stu opened his mouth to protest but his father silenced him with a wave of his hand, the sun glinting off the large gold-and-diamond ring on his pinky.

"I mean it, Stuart. It is time for you to step up and prove that you can do whatever needs to be done to protect this family. Or else you can consider yourself out of it, once and for all."

ZILYA stomped her foot. Daintily, of course. She might be peeved, but she was still a faery, and there were standards to be kept. In fact, that was the whole point, really. *Some* people, some *royal* people, might be willing to let the old ways go, but Zilya and many of her friends still thought such things were important. Plus, of course, those old ways worked in her favor. She wasn't about to let such an extraordinary and precious advantage go now.

Children were so rarely born in the Otherworld these days. At least to her people, although some of the lesser races still reproduced at an irritatingly regular rate. Even the Queen, mighty as she was, hadn't had a child in centuries.

Zilya herself had never seen the point in the whole messy, uncomfortable process, but she had no compunction against benefiting from others going through it, especially when she could turn her once-a-generation Human child into additional influence and power on this side of the doorway. The fact that she always placed "her" children with faery families who would value them and treat them well was a small weakness, one she blamed on her fondness for a long-dead blacksmith.

Zilya had been a potent force in her native Russia before most of the paranormal folks were forced to move to the other side of the doorways permanently. Once, bored with her usual forest haunts, she roamed farther afield than usual, entertaining herself by visiting her "cousins" in Britain. While there, she had been captivated by a handsome Human, a humble blacksmith with huge muscles and a gentle soul.

Although he was intrigued and flattered by Zilya's attentions, he eventually chose Rose over her. Zilya had been furious, and frustrated, and maybe even a little bit hurt.

Although her ire had mostly died down over the years (mostly—faeries had long memories and held grudges longer than sequoias were tall), Zilya had grown to enjoy the benefits she derived from being able to sidestep the Queen's rule against stealing mortal children and bringing them to the Otherworld. As far as she was concerned, she was doing these children a favor. Humans were, after all, inferior beings; their short lives and gullible natures made them either playthings or inconveniences, not equals. The babies she carried away to the Otherworld lived long, pampered lives—what could be wrong with that?

If Zilya herself was able to parlay the gift of a baby into influence at court, to offset the disadvantage of not being allowed into the Queen's precious inner circle, well, that was all to the better. And no annoying snippet of a Human girl was going to keep Zilya from what was rightfully hers.

Nor, for that matter, was some damned interfering former Rider, or even the Queen herself. There was more than one way to skin a centaur, and Zilya wasn't about to let a little thing like a royal command get in her way.

After all, this was the Otherworld, and words had power—but one had to be quite certain one used *the right words*. The Queen had very clearly forbidden Zilya to go anywhere near Jenna and her unborn child. But she hadn't said anything about Zilya sending others to do her work for her, had she?

The stomping foot began to tap a gentle rhythm on the fern-carpeted floor of Zilya's modest but elegant home. Anger wouldn't get her anywhere. Planning, on the other hand, leavened with a dollop of underhanded scheming and a dash of ruthlessness, would ensure that she would end up with everything that was rightfully hers.

It was a pity she wasn't going to be able to see the look on Jenna's face in person when the Human finally realized that there was no way to beat the curse and that history was destined to repeat itself—at least for all those in her line—until the Earth stopped spinning around the sun. Or whenever Zilya grew bored with the game, which was likely to be about the same time.

**AFTER** little Babs returned from school, she sat at the table with the other three, eating cookies by breaking them into four precisely equal pieces and dunking them into a bowl of milk. Since nobody else seemed to think it was strange, Jenna didn't bother to mention it.

"What are you all doing?" Babs asked after she finished off the last chunk and neatly drank the milk from the bowl. "Is it homework? I have homework, but I will do it after dinner."

"It is, in a way," Barbara agreed, tapping some more keys on her laptop. "We are trying to find the answers to Jenna's riddle."

"I like riddles," Babs said. "Maybe I can help."

Jenna smiled at the little girl and pointed at the pile of notebooks taking up all the space on the table not currently being used by the laptop. "See that? It's full of research. It has all the notebooks my grandmother kept, plus everything I could find in the fairy tales I devoured that might possibly be relevant. I've read about legends and myths and curses until I see the information in my sleep. But I've never found anything remotely useful. So now we're looking on the Internet. But I'm afraid we're not getting very far. It isn't easy."

Babs stared at her with round owl eyes. "Barbara says that most things worth doing are not easy. But that does not make them not worth doing."

Jenna nodded. "That's very true. And Barbara is the one who figured out the line about 'The sun's bright ray where none is slanted.' She is very smart, isn't she?"

Babs nodded. "What are some of the other lines?"

Mick gave her an affectionate smile. "Well, there's one that goes, 'A rose's cry at rock enchanted.'"

"That is silly," Babs said. "Roses do not cry."

"I know," Jenna agreed ruefully. "Not that I didn't look up every kind of rose on the planet in case there was one with a funky tear-related name. But I never found anything close."

"What about 'rock enchanted'?" muttered Barbara, typing the words into a search engine.

"Do you have any idea how many magical rocks there are?" Jenna said. She slumped over onto her pillowed arms, equal parts tired and discouraged.

"There's the Baetylus, a sacred stone endowed with life, from Greek mythology. The Hindus and Buddhists had Cintamani, which was supposed to fulfill wishes. Sir Gawain won the Stone of Giramphiel from a guy named Fimbeus and used it to protect himself from dragons." She sat up straight and held out three fingers, then a fourth.

"Then we have Singasteinn; Loki used that one. Vaidurya was worn by the goddess Lakshmi and was supposed to be the most beautiful of all stones." She put up another couple of fingers. "Plus, of course, there are the big ones, like Stonehenge, and the Stone of Scone on the hill of Tara, where the kings of Ireland were crowned. Or the legendary Philosopher's Stone, sought by alchemists for its ability to turn lead into gold." She bit her lip. "Shall I go on?"

Mick blinked, looking slightly stunned by her list. "I guess you *have* been doing your research, haven't you?"

Jenna sighed. "That's just the tip of the iceberg, the ones I could remember off the top of my head. Believe me, I've got much more extensive lists if you want to look at them. The problem is there is no hint in the curse as to which magical stone it refers to, and of course, most of them are simply legends, so I don't know how I'd find it even if I could figure out which one the rhyme is talking about."

"Mmm, I see your point," Barbara said, typing some more.

Something caught her interest as she scanned through a page. Then she surprised them all by looking up with a grin.

"I think maybe you're being too literal," she said. "Or possibly not literal enough."

"What the hell are you talking about?" Mick asked.

Jenna felt her heart skip a beat.

"Not hell," Barbara said. "Texas." She thought for a moment. "Although some would argue they are one and the same, at least in the summer."

# CHAPTER 8

**THE** look on Jenna's face was almost worth the inconvenience of having been dragged into the midst of her crazy mess at a time when all Day wanted was to be left alone.

"Texas?" she repeated, sounding incredulous. "There's a magical stone in *Texas*?"

Day cocked an eyebrow at Barbara, waiting for her to explain. This should be interesting.

"Not a magical stone," Barbara said. "An enchanted rock. Or rather, *the* Enchanted Rock. It's in a state park of the same name in Fredericksburg, Texas. According to Wikipedia, it is an enormous pink granite pluton batholith, whatever the heck that is when it's at home."

Day watched Jenna's excitement slide away like a wave into the tide. "That doesn't sound very enchanted to me," she said. "Besides, my family was living in Europe when Zilya cursed my many-great-grandmother; wouldn't the enchanted rock have to be located there?"

Mikhail swiveled around in his seat so he was facing her,

not sure how to explain the intricacies of how true magic worked. "I can see how you would think that, but it isn't that simple. Like we said, curses don't necessarily take a form that the person casting them has complete control over. Magic is more complicated than that."

Jenna shook her head. "You're not making any sense. Zilya wanted to punish my family and she set up the curse so that each generation would have to give up a firstborn child. It's spelled out in those first couple of stanzas."

"Right," he said. "She could set up with curse exactly as she wanted. But once your ancestor insisted that Zilya follow the rules and provide a way out, the power of tradition and myth took over and that part of the rhyme was out of Zilya's hands. Zilya herself may not even know the solution to the curse."

"Are you *serious*?" Jenna cried, throwing her hands up in the air. "This stuff is crazy!"

Barbara shrugged. "I don't know. Compared to daytime television, it seems quite sane to me. Either way, the answer to the curse could have been here in America all along, waiting for your people to move here and find it."

Jenna gave her a funny look. Then stared at Day.

"What?" he asked.

"That would mean that Barbara was right, and I'm supposed to be the one who solves it," she said in a shaky voice. "Because I've met you."

"Maybe," he said flatly. "Anyway, back to this Enchanted Rock in Texas. Barbara, I'm assuming you have reasons besides the name that make it seem as though it might be what Jenna's been looking for, as unlikely as that might seem."

Barbara pushed her cloud of dark hair back and shifted the laptop slightly so they could see what she was pointing to. "Here, it says that the local native tribes thought the rock had mystical and spiritual attributes, which is how it got its name. There are many legends associated with it through the years. The natives believed that the mound was a portal to another world, and once when a Spanish soldier fled to the rock when he was being chased by natives, he disappeared. When he reappeared later, he swore that he had fallen into a cavern and been swallowed up, after which he met many spirits and then was returned to where he came."

"That sounds almost like the stories they tell in Europe of people who accidentally found their way into a faery mound and then wandered into the land of Faerie itself. I mean, the Otherworld." Jenna looked intrigued. "Could there be a doorway to the Otherworld in Fredericksburg, Texas? Surely someone would have noticed by now."

Mikhail shrugged. "You would be amazed at the things that exist right under people's noses. If it *was* a portal, it should have been sealed shut when the paranormal folks retreated to the Otherworld. But that doesn't mean we couldn't get through."

"What, you have some kind of magic key or something?" Jenna asked, sounding impressed.

He snorted. "I *am* a magic key, Jenna. I can come and go through any entrance to the Otherworld. I suspect that's part of why this damned riddle includes me. The solution may lie on the other side of the doorway. Remember the third stanza: 'This curse unbroken now shall be, down into eternity. Unless you find the pathway through and solve the riddle with this clue.'"

"But I was just there," Jenna said. She scrubbed her hands over her face as if the conversation was making her head hurt. "Why couldn't I just do whatever I needed to do while I was already through the door?"

"I don't know," Mikhail admitted. "Maybe so the Queen isn't involved in any way? Or because there is something else that has to happen while you're there? Maybe there is something else in the part of the riddle we haven't figured out yet."

"How can you be so sure we've figured out this part?" Jenna asked, chewing on a fingernail. "Just because the name is right and there are stories that make it sound like it might possibly be associated with the Otherworld doesn't mean it is the right rock."

Mikhail grinned, not able to hold it in. He just loved unraveling riddles. It was like following a scavenger hunt to the treasure at the end. Alexei always used to tease him, saying it was childish, but Mikhail didn't care. He couldn't help it; finding the answers to the twisting puzzles made him happy. Even now, under these bizarre circumstances.

"Look," he said, aiming his finger at one particular note in the list of facts about the rock. He suspected it was the bit that had caught Barbara's eye too. "Do you see what that says?"

Jenna moved closer to peer at the screen and Mikhail had to suppress a shiver as a lock of her hair brushed over the back of his hand.

"A Spanish soldier named Don Jesús Navarro rescued the daughter of Chief Tehuan after she was kidnapped by Comanches who intended to sacrifice her on the rock." Jenna wrinkled her nose. "That's nice, of course, but what does it prove?"

"Look at the name of the girl the soldier saved," Mikhail said.

Jenna reread the paragraph more closely and gave out a gasp. "'The native maiden Rosa,'" she read aloud. "*A rose's cry at rock enchanted.* Oh my God, it was never a crying rose, it was a woman named Rosa crying." A single tear slid down her own face at the realization that they'd found the answer to a second line.

She threw her arms around Mikhail and hugged him hard. "Thank you, Mick. Thank you. I can't believe you did it."

Part of him wanted to pull away. Part of him wanted to point out that Barbara had found the answer, and he'd just brought Jenna to her. Part of him wanted to wrap his arms around Jenna and hug her back, feel her warmth and softness under his hands. In an instant, he was confused and happy and angry and turned on, all at once. He didn't know which one of those feelings was worse, but he did know that the next time he and fate came face-to-face, he was going to kick its damned ass.

Babs clapped her hands, breaking the spell of the moment. "This is excellent! Now can we start making dinner?" Three faces gazed at her with varying degrees of concern and no notable interest in the topic of food.

"What is the matter?" she asked, a little plaintively. "Barbara and Day helped our new friend Jenna to solve part of her riddle. That is a good thing, is it not? Why is no one happy? Why does Jenna cry? Will the nasty faery still get to steal her baby?"

Barbara gave Day a wry look and mouthed the word *insecure* over the top of the little girl's pixie-edged hair before patting Babs lightly on the hand.

Day wasn't really surprised. Babs was usually so bright-eyed and perky, you tended to forget that she'd been kidnapped by a Rusalka who had killed her parents and forced to live with a madwoman in the Otherworld, hidden away from all normal company. Until Liam and Barbara had rescued and adopted her, Babs hadn't had anything resembling a normal life. It made sense that anything that threatened to rock the equanimity of her current world would make the girl uneasy. Especially since they were talking about a faery stealing someone's baby.

"Maybe we should continue this conversation at another time," he said, raising an eyebrow in Babs's direction.

"And what time would be more convenient for Babs to learn that the world can be a complicated and difficult place?" Barbara asked softly. She gave Day's hand a tap, a slightly less gentle version of her gesture of comfort to the child. "Do we ever get old enough or live long enough for that lesson not to carry a sting in its tail?"

*No*, Day thought. *We never do.* "Fine," he said briskly. "Then let's look at the first problem: Jenna has to go back to the Otherworld."

Jenna bit her lip. "I did okay there the first time. I'll be fine. Right?" She didn't sound all that sure, though, and Day didn't blame her.

"The first time you went through an official doorway and were given a magical talisman by the guardian there, right?" Barbara asked. Day found it somewhat alarming that even the usually unflappable Baba Yaga had the tiniest hint of a worry line creasing her high forehead.

"That's right," Jenna said. "Mick said it would keep me safe from the weird way that the Otherworld can affect time, so I wouldn't pull a Rip Van Winkle."

"A who?" Barbara shook her head. "Never mind. Yes, that's a concern. I can come and go without it affecting me, as can anyone with me. Day used to be the same way, but no one really knows for sure these days if his ability still carries over to others. If you go in through an unauthorized entrance, like the one we think might be hidden within the Enchanted Rock, there is no guarantee if you will return to find that two weeks have passed, or two months, or two decades."

"Oh," Jenna said, and then shrugged. "Well, it isn't as though I have any close friends or family these days. Or a job I have to worry about being late to. If going back into the Otherworld and solving the rest of the riddle is the only way to save my baby, I'll just have to take the chance."

She lifted her chin and gazed defiantly at Day, as though daring him to argue. He wanted to applaud instead, not that he'd tell her that. He thought she was one of the bravest women he had ever known, and he'd known quite a few. The contrast between them was rather ironic; he, known for being a hero, couldn't even muster the nerve to talk to his own brothers. Jenna, on the other hand, was willing to risk everything—even fight a ruthless faery in a strange and magical land—just for the possibility to give her unborn child a normal life. He was impressed despite himself, although that didn't mean he thought she had a chance in hell of succeeding.

"What about you, Mikhail?" Barbara asked. "Are you willing to risk it too?"

"What?" Jenna said, sitting up even straighter. "But I thought Mick could come and go as he pleased. He didn't have to wear that bracelet thing when we went through the first time."

Day shrugged. "I'm fine by myself. I think what the Baba Yaga is suggesting is that we have no way of knowing if sticking close to you on the other side will somehow influence my reaction to the time variations, since we will obviously be walking through the same ebb and flow."

Babs scowled. "Thinking about this makes my head hurt. Time should not play games."

"I couldn't agree more," Jenna said, rubbing her temples. "Maybe you shouldn't come, Mick. I mean, you've gotten me this far, and I really appreciate it, but I wouldn't want you to chance losing years with—"

Mick felt the familiar grief bubbling up in his chest and the walls closing in. "I have nothing left to lose," he said in a rough voice. "We should talk about the second problem. In order to get to the Enchanted Rock, we have to drive from here to Texas. That's a long journey on the back of a motorcycle, especially if we can't use its ability to go faster than normal."

Jenna's face grew even whiter than usual. "No. Definitely not. That was . . . no."

"I didn't think so," Day said. "Baba, I don't suppose you could drive us in the Airstream?"

"Sorry, no," Barbara said with regret. "That would definitely be taking my involvement too far. Right now all I'm doing is fiddling around on the Internet. If I happened to stumble across something Jenna found helpful, that's hardly proof of intentional interference. Driving the two of you across the country, on the other hand . . ."

"Yeah, I could see how that would look a tad incriminating," Jenna said with a wan grin. "What about an airplane?

My credit card is about tapped out, but I might be able to squeeze two plane tickets out of it, if we don't mind going one way and figuring some other way back."

It was Day's turn to blanch. Not much on either side of the doorway scared him, but the idea of getting into a small metal tube and being somehow propelled through the sky without falling from impossible heights made his stomach tie itself into knots. "No," he said. "No planes. You can take one and I'll meet you there."

"I don't think so," Barbara said in a thoughtful tone, shaking her head. "I get the feeling you two should stay together." She tapped one finger on the table. "A rather strong feeling at that."

"Those feelings are sometimes called premonitions," Babs told Jenna solemnly. "It is not a good idea to ignore them. Especially when Barbara has them."

"Oh," Jenna said. "I guess we're stuck together, then," she said, looking at Day from underneath those long, dark lashes. "I mean, if you're still coming."

The walls got even closer and Day stood up from the table with a scrape of his chair legs against the wooden floor. "It would seem that is what the universe has in mind. In which case, I think I should go back to Saranac Lake, where we left the bike. I can stop by my cabin and pick up some things and then ride the fast way here, since you won't be with me. I can be back by later this evening and we can get an early start in the morning."

He tried not to hyperventilate, but he could feel his chest growing tighter, as if he couldn't draw in enough air, no matter how hard he breathed. "I'm sure you'll be safe enough until I return." Day walked to the door and looked back at Barbara. "If I could trouble you to open the passageway in the Airstream, it would be a lot faster than walking back to the Adirondacks."

Barbara gave him an inscrutable look and followed him down the path to the barn, easily able to keep up with his current rapid, almost-running pace because of her long legs.

When they were almost to the hut-turned–silver trailer, she said, "Jenna was right. You *are* rude now. I wouldn't have believed it if I hadn't seen it for myself."

Day stopped at where the door to the Airstream would be if it wasn't hiding. Out in the open, away from Jenna, he almost felt as though he could breathe normally. Almost.

"I'm doing the best I can," he said, gazing at the ground.

Barbara rolled her eyes. "I know you're having a tough time, old friend, although frankly, I think you're being way too hard on yourself. But it is clear to me that you are involved in this situation up to your neck, and the sooner you face up to that, the easier this will be on everyone."

When Day opened his mouth to argue, she added, "Jenna is no evil and insane Baba Yaga trying to lure you into danger. She's a nice girl who got dragged into a fairy tale through no fault of her own. I like her. She has backbone. You've had enough time to lick your wounds. It's time to pull your head out of your ass and get back to living your life. It seems to me that this is as good a place to start as any."

"That's a little harsh," Day said, taken aback.

"Harsh or not, it has to be said, and apparently no one else is going to say it." Barbara shook her head. "Of course, the fact that you're avoiding everyone who knows you might have something to do with that. Either way, we have known each other long enough that you shouldn't be surprised by my bluntness. Or be foolish enough to mistake it for lack of caring, when in fact, it is exactly the opposite."

"I'm doing the best I can."

"I don't think you are," Barbara said. "I think you're wallowing. I get it—a horrible thing happened to you, Alexei, and Gregori, and you feel guilty. Did it ever occur to you that Beka, Bella, and I feel guilty too, because we didn't find you faster? Especially Bella, since she tried to rescue you and actually fell into Brenna's trap too."

In fact, it hadn't. Not for a minute. "That's not her fault! Brenna was an evil, cunning old woman. I had a lot more years of experience dealing with her than Bella did, and I still fell for her lies."

"My point exactly, Mikhail." Barbara patted him on the shoulder, perhaps a tad more assertively than she'd intended to, since he rocked back on his heels from the strength of it.

"It doesn't matter what happened. What's done is done. What matters now is what you do with the rest of your life. Not being immortal anymore means you don't have time to waste sitting around beating yourself up. Maybe it is time to get back to the land of the living and do something with a little more purpose than self-flagellation of the soul."

"I swore I wasn't going to rescue any more damsels in distress," Day muttered.

To his surprise, Barbara gave him a lopsided grin, banging on the side of the trailer to make it produce a door. "What makes you think she isn't rescuing you?" she asked, and stomped inside without a backward look.

**"ARE** you sure about this?" Liam asked Jenna as they sat down over dinner. He gave her and Barbara equally dubious looks while simultaneously pouring Babs some more milk. "I mean, I realize that it sounds like the answers lie through the doorway, but aren't you worried about what being over there without a Baba Yaga or a talisman might do to your baby?" Then he said, "OW," as Barbara kicked him under the table with a heavily booted foot.

Jenna smiled at Barbara. "Thanks, but it's okay. I did think of that on my own." She curled one hand protectively over her belly. She turned to Liam. "I'm worried about that possibility, too, but I think the alternatives are worse. If I don't go, then Zilya takes my baby. I know she swears she gives them good homes, and maybe she even does. But they're raised in a strange land by people who aren't even Human. I don't want that for my little girl."

Babs gave her a wide-eyed look and nodded without saying

anything, most of her attention seemingly focused on the fried chicken on her plate, which she was devouring with single-minded determination.

"Besides," Jenna added. "This damned curse managed to make sure I got pregnant, no matter how careful I was. How am I to know that it wouldn't somehow make it impossible not to have a second child, another girl to keep the curse going? No. This thing stops with me, one way or the other."

Liam chewed on a hunk of crusty bread thoughtfully. "I see your point. Besides, you'll have Mikhail with you. If anyone can keep you safe, he can." He winked at Barbara. "I mean, if you can't have my wife."

Jenna shook her head. "I'm not sure Mick wants to go. He's been pretty adamant about not wanting to get involved, no matter how much Barbara talks about fate and destiny."

"I like Day," Babs said in a gloomy voice. "What happened to him was bad."

"Yes it was," Barbara agreed, sounding much the same as her small adopted daughter. "It was bad and unfair."

"What happened?" Jenna asked. "Does it have anything to do with how he lost his immortality and why he is living up in that cabin in the middle of nowhere?" She added, "If you don't mind me asking. He's nice to me, in his own crabby way. I like him."

"A bad Baba Yaga put him in a cage and tortured him so that he bled and bled," Babs said. "She hurt his brothers Gregori Sun and Alexei Knight too. They were hurt very much for a long time. It made them broken. It was very horrible. Now Day is all better, but he is still sad."

Jenna was taken aback by both the information and the fact that it was recited so matter-of-factly by a seven-year-old. "That's terrible," she said. "No wonder he wants to hide away in the mountains by himself."

Liam smiled at her, having caught her aghast look, no doubt. "You probably think we should have kept this kind of brutal reality away from Babs until she is older, but she had a difficult and unusual upbringing and she is a lot tougher than she looks."

"Besides," Barbara said, "she is a Baba Yaga in training, and part of that training is exposing her to all that a Baba Yaga might come into contact with, good and bad. How else is she going to learn?"

Jenna felt completely unequipped for parenthood as it was. She couldn't even imagine trying to raise a child to be a powerful mythical witch. She had a sudden fervent desire to see what her own little girl would grow up to be, a yearning so strong it made her heart spasm until she gasped.

"Are you okay?" Liam asked. "Do you need a doctor?"

"I'm fine," she said, wrapping her arms around her middle. "I don't need a doctor. I need a miracle."

Barbara gazed fondly at her husband and adopted daughter. "Lucky for you," she said. "Around here we're kind of in the business of miracles." She gave Jenna one of her small smiles, barely an upward curving of the edge of her lips. "Plus, I think I have some motorcycle gear that will fit you if I take up the hems on the pants a bit. If you're going on an adventure, the least we can do is see that you're properly dressed."

# CHAPTER 9

**DAY** was inside the cabin, throwing clothes and supplies into his saddlebags, when he thought he heard a noise outside. He swung the door open and peered out into the dimming light of early evening, but all he saw was the Yamaha, sitting in all her gleaming white glory in the clearing out front. The single bulb overhead barely reached that far, but Day's eyes were pretty good at night and he didn't see anything but some branches swaying in the wind.

He grunted and shut the door, going over to kneel in front of Jenna's duffel bag. He didn't feel comfortable rooting around in her things, but she was going to need clothes and her toothbrush and such for the trip, and he couldn't bring the entire bag. He pulled out a couple of pairs of pants and some shirts to go with them, then hesitated before reaching in to grab some surprisingly sexy underwear and bras. Somehow he hadn't envisioned her wearing such frilly, silky things. Now, of course, it would be hard not to. Dammit.

It was tough enough ignoring her luscious curves and all

that flowing straight dark hair, which he could easily imagine spread out over him as they lay together. Not that they ever would. But still, he didn't understand what it was about this woman that so intrigued and attracted him. He hadn't been even vaguely interested in anyone—Human or Paranormal— since things had gone to hell in several handbaskets and a hot air balloon. Maybe that was it. Maybe it had just been too long between lovers, and it had nothing to do with Jenna's feisty determination paired with her softness and vulnerability. Sure. Deprivation. That was his story and he was sticking to it.

The blare of a horn split the silent night, startling him into dropping the froth of underthings back into their bag. Had the bike still been an enchanted steed, it would have been an equine bugle of outrage and warning; in its metal form, it still sounded much the same.

Without thinking, Day raced out the door, a low growl forming unnoticed at the back of his throat. As he neared the motorcycle, he caught a glimpse of a thin, weedy form slinking off into the nearest stand of trees. Day chased after it, an atavistic roar pouring out of his chest and making small nocturnal animals run in the opposite direction.

After a moment, though, he came to his senses, at least enough to realize that chasing some unknown creature through the woods at night while leaving his cabin alone and unguarded was probably a bad idea. He stalked back to the motorcycle, patting her seat and talking to her as if she were a living thing. Which, in her own way, she was.

"Are you all right, my treasure? That nasty slinker didn't do anything to you, did it?" He checked her over, but everything seemed okay. "What do you think, old girl? Just some random Paranormal critter wandering around where it wasn't supposed to be, or some kind of trouble sent by our unfriend Zilya?"

Frankly, he suspected the latter, although with any luck the bike's alarm had scared it off before it could do whatever damage it had intended. Or else *he* had, with whatever *that* was. He'd never been in the habit of roaring and growling before, that was for sure.

"Do you suppose my eyes were glowing, the way Zilya said they did when I stepped in front of her magic?" he asked the bike, not really expecting any answer. But her engine purred a bit under his hand, even though technically, she wasn't turned on. Magical motorcycles rarely conformed to any technical limitations, in his experience.

"Yeah, I don't know if it matters either," he said, turning around to finish his packing, perhaps a little faster than he'd been doing it before. "It's still damned odd. And I'm not sure I like it."

**"YOU'RE** back late," Barbara said softly from the shadows. Day didn't jump. Much. "Everything okay?"

Day slung his leg over the side of the bike and grabbed the saddlebags before walking over to where she was standing, next to the darkened house.

"I think so. I caught something slinking around the motorcycle, but as far as I can tell, it didn't do any damage. My guess is that Zilya sent it; not sure what the thing was supposed to achieve."

Barbara shrugged, not moving from her position leaning against the yellow-painted wood. "Maybe it was just checking up. From what you said, Zilya had to promise the Queen not to go anywhere near Jenna. I'm guessing that she's not going to find it so easy to just stand back and do nothing. I'd keep your eyes open, if I were you."

"I will," Day said, leaning against the wall next to her. "Can I ask you something?"

Barbara didn't move, but he could feel her entire attention focusing. "Sure. Is this about Jenna?"

"No," he said. "It's about me. Something . . . strange . . . is happening. I can't explain it. I feel like something inside me is shifting. Like there is something moving under my skin. There have been a couple of odd incidents."

Barbara turned toward him, her eyes gleaming in the darkness and her expression calm and nonjudgmental. "Go on."

"Did Jenna tell you what happened when Zilya showed up looking for her at my cabin?" Day asked.

"I don't think so," Barbara said.

"You should have seen her," Day chuckled. "Jenna, I mean. She was like a wild thing; she shoved Zilya out the door and then tried to brain her with a big stick. It was epic. Alexei would have loved it." He fell silent for a moment, thinking of his brother and their long years together.

"Sounds like my kind of party," Barbara said. "Then what?"

"Once Zilya recovered from the shock of being attacked by a mere Human, she went after Jenna with magic—threw something at her that was supposed to both lay claim to the baby and cause Jenna a fair amount of pain in the process."

Barbara winced. "Sounds about standard for a pissed-off faery. What happened?"

Day gazed out at the sky, where a shooting star was winging across the heavens. "I stepped in between Jenna and the hex. I wasn't even thinking; it was just instinctive."

"Of course it was." Barbara gazed at him fondly. "You may think you have changed, but your gallantry was never just for show; it's part of who you are." She sighed. "That hex must have smarted, though."

"No, it didn't," Day said, still not looking at her. "It just . . . fizzled, I guess, and disappeared. I didn't feel a thing. Unless you count rage and a primal need to defend Jenna. I think I even growled. I know that Zilya said something about my eyes glowing, although I discounted it at the time."

"Huh." Out of the corner of his vision, he could see Barbara looking thoughtful. "That shouldn't have happened."

"No."

"Anything else?"

"When I chased that creature into the woods earlier to-night, I felt . . . different." Day didn't have the right words to describe it. "It's like I was me, but not me. Maybe it was because I'd been packing up Jenna's, um, intimate items, but somehow it felt like the thing was a threat to her and I wanted to tear it limb from limb." He turned to face his old friend. "Do you have any idea what's happening to me?"

"I'm afraid I don't," Barbara said with regret. "Maybe it's just a reaction to everything you've been through. Although that doesn't explain why Zilya's magic didn't affect you. Now that you're not a Rider, it should have. Maybe even if you still were one."

Day tried to pretend that phrase, *not a Rider*, didn't pierce him through the heart. There had only ever been three Riders to help the Baba Yagas of the world—him and his two half brothers. Now the Babas had no one to come to their aid, and neither he nor Alexei nor Gregori knew what or who they were without that title. Sometimes he thought it would have been better if the old witch had killed them, and finished the job she'd started.

"I don't suppose either of my brothers have mentioned anything unusual happening to them?" he asked, trying to sound casual. He doubted he fooled Barbara, but at least she would likely play along.

She patted him on the shoulder, her equivalent of most people's full-body hugs. "I'm sorry, Mikhail. I haven't seen either of them since I came to visit you all in the Otherworld while you were healing. They haven't been feeling any more sociable than you have, apparently."

"Oh," he said, hollowness echoing through his chest. He'd asked because he wondered if they, too, were experiencing something strange, but also because he missed them badly, and had hoped Barbara had some news of them. Of course, he could seek them out himself, but he wasn't quite ready for that.

Barbara pushed off from the wall. "Let's go into the house.

You've got a long ride ahead of you tomorrow, and I have some leftover chicken in the fridge with your name on it, if Liam hasn't gotten to it first. If you're really nice, I'll let you read a bedtime story to Babs. I'm pretty sure she's still awake, waiting for you to get back."

"And Jenna?" Day asked, trying not to care.

"Poor thing. She was exhausted. She conked out in the guest bedroom around nine, about a half hour ago," Barbara said. "If it's any consolation, she was worried about you."

"Huh," Day said. "She shouldn't have been."

Barbara opened the front door and half guided, half shoved him in. "I love you, Mikhail Day, but you're an idiot."

"Why? What did I say?" Day asked in an indignant whisper.

"Never mind," Barbara said, turning on the hall light with a click of her fingers, despite the fact that they were standing right next to the switch. Some habits die hard. "About the unusual things you've been experiencing . . . have you considered that it might be your maternal heritage coming through?"

Day stopped cold. "What are you talking about?"

She shrugged. "Well, I don't know much about your parents, of course. Your background was always sort of mysterious and vague. But Gregori said something to me once, years ago, about how your father's influence had been pretty powerful, overwhelming anything from your various mothers' sides to mold you into being the Riders. I just wondered if, now that things have changed, maybe your maternal side was somehow coming through more strongly. Of course, you'd know that better than I would. It's just a thought."

She steered him into the kitchen and pulled a plate of cold chicken out of the refrigerator. "Mind you, it could just be an unexpected side effect of the huge dose of the Water of Life and Death I had to give you to save your life. Even the Queen said she couldn't predict what that might do to you further down the road."

Day gnawed absently on a chicken leg, pondering her

words. "If it *is* the Water of Life and Death, what do you suppose it is doing?"

Barbara pushed back her cloud of dark hair with both hands. "Honestly? I have no idea. It could be releasing some gift we never knew you had. Or it could be starting to slowly kill you. No one has ever had that big a dose, so it's really hard to say."

He put the chicken down, appetite suddenly gone, and wiped his hands on a napkin. "Thanks, Baba. You are always such a comfort."

She gave him a wry look. "I know. I've been considering becoming a counselor. Or possibly a nurse."

Day shook his head. "If I were you, Baba Yaga, I'd stick to your day job."

"You know, that's what Liam said too." Barbara gave him one of her half smiles. "I do know something that will make you feel better. How do you feel about *Winnie-the-Pooh*? I hear the bear wins."

**BY** late afternoon the next day, Jenna was starting to wish she'd taken that plane after all. Mick's bike might be magical, in that it never needed gas and he never had to worry about a flat tire or mechanical problems, but that didn't make it any easier to sit on for hundreds of miles over bumpy roads. Even with frequent stops so she could pee and stretch her legs, Jenna's butt felt like someone's punching bag, and her back ached from the base of her spine to the top of her neck.

Also, it was raining.

She'd never really thought about the difference between driving through rain when you were in a car and when you were on a motorcycle. In a car, unless it was one of those rare torrential downpours, rain was simply a minor inconvenience. On the back of a bike, even a fairly light rain trickled in through every opening in your clothing, leaving you damp and cold. And then the breeze created by your own passage made you even colder.

"How many miles did you say it was to Fredericksburg?" she shouted in Mick's ear. That was the other thing about riding a motorcycle. It made casual chitchat pretty much impossible.

"About two thousand, from Barbara's house," he yelled back. "Why?"

Jenna leaned in closer to his strong back, less so he could hear her better and more for the warmth. Mick's large body gave off heat like a pile of smoldering coals. It was about the only thing keeping her going right now. "Just wondering," she said. "Also, sorry, but I kind of need to pee again. Can we stop soon?"

She could feel the chuckle resonating in his chest more than she could actually hear it over the noise of the road and the wind whistling past her helmet. Not for the first time, she sent a mental thank-you to Barbara for the loan of her second-best leather jacket and riding pants.

Fifteen minutes and about that many interminable miles later, they pulled off the road into a service station–slash–convenience store that looked like it had had its last facelift back in the late fifties. Jenna didn't care, as long as the attendant behind the counter was willing to give her the key to the bathrooms around the side.

She splashed a little hot water on her face after she washed her hands, but it didn't make her feel any warmer. Rubbing her butt to try and get the blood flowing again didn't help much either. She sighed. If she didn't toughen up, this was going to be a very long trip.

"How are you doing?" Mick asked her as she reentered the shop and handed the keys back to the clerk behind the counter. He looked about eighteen, with stringy hair and a chin full of pimples, but he gave her a shy smile as he took the long rectangle that said BATHROOM, DO NOT LOSE on it.

"Honestly?" Jenna said. "I'm feeling a little ragged around

the edges. I'm sorry. I guess it takes a while to get used to long rides on two wheels instead of four."

"I expect the rain isn't helping any," Mick said. As if his words were a signal, the drizzle they'd been driving in for the last two hours suddenly turned into a deluge.

"Oh, *come on*," Jenna said. "Now, that's just not funny."

The kid behind the counter tried to cover his laugh with one bony hand, without much success. "Not really riding weather, is it, miss? Unless you're a duck." He chuckled at his own joke.

"Quack," Jenna said weakly. She turned to Mick. "I know you wanted to make it a little farther today, but do you think maybe we could stop a little early? Maybe we could find someplace near here to stay the night. Hopefully the rain will have stopped by the morning."

Mick shrugged his massive shoulders, clearly not bothered by the ride, the rain, or the cold, but willing to do whatever she wanted. "Your quest, your call." He turned to young clerk. "I don't suppose there's a hotel or motel anywhere near here that would have a room for the night? Maybe a campground?"

The kid squinted at them doubtfully. "Only thing open this time of the year is the Come On Inn. It's mostly for truckers and such passing through. The few nice places are only open come summer, once tourist season starts. You know, them bed-and-breakfast kind of things. But the Come On Inn is okay. The Beckers—the folks who own it—are honest and the sheets are clean, if you don't mind that it ain't fancy."

"If they have hot showers and something to sit on that isn't moving, it's fine with me," Jenna said in a fervent voice.

Mick's lips twitched. "I guess you'd better give me directions," he said. He glanced at the crooked clock on the wall, which said four thirty-seven and had actual hands, not a digital readout. The big hand was a hunter holding a shotgun, and the little hand was a fleeing duck. "And maybe some idea of where we can pick up some food along the way, since I'm thinking my friend here is going to be hungry soon."

Jenna gave him a mock scowl, hands on her hips. "Just because I'm eating for two doesn't mean all I think about is food."

"There's a pizza place right down the road, about a mile from the motel," the boy said. "They make the best sausage pizza you ever had too."

"*Pizza*," Jenna breathed. "*With sausage.*"

Mick snorted. "I stand corrected. Now, about those directions."

**THE** Come On Inn was older than the gas station by a couple of decades and hadn't had a paint job in almost as long. Straggly weeds grew up amid the potholes that generously dotted the parking lot, and the neon sign at the entrance was missing the small *O* and the second *N*. There were only two cars in the lot, one in front of the door labeled OFFICE, and one way down at the end of the long, one-story building. A small ancient-looking dog of indiscriminate parentage barked at them as they walked under the overhanging porch roof in front of the entrance.

"Nice place," Mick said cheerfully. Jenna couldn't tell if he was being sarcastic or not.

The bell over the door gave a tone-deaf clang as they walked through and the skinny woman behind the desk looked up from her gossip magazine with a startled and not entirely pleased look on her narrow face. A sharp nose sniffed the air, as if trying to discern which ill wind had blown them through her door.

"Do you have a reservation?" she asked.

Jenna opened her mouth to say something (probably sarcastic), but Mick stepped forward and gave the woman the full benefit of his blue-eyed stare and white-toothed smile. "I'm so sorry," he said. "We don't mean to inconvenience you. But this rain has made traveling on kind of difficult, and the nice young man at the convenience store recommended you so highly, we thought we'd take the chance that maybe you'd have a room available for two cold, wet strangers."

Jenna thought he was laying it on a little heavily, but the woman behind the desk gave him an answering, if slightly less attractive smile, and said, "Well, I'm sure I can come up with something. We've got a couple of rooms that are already cleaned and ready to go."

She pursed her lips, gazing doubtfully at Jenna. "You folks gonna need one bed or two?"

"Two, please," Jenna said quickly. "Thank you."

The woman shook her head. "Huh. Suit yourself. But if it was me, you'd better believe I'd share with this one." She winked broadly at Mick, who took it in stride.

Of course, Jenna thought, he'd probably gotten that kind of reaction all of his life. And that was a lot of winks, all things considered.

"That's eighty-five dollars, in advance," the woman said. "And we gotta have a credit card on file in case you damage anything. Checkout's at noon sharp."

Mick's smile slid away as he patted his pockets. "I have some cash," he told Jenna, "but I didn't think to grab extra when I went back to pack our clothes. I'm sorry. I don't usually use much money when I'm on the road, and it has been almost a year since I went traveling. I guess I'm out of practice with this sort of thing." He made a face. "And I don't have a credit card."

Jenna supposed that made sense. Hard to get a credit card when there is no record of your existence, unless you count the pages of some obscure Russian fairy tales. It wasn't as though she'd expected him to pay their way anyhow. As he'd said, this was her quest. Although considering the dubious state of her account balance, she hoped that they'd be able to camp out for most of the nights of their trip, as Mick had suggested. Apparently, that was mostly what he did when he was on the road. This night under a roof was for her benefit, not his.

"Here you go," she said, handing over her card with only a tiny twinge, and then held her breath as the woman ran it through the machine.

"Okay," the woman said, smiling at Mick and handing him the key even though he hadn't been the one who paid. "You're in number eight, second down from the end. It's nice and quiet down there."

Jenna figured it was probably pretty quiet no matter which room you were in, but at this point she didn't care.

The room wasn't much to look at: faded paisley curtains, mismatched blankets with off-white bedspreads, and a cheap television chained to the dresser. But as promised, it seemed reasonably clean, and there was a lock on the door and hot water in the bathroom. Right now, that was all she cared about. That and getting into clothes that didn't drip on the flat gray carpet.

"Do you mind if I take a shower first?" she asked Mick. He'd toed off his boots, slung his black leather jacket onto the back of a chair, and was sprawled on his bed, seemingly as at ease as if he was in his own home. His long blond hair had developed a slight wave from the dampness, and his tee shirt clung to his abs in a completely distracting way that made her dart into the bathroom before he could even answer the question.

A minute later, he knocked on the door before she'd even gotten the water running.

"What?" She had the paranoid notion that somehow he'd been able to discern what she'd been thinking.

The door opened a crack and a large hand held out fringed white leather saddlebags.

"I just thought you might want some dry clothes when you were done," Mick said in a carefully neutral tone. Jenna was pretty sure she could hear the laughter underneath though. Most women probably ran toward him when they saw him like that, and not away. Well, she wasn't most women.

Nope, she was an idiot.

She grabbed the bag and muttered, "Thanks," before shutting the door. Maybe she should consider a cold shower instead of a hot one, if she could find him this unnervingly attractive even when she was soaking wet, tired, and hungry.

**DAY** fought the urge to follow Jenna into the bathroom and help her with that shower. After all, water conservation was important. He couldn't believe he found her so unnervingly attractive even when she was wet, tired, and cranky. Unfortunately, the more time they spent together, the more enchanting he found her. This was going to be a long, frustrating trip.

In more ways than one.

He couldn't believe he'd forgotten to grab money out of his stash when he'd gone back to the cabin. He'd been on his way to get it when the bike had sounded its alarm, and afterward, all he could think about was getting back to Jenna and making sure she was safe, although logically he knew that nothing would happen to her while she was under Barbara and Liam's protection.

So much for not getting involved.

It wasn't that he was one of those guys who couldn't stand to have a woman pick up the bill, exactly. It was just that he was discovering that the only thing worse than helping someone when you didn't want to was *not* being able to help them. Now that he was no longer a Rider, he couldn't protect her from the effects of the Otherworld. He couldn't get her to where they needed to be any faster than any Human guy could, and now he couldn't even help pay their expenses along the way. He clenched his hands. Maybe Zilya had been right, and he truly was worthless now.

Although there was at least one thing he could do that he was pretty sure would make Jenna forgive him, at least temporarily, for the wet and the cold. He pulled open the drawer in the bedside table and found exactly what he was looking for, then picked up the phone.

When Jenna came out of the bathroom twenty minutes later, her normally pale face pink from the heat of the shower, looking clean and absurdly sexy in a pair of pajama bottoms and a V-necked blue-gray sweatshirt, she gave a glad cry and rushed over to sit next to him on the far bed.

"You got the pizza delivered!" she said. "Oh my God, with sausage too." Anything else she might have had to say was smothered by the large wedge dripping with cheese that she shoved into her mouth.

Day smothered a grin and started in on his own piece. The odor of spicy meat and tomato sauce filled the room, making it seem homier than it had. Next to him, Jenna made sensual noises of satisfaction as she devoured her half of dinner, something Day tried to ignore as he finished off his own portion. He did love a woman who liked to eat, even if it was because she was doing it for two.

Afterward, they sat back and watched some silly television show about an author who worked with the police. It didn't make a lot of sense to Day, but it seemed to make Jenna happy, and at least it kept him from trying to make conversation. If you didn't count the running commentary inside his own head, a constant echo of grief and guilt and remorse.

"Are you okay?" Jenna asked some time later.

Day looked up, startled. "I'm fine. Why do you ask?"

"Because I turned off the TV twenty minutes ago," she said. "And you haven't said a word since then. You seem very far away. I just wondered if something was wrong."

Day scrubbed one hand across his face, feeling the end-of-the-day stubble rasping underneath his fingers. He still hadn't taken his shower, and he suspected he looked like a down-on-his-luck pirate. It was a good thing he definitely wasn't trying to seduce Jenna, since he suspected she'd run away in horror if he tried. Of course, if she knew what a screwup he was, she'd do that anyway.

"I was just thinking," he said.

Jenna turned a little to face him instead of the TV across

the room. Somehow they'd ended up still sitting on the same bed when they'd finished eating. He hadn't really noticed it before, but now she seemed too close for comfort. Despite the lingering odor of cheese and sausage, he could smell the peppermint shampoo she'd used on her hair, which was mostly dry and flowed over her shoulders like a cloak. Day knew it would feel like silk if he reached out and touched it. He didn't.

Instead, he shifted so he was a little farther away, turning to face her too. "It's been tough," he admitted. "Adjusting to not being a Rider. It is all I've ever known, and all I've been for thousands of years. I don't know how to be anything else. So in part, I was thinking about how much more useful I would have been to you a year ago, when I still was one."

To his immense relief, Jenna merely looked interested, instead of pitying. "I can't imagine living for centuries, or having a career for that long, come to think of it. I've never had a job that lasted more than three or four years. Just never found my calling, I guess. You were lucky you had one; not everyone gets that."

Day hadn't thought of things in that light. "I suppose that's true," he said slowly. "Although I'm not sure you could say it was a calling, exactly. More like what I was created to be. Maybe that's what makes it so hard to lose it. But mostly I was thinking about how much my brother Alexei likes pizza."

Jenna's nose crinkled in the cute way it did when she was confused. "Right. Little Babs said you have two brothers."

Day nodded. "Half brothers, actually, although I rarely think of them that way. We've been together so long, it is hard to imagine my life without them."

"You're close, then?"

"We used to be," he said. "There was a time when we were as close as any three brothers could be."

# CHAPTER 10

"**DID** you grow up together?" Jenna asked.

"Yes and no. As children we were often apart, living with our separate mothers. But as adults, we always had each other." His smile slid away. "It was difficult to form lasting relationships with the kind of life we led. We spent too little time in the Otherworld to make true friends there, and in a land where everything is based on where you stand in the social order, we didn't really fit in any convenient niche. Here in the mortal lands, well, those we met had lives too short for us to befriend them without suffering loss after loss. Eventually, we stopped trying. So we had the Baba Yagas, some of whom were very nice and some of whom . . . weren't . . . and we had each other. It was enough, for a very long time."

"But not anymore?" Jenna said softly.

Day shrugged, as if he could motion away the grief and the guilt and the fear that his longest and closest friends would never forgive him for what he'd brought down upon them all.

"I haven't spoken to either of them since it happened. At first I was healing. That took a long time. We were all in the Otherworld, waiting for our bodies to recover and our spirits to mend as much as possible, but each of us chose a different area to recuperate in. They came to see me at some point early on, but the faery who was tending to me sent them away, telling them I was too sick to see them."

"Were you?"

He shrugged again, taking a long drink from the beer he'd had delivered along with the pizza. "Too sick. Too cowardly to look them in the eye. Too afraid that they'd come to tell me they never wanted to speak to me again. It didn't matter. Neither of them ever returned to try a second time."

Jenna put one warm hand on his arm. "Did you ever go looking for them, once you were well?"

Day shook his head. "No. I came through the doorway and found the cabin instead. I didn't feel like I could face them until I had some answers. Until I'd figured out who I was now, and how to make amends." He tried not to sound bitter, since it wasn't truly Jenna's fault, but he was pretty sure he didn't succeed. "Of course, that would be easier if the universe could have left me alone to think."

To his surprise, Jenna didn't take offense. Instead, she just cocked her head at him and said, "How are you supposed to find out who you are sitting around staring at four walls? Don't you think it will be more useful to be out in the world and doing things instead?"

Day opened another beer. "No," he said, not quite growling. "I don't."

They sat in silence for a minute while Jenna digested what he said with her usual calm.

"I don't know," she said slowly. "It's hard for me to comprehend having brothers and not doing everything possible to hold on to them. But I guess that's just my own prejudice speaking."

She got up to go to the bathroom, and sat on her own bed when she came back. Perversely, Day felt the empty space next to him like a sore tooth.

To distract himself, he said gruffly, "Your turn. What was your childhood like?"

Jenna leaned back against the headboard behind her and closed her eyes briefly. When she opened them again, Day could see echoes of remembered pain in their depths, and he almost withdrew the question. He told himself that if he'd had to share his childhood woes, it was only fair that she share hers, but the truth was that he was also curious.

"As you can imagine," she said in a soft voice, "having a curse hanging over your head has quite the effect on people." Long pale fingers played idly with the fringe on the bed-spread. "My grandmother dealt with it by dedicating her life to trying to figure out how to solve the riddle. You've seen her notebooks. She was fierce and determined."

"That must be where you got it from," Day said, only half kidding.

Jenna sighed. "It would have to be. Neither of my parents coped with it well at all." She looked longingly at the bottle in Day's hand but shook her head when he offered one to her, patting her belly in explanation.

"How not well is 'not well'?" he asked.

"My father drank himself to death when I was eight," Jenna said flatly. "I don't know what he was like before Zilya came for my brother, of course, since I wasn't born yet. My mother always said he was a kind and gentle man, but the man I remember was mostly just quietly bitter and distant. I suppose he didn't want to get attached to one child when he'd already lost the other. He was gone before I ever got to know him well."

"That doesn't make any sense," Day sputtered. "You'd think he would cherish the one he had left even more."

"Yeah, you'd think," Jenna said. "He knew what he was getting into when he married my mom; I mean, he knew about the curse. She told me once that he was sure he could save her from it, and never forgave himself when he couldn't." She glanced at Day out of the corner of her eye. "Guilt can be a very destructive emotion."

"Huh," he grunted, not rising to the bait. "What about your mom? Was she bitter too?"

Jenna thought about it for a moment. "Not so much bitter as simply very, very sad. I think she mourned my brother every day after they had to give him up, right after he was born, and when my father died, something inside her just . . . broke. She went through the motions of living after that— went to work, cooked dinner, made sure my basic needs were met—but I never heard her laugh again. When I was a freshman in high school, she slipped away in her sleep one night. The coroner said it was a heart attack, but I think she died of a broken heart."

For a moment, Day could see fury flicker across her face, like a sudden storm in the midst of a calm afternoon, but then she made an effort to get herself under control and went on.

"After that, I lived with my grandmother, and things were better. But you can see why I was so determined not to let that damned faery and her damned curse get passed on any further than me. And why I'm willing to do anything to keep it—and her—from destroying one more member of my family, especially this baby." Jenna stared across the gulf between their beds, her eyes suddenly cold and her expression grim. "It stops with me, whatever it takes, up to and including my death."

# CHAPTER 11

**STU** fiddled with a pen with the hand not holding the cell phone while the private investigator he'd hired gave his report on the search for Jenna. For what he was paying the guy, Stu expected results. He wanted to get this mess cleaned up and the answers his father wanted to have ASAP. If not sooner.

"Well?" Stu asked impatiently. The stupid PI insisted on giving all the details in a methodical and organized manner, which was starting to get on Stu's nerves. "Did you find her or not?"

"I found her car in a ditch in the Adirondacks," the PI said. George something-Greek. Whatever. He came highly recommended. "She wasn't in it."

Stu felt a momentary flutter of alarm. "Did you check the local hospitals?" What if she really was having his baby, and she'd been hurt?

"Hospitals, police reports. Nothing. But it looked to me like the transmission gave out. The car was a piece of junk." Stu thought he detected a hint of judgment in the PI's voice.

"I'm surprised a man of your stature let his girlfriend drive around in a car like that."

Stu scowled at his cell phone before putting it back up to his ear. "Are you serious? You think I *wanted* her to be seen around town in that crapmobile? It was goddamn embarrassing. But she wouldn't let me buy her another one. I always told her it would break down someday and leave her stranded." A tiny bit of worry shifted to satisfaction. He'd told her so. She should have listened to him.

The PI grunted, an indeterminate sound that could have meant anything. "Her trail went cold then for a couple of days. I didn't turn up anything in the area at all. It was like she'd just disappeared."

"That's not helpful," Stu said, tapping the pen on his desk.

"No worries," the PI said. "I finally got a ping on her charge card. She used it to check in at some crappy motel in Pennsylvania; as soon as the proprietor ran the card to make sure it was good, I jumped in my car and drove there to check it out. Got there in the morning in time to see her leave with some handsome blond guy on a fancy motorcycle. I'm following her now, but I'm going to need to call in some backup or risk them spotting me."

Fury rose up in Stu so hot and heavy that spots actually swam in front of his eyes. That *bitch*. She'd been lying to him the whole time. He couldn't believe it. The nerve of her, coming to him with tears in her eyes and swearing that the baby was his, some kind of miracle, and all along she'd been cheating on him with some other guy. No doubt all that nonsense about not being interested in his money was just bullshit, trying to lull him into a false sense of security. And he'd almost believed her. Not quite, but almost. That lying bitch. Well, she'd see what happened to people who tried to pull a fast one on Stuart Wilmington Wadsworth III.

Now he was more determined than ever to force her to take that prenatal DNA test to prove the baby wasn't his. He'd get his father off his back and show Jenna that she had no chance in the world of getting away with ripping off him or his family.

"This backup you need," Stu said. "How squeamish are they?"

There was a pause on the other end of the conversation. "Not very," the PI said. "But we're not going to kill anyone for you, if that's what you're asking."

"Don't be ridiculous," Stu spat into the phone. "I'm a Wadsworth. We don't have people killed." That he knew of, anyway. He wouldn't put anything past his father. That man really liked to get his own way.

"I need your men to pick her up and bring her to the address I'm going to give you. It's a clinic my family has invested in heavily over the years. They owe us. Just makes sure that she gets there."

"And if the lady doesn't want to go?" George asked in a neutral voice.

"The lady doesn't get a choice in the matter," Stu said, still fuming. "And if her new friend gets in the way, tell your guys to feel free to make him a little less good-looking."

He ended the call, tossing his phone down onto the desk with a satisfying *thunk*. Everything was going to be fine. He had it completely under control.

**JENNA** was starting to get used to the long hours on the motorcycle. Kind of. Other than her numb butt, that is. At least she was learning to relax a little more and trust Mick to keep them upright and safe. And it wasn't exactly a hardship to spend hours with her arms wrapped around Mick's waist, leaning against his strong back. In some ways, she thought it was the most relaxed she'd been since she'd discovered she was pregnant, even though they were driving at high speeds down highways, occasionally passing trucks that seemed like moving mountains from her vantage point.

Not that she wasn't relieved when they stopped at a diner

outside Charleston, West Virginia, for lunch. They'd been on the road for three and a half hours since leaving the motel, and she thought they'd covered about two hundred and thirty miles. Her stomach was grumbling, and her bottom could definitely use the break. Mick had spotted the sign right before the exit and pointed at it, then pulled off the highway when she gave him a thumbs-up. Communicating on the back of a motorcycle could be a challenge, but they'd started to figure it out.

The diner wasn't anything fancy; a long L-shaped building with a country-western theme that obviously catered to truckers and locals more than any folks who might be interested in ordering some kind of venti half-caff pumpkin spice latte. But the fried chicken smelled like heaven and tasted even better. It had been a quiet meal, neither of them really feeling like talking. She suspected Mick was regretting opening up so much the night before, and she just felt odd and off balance being with someone who both knew her real history and had one that was even stranger.

She'd eaten her entire huge portion, along with all of the hand-cut fries that came with it, and a large mound of creamy coleslaw. Mick had done the same—twice. Jenna had no idea how he kept his slim waist and flat abs eating the way he did. She was about at the stage where she was going to have to find a place to stop and buy new pants. As it was, she'd given up on fastening the top button and just pulled her shirt down over it. Still, at least she had a legitimate excuse for all that eating.

Eventually, Mick waved over their waitress, insisting on paying the lunch tab out of his dwindling supply of cash. The way he glowered at Jenna when she tried to argue made her think it might be better to let him have his way on this one.

When they stood up, she said, "I'm going to hit the ladies' room before we get back on the road."

Mick was obviously getting used to her constant need to pee, although he'd been very nice about the frequent stops, and insisted he liked the excuse to stretch his legs. "Okay," he said. "I'll meet you outside." But this time he strode off without a backward look, cranky Day in ascendance again. She found charming Day a lot more pleasant, but at least Mr. Cranky was way less tempting, and that was probably a good thing, under the circumstances.

When she came out of the bathroom, she headed back down the hallway that led into the main section of the restaurant. Two burly men in worn jeans and denim jackets hurried in her direction, their faces anxious.

"Hey," the taller one said as he caught sight of her. His brown hair was a little too long and he needed a shave. "Are you the lady who was having lunch with the blond guy with the fancy white motorcycle?"

Alarm made Jenna's heart beat like a bird inside her chest. "Yes, that's my friend Mick. Why, is something wrong?"

The shorter one—who still had to be at least six feet tall, and built like a tank—gazed at her with concern. "I'm sorry, lady, but a big ol' truck just came ramming into the parking lot and smashed right into him. Someone called nine-one-one, but you better come right away. He's in pretty rough shape; it's not looking good."

"Oh no." Jenna put one hand up to her mouth. She had a dozen thoughts at once: that it was her fault he was hurt, since he was following her wild-goose chase; that she had no idea how she'd finish the quest without him; that he wasn't immortal anymore, and what would she tell little Babs if he died? Jenna had only known Mick for a short time, but already she couldn't imagine a world without him in it.

She started to hurry toward the front of the restaurant, but one of the men grabbed her arm and gestured in the other direction, farther toward the back of the building.

"He's closer to the rear of the parking lot; we can get there faster if we go out the back door by the kitchens," he said. They moved in that direction, Jenna almost running as she burst out the exit into a small area filled with reeking garbage cans, an aged picnic table where the employees obviously sat outside and smoked on their breaks, and a few cars parked in the dubious shade of some spindly trees. There was a white van idling right outside the door, but no sign of Mick or the motorcycle, and no crowds of people looking on in horror.

*What the hell?* "Where's my friend?" she asked.

The taller man shrugged, showing her stained teeth in an unpleasant smile. "Probably still out front waiting for you," he said. "He's gonna have a long wait, though, since you're gonna take a little ride with us."

"No, I'm not," Jenna said. She didn't know what these guys had in mind, but she had a pretty strong feeling she wasn't going to like it. Her kickboxing teacher once told the class that if you went with an abductor, your chances of survival were considerably less than if you fought back. And, frankly, the way things had been going, she was almost happy for an excuse to hit someone. She slowed her breathing and focused, just the way she'd been taught. There was no way she was going to be a victim. If she could survive an avaricious faery, no way in hell were two mere mortals going to take her down. No matter how big they were.

"Get in the fucking van, lady," the tank said. "Don't make us get rough with you."

Jenna grinned at him, making him blink in confused surprise. "Bite me," she said, and swiveled around to lash out with her heel, the force of her booted foot impacting against his balls making him shriek so loudly it startled a flock of birds out of the nearby trees. He fell against the van, moaning and holding himself.

"Jesus Christ!" his pal stuttered. "Chuck, get off the damned ground, ya big baby." He swung a ham-like fist at Jenna's head, the air of its passage whistling in her ears as she ducked under his arm and came up behind him. A kick to the back of his knee made one leg buckle briefly, but he recovered too quickly and turned to face her again, his teeth gritted and fury written in every tight muscle.

"Crap," Jenna said, and braced herself.

"Is this a private fight or can anyone join in?" Mick asked, strolling around the corner. "I mean, I can clearly see you have it under control, and I don't want to spoil your fun or anything, but I've been *really*, really bored." His smile lit up the entire space, although Jenna wasn't foolish enough to take her eyes off her opponent long enough to smile back.

"Be my guest," she said, aiming another swift series of kicks at the guy to keep him off balance while Mick got into position. She needn't have worried. He just threw back his head and roared, running at the tall man like a linebacker on a football field, lifting the thug off his feet with one broad shoulder and tossing him up into the air. Her attacker hit the ground with a *crunch* and rolled to avoid Mick's motorcycle boot, which came down in the spot where he'd been a minute ago. The tall man staggered to his feet, but went down again in a flurry of punches.

Jenna took a second to catch her breath, and when she looked up again, the man was dangling upside down in midair from one of Mick's large hands, shaggy brown hair nearly touching the dirty ground. Mick held his arm up with the man's full weight hanging down from it, seemingly without effort. Despite herself, Jenna was impressed. Mick's blue eyes seemed to glow an unearthly yellow for a moment, as he shook the guy so hard the change fell out of his pockets and onto the blacktop with a chiming, plinking sound.

"Put me down!" the thug said, squirming helplessly. "It ain't what it looked like."

"No?" Mick said, sounding surprisingly calm. "It looked to me like you were going to kidnap and rape my friend, maybe kill her when you got done. Shame on you."

"Jesus Christ! No way! It was nothing like that."

Jenna noted with strained amusement that the thug actually sounded offended and appalled by Mick's suggestion.

"We're just doing a job," his pal said from where he half sat, half leaned on the van, still breathing in labored gasps. "It was nothin' personal."

"A job for whom?" Mick asked, giving the upside-down man another shake, as if to jog his memory, and then dropping him on the ground with a thud.

The thug held up his hands. "Look, all I know is that some guy named Stu is paying ten grand to have the girl delivered unharmed to a swanky clinic in New York City. All we were supposed to do was grab her and bring her there, I swear."

Jenna could feel the blood drain out of her face. *Stu? What the hell does Stu have to do with this?*

Mick gave her a curious look. "Do you want me to call the police, Jenna?" he asked. "They can probably find out who this Stu guy is."

She shook her head. "We don't have time for this nonsense. I don't want to spend hours talking to the cops. I just want to get out of here and get back on the road." She could feel her body start to shake as the adrenaline rush began to wear off.

Mick raised one eyebrow, but didn't argue with her, for which she was grateful. "This seems to be your lucky day, gentlemen," he said, nudging the one nearest him with his foot. "If I were you, I'd go back to your boss and tell him that if anyone else tries to hurt my friend, this little kerfuffle is going to look like a sixth-grade dance." He glared from one guy to the next. "Am I making myself clear?"

The two men staggered into their van and took off like the devil was behind them, which Jenna supposed was answer enough. At least to that question. She had a lot more.

# CHAPTER 12

**FLAMES** danced in the middle of the fire pit Day had created
with a small folding shovel he'd pulled out of his saddlebags
and a pile of rocks. They'd agreed that until they figured out
if the goons who attacked Jenna were still coming after her,
it would be better to avoid hotels and other populated areas
and stick to back roads as much as possible. Considering the
state of their wallets, Day thought that this plan made sense
for other reasons as well. He didn't let himself admit that there
was something almost romantic about sitting under the stars
with a beautiful woman in the middle of nowhere. Particularly
a beautiful woman who looked like a sexier Snow White and
seemed to glow in the light of the fire.

He thought he'd seen a sign that said they were near someplace called Jenkins, Kentucky, but he was starting to lose
track. Frankly, it didn't much matter where they were now, as
long as Jenna ended up in Texas where she needed to be. And
he got to go back to his solitary life in the cabin. Somehow the
prospect didn't seem as attractive as it used to, but since he

couldn't think of any alternatives that suited him better, he supposed it would have to do.

Day wiped greasy fingers on a handkerchief and put down his plate, which held only the bony remains of the trout he'd caught them for dinner. Across the fire, Jenna did the same, except that she used the grass near where she was sitting. The firelight gleamed off of her black hair, making it look like a rippling curtain of silk as she leaned back with a sigh.

Day had a feeling he knew what she was thinking about, since they'd been avoiding the subject since the incident earlier in the afternoon. "So," he said. "Who is Stu? I take it you know the name?"

Jenna sat up, curling her hands protectively over her belly in what he was pretty sure was an unconscious motion. "He's the baby's father," she said in a soft voice. "My former boyfriend."

A strange pang rippled through Day's chest at the thought of Jenna with another man, although obviously he knew the baby had a father. None of his business anyway, other than to know who to watch out for. At least that's what he told himself.

"I guess this Stu wants his baby back, and that's why he sent those guys to grab you?" Day said. "I would have thought flowers might have been more effective."

Jenna shook her head. "The last I knew, Stu was insisting the baby couldn't possibly be his and accusing me of sleeping around on him. He got me fired from my job and practically drove me out of town. I hadn't expected to ever hear from him again. I certainly don't think he wants this baby. I have no idea why he would send two guys after me. I've been thinking about it since the attack, and I still don't have a clue."

"Huh," Day grunted. "Why don't you ask him, then?"

"I suppose I could," Jenna said, taking her cell phone out of her pocket and holding it up to the limited light of the fire. "It looks like I actually have a signal, for a miracle. But honestly, I really don't want to talk to him." A tiny shudder ran through her.

Day stretched out his long legs and levered himself up off the ground to go sit next to her. "Why don't you put it on speaker and then we can both hear," he suggested. It made more sense for him to sit close to her if it was just to listen to the call. He wasn't being supportive or anything.

Her grateful smile seemed brighter than the flames in front of them. "Okay, that's a good idea." She picked a number from her list of contacts and they waited through a few rings. After the fourth one, a man's voice said cautiously, "Jenna? Is that you?" To Day's ear, Stu sounded surprised and a little wary, but it could have been the connection, which wasn't great.

"Yes," Jenna said. "It's me." Her voice was even and emotionless, but Day could see the tightness around her eyes that he'd learned meant she was upset and trying not to show it.

"Oh," Stu said. "Are you okay? Where are you now?"

Day shook his head at her, but she just made a face at him, wrinkling her nose as if to indicate that she wasn't stupid enough to answer that from the guy who might be hunting her.

She glared down at the phone. "A better question might be why the hell you sent two men to kidnap me. What on earth are you up to?"

There was a sputtering sound from the other end. "I'm not *up to* anything, Jenna. I'm just trying to find out if the baby is really mine. Since the detective I sent to find you saw you with some tall blond guy, I very much doubt it."

The tall blond guy in question raised an eyebrow at Jenna, who mouthed the word *jackass* back at him.

"He's just a friend," Jenna snarled into the phone. "And it turned out to be a good thing he was there when your thugs attacked me. If you wanted to talk to me, why didn't you just pick up the phone, instead of sending Frick and Frack to grab me in a parking lot?"

"Now, now, Jenna, don't exaggerate," Stu said in a slightly condescending tone. "They were merely supposed to pick you up and take you to a clinic for a fetal DNA test to prove once and for all this baby isn't mine. And if it is mine, that there is nothing wrong with it. They never intended to harm you. I gave them specific instructions not to."

"How kind of you," Jenna said acerbically. "Are you just talking about a blood test, or something more invasive? I'm not agreeing to amniocentesis or anything. It's way too dangerous at this stage of the pregnancy, and there aren't any genetic issues in my family that I know of." Some other major issues, of course, but none that would show up on a test.

"Well, it isn't as though you wanted this baby anyway," Stu said. "How terrible would it be if something happened to terminate the pregnancy? Not that it's likely, really. You're overreacting, as usual. You clearly had some reason for being so adamant about not getting pregnant; I just want to make sure there isn't some horrible genetic trait you don't want passed on. If it's mine, which isn't likely. I don't know why you have to be so difficult about this. It's a reasonable request."

Day could hear Jenna grinding her teeth. "Of course it is. I will happily give you a DNA sample after the baby is born. You'll just have to wait another five and a half months."

A deep intake of breath. "I can't do that, Jenna. I need to know now. If the baby is mine and it has something wrong with it, it will have to be dealt with right away. And we're running out of time."

Jenna rolled her eyes. "This has something to do with your father, doesn't it?"

"Why do you say that?" Stu asked, sounding indignant.

"Because everything has something to do with him," Jenna said. "Everything you do. Everything you don't do. It all leads back to your relationship with him."

There was a pause, in which Stu didn't attempt to deny this. A telling lapse, Day thought.

"Why didn't you just ask me before you sent out your goons to take me by force?" Jenna asked.

"You would have said no," Stu said. "Am I right?"

"Yes," Jenna said. "And I'm saying it now too. Stay away from me. Stay away from my baby. I mean it, Stu. Just leave us alone." She ended the call and threw the phone into the bushes, then slumped down and put her face into her hands, quiet sobs slipping out from behind her fingers.

Day fetched the phone from where it had landed, muttering a few curses because of the brambles but otherwise not commenting on her actions. To be honest, he'd wanted to crush it with a rock after that ridiculous conversation, so he thought she'd exercised a fair amount of restraint. He also thought it was a damn good thing that jerk Stu wasn't standing in this clearing with them, since Day felt even more inclined to take a rock to him—or maybe a boulder, or an entire mountain.

He handed the device back and settled down next to Jenna, slinging one arm casually around her shoulders as if they sat that way every night. He hated it when any woman cried, but when Jenna did it, for some reason it made him want to howl at the sky like a wolf, or tear large trees apart with his bare hands. Sadly, neither of those actions would be at all helpful, so he settled for asking, "Are you crying because you're afraid Stu will send someone after you again? I promise, I'll keep you safe."

Jenna sniffed and lifted her head, wiping at her face with the back of one hand. "Thanks, but it's not that. I'm crying because it turns out that my baby's daddy is a shit. That kind of sucks. Even if I miraculously find some way to break this curse and keep my baby, my little girl is going to grow up without a father. I hate to do that to her." She sniffed again.

Day tightened his arm in a brief, almost imperceptible hug. "If it makes you feel any better," he said, "I hardly saw my father when I was growing up and I turned out okay."

"Really?" Jenna said. "Was your father a shit too?"

"No," Day said. "He was a god."

Jenna stared at him, her mouth dropping open. "Did you just say you're the son of a *god*?"

Day shrugged. "Yes. But don't get too excited; he wasn't one of the major ones. Kind of a lesser god in the Russian pantheon. His name was Jarilo, and he was the son of Perun, the supreme god of thunder. My father was a typical birth/ life/death/rebirth god, celebrated in the spring and mourned in the winter. He had clout, of course, but dying every year meant that he wasn't as powerful as some of the other gods. No one really knows if the gods are still around or not, although I've always assumed they still exist in one form or another."

"Uh-huh," Jenna said. "I'm sorry; I'm still processing the whole son-of-a-god thing. I guess I wasn't that far off thinking you reminded me of Thor after all." Then she blushed, which was sweet, although he didn't understand the reason for it.

"You've met him?" Day asked. As far as he knew, none of the old gods were around anymore, but you never knew with those guys.

"What?" Jenna bit her lip. "No, sorry, I was just thinking of the one in the movies. You know, *The Avengers*?"

Day had a feeling they were speaking two different languages. "Sorry, I don't watch many movies."

"That's probably just as well," Jenna said. "So what does your father being a god"—she blinked rapidly—"um, anyway, what does that have to do with your being a Rider? Did he create the job title or something?"

Day shook his head. "Not exactly. He created me—and my two half brothers, Gregori and Alexei—to be the Riders. Of course, we didn't know that when we were growing up."

It had been so long since he'd told this story, it felt weird to actually be talking about it. Even the Baba Yagas didn't know the specifics. It was possible that no one currently living other than the Queen and King of the Otherworld still remembered their origins. Day wasn't sure why he was telling this almost–perfect stranger, except that she'd asked, and he had no reason not to. Not anymore.

"So you had a normal childhood?" Jenna said.

Day snorted. "Sure, if you consider it normal to be raised in the great deep forests of Russia by a Leshonki, the child of a Leshy, lord of the forest and a magical forest guardian with the ability to change shape. And to spend your summer vacations with your father in the realm of the gods, playing tag with your two half brothers amid the cold white palaces in the sky."

"Holy crap," Jenna muttered. "And I thought my childhood was strange. So your brothers . . . Were their mothers, um, Leshonki too?"

Day laughed. "No, not even close. I don't know if my father chose his women on purpose to sire children with different attributes, or if he just had eclectic tastes. Mind you, this was back in the days when the gods got around a bit. Once people stopped believing in them, they apparently lost their ability to conceive children entirely." And as far as anyone knew, none of their hybrid offspring had ever had children, Greek myths aside. It was something he'd made his peace with long ago. Mostly.

"I am the youngest of the three of us," he continued. "Our middle half brother, Alexei Knight, is the son of Jarilo and a woman named Mara. Mara was the daughter of Svyatogor, a great warrior whose name meant 'sacred mountain' because he was so large. He was a great hero of the old days; probably not a Human, although no one knows for sure what he was. My oldest brother, Gregori Sun's, mother, Iduyan, was a powerful Mongolian shamaness. Maybe that's why he turned out to be so wise; I'm not sure. God knows Alexei inherited the large and warrior-like attributes of his grandfather."

"So you weren't raised together?" Jenna asked.

"Not at all. We each spent most of our time with our mothers, in their different parts of Russia. Gregori grew up on the steppes of Siberia." Day shuddered to think of the winters there. He didn't much mind the cold, but there were limits, even for him.

"But as we grew older, Jarilo brought us to the Upper Realms during the summer. In theory, it was to spend time getting to know us, but the truth is that the gods are too different from us. He was a distant father at best, always more involved in observing the world of the mortals below or enjoying the entertainments of his own world to take much interest in his children."

"That's sad," Jenna said, her expressive face creased in sympathy. "I know what it's like to grow up with parents who are too caught up in their own issues to remember they have children." Day was surprised by the bitter tone of her voice.

"I'm sorry," he said.

"It is what it is. Go ahead and finish your story."

"There's not much left," Day said. "My brothers and I weren't exactly close, growing up. We might have been the only non-gods running around in the Upper Realm, but Gregori was already a teenager when I was born, and Alexei just wanted to wrestle and break things." He smiled fondly at the memory of a nine- or ten-year-old Alexei grumbling at being saddled with a toddler brother and instructed to bring him back in one piece.

"We sometimes swam together in the great river in the sky, and explored the buildings and the land, but mostly we were taught by the other gods—how to fight and how to heal, how to speak and write in many languages, that sort of thing. Finally, when I turned eighteen, our father called the three of us to him and informed us that we had been created to play an important role in the mortal realm: to act, both separately and jointly, as the Riders, companions and helpers for the Baba Yagas. We'd heard of the Baba Yagas, of course, during the time spent with our mothers. Everyone knew the most powerful witches in the world, although there were fewer of them back then, and they only watched over Russia and the nearby lands."

Jenna gazed at him with those icy blue eyes opened wide. "How did it feel to be told you'd been born to do a particular job, with no say in the matter? Weren't you angry?"

He chuckled. "It was a very different time, Jenna. A blacksmith's son grew up to be a blacksmith. A baker's son learned his father's trade. Women married the men their parents picked out for them. Very few people chose what they were going to do with their lives; we'd simply been waiting to find out what our own father had planned for us. And in truth, it was a wonderful and satisfying job most of the time. We had plenty of freedom to explore our own interests, and then when a Baba Yaga called, we went."

"It sounds like a good life," Jenna said. "But I still can't believe you didn't mind being created for a purpose, instead of just to be yourself."

Day scrubbed one hand across his eyes, the weight of loss pressing down on his shoulders. "To be honest, I mind not having a purpose more."

They sat in silence for a moment. Then Jenna said, "The son of a god, huh? That explains a lot."

He raised an eyebrow. "Oh?"

Jenna smirked at him, a mischievous look in her sparkling blue eyes. "You know, the whole superstrong, ridiculously gorgeous thing. But obviously you've been told that a lot over the years. I don't expect it means much anymore."

A voice far in the back of his head said something faint about bad ideas, but he hit it with a large mental stick until it sputtered and shut up.

"It depends on who says it," he answered, and bent his head down and kissed her.

# CHAPTER 13

**THE** touch of his lips on hers was like an electric shock, rippling down through her body and making her tingle from head to toe—and all the important bits in between. For a moment Jenna hesitated, torn between prudence and longing, but then Mick deepened the kiss, moving his arm farther down her back and drawing her in, and for once in her life she threw caution to the wind and returned the pressure of his lips with enthusiasm.

A rising tide of desire threatened to swamp her like a tidal wave, washing away fear and doubt and leaving behind it the knowledge that in her topsy-turvy life, she was certain of only one thing: she wanted this man, right now, and she'd deal with the consequences later.

Mick pulled away, looking deep into her eyes, his own vivid blue orbs filled with a heat that turned them as dark as the night sky. "I want to make love to you," he said, his voice low and thrumming through her veins as if it were a music only she could hear. "May I touch you?" When she nodded speechlessly, he turned his other hand so that the back of his fingers barely skimmed the surface of her skin, sliding it over her cheek, down her neck and breasts, until it came to rest tenderly on her belly. Then he scooped her up effortlessly and carried her over to his bedroll.

Jenna would never have imagined that anyone so strong could be so gentle. But gentle he was, easing her shirt off over her head and then covering her with tiny kisses, as light as a butterfly's wings. Her nerve endings felt like they were on fire, each subtle touch enflaming her more than the last. She gasped out loud when he took one newly sensitive nipple into his mouth, licking and sucking as though she was a sumptuous feast, teeth nipping ever so lightly at the delicate skin on the sides of her breasts before moving down to tease the insides of her thighs.

She almost cried when he lifted himself away, only to feel her eyes widen at the sight of him stripping off his clothing to reveal the most perfect male body she'd ever seen. His chest and abs were muscular without the bulkiness of someone who worked at it, his torso slim as it tapered down to his narrow hips and the abundant display of his arousal that jutted out from between his thighs.

*The son of a god indeed*, she thought, right before he slid inside her slowly, filling her inch by inch until they were joined completely. His brawny arms held his upper body over her, barely touching, as if he was afraid of crushing her, just barely close enough so that she could feel the furnace of warmth pouring off his body. She longed for him to thrust hard, to ram himself into her, but she knew he was afraid of hurting the baby, and instead he slid his silken length in and out with a gentleness that only increased the roiling passion that bubbled up like champagne until she dug her fingernails into his shoulders and cried out, arching her back as she was lost in waves of pleasure the likes of which she'd never felt before. Over and over the tempest of sensation rolled through her, until at last she felt the ripples die away, and only then did Mick let go, emptying himself into her with a groan, clutching her tight as if she was his lifeline in an equally stormy sea.

Finally, he lifted himself carefully off of her and eased down to lie at her side, stroking her body idly as his eyes began to drift closed.

"Are you all right?" he asked softly as he pulled the blanket over to cover them.

"All right?" Jenna said. "I'm incredible."

Mick chuckled softly in the darkness. "Yes. Yes, you are."

She could feel the moment he fell asleep, his arm suddenly heavy where it lay draped across her middle. She slid her hand underneath it, cupping her belly as if to check that all was well. For a moment, she almost thought she heard a contented giggle lifting up from her womb.

*Silly woman*, she thought. *Silly indeed, to imagine such things.* But not foolish enough to imagine that this moment—this perfect moment in a time filled with so many less than perfect ones—had meant anything. Just for a heartbeat, though, she allowed herself to wish for the impossible: that the man lying next to her could somehow magically be transformed into a retroactive father for her baby.

Not that she thought he would stay, even if that were possible, but how much better it would have been to have a little piece of this sometimes cranky, sometimes charming magnificent beast of a man inside her, instead of a fragment of a selfish, self-involved so-called gentleman. As she drifted off to sleep, Jenna was visited by a vision of a tiny laughing toddler with blond curls and bright blue eyes, running toward her with open arms. If there was anyone behind her, following to make sure the little girl didn't fall, Jenna couldn't see him.

**DAY** woke with the sunrise, as he had for thousands of years. Alexei had always been able to carouse deep into the night and sleep all day if he so desired, but Day had never mastered the knack. Once the sun was up, so was he.

Red-gold light glowed in the eastern sky and gilded the clearing with touches of pink and yellow, making the form lying next to him seem momentarily like the enchanted statue of some mythical goddess. Of course, Day had a certain acquaintance with mythical goddesses, and he'd never met one quite like Jenna Quinlan.

The morning was silent, other than the musical twittering of birds and the distant murmur of the stream where he'd caught last night's dinner. It felt as though the world was allowing him a tiny space of time in which to catch his breath before the rest of the day came crashing in on him. He appreciated that, since he was pretty sure that what came after was going to be a lot less pleasant.

He leaned over and brushed a long black strand of hair away from Jenna's face, as dark as the lashes that lay against her pale skin like the wings of some delicate and elusive creature. If anything, she was even more beautiful now than when he'd met her; with the morning sickness behind her, she was beginning to display that glow some pregnant women had, and the slight curve of her belly only made her more attractive to him.

Which is precisely why he was kicking himself for his actions last night.

This whole mess was complicated enough without him being foolish enough to have sex with her. Bad enough that he'd been pulled into her problems, but now there was going to be that awkward *what does this mean?* conversation, and she would start wanting things from him he simply didn't have to give. He'd always managed to avoid that in the past because his role as a Rider meant that he was constantly on the move.

Riders didn't settle down or have relationships. It simply didn't come with the job. Or the men who had the job. Either way, it was the truth.

He'd had plenty of dalliances with women, of course, both Paranormal and Human. But that's all they ever were, brief encounters between consenting adults, because he was always just passing through and the women knew that. Not that he was just using them for sex—far from it.

Day knew that some people thought of him as a flirt and a playboy, but the truth was, he simply loved women. He loved everything about them: the way they looked, each of them beautiful in her own way, their softness, and the sound of their laughter. He loved all their different shapes and sizes, thin and fragile, tall and tough, abundantly curved and round of cheek. He enjoyed them and they enjoyed him, and if it wasn't something that could last and grow, it was still enough to sustain him through the long and lonely years. He had never looked for more, and he certainly wasn't going to do so now, after everything that happened.

He had nothing to offer anyone, especially someone like Jenna, so full of life and light and passion. He didn't even know who he was now, or what he was becoming, or what his limited future might hold. But he knew that Jenna probably wouldn't understand that. She'd think their making love meant something in the long run, when there could *be* no long run. Not for them. And yet they would be stuck traveling together until Day could get her to the Otherworld and safely back again. He groaned quietly, foreseeing long, awkward hours ahead.

A long yawn interrupted his agonized self-flagellation, and Jenna gazed at him sleepily.

"Good morning," she said.

Day cleared his throat, which was suddenly dry. "Good morning. I hope you slept well."

"Like a baby," she said, sitting up and grabbing her shirt to pull it unself-consciously over her head. She giggled and patted the slight swell of her midsection. "Or, like a baby incubator, more accurately."

He braced himself. Any second now it was going to get mightily uncomfortable. He'd have to be kind, to let her down easily. He could do that, even as grumpy as he felt most of the time these days.

Jenna stood up and put on her panties (a surprisingly dainty pink lace) and her pants, then stuck her feet back into her boots. "I'm starving," she said, giving him only a passing glance. "I'm going to go find a convenient tree, and then maybe we can hit the road? I'm keeping my fingers crossed that there's a diner somewhere not too far down our path. Suddenly, I've got an incredible craving for bacon and sautéed onions with maple syrup on them."

Day was pretty sure his mouth was hanging open as he watched her walk toward the nearest stand of trees. So much for the fuss he'd been expecting and the difficult conversation he'd been bracing himself for. Jenna was apparently fine with acting as if the whole thing had never happened and getting on with their journey without so much as a *where do we go from here?*

That was great. It was going to make things much easier. If only he could figure out why her not making a big deal about it made it feel like an even bigger deal than it had before.


**THAT** night they camped in the Prentice Cooper State Forest, somewhere in Tennessee. There was an official campground, but Mick had insisted on leaving the path and delving deeper into the woods. Better, he said, to be scolded by park rangers, than to be found by their enemies. Jenna still found it remarkable that she had enemies, so she just followed his lead.

Things seemed fine between them, on the surface. At least as much as she could tell when they'd spent about six hours on the back of the bike, with a couple of breaks for food and for Jenna to stretch her legs. Apparently Mick's legs were just fine. Bah. Jenna's back hurt, her butt ached, and the rest of her wasn't all that happy either. She'd be longing for a nice comfy car, except then they'd be able to talk, and she wasn't sure if that was a good thing or not.

Last night had been wonderful. Amazing. Practically world-shattering. But it wasn't as if he'd offered up a declaration of undying love afterward. Of course, neither had she. The situation—and where they were both coming from—was just too unsettled and strange. So for the moment, she was just playing it cool and leaving the next move up to him.

Although she had to admit, if only to herself, that she wouldn't have minded a repeat, if things were just a little less complicated. Of course, if things were less complicated, she would never have met him.

She watched as he finished setting up their camp with competent efficiency and a minimum of unnecessary movement. Everything he did seemed to be imbued with grace and a sense of restrained power; he was a pleasure to watch, like a leopard pacing out the confines of his territory with confident strides.

"That's as good as we're going to get for tonight, I'm afraid," he said, dropping down to sit about a foot away from her. "We don't dare risk more than a tiny fire tonight, since we're camping outside the regulated zone, but it should be warm enough for sleeping as long as it doesn't rain."

Jenna had a momentary thought about shared bedrolls and ways of generating warmth that didn't require a fire and blushed, grateful for the darkness.

"It's a good thing we ate dinner on the road," she said, voice only slightly breathy. "All we have to do now is curl up and get some sleep, and we can be on the road first thing in the morning. How much farther is it to the Enchanted Rock, do you think?"

Mick shrugged, his face barely visible in the light of the small lantern he'd set up between them. "It's a little over a thousand miles still," he said. "We've been on the road for three days. I'm guessing we could do the rest in another three days if we really pushed it; four might be more comfortable." He glanced at her, catching her in the act of rubbing her bottom with both hands to try and ease the ache. "How are you holding up?"

"The baby is okay," she said, pulling her hands away and

putting them in her lap instead. "At least as far as I can tell. I'm sore, but I'm managing."

Mick grunted, not buying it. "We'll do it in four," he said. "We'll find a place along the way to rest a bit, so we're reasonably fresh when we get there. After all, we have no idea what we're walking into."

Jenna had the feeling that he would handle it just fine, no matter what they ended up facing. But if he wanted to cut her a little slack, she'd take it. Gladly.

"Okay," she said. "You're in charge. I'm just going to, uh, go relieve myself before bed. I'll be right back." She got up creakily and headed toward the cover of a clump of trees. Jenna understood the multiple reasons they were avoiding hotels, and really, she had nothing against camping, but she was never going to be a fan of peeing in the woods. Every time she did, she swore that in her next life, she was coming back as a man.

On her way back to the campsite, Jenna thought she heard a rustling in the woods behind her. She stopped, listening, the hair standing up on the back of her neck. Probably an animal—a raccoon or a deer, or something equally harmless, but even as she told herself that her heart rate sped up and she could feel her breathing become tight and rapid.

Something scuffed in the leaves off to her left side, and a piece of wood broke with a sharp *snap* off to her right. That was enough for her and she let out a shriek, leaning down to grab a thick branch that was lying at her feet. And just in time, because no sooner was the stick in her hands than three, four, five creatures swarmed out of the forest to surround her.

Panic rose in her throat like lava from a volcano, hot and bubbling. The creatures were like nothing she had ever seen before: nightmares of long fur-covered limbs, flat simian features, and slitted goatlike eyes that gleamed at her out of the darkness. It was hard to tell, since they walked slumped over and shambling, but they must have been four or five feet tall. Sharp teeth protruded from the jutting jaws, and low brows hung over the deep-set eyes. Slavering and drooling, they gazed at her without discernible emotion or intelligence, but a quick glance showed that the largest male—they were all obviously male—wore a kind of loincloth, although the others were naked. She didn't know if that meant he was in charge, or just had better fashion sense than the rest.

She waved the branch at them, wishing it were a gun, or maybe a lightsaber, and yelled, "Get away from me!"

Unimpressed, they crept in closer, moving in a complete silence that was far more unnerving than any sound would have been. "*Shit!*" she breathed, and then ran forward to attack the one closest to her, before they could all come after her in unison.

She hit it with all of her might, swinging the tree branch like a baseball bat. She would have aimed at its head, but the angle was wrong for the blow to have enough force behind it. So instead, she targeted its knees, which made a satisfying cracking noise as the branch impacted against the bony protuberances.

The creature, whatever it was, went down with a high keening cry but unfortunately, its comrades were already pressing in to take its place. Jenna swung the branch around her in a circle, trying to maintain a clear space, and screamed Mick's name at the top of her lungs.

# CHAPTER 14

**DAY** was wondering what was taking Jenna so long when he
heard her scream. To his experienced ear it sounded less like
pain and more like fear, but the frantic tone in her voice had
him up and moving before his conscious mind had even pro-
cessed the fact that she was calling his name. He covered the
space between their camp and where he'd seen her go into
the woods impossibly fast, not stopping to question where the
speed was coming from.

Just inside the tree line, he spotted her standing with her
legs braced in a fighting stance, her face set in lines of defiance as she swung a large stick back and forth at the creatures
who had her surrounded. He noted and dismissed the one
already lying on the ground, and raced across the space between them to take on the rest.

Furry bodies went flying like bowling pins as he barreled
into their midst, growling and snarling and knocking heads
together, filled with a rush of glorious fury. With a high-
pitched yelp, the tallest of the beasts hightailed it into the

woods, his companions scattering and then bounding off in his wake, dragging their fallen fellow with them.

Day dusted off his hands in satisfaction. "Are you okay?" he asked, turning to Jenna.

She nodded silently and took a step back. "Uh, yeah. Thanks for coming to my rescue."

He started to move closer to her, and she took another backward step, still gripping her branch between both hands. It suddenly occurred to Day that she was still looking frightened—and she was staring right at him.

"What's wrong?" he asked, the words coming out in a strange lisp he hadn't noticed before.

Jenna bit her lip. "Um, did you realize that your hair is kind of greenish right now, and your eyes are glowing? Plus, I don't know how it's possible, but I'm pretty sure you're about a foot taller than usual. Not to mention that your teeth are kind of large and sharp. What the hell is happening, Mick?"

Day picked up a hank of his shoulder-length hair and looked at it in the shaft of moonlight that slipped through the trees into the space where they stood. Unless it was a trick of the light, his hair was in fact about the color of new leaves, although it started changing back to his normal blond as he watched. He ran his tongue cautiously across his teeth and found them distinctly fanglike, although they, too, shrank back to their normal size and shape almost as soon as he took note of the change.

*Well, shit.*

"It's okay, Jenna," he said, holding out one hand. "I'm pretty sure I can explain. But I'd rather do it back at camp, where we're less likely to be attacked. I've seen those creatures before, and they prefer to stay away from open spaces. Not that I think they'd come back again tonight anyway. I think we scared them sufficiently to make them more cautious for now."

Jenna hesitated, then dropped the stick on the ground and moved forward warily. But she didn't take his hand, and kept a watchful eye on him as they settled back into their places on opposite sides of the meager campfire. It made Day's heart ache to see the way she looked at him, as if he might turn on her at any moment, but he thought he understood. After all, she'd been raised her entire life to think of the Paranormal world as frightening, with a faery as her own personal boogeyman. Whatever had happened to him back there, it had clearly reminded her that no matter how Human he looked, he wasn't someone like her. And therefore, he might be a threat.

He was surprised to discover how much that hurt.

Jenna cleared her throat. "So, what were those things? Do you think Zilya sent them?"

"They're called *biesy*," Day said. "They're a kind of minor demon being, the type that used to prey on innocent travelers in the forest, back in the old times. I've never seen them on this side of the doorway since the exodus to the Otherworld, so yes, I would think it is almost certain that Zilya is behind their appearance now." He scowled, then reset his features into a more neutral expression when Jenna twitched. "It was probably too much to hope for that she would play fair. At least now we're forewarned."

He watched Jenna's shoulders slump. "So now we have Paranormal demons and Human thugs after us too? That's just swell." She swallowed hard. "Plus, of course, whatever that was that happened to you back there. Should I be worried?"

In other words, *Are you going to turn into some kind of monster too?*

He sure as hell hoped not.

"I don't think so," Day said in a calm tone. "Although, to be honest, I'm not much more certain of what is occurring than you are. But I may have a pretty good idea."

Jenna leaned forward a little, at least willing to listen, which he appreciated. "Tell me. Zilya didn't curse you, too, did she?"

Day gave a short laugh, tinged with bitterness. "No, I believe that in a way this is the parting gift of Brenna, the insane Baba

Yaga who tortured me and my brothers and almost killed us. In order to heal us, Barbara had to give us a huge dose of a substance called the Water of Life and Death. The Baba Yagas use it to extend their lives and boost their magic, and even they only take a small amount over measured intervals. The dose Barbara gave us was many times greater than normal—especially mine, since I was the most sorely injured."

"Little Babs said you were broken," Jenna said, giving him that pitying look he'd come to hate so much. Somehow coming from her he didn't mind so much. "How bad was it?"

He shrugged. "Bad enough that Barbara risked the Queen's wrath by giving us all a massive dose of something not meant for us. Fortunately, Her Majesty was kind enough to decide that our many years of service had earned us the right, but even she couldn't say if there would be any repercussions or side effects later on down the line."

Jenna bit her lip again in that way he found so adorable, no matter how hard he tried not to. "Is that what you think this is? Some kind of delayed side effect of this Water?" Concern *for* him seemed to override any fear she had *of* him, at least for the moment. "Are you going to be all right?"

He wished he knew. They were deep into uncharted territory now. But the last thing he wanted was for her to worry about him, when she should be concentrating on herself and her baby.

"I expect I'll be fine. My best guess, from what's been happening and your description of the way I looked in the woods, is that the maternal side of my heritage is making a long-delayed appearance. Maybe it's a result of drinking so much of the Water of Life and Death, or maybe it is simply because I am no longer a Rider, and that role took precedence for as long as I was."

The usual wave of loss and sadness threatened to swamp him, and he had to clear his throat before he went on. "The Leshy are shape-changers, you see. And while they are described in various ways in the old Russian tales, the few I met, including my mother's father, my grandfather, seemed Human most of the time, but when they assumed their guise as forest guardians, they usually had green hair and glowing eyes, and could grow larger or smaller at will." He ventured a brief smile. "Somehow I don't see myself running around as a cute, tiny forest gnome, so I suspect I'll stick with getting larger."

As he'd hoped, that image elicited a hesitant smile in return.

"Were the Leshy dangerous?" she asked.

*Are* you *dangerous?* was what she really meant, he suspected. Day wished he knew the answer to that question for sure.

"They didn't react well to those who threatened their forests or those who lived within them," he said, for lack of a better response. "But I'm not a mythical creature. I'm me. And I would never hurt you, Jenna."

She gazed at him steadily and said in a soft voice, "How can you be sure, when you don't even know what is happening to you or how to control it?"

Because he knew in his gut that he'd rather rip his own arm off than use it to harm one hair on her head? "I just know," he said. "I don't blame you if you don't believe me, but all I've done is try to help you since I've met you."

"And grump around like a bear with a sore paw," Jenna said with a laugh. But she still went to sleep in her own bedroll on her side of the fire, and not in his arms. He lay awake all night on the other side, trying to persuade himself he didn't mind, and failing miserably.

**TWO** hundred and sixty miles down the Natchez Trace Parkway, then a night spent in one of the parkway campgrounds in Mississippi. The next day saw them driving about three hundred miles, stopping to rest near Sarepta, Lousiana. Their sixth night was spent in the Davy Crockett National Forest, near Crockett, Texas. They'd only gone one hundred and seventy miles that day, but Mick insisted that Jenna needed the breather he'd promised her, and she couldn't really disagree. It was nice to be about to take a hot shower at the campgrounds, and take a few hours to sit on the shore of the Ratcliff Lake, enjoying the feeling of not having the ground moving underneath her.

The next morning they got on US-79, which would take them most of the rest of the way to their destination. Mick decided to stop taking back roads, as they had for much of the way since the attack in West Virginia, and stick to the highway for the last leg of the journey. There had been no sign of either Paranormal or Human adversaries since that night in the forest, and with a five-hour trip ahead of them, he wanted to make as good time as they could, so they would arrive at the Enchanted Rock park while it was still light out.

Jenna was torn between eagerness to get to their goal and fear that once they arrived, it would turn out to be another dead end. If that was true, she had no idea what she'd do next.

They stopped for lunch at a small diner along the way. Jenna looked up from her cheeseburger (with extra pickles and jalapeño peppers) to see Mick cast a slightly worried glance out the window at the road that ran past the parking lot. She looked, too, but didn't see anything other than the usual cars and trucks whizzing by, the same sight she'd been enjoying from the back of the motorcycle for days.

"Something wrong?" she asked, snagging a curly fry off of his plate and dragging it through a pile of ketchup.

He gave her a crooked grin and pushed a pile of fries onto her plate. "No, everything is fine," he said. "Except for the fact that you keep stealing my food. I know you're eating for two, but at the rate you're going, you're going to need even bigger clothes than the ones we picked up at that Walmart three days ago."

"Nice," she said. "You'd think after all these centuries you'd know better than to insult a woman's weight. Jeez." She ate another fry. "Also, points for trying, but you're not distracting me from my question. You look worried. Why?"

Mick shrugged, polishing off his third chili dog in a single bite. "I might have spotted the same car behind us a few times. But it was one of those black Ford Explorers, and there are a lot of them around, so I'm probably just being paranoid. Besides, even if it was the same car, we're on a main highway. With pit stops and such, we could be playing tag with the same vehicle most of the day without it meaning anything sinister."

Jenna put down her last bit of burger, appetite suddenly gone. "Uh-huh," she said, wiping her mouth with a napkin decorated with the bull's horn symbol that adorned the entire diner. "So you're not worried at all?"

"Let's just say that I'm not *very* worried. But maybe we should get back on the road."

She nodded. They were so close, there was no way she was going to let anyone stop them from reaching Enchanted Rock. Even if it meant dodging every dark-colored SUV on the road.

**ONCE** they got to the Enchanted Rock State Natural Area, Jenna began to realize the scope of the problem. It was a *big* place. The whole area was six hundred and forty acres, according to the guidebook, although they were only looking for a spot on the top of the rock. But even that covered a lot of territory.

Thankfully, much of the area was accessible by motorcycle, even if technically there were no vehicles allowed, and they had some idea from Barbara's research of where to look for the place that Spanish soldier Don Jesús Navarro had rescued the maiden Rosa, daughter of Chief Tehuan, after her kidnapping by Comanches who intended to sacrifice her on the rock. In theory, this spot also coincided with a couple of the locations where people had reportedly disappeared, so they were hoping that the mention of *rose* in the riddle was a clue to the site of the doorway they were looking for that would lead to the Otherworld.

Mick seemed pretty certain he knew where he was heading, so Jenna just held on tight and prayed quietly under her breath as they bumped their way over the rough paths.

But the prayers turned into cursing when she looked over her shoulder to see a massive black vehicle parked on the road underneath them. She tapped Mick on the shoulder and gestured. He took his eyes off the path long enough to squint behind her and add his curses to her own. Then he revved the bike and took them up and around the next curve at speeds that made her grab on even tighter.

The men from the SUV pursued them up that incline and all those that followed, no matter how rapidly they went or how many turnoffs they took. The bike's speed was limited by the roughness and incline of the rock, but even so, the wind cut into Jenna's face and tiny bits of gravel bounced up to nip at her ankles and lower legs. Mick drove the bike faster and faster, pushing it to speeds that would have seemed unsafe on regular roads, much less the top of a large hunk of pink granite covered with smaller stones, rutted gullies, and the occasional startled tourist.

"Do you know where you're going?" Jenna screamed in Mick's ear. "Or are you just trying to lose them? Because if that's your plan, I don't think it's working."

"Trust me," Mick hollered back. "And hang on. Things are going to get dicey in a minute."

Jenna swallowed hard. Things seemed pretty dicey already. She wasn't sure she wanted to find out what Mick thought was going to be even more dangerous. But a few seconds later, she found out, as he rode the motorcycle straight toward a solid wall of rock.

# CHAPTER 15

**"WHAT** the hell are you doing?" Jenna shrieked, and then she didn't have any breath left to yell as Mick tilted the bike down at a reckless angle, seemingly keeping it upright through will power and determination alone, and slid them—bike and all—through a hole in the rock wall she hadn't even seen. As they went through, the stone edges of the entrance came so close, they tore down the leather arm of the jacket Barbara had loaned her, and a tiny shard scraped at her cheek like a claw reaching out to stop her.

There was the sound of yelling behind her and Jenna risked turning her head long enough to see two large and familiar figures pounding down the track after them, with what looked like the flashlight app from a cell phone wavering up and down in the dark. One of them was holding a knife the size of a small sword and the other one was waving a gun around and shouting something threatening in their general direction.

Jenna was a lot less worried about the men following them

than she was about the fact that Mick was actually riding them through an underground cave on a Yamaha. She was pretty sure they were about to be killed, and she was just whispering, "Sorry, baby girl," when Mick drove the bike into a crack even narrower than the one they'd come in through, which looked as though it might lead directly down into the center of the Earth.

She swallowed a scream and closed her eyes, feeling as though the earth was rippling around her, only to open them a minute later when she realized they'd stopped. Everything was quiet; she couldn't even hear the sound of the Yamaha's engine. But she couldn't be dead, because in that case, she doubted that her heart would be hammering hard enough to burst through her chest.

She opened her eyes again and said in a strangled whisper, "What the hell?" as she found herself looking at a lavender-gray sky and sitting atop a glorious white horse with gleaming silver eyes. Jenna had the strangest feeling that the horse's expression was ridiculously smug.

**DAY** patted his horse on the neck and bent over to whisper, "Good girl, Krasivaya; well done," before sliding off onto the ground and offering a hand to a stunned-looking Jenna. The dark-haired woman wobbled a little bit once her feet hit the grass and her face was even a paler shade of white than usual, but other than a tiny scrape on one cheek she seemed otherwise unharmed.

"Welcome back to the Otherworld," he said. "Sorry about the rough ride."

Jenna's mouth opened and closed without any words actually making their way out. Finally, she simply shook her head. Then she jerked around, almost knocking herself over, and pointed back at the area they'd just come through.

"Don't worry," Day said, steadying her so she didn't fall

down. "They shouldn't have been able to follow us through. This gate has been closed; I only got through because it recognized me as a Rider."

He didn't bother to mention that he hadn't been completely sure until the last minute that it would still do so. His original plan had been to check it out cautiously before they tried to pass the barrier, but then, his original plan hadn't included being chased through the cave by armed men. He could have taken them, of course, but he was worried about Jenna's safety in a fight in such tight confines, plus he had been afraid that he would change forms again and scare her so much she wouldn't want to stay in his company at all.

So in the end, he'd just trusted fate, figuring that destiny wouldn't have dragged them all the way here just to let them get smashed into a million bits against an unwelcoming rock door. He sent up silent thanks that he'd guessed right, and then turned back to Jenna, who was gazing around with wide-eyed wonder.

Day took a look around himself and smiled, recognizing the place they'd come through as one he'd been to many years before, although it was too far off the beaten path for most denizens of this side to visit it often.

"I don't understand," Jenna said. "This doesn't look anything like what I saw on our way to the Queen's castle."

She was right about that. Unlike the more polished region around the royal grounds, this area was much more overgrown and wild. Without any regular residents to guide its design, the more desolate spaces in the Otherworld tended to simply do what they wanted.

In this case, that meant lots of short, stubby trees with gnarled limbs in various shades of blues and grays, most of them draped with dark green hanging vines that twisted and braided themselves into complicated patterns. (And occasionally dropped down to ensnare an unwary creature for dinner. Day thought maybe he'd wait a minute to mention that little tidbit.) The sparse grass was tough and fibrous, and made a subtle whistling sound as you walked through it. Day's horse bent its head down to nibble on it and gave up in disgust after one unpalatable mouthful.

There were no paths or roads, simply places where the trees hadn't bothered to grow. But if they wound their way through the narrow spaces, Mick knew they'd come out the other side to a slightly more hospitable area. Of course, the problem with that was there would be more people there, which meant a greater chance of being seen, which wouldn't be a good idea under the circumstances.

"We're in a completely different part of the Otherworld," he explained. "It's not nearly as large as the world on the other side of the doorway, but we've still traveled quite a way from where we were the last time you were here. This is a less civilized section, with a much smaller population, but we're still going to want to keep a low profile."

"Why?" Jenna asked, starting to regain her usual poise.

"A couple of reasons," Day answered, reaching up to rearrange the saddlebags so they sat a little more comfortably on the horse's back. "For one thing, we're on Zilya's home territory now. She'll have more power here than she would back in the Human lands, and I'd just as soon she didn't find out we were here."

"Oh," Jenna said in a small voice. Clearly, the thought of her nemesis with ever more power was unsettling, to say the least. Still, she stuck her chin in the air and asked, "What's the other reason?"

"That's the more important one, in some ways. We don't want word to get back to the Queen that we're here without her permission. She might be just fine with it, or she might decide to send you home." *Or worse*, but he wasn't going to mention that either.

Jenna wrinkled her brow, staring at his steed. "I don't know, Mick. I'm thinking that a horse like this will kind of stand out. There can't be that many this beautiful, even here."

The horse tossed her head and stamped one foot, obviously

pleased with the compliment. Day rolled his eyes but patted her gleaming sides anyway.

"That shouldn't be a problem," he said. "As long as I ask nicely and she's feeling cooperative." He stroked the horse's long nose and whispered into her ear. She whinnied and then shimmered from her tail to the ends of her mane, and slowly changed color from shining white to a drabber, although still pretty, dappled gray.

Jenna blinked. "Well, that's a handy trick," she said.

"She can change from a steed into a motorcycle; a superficial alteration of her hue is hardly a big deal." As long as they were in the Otherworld. Trying such a thing on the other side of the doorway was nearly impossible. Day glanced down at his black leather jacket and boots, and the brown pants and cotton shirt he wore with them. "We can't pull off the same trick, alas, but hopefully my different attire will throw off anyone who sees us at a distance."

At Jenna's questioning glance, he explained, "As the White Rider, I used to wear all white. Few people here have ever seen me dressed in any other way. I wouldn't wonder that most of them could be standing right in front of me, wearing these clothes, and not even look twice."

Jenna grinned at him. "Not if they're female, they won't. I doubt there's a woman alive who would not look twice at you, babe."

He snorted, absurdly pleased by the flattery, although he tried not to show it. "We'll just have to try and stay away from women, then, won't we?"

"What exactly *are* we going to do, now that we're here?" Jenna asked as they started walking alongside the newly re-tinted horse, ducking occasionally to avoid a particularly enthusiastic vine.

"We've followed the part of the riddle that said to find 'a pathway through,' but I'm not sure how that helps us." She stroked her belly absently, a nervous habit Day had noticed recently. "What do we do next?"

"I suspect we need to find the 'magic key to a gift divine' mentioned in the riddle," Day said. "But the Otherworld is vast and changeable, with lots of places to hide things. We obviously can't just wander around looking for something that might or might not be the right key, and could be either hidden or sitting right out in plain sight." His feet slid a bit as the ground underneath them changed from grass to a kind of silty sand that seemed to shift and move on its own. The tiny black grains sang quietly to themselves, with sharp dissonant notes whenever walking feet disrupted them.

"Oh," Jenna said, grabbing on to his arm for balance and then letting go as soon as she realized what she'd done. Mick shook his head and took her arm back. She hesitated, and then left it there.

"Is there anyone here who might be able to help us figure it out?" she asked. "You know, like some kind of an Other-world version of a reference librarian? Or a scholar?"

Day could feel his face set into grim lines—lines that had become habit recently. At least until Jenna came along. "I know someone who might be able to use the journals and books you brought along to help us find some answers," he said reluctantly, patting the saddlebags with the hand not holding on to her. "But . . ."

"But what?" Jenna asked, turning to face him. She stopped in her tracks, no doubt catching a hint of something in his voice. She was getting way too good at reading him.

Day grimaced. "But I'm not sure if this person is even still in the Otherworld. Or if he would be willing to speak to me, even if he is."

"Why?" Jenna asked. "Is he some kind of old adversary?"

"No," Day said, shaking his head ruefully. "He's my brother."

# CHAPTER 16

**EVENTUALLY,** they reached a place where the footing was more dependable, and Day lifted Jenna up so she could ride in front of him on the horse. Krasivaya was plenty tough; she could have taken Jenna's slight weight in addition to his own and still trotted for days without getting tired. The horse *was* magical, after all.

And it was a good thing, because the last place he'd heard Gregori was living was pretty much on the ass end of nowhere. His eldest brother had picked one of the most inaccessible spots in the Otherworld, and that was really saying something. But that was Gregori for you. It was likely to take them days to get to him, traveling through some fairly desolate lands.

"I don't understand," Jenna said after they'd been traveling for a couple of hours (or what seemed like hours, since time was both fluid and difficult to track on this side of the doorway). "Why wouldn't your brother talk to you? I thought you told me that you and your brothers got along well."

Day had been afraid she'd get around to asking that. In fact, knowing Jenna, he was pretty sure she'd been holding the question in since he'd made his original comment. It wasn't that she was nosy, as far as he could tell, but that she was genuinely interested in other people. Which would have been fine, if "other people" had been anyone other than him. Or if he'd been *normal* other people.

"We did," he said, reluctant to tell the story. "But things happened. Brenna happened. Except that everything she did to us could have been avoided if it hadn't been for me."

"I don't understand," Jenna said, twisting around on the horse so she could look at him.

"Brenna trapped me because I fell for her damsel-in-distress routine. She played on my well-known weakness for rescuing women, and used it to sucker me into lowering my guard. My brothers got caught when they came looking for me. So you see, she used my stupidity to capture us all. It was my fault we got caught in her trap, and my fault that my brothers were tortured day after day, nigh on to the point of death." He fell silent, overwhelmed as always by the crushing reality of what he'd done to those he loved the most in all the world. In both worlds.

Jenna was silent for a minute, and he thought maybe he'd finally made her understand the magnitude of his crime. He should have been happy if that was true, but a part of him hated that she would look at him differently from now on.

"I heard a little of the story at Barbara's house," she said finally. "But nobody seemed to think it was your fault."

"They weren't there," Day said shortly. "I was."

The two of them rode along for a while through a grove of what looked like apple trees, if apples were purple and covered with soft fuzz like a peach. Day reached up and plucked a few, tucking them into one of the saddlebags for later.

"So your brothers blame you for what a deranged Baba Yaga did to them?" Jenna said. "That hardly seems fair. After all, you had no way of knowing she wasn't genuinely someone in trouble, did you? Did they expect you to just keep going?"

"Well, they probably would have," Day said. "The two of them have always believed it is better not to get involved with the affairs of the Human world, except when under the express orders of a Baba Yaga." He shook his head, giving her a rueful half smile. "Truth is, they'd been teasing me about my weakness for years. It just turned out not to be so funny in the end."

Jenna narrowed her eyes, then swiveled back around to face front as the going got a little rougher. "So neither of them had any flaws at all? That doesn't seem likely."

"I guess it depends on what you consider a flaw," Day said. "Alexei loves a good bar fight, and he was always dragging us into them. But to be honest, Gregori and I find them fairly amusing, too, so it wasn't much of a hardship. And Alexei's grandfather was a great warrior who was always fighting one battle or another, so it was probably to be expected."

"What about Gregori?" Jenna asked. "Surely he had some kind of failing. Nobody is perfect."

"Gregori came awfully close," Day said. "It could be damned irritating at times. Maybe it was because he was raised by a mother who was a powerful shamaness, but Gregori was always cool and unruffled. Even when we were trapped in that horrible cave, he drove Brenna crazy with the fact that she could never break his calm serenity. Some days, I think that was all that kept Alexei and me from losing it entirely."

"Huh," Jenna said.

"What?"

"Oh, that just doesn't sound to me like the kind of man who would blame his brother for a situation that was primarily the fault of a crazy woman. I'm surprised, that's all."

Day didn't see how anyone could *not* blame him. Which is why he'd never tried to ask either of his brothers how they felt about it. He couldn't bear to hear what they had to say.

"Gregori is very good at keeping his feelings hidden," Day said. "Besides, we haven't seen each other since right after it all happened, remember. He could be thinking anything."

"Then why assume the worst?" Jenna asked in a mild tone. "After all, you have a lot of shared history. A *lot* of shared history." She turned back around and stared at him. "I still can't believe you're the son of a god. That's just incredible."

Day snorted. "Really, Jenna, it wasn't all that great. I mean, sure, it was fun when you got to throw a thunderbolt or create a silly new bird. Alexei came up with the duck-billed platypus, by the way, so don't blame that one on me." He tried to muster a smile. "But mostly our father was busy, preoccupied, and arrogant. About what you'd expect from a god, but not a hell of a lot of good as a father. It's not as though he spent time playing catch or reading us bedtime stories."

"Oh," Jenna said, sounding disappointed. "I hadn't thought of it that way. So you really didn't have a father at all. That's sad."

"It was okay," Day said. "It's not as though I had a bad childhood. But Gregori was probably more of a father to me than my own was." Maybe that was part of why it was so painful to have let him down.

"We were always very different from each other, but it didn't stop the three of us from getting along. It was almost like we were each pieces of a great puzzle, but together we made one picture. Alexei was fun-loving and looked at life very simply, and Gregori was always the deep thinker whose passions ran deep and quiet." He sighed. "Of course, that was before our ordeal. We're all changed now."

"Changed how?" Jenna asked.

Day was glad she was facing away from him again, so he wouldn't have to see the pity in her eyes.

"Alexei lost his joyful exuberance," he explained. "And Gregori lost his inner peace. I haven't seen them in months, but from all reports, they are both still searching for answers, just as I am."

"What did you lose?" Jenna asked softly, looking straight ahead.

"Everything else," he said. He knew he sounded rude and abrupt, but there was no way he was going to tell her that he'd lost his never-ending faith in his own judgment, especially when it came to women. Now, instead of looking at women and finding them each glorious and beautiful, as he once did, he always saw a shadow of Brenna staring out from behind their eyes, lurking in hiding and waiting to pounce.

Jenna was the first exception to that, although he wasn't sure why. Maybe it had something to do with her being pregnant—a state Brenna would never have been able to duplicate—or maybe it was merely her open heart and blunt directness. It was impossible to imagine subterfuge within those light blue eyes, no matter how paranoid one might be.

"You all suffered at the hands of that evil Baba Yaga," Jenna said. "From the sound of it, you came out worst of all. Maybe your brothers were upset with you at first, but surely they must be over it now, even if they are still suffering."

"I wouldn't know," Day said coldly. "I haven't spoken to either of them since we went our separate ways to heal. For all I know, they hate me. I wouldn't blame them if they did." Gods knew, he hated himself. And he had heard the whispers in court . . . He knew that others blamed him as well, no matter what they said to his face.

The Queen herself had been silent on the matter, but he doubted she was as sanguine about the loss of her Riders as she seemed.

**NIGHT** fell quickly, as though someone somewhere had thrown a switch. Jenna wondered if that was how it worked, but she wasn't going to ask Mick. He'd been silent and brooding since their conversation about his brothers and had refused to talk at all for the last few hours. Or however long it had been. It was hard to mark time without a sun overhead and her watch had quit working as soon as they'd crossed over into the Otherworld. But the clear daylight had faded within minutes to a dusky evening, although the three moons now glowed more brightly overhead, lighting their way.

"We'll stop now," Mick said, bringing the horse to a halt and dismounting with ease.

He had to give Jenna a hand down; her hips and knees felt creaky and stiff, no matter how smooth the horse's gait had been. She worried a little that all this bouncing was bad for the baby, but since there didn't seem to be any choice, she tried to shove that thought to the back of her mind, along with its fifty thousand fretting cousins.

"We can have some dinner and get some sleep, and be on our way whenever the Queen decides she wants it to be morning."

*Aha, there is a switch, of sorts. It figures.*

"How long is it going to take us to get to where you think your brother is living?" she asked, a little afraid to hear the answer.

"Another day or two, probably. Hard to say. Some parts of the Otherworld stay more or less static, but others can change around periodically, and it has been a long time since I have been out this way. Maybe tomorrow. We'll have to see."

Jenna thought she could really come to resent the Otherworld. Sure, it could be really beautiful, and it was certainly fascinating, but she much preferred a place that was a little less unpredictable. On the other hand, she couldn't fault the scenery. The moons overhead gleamed like polished silver, even the smaller crescent with the slight tilt to the right. They'd camped on a rocky outcropping covered with blue moss that glowed softly in the darkened landscape. Something that probably wasn't a bird twittered in the distance, singing a song that sounded like church bells.

Mick built a small campfire using twigs and branches that he politely asked a small tree to donate, and they had the last of the supplies he'd packed in for a hodgepodge kind of dinner—a hunk of cheese paired with a marginally too-chewy heel of bread, plus a handful of figs he'd had stowed away somewhere. When they finished, he offered her one of the not-quite-an-apple fruits he'd plucked off the tree they'd passed earlier.

Jenna gave it a dubious glance and shook her head.

"I know it looks a little odd," Mick said. "But I promise, it tastes delicious."

"It's not how it looks," Jenna said, although it was, a little. "I'm more worried about what will happen to me if I eat it. The tales are full of warnings for those who venture into the land of Faerie, and they almost always tell you not to eat anything."

Mick snorted. "You can't believe everything you read in fairy tales," he scoffed. "Mostly those stories come from the fact that the food is so perfect here, nothing in the Human world ever tastes good enough in comparison."

"Very reassuring," she said. "Thanks so much."

He gave her one of his crooked grins, flashing a dimple in a way that always made her heart beat a little too fast. "Seriously, there are certain plants that you should avoid, and if a faery offers you anything—food or otherwise—you should probably think twice about accepting it, but since you're traveling with me, I can steer you away from anything dangerous."

"Well, if you're sure . . ."

"Nothing about the Otherworld is ever certain," he said. But then he added in a practical tone, "We're out of food from the other side, so if you don't eat whatever we find here, you're going to get awfully hungry. And so will your baby."

She had to admit he had a point there. "I hope this is okay for you," she whispered, rubbing her belly, and then she held her hand out for the not-apple and took a big bite. It tasted like vanilla ice cream with swirls of chocolate and caramel and a hint of amaretto. "Okay, I see what you mean about the problem with going back to eating regular Human food. And, um, can I have another?"

* * *

**THEY** traveled throughout the next morning without incident until they rounded a low hill and found themselves facing a giant lizard. Mottled blue and green in color, it almost blended into the mossy hillside; only its embroidered orange waistcoat and gleaming white teeth made it stand out from the background. That and the fact that it was over twelve feet tall and had smoke trickling out its nostrils.

"Eek!" Jenna said, grabbing Mick's arm involuntarily. "Is that a dragon?" she asked in a quieter tone, hoping not to attract its attention.

Too late. "A dragon?" the lizard said in a deep husky voice, sounding indignant and slightly British. "Do you see any wings, young lady?" He glared down his outsized snout at her. "Dragon, indeed. How rude."

Jenna could feel Mick's chest shaking; she had a feeling it was laughter and not fear, and relaxed a little bit. Although not much, since the lizard was *very, very* large and she'd clearly already said the wrong thing. Not a good idea when facing a creature whose teeth were longer than your forearm.

"I apologize for my companion," Mick said, sliding off the horse and executing a graceful bow in the lizard's direction. His expression was perfectly composed as he helped Jenna down, too, but the corner of his mouth was twitching ever so slightly. "She's new around here."

The lizard huffed, causing more smoke rings to create curlicue clouds in the air above his massive head. "Ignorance is no excuse for rudeness, my lad. Dragon. Pfft. I will have you know that I am a descendant of the great gorgonopsid, the most dangerous lizard species that ever roamed the other side of the doorway. Dragons cower before me."

"Don't tell that to my friend Chudo-Yudo," Mick suggested. "Although I am sure that lesser dragons find you very intimidating."

"Hurumph," the lizard said, apparently mollified for the

moment. "Friends with Chudo-Yudo, are you? Then you know the Baba Yagas?"

Day bowed again, but Jenna could see the smile sliding out of his eyes, leaving them misty blue with sadness. "I know them well, sir. My name is Mikhail Day, and I am—that is, I was—the White Rider. My companion's name is Jenna. Pleased to make your acquaintance."

The lizard gave a brisk nod. "Bob."

"Excuse me?" Mick said. Jenna wondered if the creature was ordering Mick to bow again, although it seemed an unlikely way to do so.

"Bob. My name is Bob," the lizard repeated. "I have heard of the Riders, of course, but I rarely leave this valley. I believe you are the first one I have met."

Jenna thought Mick looked relieved that Bob the lizard wasn't familiar with the story of his current situation, although she would have felt better if the giant reptile weren't completely blocking their path forward, and showing no signs of moving.

"I couldn't help but notice that you seemed to be in some distress before we came around the corner," Mick said, undoubtedly thinking the same thing. "Is there anything we can do to assist you, before we get on our way?"

Jenna hoped that Bob's problem didn't have anything to do with wanting an unusual entrée for lunch.

Bob patted his waistcoat pockets, his long snout wrinkling so that his white teeth were even more obvious. "I seem to have misplaced my pipe, as it happens. I am quite desolated."

Both Jenna and Mick swiveled their heads around, looking for the missing object, but there was nothing obvious to be seen.

"Isn't a pipe rather redundant for a lizard who can breathe fire?" Jenna asked. "Not that I'm criticizing, or anything. Pipes can be quite distinguished."

"Whatever is she talking about?" Bob asked Mick. "What does a pipe have to do with fire?"

Mick blinked. "Uh, you weren't looking for the kind of pipe you smoke tobacco in? Or, I don't know, a hookah?"

Bob's tiny eyes narrowed even further. "What on earth would I want such a silly thing for? No, I am looking for my bagpipe. It is a lovely day, and I was in the mood to make a bit of music."

*A bagpipe. Oh, sure, that makes* so *much more sense.* Jenna glanced around again and noticed what looked like a deflated green balloon peeking out from underneath a bush of almost exactly the same hue. "Is that it?" she asked, pointing in the bush's direction.

"My pipe!" Bob cried in a clarion voice that shook a birdlike creature off a nearby branch. "There it is!"

He stomped over to the bush and pulled out a giant set of bagpipes that still looked small in his clawed hands. Instantly, he set them to his lipless mouth and took a deep breath, ignoring Mick and Jenna completely as he focused all his attention on the instrument. After a few discordant notes, a cheerful tune began to take form. As they rode on, carefully skirting Bob's immense tail, they were followed by the droning sound for miles. Bob was actually surprisingly good, considering he'd never been to Scotland.

As they sat around yet another campfire that evening after a meal made up of things that bore even less resemblance to the food she knew than the apple she'd eaten, Jenna stared into the crackling black and maroon flames and gnawed on her lip as she worried.

"If you're still hungry, I could probably find some nice roots by the riverbank we passed," Mick teased. "Mind you, some of them insist on yodeling while you eat them, but you get used to that after a while."

Jenna rolled her eyes. "Very funny," she said. "I'm just thinking."

Mick scooted closer to her, so they were sitting near enough to touch, although they didn't. In fact, Jenna had been careful to keep her distance as much as possible since the night they'd made love. Or he was keeping his distance from her. It was hard to tell. Better to think it was mutual.

"What?" he asked. "I can tell something is bothering you. If you're fretting about our being seen by someone, I can assure you that I haven't caught so much as a glimpse of anyone since we passed those first few small huts the day we got here. Plus Bob, of course, but he didn't strike me as the chatty type. And as far as I know, none of the more predatory denizens live out in this direction. I think we're pretty safe."

"That's not it," Jenna said. To be honest, her biggest concern wasn't that she might be in danger from any of the Paranormal creatures, no matter how odd and ominous some of them could seem. Something about having Mick around made her feel protected. At least from the more obvious threats.

"Then what is it?" he asked. "You've been quiet all day."

Jenna put her hands over her belly, which seemed slightly rounder than it had been. She was surprised by how fierce she felt about defending this little being she hadn't even met yet.

"I'm just worried about what being in the Otherworld might be doing to my baby," she admitted. "They have all kinds of warnings on medicines and booze and cigarettes back home, but nobody seems to have put a handy label on the Otherworld listing possible side effects."

Mick chuckled. "Well, we don't get a lot of babies here, so they probably haven't done enough studies to be sure. But I'm certain it's okay. You don't feel sick, do you?"

"Actually, I feel pretty good, now that I've moved out of the morning-sickness phase," she said. "Oh!"

Mick shifted closer to her faster than she could see him move, leaning in but still not touching. "What's the matter?"

"Nothing," Jenna said in a marveling voice. "I just felt the baby kick for the first time."

His thick brows drew together. "Isn't it a little early for that? I admit, I haven't spent a lot of time with pregnant women, but I thought it started with a little flutter, and even that came later."

Jenna pressed her hand against her belly, waiting to see if it happened again. "I'm pretty sure the fluttering thing is supposed to happen around the fourth month, and I'm not quite there yet. I don't know about the kicking. Maybe I imagined it." She rubbed her stomach again, as if doing so would encourage a response.

"To be honest, I had to abandon the one baby book I bought in order to make enough room for my grandmother's journals and notebooks, so I might be confused about the timing." There was a tiny movement under her fingers, subtle but unmistakable. "No! There it is again!" She giggled a little, both thrilled and slightly intimidated by the experience. "I have to admit, I don't really know anything about pregnancy and babies. I was so sure I'd never need the information."

Mick held out his hand hesitantly and then withdrew it again. He peered at her through the dim quasi-night. "It must be tough," he said quietly. "Being pregnant when you never wanted a baby."

Jenna shook her head. "On the contrary. There is very little I wanted more. Maybe because you always want what you can't have, or maybe just because it is built into the genes, I don't know. But I always avoided pregnant women because seeing them made me so sad and jealous. Petty, I guess, but there you have it."

"I don't think that's petty at all," Mick said, and there was something odd about the tone of his voice.

"Did you ever want children?" she asked.

"It was never a possibility," he said, and she thought she recognized the tone now as the same slightly wistful note that used to color her own words on the subject, on the rare occasions she spoke about it.

"Why not? I can't imagine there was a shortage of women who would have offered to be your baby mama."

Mick grimaced, although she thought it was more for her use of silly slang than anything else.

"It's not that," he said. "None of the Riders could have

children. Maybe it is simply that our father didn't see fit to design us that way, but it is also true that Paranormal creatures usually can't crossbreed with Humans, and they can only mate with their own kind to produce offspring. My brothers and I are the only ones of our kind, at least that we know of. Presumably other gods produced children as our father did, but we have never met any other demigods in all our travels."

He ran one large hand through his long blond hair. "The gods usually only had children when they needed them for some particular reason, such as creating the Riders to be companions to the Baba Yagas. Apparently, doing so took a lot out of them, and most of them didn't want to lose even a fraction of their power."

Jenna was so astonished, she could feel her mouth drop open, and she had to force herself to shut it with a *snap*. "But mythology is full of stories about the Greek gods mating with Humans right, left, and center,"

Mick rolled his eyes. "Oh, well, the Greeks," he said, as if that explained everything.

"If you don't mind my asking," Jenna said, not wanting to raise a sore subject, but too curious not to, "did you and your brothers mind not being able to have children of your own?" She sure as hell minded—every single day until the impossible happened.

"We never discussed it," he said, as if it was normal for such an important topic never to have come up in centuries spent together.

*Men.*

"No?"

"I was always a bit sorry, myself," Mick said, looking down at the ground as though it held some fascinating clue to the questions of the universe. "I like children. I've enjoyed being around the Babas in training when they were young. You'd never believe it to see her now, but Barbara was cute as a button."

He sighed, and added so quietly she barely heard it, "One

of the things I regret the most about everything that happened is that now I won't be able to watch Barbara's little Babs grow up. I just don't feel right being around the Baba Yagas anymore, now that I'm not a Rider."

"But you could still be a friend," she said.

"It doesn't work that way."

"Why not?"

"It just doesn't," he said, as if the last bell had tolled on the subject.

"You're being ridiculous," she said, not able to understand how he could walk away from brothers he'd spent over a thousand years with, when she would do anything to get back the one she'd never even had a chance to meet. Not to mention the Baba Yagas, who seemed as close as family. "And stubborn."

"And you're butting your nose into something that is none of your business. Just drop it."

Jenna put her hands over her belly and patted it gently, then they both sat in silence, staring into the fire and thinking their own thoughts until it was time to curl up in their bedrolls to sleep. More separate than ever, alas.

# CHAPTER 17

**EVENTUALLY,** they arrived at the edge of a small lake. The landscape was sere and silent, with few birds and little wild-life. There were some reeds and cattails, which actually made a quiet purring noise as Day petted them in passing, and some dry grasses, but not much else other than rocks and sand. Near the shore was a small brown hut with windows that looked as though they'd been made from some kind of shell, like an iridescent bubble stretched not quite flat.

There was no smoke rising from the chimney; in fact, no signs of habitation at all. The hut could have been deserted for years, and Day began to worry that they had made the long trek for nothing.

"It doesn't look like anyone is here," Jenna said in a voice barely louder than a whisper. It was that kind of place where hushed tones felt appropriate. Her face fell. "What do we do now?"

But as they approached the hut, the curtain hanging over the low doorway was swept aside and a slim, handsome man stepped out. He was of medium height, with long ebony hair pulled back in a tail, a Fu Manchu mustache, and dark slanted eyes set in a face with flat cheekbones that reflected his Mongolian heritage. As always, his expression was calm but closed, giving Day no hint as to what was going on behind those dark eyes. He still wore the head-to-toe red clothing he'd always favored, but he'd traded in his leathers for loose silk trousers and tunic, and instead of boots his feet were bare.

He and Day stared at each other for a minute, and then Gregori said, "It took you long enough, brother," and held the curtain aside to invite them in. Day heard Jenna let out a sigh of relief.

The interior of the hut was as austere as the exterior. It couldn't have been more than about twelve feet square and most of that space was empty. The walls seemed to have been formed out of some kind of mud, smoothed more or less flat, and the floor was rough wooden planks covered with woven reed rugs. In contrast to the usually colorful Otherworld, it was a monochromatic brown and tan, although not unpleasantly so. Peaceful, Day would have called it. Neat, certainly. A nice cave to hide out in, even, if one was in the mood for hiding. He knew the feeling.

Gregori pulled a couple of flat cushions from a plain wooden chest for them to sit on at a low stone table, and poured tea from a kettle sitting on a tiny stove. Day could see a tiny orange salamander curled up underneath the stove, keeping it hot, which was undoubtedly why they didn't see any smoke from the chimney. Salamanders were elemental creatures, usually volatile and hard to control, although this one seemed as content as any hound sitting at his master's feet.

Other than the chest and table, there was only a low platform in one corner that probably served as a bed, if the thin blanket resting on top was any indication, and a curved wooden bench near the stove. Even for Gregori, who tended toward the simple and unadorned, this place was drastic.

Peaceful it might be, but Day found it bleak and depressing. Hopefully his brother did not, since he seemed to have chosen to be there of his own free will.

Once they were all seated around the table, Day waved his hand to make the introductions. "Jenna, this is my eldest brother, Gregori. Gregori, this is Jenna." He stopped for a second, stymied as to how to refer to her. "We're traveling together for the moment."

Gregori raised an eyebrow at that but didn't say anything more than, "Welcome. It is very pleasant to meet you. Is this your first visit to the Otherworld?"

"Technically, my second," Jenna answered. "I went with Mick and Barbara to see the Queen briefly, a little while ago. But I didn't get to see much of the lands here. Traveling through them this time has been . . . interesting."

"I would expect so," Gregori said. "Although there is very little of any note out here at the far reaches."

Day appreciated that his brother was being gracious to Jenna, but he thought he detected a note of strain in his voice.

"How are you doing?" he asked.

"I am well," Gregori said. "And you?"

"I am also well," Day said. It was a dreadfully stilted conversation, far removed from their previous cheerful banter, and it made his heart hurt to have it. Especially since he knew they were both lying about being fine. Neither one of them was any such thing. He thought it might ease the uncomfortable situation a little if he provided a distraction from the elephant in the room that was their last horrible shared experience.

"Jenna is here searching for the answers to a riddle," Day said, a little desperate. "She has to break a curse that has been passed down in her family for years. I told her that you were the wisest, most knowledgeable person I knew, and that you might be willing to help her solve this puzzle."

"Still running to the rescue, I see," Gregori said. His flat tone made it impossible to tell if he thought that was a good thing or a bad one.

"Barbara made me," Day explained.

"Ah. That does put rather a different complexion on things. So, tell me more about this curse."

Jenna gave him the specifics, including the general details of everything that had happened since she'd stumbled onto Day's cabin in the woods. There were a few nonpertinent specifics that she left out, for which Day was grateful. His brother didn't need to know about their one passionate night together—it would just confuse the issue and make him think that Day had an emotional involvement, when he didn't.

"Zilya, eh?" Gregori said when Jenna was done. "I never liked her. But then, I find most of the Queen's court less than appealing, no matter their physical attractiveness." He lifted one shoulder in a minute shrug. "I would be happy to assist you, if I could, but as you can see, I have no resources in this hut. It was designed as a retreat, not a library. I'm afraid I am not going to be much help to you."

For a moment, a shadow slid across his face, and Day knew exactly what he was thinking: now that he was no longer the Red Rider, he was of very little help to anyone. Day recognized that look as one he saw in his own mirror every day, and he wanted to beat his fists against the wall until they were bloody to punish himself for having done this to his brother. But that would change nothing.

"I brought my grandmother's books and journals with me," Jenna said, sounding less discouraged than Day would have expected. "They're out in the saddlebags on Day's horse. He said that you might be able to get an idea from taking a look at them."

Gregori's expression lightened, intrigued as always by a puzzle to be solved. "That does change things. You should have said so from the start." He rose from the table with one smooth motion, not using his hands. Day was gratified to see that at least physically, Gregori seemed to be back to his old self, although he seemed perhaps a little sad and tense underneath.

"My bad," Day said, meaning a lot more than the omission. "I hope you'll forgive me."

Gregori gazed at him steadily with his dark eyes. "There is nothing to forgive, brother. Nothing at all."

For a moment, it was all Day could do not to weep, although whether from guilt or relief or both, he couldn't have said.

"Well?" Jenna demanded, breaking the mood. Probably on purpose, bless her. "Are we going to solve this riddle or not?"

"Definitely," Day and Gregori said in unison, and each one's mouth curved up in a tiny smile. It wasn't much, but suddenly Day felt better than he had in months.


**"THAT'S** impossible," Jenna said the next morning.

Mick yawned from his bedroll across the room, and Gregori opened one eye from where he sat cross-legged near the sleeping salamander.

"It's the Otherworld," Mick said, still not quite awake. "Nothing is impossible. But, that being said, what are you talking about?"

Jenna pushed aside the blanket and sat up, pointing to her stomach. "This," she said. She'd been able to tell something was off as soon as she woke up, even before she moved.

Mick blinked a couple of times and rubbed his eyes. "Is your belly noticeably larger than it was yesterday? I swear, you look about five months along now. The baby is growing as fast as a turnip. That's impossible."

Jenna glared at him. "That's why I said it."

Mick turned to his brother, who looked completely unperturbed. Even though Jenna had already figured out that this was a normal state for him, it made her kind of cranky. Hormones, maybe. Or else it was a side effect of waking up in a strange world with her baby growing at an alarming rate.

"It is unfortunate," Gregori said calmly. "But not completely unexpected, given the odd way that the Otherworld can affect Humans."

"Will it hurt the baby?" Jenna asked, trying not to sound as anxious as she felt. The tiny hut suddenly seemed claustrophobic and she had to tamp down the desire to run screaming out into the pseudo-daylight and all the way back to the dubious safety of her own familiar life.

"I think it unlikely," Gregori said. "I suspect that time is simply moving faster for you than you can perceive. If you weren't pregnant, you wouldn't have noticed it at all until you returned home. But if you aren't experiencing any pain or discomfort, I would assume the baby is fine."

*Just growing at the speed of light. Great.*

"Would you take a look at her, Gregori?" Mick asked. He turned to Jenna and explained, "My brother has always had a knack for healing, which came in pretty handy, considering how often the three of us ended up getting into fights."

Gregori shook his head slowly. "I'm sorry. I cannot. I no longer have my connection with the universal energy that gave me the healing gift. Apparently I lost it along with my immortality." He shrugged, trying to make light of it, although Jenna could see the sadness in his eyes. "Since we will no longer be brawling so much on behalf of the Baba Yagas and our own entertainment, I probably won't even notice it is gone."

Mick let out a strangled groan and stood up with his fists clenched at his side. "Why didn't you tell me? That connection with universal spirit was a huge part of who you were. No wonder you seemed so strained."

"I am fine," Gregori insisted. "It is nothing."

"It's not nothing," Mick said through gritted teeth. "I did this to you. I'm responsible for you hiding out in this shack on the ragged edge of nowhere. I am so sorry."

"I don't hold you responsible," Gregori said. "Brenna did this to us. Only she is to blame, and she paid the price for her crimes. It is what it is. There is no point in continuing her work and torturing yourself over that which cannot be changed."

Mick shook his head and stalked out of the hut, flipping the curtain over the door aside so abruptly it continued to flap even after he was gone. Krasivaya's hoofs clattered on the rocky soil outside and then faded into the distance.

Stunned, the other two stood in silence.

"Do you think he's coming back?" Jenna asked, almost afraid to hear the answer.

"Who can say?" Gregori answered, as calm as always. "Each of us fights our own demons these days. And none of us seems to be doing it very well, or at all gracefully."

But after a moment he added in a more gentle tone, "I would not worry. My brother has never been able to walk away from a woman in need."

"I wouldn't be so sure," Jenna said. "I think he's trying to learn how."

WHEN it became clear that Mick wouldn't be returning any time soon, Jenna finally turned away from the window where she'd been watching for him, rubbing her back where it had begun to ache. Gregori, who was sitting cross-legged on the stool, gazed at her with his fathomless black eyes.

"Which bothers you more?" he asked. "Fear for my brother or fear for your babe? Clearly, you are troubled."

Jenna sighed. "Obviously, I'm worried about Mick. He's beating himself up with guilt for everything that happened to you all. But he's a grown man and I suppose he's going to have to work this out for himself." She rubbed one hand over her newly enlarged belly. "I'm a lot more concerned about what this rapid growth means for the baby."

Gregori shook his head, rising gracefully and coming over to stand in front of her. "I believe what I said before, that the child—and you—are unlikely to come to any harm from this phenomenon, no matter how disconcerting it might be."

"It's not just that," Jenna said. "Although god knows, that would be enough. But when we went to see the Queen, she made Zilya promise to leave us alone. For now. Once the baby is born, she can claim it. I thought that meant we had almost six months to find a solution, but if the baby continues to grow at this rate . . ." She clasped both hands over her belly, trying hard not to give in to despair. But one hot tear escaped to creep down her cheek.

"Ah. That explains much. And changes everything."

Jenna jerked her head up to look at him, surprised by the bleak tone in his voice.

"I don't understand," she said.

He gave one of those minute shrugs again and turned his back on her to walk over to the chest against the far wall, tension visible in the set of his shoulders. The chest creaked open and he knelt there silently for a moment, rummaging around its interior before pulling out a small packet of what might have been herbs, a wide-bottomed glass flask, and a sharp-looking knife.

Jenna could feel her eyes widen as he placed everything on the floor in front of the little stove and gestured for her to take a seat on the cushion he put down next to it. A whispered command to the tiny orange salamander woke it from its doze, and it turned in circles rapidly until its heat flared into renewed life.

"What's all that for?" she asked, settling onto the cushion. Her changing center of gravity was hard to get used to, and she almost tipped over and slid right back off. It wasn't so much that the physical differences were dramatic, but that her body barely felt like itself anymore. She assumed it was easier for the average expectant mother, since the changes were more gradual, but she still wasn't quite sure how they did it. She'd find out for herself soon enough. Too soon, in fact.

"I told Mikhail that I was no longer able to use the universal energy to heal, and that is quite true." His lips compressed into a thin line momentarily, before he gathered himself together and went on. "However, I do have a few other limited options at my disposal."

He placed the flask on top of the stove, a flat thin pottery disk sandwiched between it and the direct, albeit subtle heat generated by the salamander. It peeked up at Gregori, a small forked tongue darting out as if to taste the air, surprising intelligence in its glowing yellow eyes, before giving a minute sneeze and retreating to its spot underneath.

"Sorry, Ziva," Gregori said, bending down so he was at the same height as the fiery orange creature. "I know the herbs tickle your nose. Don't worry; this won't take long."

"His name is Ziva?" Jenna said. She hadn't realized it even had a name. "And what are the herbs for?"

"Her name," Gregori said absently, tapping a minute portion of a powdery substance into the flask and adding a splash of water from the kettle sitting next to his hand. He swirled the mixture together and then popped a cork into the top, so the flask slowly began to fill with a misty vapor the color of a blue jay's feathers.

"Right, sorry. *Her* name." Jenna wasn't sure how you were supposed to be able to tell a male salamander from a female one, and wasn't about to ask. "It's pretty."

"The word translates to 'living' or 'alive,' near enough," Gregori said. "Which a salamander certainly is." He turned back to face her, his visage revealing nothing of the thoughts behind it. "As for the herbs, I've thought of something that might help, if you're willing to trust me."

Was she? She trusted Mick, and Mick clearly trusted his brother. Besides, she was so far out of her depth, she might as well be in the Bermuda Triangle. "What are we talking about here?"

"Did Mikhail happen to mention anything about my mother?" Gregori asked, flipping his long dark ponytail over his shoulder to keep it away from the stove.

"Um, he said she was a powerful shamaness," Jenna replied. "But to be honest, I'm not quite sure what that means."

Gregori gave a brief laugh, his tan face brightening. "Yes, well, where my mother is concerned, I am not sure anyone *really* knew what that meant. She pushed the boundaries well past what the term normally encompassed."

He took the flask off the heat and set it aside for a moment while he continued, "A shamaness can be many things. It is the female term for a shaman, who is generally considered to be a priest or spiritual leader of some kind, or a medicine man, or both. They are often believed to be able to heal and predict the future. Sometimes they do magical work. My mother was all that and more."

"She sounds impressive."

Gregori snorted. "She was scary as hell, to be honest. Not that she meant to be. Iduyan was gentle with the sick, kind to the beasts of the forest, and a wise leader. She was also so far along her spiritual path, she had left most of her humanity behind her well before I was born. I have always suspected that I was an unwelcome surprise from her dalliance with Jarilo; children are messy and emotional and hard to control, none of which are conducive to a spiritual practice. Certainly no man, god or Human, ever tempted her to take such a chance again, that I know of."

"Huh. It doesn't sound like she was likely to be a warm, fuzzy mom."

"Hardly." Gregori shook his head. "Don't get me wrong— in many ways, she was a fabulous parent. She taught me many things, not the least of which were many techniques of healing and meditation, and also helped me to hone my bond with the universal energy she worked with so well. But I quickly learned to be silent and stay out from underfoot when she was busy with more important things."

"More important than her own child?"

"You have to realize that by this time, my mother had become a great spiritual leader. A select group of disciples had gathered around her, creating a small but dedicated community, all of them with powerful abilities of their own. She spent most of her time either teaching or off on her own meditating or speaking with the spirits. It wasn't that I was unimportant; merely that her work was so much *more*. What she achieved was unparalleled in Human history."

"Sort of like being raised by Gandhi, I guess," Jenna said, feeling sorry for him. Her family life was starting to look positively normal, compared to the stories he and his brother told her.

"Gandhi crossed with Einstein and mixed with Merlin," Gregori said with a small smile. "Please do not think I am complaining in any way. It was a great gift to be born to such a woman and raised in that community. But we are straying from the point, I fear."

Jenna stared at the flask dubiously. "Right. That."

"As you say: that." He tapped the side of the flask and the smoke inside slowly started to transmute from blue into a dark indigo, and from that to a lighter lavender color. "Much of what my mother did might be considered by some to be a form of magic, although she despised that label. I still carry some of the remedies and elixirs she made so long ago, and none of them have ever lost their potency, from what I can tell. I use them infrequently, since I have no way of replacing or re-creating them, but this mixture could prove effective in slowing your baby's growth, at least temporarily."

Jenna's eyes widened. She wasn't sure which part of this impressed her more—the fact that he might be able to help her control her bizarre situation or the fact that he was willing to use up some of his precious, irreplaceable supply of remedies handed down from his mother in order to do it.

"Could?" she asked doubtfully. "You don't sound very certain."

"This particular elixir was designed to return a body to its rightful rhythms," Gregori said. "It was purposely made to work on a wide variety of conditions; whether or not it will do so in this case remains to be seen. Additionally, even if it does work, I have no idea how long the effects will last.

Normally, it would remedy the issue and the problem would stay fixed. But it was created for use on the other side of the doorway. Here you will be fighting the energies of the Otherworld, and I am not certain there is any potion made that can do that for long."

"Oh." None of that sounded terribly encouraging. "Are there any negative side effects I should worry about?"

One slim shoulder rose and fell. "I suspect it will do either what you wish, or nothing at all. But there are no guarantees."

*When are there ever?* "Okay," she said. "Let's do this."

"Very well." Gregori took the now-cooled flask and pulled out the cork rapidly. In almost the same moment, he used the knife to prick his finger so that three precise drops of blood fell into the mixture. Instantly, the lavender mist turned green, then pink, then condensed into a ball, so that when he tipped the flask over, a single pink pellet, about the size of a large vitamin, lay in the palm of his hand.

"Ow," Jenna said. And, "Ew. That has your blood in it."

Gregori sighed, clearly unimpressed by her squeamishness. "A shaman activates a medicine with his or her own vital energy. Normally, that could be done by channeling the universal energy, but since I can no longer access that source, the fastest and easiest alternative was a bit of my own essence. Believe me, three drops of blood is nothing."

For a moment, his eyes were bleak, lost in the past, and Jenna remembered what little Babs and Mick had told her about what the evil Baba Yaga, Brenna, had done. That made this small gesture mean even more, and she certainly wasn't going to waste it.

"Right," she said, holding out her hand. "Do I just swallow it?"

He nodded, and she took a deep breath then tossed it back. He handed her a pottery cup full of water to wash it down with.

"Hey! That tickles!" Jenna tried not to giggle as the feathery feeling went from her mouth, down her throat, then settled into her stomach, where it buzzed and fizzed for a moment before settling down to a small but discernible hum.

"Does it?" Gregori raised one feathery eyebrow, looking pleased. "That means it is working. Or at least, it is doing something. To be honest, I thought there was only about a fifty–fifty chance of even that. Excellent."

"How will we know if it is working?" she asked, smiling back at him, glad that his sacrifice hadn't been in vain, and hoping that maybe this tiny bit of healing work would make him feel less broken.

He nodded in the direction of her belly. "I suspect we'll be able to tell one way or the other when you wake up in the morning. With any luck, you will still look much as you do now."

Behind her back, Jenna crossed her fingers.

SINCE it was the whole reason for seeking him out in the first place, Jenna and Gregori spent the rest of the morning going over her grandmother's notebooks and journals, while Gregori tried to remember if he'd ever heard mention of a magical key that might possibly be helpful, and Jenna tried not to worry about Mick.

They hadn't made any particular progress, and they were surrounded by crumbs from the simple bread and cheese he'd served her along with numerous cups of strong black tea. Jenna put her hands against her back and pressed hard, feeling the strain of sitting on an unyielding cushion on top of a barely harder floor. Her eyes ached from trying to read in the dim light, and the inside of her mouth tasted like tannin and sawdust.

Gregori rose to his feet with grace, making her feel even crankier, and put out one golden brown hand to help her up. "Why don't we go outside and stretch our legs. The mind often works better with a little exercise for the body."

"I know what you mean," Jenna said, squinting a little as she walked outside into the bright light. "I do kickboxing, and I often figure out the solution to some problem I've been stuck on when I practice."

The hint of a smile made Gregori's face even more handsome than usual, and for the first time Jenna could see a slight resemblance between him and his brother.

"Ah, kickboxing. I have seen some interesting exhibitions, although I haven't done much of it myself. Would you be interested in showing me some of your moves?"

"Well, we'll have to be careful because of the baby, but I don't think the pregnancy has thrown off my balance too much yet," Jenna said. She was happy to do something that didn't involve thinking about her issues for a while. "Let's see what you can do."

They sparred for a while, in a kind of slow motion, and then when he asked, Jenna demonstrated how she'd taken down the men who had attacked her. Suddenly, Mick galloped up and jumped off his horse, growling at his brother and standing protectively in front of Jenna. His hair had already begun to take on a greenish tint, and his eyes sparked yellow.

"For the love of God," Jenna said with some exasperation. "Will you cut that out? We were just fooling around."

"Oh," Mick said, standing down and taking a couple of steps away from them both. "Of course you were. I just saw him attacking you and thought—"

"Yeah, I know. Thank you for that, but you know Gregori would never hurt me."

"No, he wouldn't," Gregori said, raising one feathery black eyebrow. "But I think you left out part of your story. A very important part, I would say."

# CHAPTER 18

**OVER** dinner, Day told his brother about the strange new abilities he'd been developing, with Jenna chiming in occasionally with her own, usually snarky, observations as she ate more than the other two put together.

Apparently, the baby's fast growth was making her even hungrier than usual for a pregnant woman. Luckily, Day had come across some edible (and nonsentient) critters on his way back, so they had something that resembled a cross between a chicken and a chartreuse pigeon roasting on a spit out in front of the hut. He'd brought home a string of the ugly things slung across the back of his horse, and all that was left was a pile of hollow bones and some sharp-edged feathers. Gregori had contributed a salad of ferns, thistles, and dried grasses, which had tasted surprisingly good, despite its weedy appearance.

"That is a strange tale," Gregori was saying, wiping his hands neatly on a square of rough cloth. "Glowing eyes and green hair. How very curious."

Jenna snorted indelicately at his choice of words, but didn't say anything.

"Have you shown any signs of any new abilities or odd changes?" Day asked. Part of him hoped the answer would be yes, since then he wouldn't be alone in this unsettling transformation, but on the other hand, then it would just be one more problem to add to the list of things he'd done.

Gregori shook his head. "Nothing like that, no. And I saw Alexei before he returned to the other side of the doorway and I headed here, and he didn't mention anything unusual either. Although he might not have; he wasn't very talkative."

Day's food sat in his stomach like a boulder. Alexei wasn't exactly chatty, but he could tell from the way Gregori said it that their middle brother was having as much trouble adjusting as the others.

"Maybe this is because I got the largest amount of the Water," he said, his lips twisting. "Or maybe it is just some kind of punishment."

"I doubt it," Gregori suggested mildly. "I think you are punishing yourself enough. It hardly requires any outside intervention from the gods in addition."

Jenna nodded in agreement, putting down the last of the bird she'd been gnawing on. Gregori passed her his piece of cloth wordlessly, almost managing to hide his small smile. She had grease spread over much of her face and both hands. Day thought it was a remarkably good look for her, all things considered. Of course, he thought she looked good no matter what, as much as he tried not to acknowledge it.

"Do you know anything else about the Leshy?" she asked Gregori. "Any old lore that might help us figure out what's happening to Mick and how to stop it?"

"Why would you want to stop it?" Gregori said. "I'm actually a little jealous that my brother has this new and fascinating gift."

Day rolled his eyes. "More of a curse than a gift," he said. "I don't seem to have any control over it at all, and it scares

Jenna." He hated that part most of all. It wasn't as though they were *together* or anything, or even likely to see each other after this adventure was over. But for some reason, the thought of her being afraid of him stung worse than anything else. "That's the last thing I want to do."

"I know you aren't doing it on purpose," she said. "And really, I'm trying not to let it frighten me. It's just that I grew up with all these horror stories about the faeries and other Paranormal people."

Day grimaced. "I know. And here you are, knee deep in your personal nightmare. Maybe I should leave. I'm sure Gregori can help you figure things out, and he can guide you through the Otherworld as well as I can. Maybe better."

Jenna and Gregori exchanged glances.

"If that is your wish, Jenna, I would certainly be willing to help. Although I do believe this task belongs to my brother. Especially if Barbara said it did. I have rarely known her to be wrong."

Jenna put one hand gently on Day's arm, sending tingles through the rest of his body.

"No," she said. "I don't want you to go. Please stay. We're in this together, aren't we?"

Day tried not to show how ridiculously pleased he was by her answer, so his voice was a little gruff when he said, "If you say so. By the way, you just got grease stains on my shirt."

She grinned at him. "I know. That's what you get for threatening to abandon me, dude."

He grinned back, not even knowing why, except that it was hard to resist Jenna when she smiled.

**DAY** sipped dubiously at the black sludge his brother called tea and grimaced. There were many reasons he preferred living on the other side of the doorway, and a decent cup of coffee first thing in the morning was one of them. From where he sat at the low table, he could see Jenna sleeping across the room, the growing mound of her belly clear under its covering of blanket, her pale face framed by a fall of dark silky hair. Day tried to tell himself that she wasn't any more beautiful than all the other women he'd ever met, but he knew, at least in his eyes, it was a lie.

He glanced toward the doorway, its curtain slung back across a hook to let in the light and air. Gregori had gone out an hour before to meditate—or at least to attempt to; his brother had admitted with some reluctance that he hadn't been able to manage it successfully since they were tortured, although he refused to stop trying.

Day had stood outside and watched Gregori for a while, sitting cross-legged on a large rock by the edge of the turbid lake, completely still except for his slow breathing. Finally, Day had given up and gone back inside. He wasn't sure how you were supposed to be able to tell the difference between someone who was meditating and someone who was only trying to—they looked exactly the same to him.

So instead, he sat on a low stool and watched Jenna sleep. Probably not an improvement as far as his mental state was concerned, but at least the scenery was better.

Suddenly, Day heard a loud splash, followed by the sound of bare feet hitting the ground rapidly. A moment later, Gregori burst into the hut, his face intent with the alertness of a natural warrior preparing to go into battle. He grabbed a curved sword from where it hung on the wall, tossing its fellow toward Day, who caught it effortlessly with one hand as he rose from the table. Day's abandoned teacup rolled onto the floor with a thud.

"What's going on?" Jenna asked, struggling to untangle herself from the woven embrace of her blanket as she sat up. "Why do you two have swords?"

"Yes," Day asked. "Why do we?" He headed toward the door without waiting for the answer.

"There is a gigantic beast rising from the lake and coming toward the hut," Gregori said, as if he'd just told them the neighbors were coming for breakfast. "We should probably stop it before it gets here."

"Do you think Zilya sent it?" Day asked, pushing his feet into his boots and peering outside. Nothing but morning mist and empty ground.

"I wouldn't be surprised," Gregori said. "I've been here for some time and there has never been anything in that lake except the occasional fish and one seemingly depressed otter." He shook his head. "I told you I never liked that faery."

"I'm coming too," Jenna said, pulling on her own boots. She and Day had both slept in their clothes, since they'd packed only one change each, and there had been no room for niceties like pajamas. (Not that Day owned such a thing, but he hadn't felt it necessary to mention that.)

"No." Both brothers spoke in unison, and she glared at them equally. Outside, the ground shook and a muffled roar reverberated through the air.

"Jenna, think of the baby," Day said. "Please stay in here, where it is safe. Gregori and I can handle this."

He could see her waffling, torn between wanting to stand up for herself and the need to protect her unborn child.

"If we need help, we will yell," Gregori reassured her. "At which point, feel free to throw the teapot at it. It makes dreadful tea anyway."

Jenna gave him a reluctant smile and the two men ducked out through the low doorway. For Day, it seemed almost like old times, and he felt a grin of his own spreading across his face as he and Gregori raced toward the lake.

They didn't have to go far before they came upon the monster. Its huge green-and-yellow-striped form rose at least ten feet above them, still dripping acrid water and draped with noxious crimson weeds from the shoreline. Jagged teeth gnashed at the air in front of them and clawed arms waved closer and closer, menacing them as it clomped its ponderous way in their direction. Its large tail, tipped with venomous spikes, slithered behind it, whipping to and fro as though it had a mind of its own and intended to attack them too. Since this was the Otherworld, Day knew that was entirely possible.

Luckily, it appeared to be as stupid as it was large, and while it was certainly dangerous, its movements were slow and its reactions instinctive rather than the planned attack of a more cunning creature. It took Day and Gregori working in unison less than five minutes, dancing and weaving around it, hacking and slashing at its leathery hide until they finally wore it out and killed it.

Triumphant, albeit covered with yellow-tinged blood, they returned to the hut to tell Jenna the good news.

But when Day ducked back into the hut, the place was empty. Jenna was gone. "Shit," Day said. "Jenna?" But she clearly wasn't there. Her bedroll was empty, and there was no sign of her. He'd told her to stay there because he'd assumed it was safe. Apparently he'd been wrong. Again.

"I don't think she left voluntarily," Gregori said, pointing at faint signs on the floor. "These look like drag marks to me."

When they ran outside, Day saw that the scuffed spots continued in the dirt in front of the hut, leading off into the direction opposite the one they'd just come from.

"Son of a bitch," he said. "No wonder the creature wasn't more threatening; it was just supposed to be a distraction."

"One that worked," Gregori said, a touch grimly. "While we were off bouncing our swords against its tough hide, someone or a number of someones grabbed your girlfriend."

They took off running toward where it looked as though Jenna had been taken. "She's not my girlfriend," Day growled, his own voice sounding strange and hoarse to his ears. "And if they've harmed one hair on her head, they're going to pay, whoever they are."

He and Gregori sprinted down a barely discernible trail, pushing aside lavender ferns and tall silvery grasses until they came upon a small break in the underbrush. Jenna was surrounded by a bunch of weedy little creatures like the ones who had attacked her before. She had clearly been putting up a fight. More than one of her kidnappers was bleeding, and a couple of them had limbs that bent at angles it was unlikely even a Paranormal designer had in mind. But their superior numbers had gained them the upper hand, and a disheveled Jenna was fighting like a wild woman as two of the things held on to one arm each, attempting to hold her still enough for a third to put a bronze medallion over her head.

"Jenna!" Day yelled, and changed in midstep, feeling his spine crackle and expand while greenish fur crept down to cover his arms and hands, and probably other surfaces he couldn't see. Ignoring his brother's startled look, Day charged the huddle of creatures and tossed them around like so many rag dolls, a part of him rejoicing in the sound of their screams. Thankfully, there was enough of his rational brain left to bring him to a halt once the last one still capable of movement had run off.

Jenna stared at him with an expression that could easily be read as mixed relief and trepidation, and Gregori, his face as impassive as always, said in an awed voice, "My brother, are you aware that you are presently taking the form of a rather large and distinctly emerald-hued bear? Not that it isn't an improvement on your usual excessive good looks, but could you perhaps change back to what we laughingly refer to as normal? I believe you are alarming poor Jenna."

"Not nearly as much as being hauled off by that bunch of undersized ninjas did," Jenna said, although she gazed at Day with wide eyes and a cautious gaze. "What the hell was that thing they were trying to put on me?"

She bent down to pick up the medallion, which had been dropped into the dirt and left behind by her erstwhile captors, and Gregori shouted, "No! Don't touch it!"

Jenna backed away from the piece, still staring at Day. "Here I was thinking that I was Snow White, and it turns out that the story was *Beauty and the Beast*," she said faintly. Then she passed out, crumpling to the ground in a heap.

* * *

**JENNA** woke up back inside the now-familiar confines of the wooden hut to see Mick packing up their few belongings and Gregori sitting at the table examining the medallion with a fascinated expression. A small scroll and a pot of ink sat at his elbow, and a smudge of black ink adorned his wide nose. Mick was back to his usual gorgeous blond self, with nary a hint of green anywhere, and she noticed, as she watched them unobserved for the moment, that despite a few bruises, both men looked more cheerful than at any time she'd ever seen them.

It occurred to her that neither of the men was truly suited for the quiet solitary lives they'd been leading. She wondered where the third brother was and what he was doing; not trying to become a librarian or a monk, she hoped. Apparently fighting off lake monsters and hordes of unpleasant Paranormal creatures had perked them right up.

Unfortunately, it had the opposite effect on her. Jenna spent a quiet moment freaking out that this was her life now. How the hell had this happened? It was bad enough growing up with a faery curse hanging over her head, but now she was actually *in* the land where such people lived, plus all sorts of other frightening beings, many of whom seemed to be coming after her. She squeezed her eyes shut, as if she could shut out reality—or whatever one wanted to call the insanity that was her current existence—and transport herself back to a boring job and a boyfriend who didn't make her heart beat fast.

Then she opened them again and looked across the room at the two handsome brothers who were trying to help her despite their own issues. Suddenly, her situation didn't feel quite so grim. A tiny kick from the region of her navel reminded her that not all the changes were bad ones either.

"Is everything okay?" she asked, sitting up carefully. Her head had stopped spinning and she felt perfectly fine. She wasn't sure why she'd fainted; shock, maybe, at seeing Mick morph into a giant pale green bear, coupled with an overabundance of pregnancy hormones. She suspected, from the look on his face as he turned in her direction, that Mick found her passing out almost as alarming as she'd found his transformation.

"I think we should ask you that question," Mick said, coming to squat down next to her. "Are you feeling all right? Are you dizzy? Is something wrong with the baby?"

Gregori followed him over and peered into her eyes. "Have you ever passed out before? Is this a recurring problem?"

Jenna brushed them both off with a smile. She wasn't used to being fussed over, and it was kind of sweet. "I'm fine," she said. "And no, I don't have a habit of fainting, but then I've never had a magically accelerated pregnancy before. Maybe this is normal for one of those."

Mick took a couple of steps back. "It would probably help if I didn't keep scaring the daylights out of you," he said in a grim tone.

"Since you always seem to be running to my rescue when you're doing it, I think I can probably forgive you," she said lightly. She wished she could honestly tell him that he didn't frighten her, but in truth, seeing him like that, and knowing that he could turn into whatever the heck that was at any moment, made it hard not to be on edge around him. And he knew it. That fact made her feel sad and guilty, but she didn't know what to do to change it. She just knew she had to. Maybe she needed to find some different way to think of the experience.

"Is that thing that came out of the lake gone?" she asked, both to alter the topic of conversation and because she wanted to know if she needed to be prepared to jump up and run for her life at any moment.

"Rather permanently," Gregori said, not without satisfaction. "Although it is going to be quite the task to dispose of the remains." He looked thoughtful. "I wonder if it is edible."

Mick made gagging noises. "It would probably go perfectly with that toxic liquid you call tea," he teased. Jenna was happy to see that he and his brother seemed less uncomfortable around each other than they had. Apparently the family that fights together stays together. At least in this case.

Gregori ignored him. "There is also no sign of Zilya's minions, but I doubt this will be their last attempt."

"They know we're here," Mick said, placing the saddlebags containing her grandmother's journals by the door. "We can't stay. But it seems as though they can track us down somehow; I don't understand it."

Gregori rolled up the parchment he'd been writing on and tied it with a scrap of leather. "I believe I do," he said. He pointed at Jenna's ever-more-prominent belly.

"What? She's tracking me?" Jenna said. "But how?"

"Not you," Gregori clarified. "Your child. I think it is likely that because of the curse, Zilya has some kind of magical connection to your unborn baby. Through that connection, she can follow your movements—like a needle pointing to north on a compass."

Mick's expression was grim. "That means we'll have to keep moving so she can't keep up. Clearly Zilya has no intention of losing that child."

Gregori nodded in agreement. He held up the medallion dropped by the creatures who had attacked Jenna. "I cannot be sure, but I suspect that this is a talisman designed to remotely activate Zilya's claim. If they had been able to place it over your head, the baby would have belonged to her." He dropped it into a leather drawstring bag and tucked it into a side pocket of the saddlebags. "You had better hang on to this."

"But the Queen made Zilya promise to leave me alone until the baby is born," Jenna protested.

"No doubt she is trying to get around that vow by having someone else act in her stead," Mick said. "Remember, you're in the Otherworld now. Faeries are tricky and bound by rules only if they can't figure out a way to get around them."

His expression grew more forbidding. "Hopefully, if we can keep moving, anyone or anything she sends after us will always be one step behind. But once the baby is born and you reach the deadline the Queen set for you to have solved the riddle, nothing will stop Zilya from laying her claim." His lips tightened as he looked at Jenna's growing baby bump. "Unfortunately, it looks like we won't have nearly as much time as we'd thought, since the Otherworld is having this unexpected effect on your pregnancy. At this rate, we'll be lucky to have weeks instead of months."

Jenna blinked rapidly, trying not to cry. She realized they'd never had a chance to tell him about the experiment she and Gregori had done.

"I know," she said. "Your brother had some kind of magical healing elixir his mother gave him. We used it while you were gone. He thinks it might help the baby's progress go back to normal." She placed both hands over her womb, as if she could beg the child inside to wait, slow down, stop growing so fast. "At least for a little while. But he couldn't be sure."

Mick took a cautious step closer, clearly torn between wanting to comfort her and being afraid of alarming her with his nearness.

"Do you want me to take you back to your own world?" he asked. He didn't sound as happy about the prospect as she would have expected. "Once you're back there, the pregnancy will probably go back to its normal pace." He looked at his brother for confirmation and Gregori nodded.

Jenna thought about it for a minute and then shook her head. "That doesn't really gain us anything, does it? Yes, I'd have more time, but we came here because that's where we think the answers are. What good would it do me to gain months if at the end of them I'm not any closer to solving the riddle?" She patted her belly again. "I feel fine, and the baby feels fine, and unless I can find this key we're looking for, all I would be accomplishing would be putting off the inevitable. I'd rather be here, actually *doing* something."

"In that case," Gregori said, gazing at her with approval, "this might be of some help." He held up the scroll of parchment paper. "I have come up with a list of three different magical keys, each of which I believe to be located somewhere in the Otherworld, and whose properties might make sense within the context of your riddle."

"What do you mean?" Jenna asked, standing up with a slight wobble.

"All of these keys have something to do with the gods," Gregori said. "So they might fulfill the line that says, 'a magic key to a gift divine.'" He handed the scroll to her with a graceful bow. "I have included a small map as well. I hope it turns out to be helpful, Jenna. I have been most charmed to make your acquaintance."

She leaned forward and hugged him briefly, mindful of his steadfast dignity. "Thank you for everything," she said.

"Not at all. You brought my brother back to me. For that alone I would have been pleased to be of assistance." He gave her that gentle smile that so lit up his otherwise serious countenance. "Plus, of course, I like you."

He turned to Mick, and the two exchanged a short hug of their own. To Jenna's eyes it still seemed stilted and a little uncomfortable on both sides, but it was a vast improvement over their demeanor toward each other when she and Mick had first arrived.

"Keep her safe, Mikhail," Gregori said. "I believe that while the two of you seek out the first key, I shall return to court and attempt to speak to the Queen and King about Zilya. I doubt it will do much good, but with the Queen, one never knows. Once I have finished that errand, I will try to catch up with you later."

Her heart swelling with gratitude, Jenna thanked him. "I

really appreciate it, Gregori, but I feel terrible about interrupting your retreat."

Gregori's expression didn't change in any notable way, but Jenna could see the sadness in his eyes.

"It does not matter," he said softly. "It was doing me no good anyway."

# CHAPTER 19

**DAY** lifted Jenna onto Krasivaya's broad back and swung up into the saddle behind her. It was impossible to keep his body from touching hers, under the circumstances, which was both a pleasure and a trial. Plus, of course, he knew it must be torture for her, feeling as she did about him now that she'd seen what he was becoming. He could just imagine her cringing inside as his legs wrapped around the outside of hers.

"I'm sorry," he said quietly. "If there were any other way for us to get there quickly, I would choose one that didn't force you to be so close to me. Are you okay?" He wouldn't blame her if she wasn't. After all, what woman would want to be traveling through a strange land with a man who turned into a bear—or worse—at a moment's notice?

Jenna was quiet for a minute, clearly thinking before giving him an answer. He held his breath, hoping that she wasn't going to tell him that she'd changed her mind about going back to the Human lands.

It had already occurred to him long before this that he

could take her home and continue the search for the mystery key or keys on his own in the Otherworld, but he hadn't suggested that option to Jenna. In part, it was because he was concerned for her safety; if she was on her own it would be too easy for either Zilya's minions or the thugs her idiot ex-boyfriend had sent after her to capture her. But doubtless, Gregori would have been willing to take on the task of guarding her. If Day had been willing to give it up.

That was the real reason he hadn't suggested it. The reason he hadn't even wanted to admit to himself. He wanted her around.

Oh, he knew that as soon as the riddle was solved and her baby was saved, Jenna would be on her way. She tolerated his presence now because it was necessary, an evil only slightly less frightening than all the others she faced. Not to mention that she had a life of her own, one that didn't involve Paranormal weirdness and men who had no idea how to have anything that resembled a normal relationship.

Not that he wanted a relationship, of course. That would be absurd. But that didn't mean he was ready to give up being with Jenna, soaking up the glorious brightness that was her spirit, enjoying the swings she made from gentleness to fierceness and back again. Not yet. Not yet.

He was almost grateful when her voice jarred him from his disconcerting thoughts, although he braced himself to hear what she would say.

To his surprise, she turned around and gave him a brief smile before facing forward again. "I've been thinking," she said, speaking slowly as if choosing her words with care.

"Have you?"

"I have. I realized I'm not afraid of you anymore." She leaned back against his chest a little more, relaxing into his hold. Day was so startled, he almost dropped the reins. Not that it would have mattered, since Krasivaya pretty much steered herself, once he pointed her in the direction he wanted. Still, it would have been embarrassing.

"You're not?" he said, not quite believing her. "That doesn't seem likely, given the way you feel about the Paranormal world."

Jenna gestured at the lands they were passing through at the moment, a gentle rolling hillside covered with brilliant poppy plants as high as the horse's withers in vivid shades of crimson, violet, and lapis blue. In the distance, a pair of young Pegasus flew figure eights through the lavender-tinged sky.

"It's not all bad," she said. "You have to admit that the scenery can be pretty glorious."

Day looked down at the silky fall of her hair and the gentle curve of her body tucked into the saddle in front of him. "Yes, it certainly can be," he said. "But I don't see how the beautiful scenery makes me any less scary."

"Oh, you're still scary," Jenna said with a tiny laugh. "But you're *my* scary."

"Huh?" He was definitely missing something here.

Jenna patted his large hand with her smaller one, and then left it there, the paleness of her skin a pleasing contrast with the darker tan shade of his own.

"It finally came to me that the only times I've ever seen you change into . . . well, whatever it is you become, were when you were coming to my defense. Other than that, you've never been anything other than kind and gentle with me. Okay, and crabby and rude, but I think I understand that better now."

Day shook his head, knowing she couldn't see it. "I'm glad you do," he said in a short tone. "Because I don't understand anything at all anymore."

**A** few mornings later, as they neared the first place marked on Gregori's parchment map, Day unraveled the scroll his brother had given him and peered again at the tiny, precise, flowing script. "Huh," he said. "Apparently we're looking for something called 'Merlin's Key.' Have you ever heard of it?"

Jenna shook her head, causing the silk of her hair to flutter across his arm in an absurdly distracting way. "I don't think so. I've heard of Merlin, of course. I always loved the stories about him and King Arthur." She sighed. "I know that historians mostly think Arthur was a myth, or at best a conglomeration of a number of kings who ruled back in the day, but I always wished that he and Merlin were real."

Day rolled his eyes. Humans. They had such short memories. "Of course they were real," he said. "Although Merlin was actually a powerful faerie who spent a lot of time messing around in the Human world when he wasn't supposed to. Eventually, the Queen lost patience and locked him up in a crystal cave. For all I know, he's still there. Too bad; he was actually very nice, as faeries go. A little too fond of creating chaos and chasing nymphs, but amazingly powerful, and I think he mostly had good intentions."

Jenna twisted around, her icy blue eyes wide and amazed. "Seriously? Merlin was real? What about King Arthur? Did you ever meet him?"

"Once or twice. Huge guy, red hair, needed to bathe more, but, hell, they all did back then." Day thought for a minute. "He really did have charisma, in that rare way you see only once in a generation in a true leader. Didn't say much, but man, could he fight. Even Alexei was impressed, and that's really saying something."

"Wow. That's so cool." She chewed on her lip. "And the romance between Guinevere and Lancelot that broke up the kingdom? Was that true too?"

Day laughed out loud. "Oh, hell no. Lancelot was incredibly handsome and charming, but he didn't have any interest in the queen. He was more of a man's man, if you know what I mean. No, Arthur and Guinevere never had eyes for anyone other than each other. It all just fell apart because of war and politics, like so many other ideal societies before and since. Although by then Merlin was out of the picture, so that probably didn't help."

"Does Gregori think this key of Merlin's is something magical? He said all the keys had something to do with the gods, but if Merlin was from the Otherworld, that doesn't make a lot of sense." Jenna twisted back around and shifted in the saddle a little, trying to get comfortable. The baby hadn't shown any more signs of unusually rapid growth since they'd left Gregori's hut, for which she was grateful, but she clearly still wasn't used to having a bump where her flat belly used to be.

They'd been on the road—or path, or whatever—for a couple of days. But at least they should be getting close. There were more odd-looking houses scattered about the landscape, their shapes somehow distorted from what a Human would be used to: too big or too small or too slanted, their colors bright and cheerful in the unnatural brightness. The occasional tilled field planted with mostly unrecognizable fruits and vegetables or inhabited by six-legged cattle broke up the space in between.

"Depends on which god, doesn't it?" Day said. "But, in fact, Arthur converted to Christianity in his later years, after being born and raised a pagan. According to what Gregori has written down here, Merlin gave him this key and told him it was a symbol of divine power. He probably just never bothered to mention to Arthur *which* divine power. Sneaky old fae."

"If he gave it to Arthur, how did it end up back in the Otherworld?" Jenna asked.

"Who knows? Maybe some Paranormal creature stole it and brought it back here after Camelot fell. Or before. The worlds weren't as separate then, remember, and lots of magical folks are attracted to shiny or valuable objects."

He lifted one hand and pointed at a tall, crooked house directly ahead. "I think this is it. Gregori said to look for a cottage trying to be a castle, and this certainly fits the bill." He blinked, trying to take it in. Whoever lived there should ask his decorator for a refund.

The house was one story high, but its proportions were all off, so it looked very tall and yet somehow squat at the same time. Something that was trying to be a crenellated tower hung off one side, and there was only one window at the front, set crookedly over an oval door set into a crumbling stone exterior. The stone was a jumble of variegated hues, which didn't add to either its beauty or its dignity, and there was a crude attempt at a moat dug right in front of the entrance that had turned into a mud pit. A pair of wide splintery planks took the place of a drawbridge.

"Well, that's . . . colorful," Jenna said.

"That's one word for it," Day agreed, helping her to dismount. "I'd say we've got someone here who was around on the other side during Arthur's time and still thinks of it fondly. Either that, or his mother read him some very strange bedtime stories."

Before they could walk up to the door, it was yanked open with a loud creaking noise and a deep voice yelled out, "Go away."

"Oh, good," Day said in a cheerful voice. "It sounds like he's friendly."

Jenna stuck out her tongue at him, and then turned back toward the house/castle. "Hello? Could we talk to you for a minute, please? We don't want any trouble, I promise."

"Speak for yourself," Day muttered under his breath. He had a pretty good idea who (or what) lived there.

Sure enough, the creature that came thumping out across the erstwhile drawbridge was large, wide, and ugly as a bad date on the morning after. In short, a troll. It had a blobby snout of a nose, lanky hair that fell into its tiny, beady black eyes, and sharp snaggly teeth that seemed to go every which way inside its gaping mouth. It wore a ragged shirt and a loincloth, with a rusty but still dangerous-looking sword hanging from a moldy leather belt around its waist.

"What the hell *is* that?" Jenna whispered, clutching Day's

arm as it came closer, twitching its nose in the air. Trolls had lousy eyesight but a very good sense of smell.

"Rider," it said in a hoarse voice as soon as it got close enough to recognize at least one of its visitors. "And dinner?"

Jenna squeaked but gamely held her ground.

"Not dinner," Day said firmly. "My friend Jenna. She is under my protection. And that of the Queen."

The troll grunted, in acceptance or disappointment, it was impossible to tell.

"What does Rider want?" it asked.

He debated going into the entire *I'm not a Rider any longer* speech, but decided it would be wasted on the troll. It was best to stick to the basics with such folks.

"We're looking for something called 'the Key of Merlin,'" Day said. "Do you know of it?"

The troll spat something green and viscous onto the ground. "I know it. It is mine. You go away now."

Day sighed. It wasn't as though he'd really expected the Key's owner, whoever it had turned out to be, to just hand it over without a protest. But this would have been a lot easier if it had been in the possession of something cute and cheerful, like a sprite. A sprite he could have bargained with. Something told him that dealing with the troll wasn't going to be that simple.

Jenna started to open her mouth, but he put one hand warningly on her arm. "I know you like to handle everything yourself," he said. "And I respect that. But I am a lot more familiar with this land and its denizens, and how things work. So let me deal with this one, if you don't mind."

She hesitated, and then reluctantly nodded and stepped back.

*Would miracles never cease?*

"I have need of the object called 'the Key of Merlin,'" Day said in a formal tone. "I am willing to fight for it. What are your terms?"

The troll stuck one blunt finger into its nostril and dug around for a moment as it thought. "Challenge of wits," it said finally. "Very traditional. You win, I give you Key. I win, I kill you."

Jenna let out a muted protest, but Day ignored her. "I win, I get the Key. You win, I give you my magical steed."

This time there was nothing subdued about Jenna's response. "Mick! You can't!"

He didn't have time to tell her that Krasivaya could take care of herself, so he just concentrated on the bargaining. As the troll said, it was traditional.

The troll eyed the horse avariciously. "Deal. Challenge of wits. I give three riddles. You answer right, you win. You answer wrong, horse is mine." Its thick tongue licked its chops.

"The Key first," Day said, and they waited for the troll to stomp inside, root around noisily, then stomp back outside with a small ebony box that almost vanished inside its huge fist.

There was, Day thought, a certain irony to having a challenge of wits thrown down by a barely verbal troll. But there was no question that it knew its proper folklore forms. No doubt something it had picked up when it lived on the other side of the doorway.

"Very well," he said. "What is the first riddle?"

The troll gave a wide and dreadful smile. Day was guessing that it had seen this very riddle used on someone else, and that someone had failed the test.

*"My life can be measured in hours,*
*I serve by being devoured.*
*Thin, I am quick*
*Fat, I am slow*
*Wind is my foe."*

"What is the answer?" the troll asked.

Day and Jenna exchanged looks. Jenna mouthed, *I have no idea*, but he just smiled at her.

"The answer is 'a candle,'" Day said.

The troll growled and gnashed its crooked teeth. "Next riddle," it said.

> *Every dawn begins with me,*
> *At dusk I'll be the first you see,*
> *And daybreak couldn't come without*
> *What midday centers all about.*
> *Daisies grow from me, I'm told*
> *And when I come, I end all cold,*
> *But in the sun I won't be found,*
> *Yet still, each day I'll be around."*

The troll's smile grew even more gruesome. "What is answer, Rider?"

Day laughed. "I would be a fool not to get that one, since it is the letter that starts my own name. The answer is the letter *D*."

"Wow," Jenna said. "I never would have gotten that one."

"LAST ONE," the troll trumpeted in a loud voice. Day could practically see the steam coming out of its hairy ears. "You not get this one, I think.

> *"I grow more in darkness than in light,*
> *Can lead the weakest to stand and fight.*
> *I can't be seen, but can make the heart sing,*
> *I can lift the heaviest burden though I don't weigh*
>     *a thing.*
> *Not even death can cause me to shatter*
> *If I am lost, nothing else will matter."*

*Uh-oh.* Day pondered asking the troll to repeat the riddle, but he doubted it would help. He had no idea.

"What's the problem?" Jenna whispered.

"No answer, Rider?" The troll took two giant, er troll, steps forward.

He racked his brain, but Day still couldn't come up with it. He'd never heard this particular riddle before, and for the life of him, he couldn't think what it meant.

"I'm sorry, Jenna," he started to say, but before the words could leave his mouth, she said, "The answer is hope."

It was like a lightbulb went on in his head. Once she'd said it, the riddle was perfectly clear.

"Hope," he said to the troll.

"No fair!" it yelled. "You cheat! You not answer, girl answer. No fair. No get Key." It hopped up and down, making the ground shake. "Go away. You lose."

"What?" Jenna put her hands on her hips. "You never said he had to come up with the answers himself, just that he had to solve your riddles. He has, so give us our prize."

Day would have explained to her that trolls rarely kept a bargain if they could find any way to weasel out of it, but he was too busy drawing his sword, since the troll had drawn its own and was waving it menacingly through the air.

"Yikes!" Jenna jumped back, getting out of the way just before the tarnished blade whistled past Day's ear.

Then it was just the dance of the battle, dodging and weaving, the clanging of sword against sword, grunting and cursing. It was wonderful. Day hadn't felt this alive in ages.

Then it was over. With a twist of Day's wrist, the troll's sword went flying to land in the muddy moat with a splash. Something with tentacles reached out and dragged it farther into the muck, leaving nothing but fetid bubbles behind.

"Drat," said the troll. "Liked that sword."

Jenna gave a tiny giggle of relief from behind him as Day walked up to the creature with his hand out. Up close, the troll smelled as bad as he looked, but with a final reluctant glare he dropped the ebony box into Day's outstretched fingers. Then he crunched his way up the stone walk to his lopsided house, stomped inside, and closed the door behind him with a vicious thud. The tower on the side tilted even more precariously toward the ground as they left.

"That was interesting," Jenna said, wrinkling her brow.

"Which?" Day asked. "The riddle challenge or the sword fight?"

"Neither," she said. "I'm talking about the fact that you didn't change shape."

He hadn't even noticed. Too busy with everything else, he supposed. But she was right, that *was* interesting. Not to mention something of a relief.

"I suppose it was because you were never in any actual danger," he said thoughtfully. "I knew that I could handle the troll no matter what. The shape-changing seems to be instinctive; obviously my instincts knew the troll wasn't a real threat." He cleared his throat. "To be honest, I was too busy enjoying myself. I know the situation is dire, but this is the kind of thing I do. I mean, that I used to do. It felt natural." *Hell, it felt great.* He felt a little guilty that he was having fun while Jenna was in the middle of a crisis.

"I'm glad," she said, sounding almost as cheerful as he felt. "I have to admit, it was pretty entertaining. Now can we have a look at that Key, since we went through all that fuss to get it?"

"Sure," he started to say, when the water in the moat began to roil and churn. Six long tentacles rose up out of the murk with a sucking sound, one of them holding the troll's sword and all the others being ridden by the thin, scrawny creatures they'd run into before. As soon as Zilya's minions cleared the surface of the water, they began to let out a high keening sound that seemed to agitate the moat monster even more.

"You have *got* to be kidding me," Day said, pulling his sword out of its sheath again. "Don't you things ever give up?"

"Shit," Jenna said, not sounding amused anymore. "You are seriously going to have to teach me how to use one of those."

"Good idea," Day said through clenched teeth. "Maybe later. For now, take this, but go stand by Krasivaya, please. She'll kick those bastards into next week before she lets one get close to you." He handed her a large knife and gave her a gentle shove in the right direction before he went charging into the midst of this newest attack.

Fortunately, this batch wasn't any better at fighting than the last ones had been—assuming it was even a different bunch, since they were impossible to tell apart. The trickiest bit was avoiding being herded toward the sword-wielding tentacle while swinging his sword in the direction of whichever *biesy* came closest to him. They displayed a kind of animal cunning, working as a pack, but it didn't last long against a well-armed Rider—former Rider—with someone vulnerable to defend.

A bobbing, weaving movement brought him up underneath the tentacle holding the sword, and his own sharp edge went whistling through the air to send both sword and tentacle flying. They slammed into one of the *biesy*, skewering it as an incidental bonus, as the moat creature slithered back below the surface with a bubbling groan. After that, the rest of the demons ran off, leaving their dead and wounded behind them. A different tentacle snaked quietly up to snag the one closest to the water and disappeared again.

As requested, Jenna stood next to Krasivaya, holding the knife in one clenched fist, her tense expression loosening a little as he approached.

"You're hardly green at all this time," she said, handing him back the knife. "Either that or I'm getting used to it."

"Very funny," he said. "I think we're safe for now. Did you want to have a look at our prize?"

Day wiped the box off with a large leaf and opened it up to peer inside, Jenna leaning over his arm to see too. Inside, on slightly dingy velvet, there was a shiny blue stone on a delicate chain.

"Oh," she said. Her face fell. "That's not a key. He gave us the wrong thing." She looked at the troll's house, but obviously didn't seem inclined to go try again.

Day gave a small laugh. "Remember, in fairy tales, things

are rarely as they seem. A key doesn't necessarily mean the kind of key you were thinking of. If this is the Key of Merlin, it is almost certainly magic. There's no way of telling what it might unlock." He handed the Key to Jenna, who tucked it away safely in her pocket, and they rode on to find the next one.

# CHAPTER 20

**BY** the time the abrupt Otherworld night fell, even Day was ready to get off his beloved steed and rest for a bit. The loss of his immortality hadn't made him as weak as a normal Human mortal, but he certainly wasn't as tireless as he used to be. Or perhaps he simply hadn't healed as completely as he'd thought from his terrible wounds.

Either way, he could tell Jenna was starting to grow uncomfortable, so he led them to a spot along their path that had always been one of his favorites. Her gasp of wonder was a gratifying indication that she liked it as much as he did.

"Oh my," she said as Krasivaya picked her way carefully down the incline that kept their destination hidden from sight until they were almost upon it. "It's lovely."

If this place had been on the other side of the doorway, it would have been called an oasis. Here in the Otherworld, there was a circle of low hills instead of sand dunes, but inside them, there nestled a serene pond, surrounded by softly swaying trees that bore various fragrant fruits. The ground was lined with a mossy grass that felt like velvet under the feet, and the three moons reflecting off the pristine waters made the entire dell glow as if lit by candlelight. Tiny azure nocturnal birds with topknots that twinkled like fireflies flitted from branch to branch, making a melodious chiming noise as their feathers moved through the air.

"This is just amazing," Jenna said as she dropped to the ground. She immediately took off her shoes and walked through the soft grasses with delight.

"It is," Day agreed, relieving Krasivaya of her burdens and plucking a few fruits down for her to eat along with the grass. There was no need to tie her up, of course. She might wander a bit, but she would never go far.

He started setting up their minimal camp as Jenna gazed around her.

"This is one of the most magical places I've ever found in either world." Day paused for a moment before adding, "I have never brought anyone here before. Not even my brothers." Somehow it had always seemed too special and peaceful a spot to share with them. He couldn't have said why it seemed so right to bring Jenna here, but now that he had, he suspected it would never feel the same without her presence.

"I'm honored," Jenna said, sounding like she meant it. "It truly is magical." She looked longingly at the water. "I don't suppose the pond is safe to bathe in. I feel like it has been forever since I've been clean."

Day chuckled. "That water is purer and softer than any you have ever felt in your life; it is even warm. Go ahead and bathe to your heart's content. I'll put together dinner for when you are done. I'm afraid it will just be some cold fruits and vegetables, but I assure you, they'll be delicious."

She hesitated for a moment. "Are you sure we'll be safe? I keep expecting those creatures to leap out from behind every bush."

"We've kept moving," he answered. "I expect they are still trailing far behind us. And it should take them some time to regroup after that fight earlier. But I'll stand guard, nonetheless. Go, have your bath."

Apparently that was all the encouragement she needed, since she ran down to the water's edge, shedding her clothing as she went, sinking into the water with a sigh of unfettered satisfaction.

Day tried not to look, but it was impossible not to stare. Jenna was incredibly beautiful under the moonlight, the rounded curve of her expanding belly only making her more attractive in his eyes. He drank in the sight of her as if it were the finest wine, stowing the memory away for the time when she would no longer be his to gaze at.

She ducked her head under the water and then rose up laughing, her joyous mirth filling the glade with music as she pushed streaming wet hair back out of her face. White skin glistened like satin, tiny jeweled droplets gleaming with golden light. As magical as this place was, it was nothing compared to the enchantment that was Jenna.

Finally, she emerged from the pond, leaving a dripping trail behind her. She smiled at Day when she saw him standing there, seemingly unself-conscious about her nakedness.

"This is what you call guarding?" she said with a smile. "Anything could have snuck up on us while you were staring at me."

"Yes, but I would have noticed them as soon as they blocked my view," he said.

Jenna snorted, wringing her hair out with her hands. "You can have a turn now," she said. "I'm guessing I could guard you at least as well."

Day took three long strides toward her, bringing him close enough to reach out and touch her. But he didn't. Not yet.

"I could take a bath," he said softly. "But I would rather kiss you." He held his breath. "May I kiss you, Jenna?"

She put damp arms around his neck. "I was rather hoping you would," she whispered. "After all, I can always get clean again later."

Day bent his head down until his lips brushed hers in the gentlest of kisses. She tasted sweet, like berries under the summer sun, and her lips were soft and yielding as she opened them to his exploring tongue. For a long time, they did nothing but kiss, her wet naked body pressed up against his dry clothed one, his arms draped loosely around her shoulders.

Finally, he could stand it no more and he began to move his lips slowly down her body, worshipping her like the goddess she was with featherlight kisses that trailed down her neck, over the line of her collarbone, pausing to tease and suck on her rosy nipples. When she sighed and moaned, he moved down even lower, kneeling before her and pressing his lips to the glorious abundant roundness of her stomach before laying her gently on the soft, soft grass.

Then she reached up and removed his clothing, piece by piece with trembling hands until they were both bare to the night's light breeze and to each other. Hands explored, mouths tasted, until finally their bodies were joined together in shared ecstasy, their cries rising up together to reach the starless skies.

They lay together for a while in breathless bliss, then, laughing, Jenna pulled him down to the water, where they bathed together before doing it all over again. Apparently, pregnancy had lent her an even greater hunger for sex than it had for food, a fact that delighted them both.

Later, Day carried her to the bedroll as she yawned.

"This place really is enchanted," she said in a sleepy voice. "It makes the real world seem so far away. I don't think I have ever felt so safe."

Day stroked her silky hair, now almost dry again. "It is you who are enchanting," he said. "You are the most beautiful woman in two worlds."

"I'll bet you say that to all the girls," Jenna said, not sounding like she minded.

In truth, he probably had. But he'd never meant it as he did now. Not that he would admit that to Jenna. It was painful enough to admit it to himself.

"Hush," he said. "Reality will come for us soon enough. Sleep now. I will guard you and keep you safe through the night. Rest."

He pulled a small wooden flute out of his saddlebags and started to play, watching her eyes flutter closed, inky lashes covering those striking blue eyes. It wasn't until he was sure she was asleep that he allowed himself to sit very, very still and mourn for that which was only his for this moment out of time, and could never be more.

**THE** next morning, Jenna's belly had grown again. It seemed as though whatever magic Gregori's elixir had worked had worn off. Worse yet, it seemed as though her body had caught up with all the days of unnatural time it had missed, since it was considerably larger than when they'd gone to sleep. Day could see her struggling not to panic as they both stared at a tiny hand or foot pushing outward in the area near her belly button.

They rode even faster to the location where Gregori's map told them to look for the second key, the Key of Solomon. Not even a day's ride from the troll's tumbledown castle, their next stop might well have existed on a different planet. They came to a stop and dismounted outside a small, almost painfully neat house. Its wooden siding was painted a pristine white and the thatched roof had not one piece of straw out of place. Windows set with tiny faceted glass panes looked out onto a tidy lawn bordered on two sides by orchards, and the red door had a shiny brass knocker and an engraved plaque that read SMYTHE.

Day and Jenna walked up the flagstone path and he rapped the knocker briskly against the door. The *clomp, clomp, clomp* of wooden clogs sounded on the other side and then the door opened. Day quickly adjusted his gaze about two feet below where he'd been looking.

"Good afternoon," he said politely to the dwarf who stood

in front of him, a quizzical but not unfriendly look on his wrinkled, bearded face.

"Whatever you're selling, I already have it, I don't want it, or I never heard of it. Go away, if you please," the dwarf said. "It's almost time for tea. Or anything that isn't talking to strangers." He started to close the door.

Day blinked. "We're not selling anything," he said. "And we're terribly sorry to bother you, but we're searching for something called the Key of Solomon. I don't suppose you are familiar with it?"

The dwarf's bushy brows pulled together, almost meeting over his doughy knob of a nose. "Of course I am familiar with it," he said. "It used to be mine, didn't it?"

"Used to be?" Jenna said. "Did you give it away?"

The dwarf looked as though he was going to spit, although he thought the better of it when he took in Jenna's condition, and swallowed hard instead, his face turning an alarming shade of red that almost matched the open door behind him.

"Give it away! Give it away!" he sputtered. "As if I would be foolish enough to do such a thing. Nay, missy, I did not give it away. I hid it to keep it safe, didn't I? Hid it so well I might as well have thrown it into a bottomless pit, idiot that I am." He smacked himself on the head so hard, the pointed green hat he wore wobbled back and forth. "Go away now. I have no wish to discuss my stupidity with traveling salesmen."

Day blinked again, feeling like he was missing something. "I'm sorry, are you saying you lost it?"

"Pfft, lost it. I'm an idiot, but I'm not a moron," the dwarf said. "Nay, I put it up in yonder tree, didn't I?" he said, pointing to the tallest tree in his orchard. "No one would ever look for it there, I thought. And no one did. But then a damned fool phoenix built its nest in my tree, and cached the Key of Solomon away with all its other treasures. It guards that nest so well, my Key might as well be on one of the moons for all the good it does me."

The dwarf shook its head in disgust, putting one gnarled

hand up to catch its hat before it slid off. "I gave up all hope of recovering the damned thing years ago. If you can take it away from that benighted bird, you're welcome to it. Good day to you." With that pronouncement, he shut the door briskly in their faces. They could hear him clomping off toward the back of the house.

"Okay," Day said, slightly bemused. "Let's take a look at this Key-stealing phoenix, then."

He and Jenna walked through the meticulously straight rows of the orchard until they stood near the tree the dwarf had pointed out. There was no telling what kind of fruit it bore, since at the moment it was adorned by slightly prissy chartreuse blossoms in neat clusters of exactly three flowers per branch, but it smelled oddly like a mix of Brussels sprouts and juniper berries, so Day wasn't entirely sorry to have missed the harvest.

The tree was tall, and the phoenix's nest high in its branches, but that wasn't the worst of their problems. Not by a long shot.

The base of the tree was surrounded by a circle of flaming scarlet-hued rosebushes, all of them seemingly burning without any harm to themselves, although there was no way to get to the trunk of the tree without somehow wading through the four-foot-high thicket of bright red flowers, snapping orange flames, and long, menacing thorns. The strange aroma of smoke and rose blossoms mingled together and hung in the air like a wall of its own.

"Crap," Jenna said, looking up through the branches to the large nest resting securely in a fork high, high up in the tree, and then at the merrily blazing bushes. "How the heck are we going to get the Key down from there?"

*Damn good question.*

"I have no idea. The last time I came across something like this, there was a slumbering princess on the other side."

Jenna gazed at him with wide eyes. "Are you telling me you rescued Sleeping Beauty?"

Day shook his head. "Even I'm not that crazy. I kept riding and let some other poor schmuck impale himself in the name of true love." He drew his sword. "In this case, I think we're going to have to take the direct approach and just hack our way through."

Jenna opened her mouth to tell him that she didn't think that was a good idea, but he was already part of the way in, holding the sword out in front of himself as he chopped at the branches so he wouldn't get singed.

For a moment, it almost seemed as though it was going to work.

Then Jenna's heart filled with dread as she noticed the briars growing back up behind him, jagged thorns entwining to fill in the spaces he'd just cleared.

"Mick! You have to get out!" she yelled, but it was too late. The path behind him closed and fiery branches crept toward him, a few reaching out to wrap themselves around each booted ankle.

He hacked even faster, but Jenna could see the moment when the first thorn sank itself into the flesh of his arm, another grabbing at the wrist that held the now-useless sword. Flames spread up his clothing and nibbled at the edges of his long blond hair.

Mick struggled wildly, but she could see the panic rising in his eyes like a tide of madness as he felt himself being engulfed. She wasn't sure if his hoarse cry of agony had more to do with the inferno and sharp thorns that currently attacked him or the memories of the last time he was so helpless.

"Mick! Mick!" Jenna didn't know what to do, couldn't stand the idea of him dying in pain and terror because of her. She tore at the briars with her bare hands, trying hopelessly to reach him, tears of frustration and grief streaming down her face.

The tears sizzled when they touched the velvety red roses, and the wall of thorns quivered silently and then disappeared.

Jenna gazed around in amazement. One minute they were

fighting for their lives amid a living wall of writhing, burning branches and daggerlike thorns, and the next Mick stood a few yards away from her, completely unharmed. Only the lingering scent of rose petals remained behind to prove the wall had ever been there.

Mick patted at himself wildly, checking for the charring and wounds that had been there only moments before. His breathing was labored and his face pale; it took a clear effort for him to gather together the remnants of his shredded nerves, and even when he was done, Jenna could see the tremor in his large hands.

By now she knew him well enough to be certain that he would rather be torn apart by giant thorns than be seen by her in a moment of weakness, so she ignored his shaking and allowed him the space to pull himself together, when what she really wanted was to run to him and hold him close.

"Was it just an illusion all along?" she asked, staring pointedly at the tree and not at him.

He took a deep, shuddering breath. "Illusion it might have been, but I suspect it would have killed me nonetheless. It was a test. Apparently, you passed it." Another breath. "I did not."

"All I did was burst into tears," Jenna said. "I don't understand how that was helpful." She finally took another couple of steps closer. He was pale, but seemed otherwise back in control.

"It's *why* you burst into tears that seems to have made the difference," he said, gazing at her thoughtfully. "I suspect if you had been crying for yourself, you would have burned up with me. Instead, you saved me." He sounded both grateful and a tiny bit resentful, no doubt more comfortable doing the rescuing than being rescued. "Is the little turnip okay?"

"I think so." Jenna put her hands protectively over her belly. In the moment, she had just reacted. If she had had more time to think it through, would she have risked her baby to save Mick? She had no idea.

She didn't want to think about it either. "We got past the first obstacle, but there is still the phoenix itself to deal with."

She pointed up at the nest, proud to note that the finger she used was hardly trembling at all. "What do we do now?"

"Well," Day said, thinking out loud. "The phoenix is entranced by music; maybe we can use that somehow to lure it off its nest."

"Great," Jenna said. "You can play your flute and distract it while I climb up and grab the Key. I was a great little tree climber when I was a kid."

Day choked back a laugh and looked pointedly at her belly, which today resembled that of a woman closer to six months pregnant than three or four, or whatever she actually was. "I'm not sure that's the best idea," he said. "Under the circumstances."

She glanced down at the large bump under the peasant blouse she'd picked up on their last shopping trip before leaving the Human world. She'd figured she would need something expandable. She'd had no idea how much. "Oh. Right. Good point. But unfortunately, I can't play a flute."

"Oh," Day said. "That's a problem." He thought for a minute. "I don't suppose you can sing?" he asked hesitantly. He'd once had to jump from a second-floor balcony after questioning a woman's ability to sing. Mind you, her voice could have cracked glass.

Jenna shrugged. "Sure. I mean, I mostly sing in the shower and when I'm driving alone in the car, but the neighbor's cat seems to like it when I serenade him." The twinkle in her eye was the only thing that gave her away.

"Fine," Day said. After all, what did they have to lose? Worst-case scenario, he played the flute and the seriously pregnant woman climbed a very tall tree. "Let's hear something soothing, then, fit to entrance a Key-stealing bird."

Jenna smiled at him and lifted her face to the sky. When she started to sing, the purity and sweetness of her voice almost knocked him off his feet.

"Amazing grace, how sweet the sound, that saved a wretch like me. I once was lost but now am found, was blind, but now I see," she sang, the clear piercing notes rising up like dust motes in a ray of sunshine. "'Twas grace that taught my heart to fear. And grace my fears relieved. How precious did that grace appear the hour I first believed."

Up above them, the huge nest shook as a glorious red-and-orange bird appeared, its feathers flaming as it rose into the air and then sailed gracefully down, coming ever lower until it was perched on a nearby stump. As it listened with an intent look on its beaked yellow face, chirping along melodically, Day grabbed the closest branch and began to climb.

His biceps strained as he moved from branch to branch as quickly as he could, trying to find the most direct route up to the nest. Bits of twig scratched his hands and caught in his hair, but he kept moving. Below him, Jenna started in on "Swing Low, Sweet Chariot," and the emotion in her voice as she sang the bittersweet old spiritual distracted him so much he missed a handhold and almost fell out of the tree. He could only hope the phoenix was just as distracted.

Finally, he drew even with the nest, its slightly charred interior still smoking a little where the phoenix had been sitting. The mass of closely knit branches, no doubt culled from some reasonably fireproof shrub, was filled with shiny bits and pieces. From where he hung precariously from a limb that ran parallel to the crook of the tree where the nest was situated, Day could see a tarnished brass pocket watch, a gold spindle, a pair of jeweled hair combs, and yes, a faceted gem hung on a thin chain that looked like a match to the other Key they'd taken from the troll. This one was larger, rougher in cut, and a rosy peach color rather than the bluish green of their previous acquisition, but Day was pretty certain he'd found what they were looking for. He certainly didn't see anything else that fit the bill.

Thanking his mother silently for bringing him up to believe that a gentleman always had at least one handkerchief on him at all times, he reached into the smoking embers of the nest's interior and wrapped the piece of cloth around the necklace, careful not to touch any of the surrounding area with his unprotected flesh. He thought he heard a tiny chiming sound as he picked it up, but he couldn't be sure.

Then he tucked the handkerchief into his back pocket and shimmied rapidly down the tree. Jenna wound up her song, then bowed gracefully in the direction of the phoenix. Day braced himself in case the creature realized that it had been robbed, but it only bobbed its head in return and flew back up to its perch, leaving one glowing feather in its wake. Cautiously, Day picked that up too. Luckily, it had cooled off quickly; phoenix feathers were too rare to leave behind. Besides, he rather thought it might have been a purposeful gift, in thanks for the entertainment.

As they beat a hasty retreat, Day said to Jenna, "You have an incredible voice. That was just wonderful."

A hint of pink crept across her cheekbones, and Day thought, not for the first time, that it didn't seem as though she'd gotten many compliments in her life. He would have liked to have remedied that, if things had been different.

"Thanks," she said. "My grandmother used to go to church pretty regularly, and she often dragged me along with her. I didn't get the religious part, but I always liked the music. Who knew it would come in so handy for dealing with magical creatures."

Day smiled at her. "Music has a magic all its own," he said. "Especially when you sing it."

Jenna ducked her head, as though to hide her answering smile. "That's great, but did you get the Key of Solomon? I'd hate to think I put on that show for nothing."

Now far enough away from the orchard that he figured it was safe, Day pulled out his prize and unwrapped the cloth to show it to her. Less flashy than their first acquisition, it mostly looked like a chunk of pretty rock on a flimsy silver chain, and Jenna's face reflected her disappointment.

"Are you sure you got the right thing?" she asked. "That looks even less like a key than the first one."

Day shrugged. "It was the only piece in the nest that looked like it had even a possibility of being what we were looking for. But if you want to climb up there and check for yourself, be my guest."

From the way she stalked off toward the horse, he was guessing she wasn't interested in taking him up on his proposition.

"You're welcome," he muttered, sucking on a scratch. "Next time I'm letting you go up in the tree and I'll sing. I'm pretty sure I remember all the words to 'Froggy Went A'Courting.'"

# CHAPTER 21

**IT** took them a few more days of traveling to reach the place on Gregori's map that they hoped marked the location of the third and final key, the Key of Zoroaster. Every night Jenna considered curling up with Mick when they set up their bed-rolls, and every night she wound up sleeping on her own. It was as if the magic of the oasis had only worked while they were within its enchanted confines, and now that they were back in the less secluded environs outside its borders, their previous awkwardness toward each other had returned.

It didn't help that she was waking up each morning a little bit larger than when she'd gone to bed the evening before. She could no longer find a comfortable position to sleep in, no matter how many times she rolled from side to side or onto her back, and she kept having to get up in the middle of the night to pee. When she did get to sleep, the baby would shift or kick and wake her right back up again.

Mick clearly tried to locate the most accommodating places for them to camp, but she was starting to dream about actual beds and running water with a passion she'd previously reserved for chocolate.

Also, there was apparently no chocolate in the Otherworld, which just made her crabby since she'd been craving it for days. Truth be told, almost everything made her crabby, including Mick, which was hardly fair and she knew it. She'd dreamed her whole life of being able to experience the magic of pregnancy, and now a different kind of magic was stealing away days and weeks and months and compressing what should have been a long and wonderful journey into a few short moments. That wasn't fair either, and yet it wasn't as though she could complain, since she'd made at least this particular choice herself.

Her rapidly advancing pregnancy was harder and harder to adjust to, and she was starting to worry about the health of the baby. It was difficult to imagine how this kind of insane growth could be good for her daughter, no matter what Gregori had said.

"You're brooding," Mick said, his breath stirring the small hairs on the back of her neck as they rode along a pale orange stream filled with speckled blue fish that swam backward instead of forward. Jenna could identify.

"I'm not brooding," she said. "I'm just thinking."

"Right, thinking dark, grim thoughts in a circular fashion for hours on end," Mick said. "Where I come from, we call that brooding. And you've been doing it for days."

Jenna sighed, sagging back against him for a minute to try and relieve her aching back. "I'm sorry. I'm just worrying. About the baby and, you know, everything else."

"The baby is fine," Mick said, taking one hand off the reins and putting it on her stomach. A tiny foot kicked as if in agreement.

"Nobody likes a wiseass," Jenna told her stomach. "I wouldn't start taking his side if I were you."

Mick chuckled, patting the foot. Or hand, or whatever it was. "Look, I know this has to be scary, but there aren't any signs that the rapid pregnancy is having any ill effects on either you or the baby. You should stop worrying and just enjoy the experience." The foot kicked out again.

"Oh, shut up, Turnip," Jenna said, but she rubbed the spot affectionately anyway. She couldn't believe Mick had her calling her unborn child after a root vegetable. "Besides, that's part of the problem."

"Sorry? You lost me."

"I've been wanting to be pregnant my entire life, even knowing it wasn't possible. I used to spend hours imagining what it would be like: each little change, every step in my unborn child's development. I didn't know all the facts, of course, since I avoided learning any more than the minimum, but still, I would lie in bed at night and wonder about what it would be like to feel a baby growing inside me for nine months. And now it's all rushing by at the speed of light."

To her embarrassment, Jenna started crying. Not just subtle little tears that streaked delicately down her face one at a time, but great heaving sobs that shook her whole body and poured over her cheeks as though someone had unleashed Niagara Falls.

Mick let her cry for a few minutes, tightening his hold around her and handing a handkerchief over her shoulder. He didn't try to tell her she was being silly, which she greatly appreciated. Just rubbed one hand up and down her arm and let her get it out.

Finally, she snuffled and blew her nose, tucking the now-sodden scrap of cloth into her pocket. "Sorry. I didn't mean to make a scene."

He laughed softly, gesturing around the deserted countryside. "Hard to make a scene when no one is watching. Besides, you're entitled. I hadn't thought about that aspect of things. I guess I just figured that most women would be happy to have the entire experience over more quickly, since it looks so uncomfortable."

Jenna wiped her eyes. Mick might be a kind of Paranormal

superhero, but sometimes he was such a guy. "There are probably some women who feel would that way," she said. "Sadly, I'm not one of them. Mostly, though, I can't help worrying if spending most of her gestation time in the Otherworld is going to affect my little girl somehow. What if she keeps growing so rapidly once she's out of my womb? Could that happen?"

"I don't think so," Mick said, but he didn't sound sure. "If Gregori is right, then the baby is somehow manifesting the odd effects of time in the Otherworld in a more obvious way than would happen to someone who is already mature. Which would mean that once she is born, we will know that we've missed about six months on the other side. He seemed to believe the whole thing was actually likely to be a mechanism that is keeping her safe, rather than something that might hurt her. Whether she will continue to age faster after that, even Gregori didn't venture to guess."

"Oh," Jenna said. "You know that just confused me more, right?"

"Don't worry," Mick said, patting her shoulder and then loosening his hold on her. "I don't understand it either. Most Humans who come to the Otherworld seem to age more slowly, not more rapidly. But I know little Babs did the opposite. She was brought here when she was a baby, and when Liam and Barbara rescued her, she looked as though she was about five years old, even though only a year or so had passed since she'd been kidnapped. Like we said, time can be unpredictable in the Otherworld."

"Maybe it affects children differently," Jenna pondered. "This is just crazy. How can I not worry about this stuff?"

There was a marked silence from behind her.

"What?" she said. "What aren't you saying?"

"I think we have bigger worries, that's all."

"Bigger worries than how fast my baby is going to age once she's born? Seriously?" Jenna tried not to hyperventilate at the thought she might end up giving birth in the middle of a strange land with no doctors and no hospitals. "Oh Lord. You're worrying about the actual labor, aren't you?"

"Shit," Mick said. She could feel the muscles in his thighs tense where they curved around hers. "I hadn't even thought about that. I don't know how to deliver a baby. Shit. Maybe Gregori will know someone. It's not exactly a skill set that's in high demand on this side of the doorway. Some Paranormal creatures still have babies on occasion. Like Brownies. Maybe we can find a sprite to help."

Despite her concern, Jenna had to stop herself from laughing out loud. Now Mick sounded like he was going to start hyperventilating. Definitely a guy, even if he did occasionally turn into something large, furry, and light green.

"Hopefully, we'll find the third Key and solve the riddle and get me home before the baby is born," she said, trying to reassure them both. "Right?"

"Right," he said. "Because otherwise we're running out of time a lot faster than we thought we would. The Queen told Zilya she could claim the baby two weeks after it is born, if you haven't solved the riddle by then. We thought that gave us six months, but at the rate you're growing, we may only have a few days, and then the clock starts counting down. *That's* what I've been worrying about."

"Shit," Jenna said, no longer feeling the slightest inclination to laugh. "Is that two weeks here or two weeks back in my world? And how will we know?"

"I have no idea," Mick said. He gave the reins a little flick and Krasivaya picked up her pace. "Either way, we need to hurry. Hopefully, Gregori will meet us at the third Key as planned and have some kind of good news from the Queen. She could decide to penalize Zilya for skirting the rules, even if she didn't technically break them. But we can't count on that."

Jenna put one hand protectively over her baby, knowing Mick wouldn't let her fall. She knew they were running out of time, but no matter what happened, she wasn't going to

stand passively by and hand her child over to Zilya. Jenna
was not going to be like her mother. She would fight the faery,
fight the Queen, fight everyone in the Otherworld if she had
to in order to keep her baby safe. They were going to take her
child away from her over her dead body. Literally, if need be.


**THEY** rode through lands that transitioned from desert dunes
to vivid green rain forest, and then turned into rolling hills
that might have been somewhere in England if the grass
hadn't been purple and the cows—or whatever it was that
grazed in the open fields—had fewer legs and smaller horns.
Cottages the size of shoe boxes gave way to thatched huts that
could have housed entire families of giants. And probably
did. The odor of Otherworld manure made her wrinkle her
nose; apparently, even here, nothing could make *that* particular smell less pungent.

Actual paths started to appear in the previously trackless
meadowland; Day began to worry about being spotted as they
grew closer to something that resembled populated areas. He
unrolled the scroll and peered over Jenna's shoulder at the
map his brother had drawn in meticulous black lines.

"I think we're getting close to the location of the third
Key," he said, trying to ignore the scent of her hair as it blew
into his face. It was a kind of sweet torture sitting this close
to her every day and then not being able to touch her at night,
but he didn't blame her for keeping her distance when she
could.

He still had no idea how to control the beast he became
when he felt she was threatened, and he couldn't be completely sure the change wouldn't happen under other circumstances. They both knew that their journey together was only
temporary; she was probably smart not to let things get any
more complicated than they already were.

"What's that?" Jenna asked suddenly, pointing at what
looked like the tip of a white tower poking out of a mass of

smoky gray shrubbery. "Please tell me it isn't another wall of thorns, I'm begging you."

As they drew closer, Day got a sinking feeling he was about to get nostalgic for their previous challenges. "Worse," he said. "I'm pretty sure it's a maze. I'm guessing that the owner of the third Key takes its possession a lot more seriously than the troll and the dwarf did theirs."

Jenna twisted around to look at him, her nose wrinkled. "What's the big deal? There's usually a trick to figuring out a maze, like taking every other left turn, or something. I'm sure we can figure it out."

"This is the Otherworld, Jenna, not Hampton Court in London. There's no friendly groundskeeper to come fetch you out if you get lost, and there are likely to be a lot of unpleasant surprises. Whoever owns that tower in the middle is sincere about discouraging unwanted visitors."

"Oh." She looked thoughtful, but not as discouraged as he would have liked. Day tried scowling at her, but she just shook her head.

"No," she said, as they got closer to the entrance.

"No, what? I haven't even said anything yet."

"No, I won't stay out here." Her pale face set into a stubborn look he was beginning to become all too familiar with. "No, I will not wait with the horse while you wander around in a potentially dangerous maze trying to find the Key *I* need to solve *my* riddle. So, no."

Day ground his teeth. "Do you hear yourself? 'Potentially dangerous.' You're making my point for me. I will manage a lot better if I don't have to worry about you."

Jenna smiled up at him sweetly. "You mean the way you managed that rose barrier without my help?"

He was pretty sure he was going to break a molar. "Jenna—"

Her smile melted away. "And what if those *biesy* creatures catch up with us while you're inside the maze and I'm out here?" She slid off the horse and stood on the ground, her arms crossed in front of her chest, blocking the narrow path into the maze. "You really think I'm safer on my own than I am with you? Or that you are more capable of solving this task by yourself than we are as a team? Michael Day, you have a serious problem. And we're not going one step farther until you and I talk about it."

*Great gods on high.* What was it about women that always made them want to talk about things? His brothers had never wanted to talk about things. Even the Baba Yagas weren't prone to insist on picking everything apart, being much more likely to charge into action and blow things up. No wonder he'd always avoided spending more than a few days with the same woman. It always ended up with TALKING.

"Jenna, we're in the middle of a quest," he said in what he hoped was a patient voice. He dismounted, too, and Krasivaya swung her great equine head from one to the other, rolled her brown eyes, and started cropping at the grass near her metal-shod feet.

"Yes, we are," Jenna said, chin raised. "*My* quest, if I'm not mistaken."

"Of course it is your quest," Day said. "But can't this conversation wait until we've actually completed it? That might make a little more sense, don't you think?"

The chin went up a little higher. "What I think, Mick, is that you are so afraid that someone else will get hurt on your watch that you aren't going to allow anyone close to you to take a risk again. Or worse yet, that you won't let anyone ever get close to you at all. Which is why every time we start getting intimate, you push me away."

Day shook his head. "I'm not pushing you away, Jenna. You're afraid of me—of this thing I'm becoming, and whether or not I can control it—and I can't stand to see that fear in your eyes."

She took a step closer, standing right next to him until she was so near he could feel the heat coming off of her body and smell the scent that was so distinctly Jenna. As always, his body responded with longing, despite the circumstances. Her icy blue eyes stared directly into his. "Do you see fear now, Mick? I don't think so. I told you before, I stopped being afraid of you long ago. You're the one who is afraid, not me."

He fought not to look away, not to step back—hell, not to turn and run as far and as fast as he could from this woman, whose gaze held only affection, frustration, and defiance. She was right, of course, although he didn't want to admit it. The great Mikhail Day, once hailed as one of the heroes of the Otherworld, was afraid.

Not of action or fighting. Not of getting hurt or even dying, although these days such a fate was much more likely than it used to be. He would face such things as gleefully as ever, running toward the danger and not away.

But to watch those he loved and valued put themselves in harm's way, knowing that he might not be able to save them? Jenna was right; the terror that induced was almost enough to freeze him in his tracks and make him wish never to take another step again, lest it be the wrong one and invite disaster.

"You can't live your life like this," Jenna said more softly. "Being connected to others always carries the risk of grief and loss. Believe me, no one knows that more than I do. But what kind of existence will you have if you shut everyone else out?"

*One without the kind of horror that comes from watching those you loved beyond measure being tortured beyond endurance—all because of you?*

"I can't live through that again," Day said. "Not for you. Not for anyone."

Jenna lifted one hand and touched his cheek gently. The gesture almost broke him on the spot.

"I doubt that anyone could," she said. "What happened to you was terrible. But Brenna is gone. You and your brothers survived. Bella survived. You won. But if you allow what you experienced to deprive you of a full and rewarding life, then Brenna wins after all. That's not what you want, is it?"

He shook his head, long blond hair falling into his eyes

and mercifully blocking the compassion in Jenna's gaze. "It's not. Of course it's not. But I don't know what I do want. That's part of the problem."

"I don't agree. I think you know exactly what you want, but you're afraid to allow yourself to try for it." The hand dropped and Jenna took one step backward, taking all her heat and warmth with her.

Day lifted his head, pushing his hair back out of the way. "What are you saying?"

"I'm saying that you already found what you want," Jenna said. Her expression was firm, but her voice trembled slightly, revealing how much this conversation was costing her. "And so have I. But while I'm no longer afraid of the beast, I'm not sure I can trust the man. What are you going to do when this is all over, Mick? When we've finished this quest and come through to the other side, whichever way it turns out. Are you going to run away again and hide in a cabin in the woods? Or are you going to stay?"

*Stay? With Jenna?* For a moment, he allowed himself a glimpse of the future she offered him: a greater gift than any he could ever have imagined. A life with a woman who was smart and funny and gentle and fierce. And perhaps a child to raise as they grew older together, laughing and crying and doing all those Human things he'd never had a chance to experience. Building a true family, maybe even reaching out to his brothers and inviting them in.

For that one moment, he could see the vision as clearly as if a crystal ball hung in the air before him. Then reality hit with the power of a giant's fist, rocking him back on his heels. What if they couldn't break the curse and Jenna lost the baby after all? Would she still want him around then? Even if she did, how could he possibly ever face her again, knowing how he had let her down?

And what if they *did* succeed? What if they saved her baby and being with Jenna meant raising a child too? What did he know of being a father, when he'd barely had one himself? If he couldn't keep his strong, capable brothers safe, how could he be trusted with a tiny baby?

Day clenched his hands. He couldn't have this conversation now. Couldn't deal with these thoughts crowding his brain, distracting him from the task ahead. It would have to wait until later, if there was a later. If after they reached the end of their travels, whatever and wherever that was, she still wanted him. Then he'd see if he had an answer for her question. Right now, all he had was the ability to keep moving forward, so that was what he was going to do.

"We have more important things to deal with right at the moment, don't you think?" he said firmly. "You're right though. It's your quest and your choice, and probably too dangerous to leave you behind anyway. So if we're going to find that third Key and solve *your* riddle, we'd best get on with it." He picked her up as if she weighed less than a feather and moved her out of his way, clicking his fingers for Krasivaya to follow. "Come if you're coming," he said, and stalked off into the maze without a backward look.

# CHAPTER 22

JENNA stared after him for a moment, torn between grief and anger. She couldn't believe it. She'd offered him her heart on a plate and he'd simply turned and walked away.

Maybe she'd been wrong, and he didn't really want her after all. Who could blame him? She certainly came with enough baggage, although she doubted that was the issue. Maybe when he said he liked children, he'd meant other people's children, and simply wasn't interested in a woman with a baby. Or maybe it was because the baby was another man's?

She hadn't thought Mick was that shallow, but then, she hadn't known him for that long, and no matter how much they'd shared in the course of their journey together, perhaps she didn't really know him at all.

Or maybe she'd been right the first time, and he was too scared to take the risk on love.

She didn't suppose she'd blame him for that either, although she didn't know where that left her, since somewhere along the line, she'd fallen madly, deeply, truly in love with this blond son of a god with his strong muscles, huge heart, and broken spirit. Perhaps he was just too broken for anyone to fix, no less a woman with her own scars and hidden damage.

*Well, Jenna, none of this brooding is going to get the job done, is it, now?* She could hear her grandmother's voice ringing in her ears as if the old woman stood right in front of her. *Worry about Mick later. Find the third Key and save your baby now.* She straightened her back and marched off after him, more determined than ever to save herself, since it looked as though she'd be doing it on her own for the rest of her life.

**AT** first, there was nothing to see but the tall sides of the maze, a monotonous vista of grayish white, slightly glittery shrubbery that grew taller than Day's fingertips stretched up over his head and thickly enough that neither one of them could reach a hand through it. The shrubs had long drooping needles, much like a pine on the other side of the doorway, but thicker and with a vaguely citrus scent that grew stronger when they brushed against it.

The plants grew toward each other in the middle, so all Day and Jenna could make out was a sliver of sky up above them, and soft, mossy ground under their feet. Even Krasivaya's hooves made no sound as they walked, and Day began to wonder if they had all turned into ghosts, doomed to wander forever. It would have made a very suitable Russian tale, but not one he particularly wanted to star in.

Time seemed to blur as they walked, but eventually they came to a place where the path forked: one part veering off to their right and looking much like the way they'd come, and the other turning to the left and becoming paved with flat cerulean stones of varying sizes. Some were as large as the saddlebags slung over Krasivaya's withers, and others were as small as the palm of Jenna's hand. Day had a bad feeling about that path. Of course, he didn't have a better one about the other choice. That was the problem with mazes.

Jenna looked from one option to the other, gnawing her lower lip. "What do you think?" she asked, suddenly sounding less sure of herself. "Do we stick to the path that looks just like the one we've been slogging down forever, or take the one that looks like it should lead to civilization? Maybe that one is too obvious, and it is a trick."

*Maybe they are both a trick. This is the Otherworld, after all.* "Or maybe it is so obvious, you're meant to think it is a trick and take the other path," he said.

"Oh. Crap." Jenna rubbed her belly, then stretched her back out. Clearly, the long walk was starting to bother her, but she'd refused to get back on the horse, who seemed to be feeling even more claustrophobic than her companions. "How are we supposed to choose?"

"We could try one direction for a while and then turn back if we don't get anywhere, but I don't like the idea of spending any more time in here than we have to," Day said.

"Flip a coin?" Jenna said, trying to sound lighthearted.

Krasivaya tossed her head, snorting loudly, and trotted off to the left, her hooves making clicking noises as they struck the stones. She was soon out of sight around a curve in the shrubbery.

"Or we could let the horse decide," Day said, his lips compressed. *This is what comes of allowing your transportation to be both magical and sentient.* They set off after her at a brisk walk.

Only to discover after a few steps that the stones were neither as random nor as steady as they had appeared to be. Day took the first wrong step and jumped quickly to the next rock as the one under his feet tilted as soon as his boot was upon it. Behind him, Jenna gave a surprised squeal, then had to hop quickly over to his side as the rock under her right foot simply disappeared into thin air.

"Crap squared!" she said. Day muttered something a lot worse than that, and hoped she didn't understand Russian.

They went forward another few yards without incident,

but then the stones started to sink when trod upon. Not every one, or even every other, but just enough so they were constantly off balance—especially Jenna, who was already struggling to keep herself upright with the unaccustomed weight from her belly throwing her off. For a bit, Day tried carrying her, but that was even worse. The rocks sank faster under their combined weight, and he couldn't carry her and jump safely, too, and eventually he had to put her down again.

Finally, they both found solid footing at the same time and stood still for a moment to catch their breath.

"Well," he said, trying to cheer her up. "Look on the bright side. If this was the wrong path, it probably wouldn't be so difficult."

Jenna scowled at him. "That's very encouraging. Not." She glanced down the way ahead, where they could hear Krasivaya whinnying. She didn't sound like she was in distress, which Day found reassuring.

"How the hell is the *horse* doing it?" Jenna asked, sounding put out. "She's much heavier than we are, and yet she didn't seem to have any problem at all. I don't get it."

Day thought about it for a minute and then grinned at her. "We're doing it wrong," he said. She rolled her eyes at him. "No, really, the horse got it right. She started moving and kept moving. Can you run?" He stared at her belly dubiously.

"Will it get us out of here?" she said. "You better believe it."

Day grabbed her by the hand and said a silent prayer that he'd guessed correctly, and they took off running, jumping from rock to rock so quickly that their weight was never on any individual stone for more than a few seconds.

Not long after, they came to the end of the paved stretch, racing between the narrow opening between the shrubs, and out into the light. Krasivaya stood nearby, chewing placidly on some bright yellow flowers and looking distinctly smug.

"Whew," Jenna said, leaning over with her hands on her knees. "Thank God that's over."

Day turned his head back and forth in either direction and groaned. "It's not," he said.

"What?" What are you talking about?" Jenna straightened up so fast she wobbled. "We made it through that part of the maze."

"Yes, we did," Day agreed. "And look where we are." He watched Jenna glance around her wildly and then back toward the center of the maze, where the white tower could still be seen, standing upright like a raised middle finger.

"You have *got* to be kidding me," she said. "We're back on the outside? Right where we started?" She let out a small laugh, tinged with a touch of hysteria. "We have to do it all over again?"

Day nodded, feeling grim. "I suspect that there are different paths depending on where you enter the maze. Each one will probably have its own tricks to master. Depending on how many entrances there are, it could take us days to master them all until we finally stumble on the one that actually gets us to the heart of the maze."

Jenna peered up at the sky, then down at her stomach again, her face drawn and white. "It's worse than that, Mick. Look at the color of the sky. When we went in, it was afternoon. I'm pretty sure that's the dawn, or at least as close as you get to it in a place with no real sun. I think that something weird happened to time inside that place." She pointed at her belly, which Day could see was noticeably larger than when they'd gone in. "I don't know how many times we can attempt it before we run out of time altogether."

THEY tried three more times before they had to give in and rest for a while. Each time it seemed as though only an hour or two had passed, and each time the moons had shifted position in the sky by the time the maze spat them back out again. Jenna was so tired she could have wept, but they'd used up most of their water by then, and she didn't want to waste a precious drop of moisture. She leaned against Mick's strong shoulder, nibbling halfheartedly on a piece of fruit for the sake of the baby, who she wished would repay her by taking that tiny foot off of Jenna's rib cage. Or at the very least, stop kicking with it. Nice to know that one of them was feeling just fine.

"Why don't you try and sleep for an hour or two, and then we'll walk in the other direction and try to find another way in," Mick suggested, his voice unusually gentle. She wasn't sure, but she thought she felt his hand brush over her hair, so light she could barely sense it.

She didn't know how she could possibly sleep. But she couldn't go on much longer without it either. "Maybe we should just give up on this Key," she said. "Take a chance that we can somehow make the riddle work with only two."

Mick didn't even bother to answer that. She didn't blame him. For now she'd rest. In a little while, they'd try again.


**THEY'D** gotten closer than last time, Day thought. He had seen the sides of the tower rising up over the nearest bank of shrubs, so close he could almost touch it. But then they'd had to duck away from some kind of bird that spat acid from a funnel-shaped beak, and they'd found themselves back on the outside again, facing, as far as he could tell, in a completely different direction. He sincerely hoped that someday the people who lived in that tower got turned around in their own maze and had to go through this ordeal themselves. It would serve them right.

Jenna jarred him out of his unproductive train of thought by lifting one hand and pointing off toward one distant corner of the maze's exterior. "Mick? Look. Isn't that Gregori?"

Sure enough, his brother was riding toward them on the back of his glorious red steed, a horse the color of the sunset over the ocean, whose beauty came close to rivaling that of Day's own magical companion. Not just riding, but racing fast, the horse's strong muscles bunching as he strode across the land, his golden hooves striking sparks of rocks as they flew over the landscape at speeds faster than any normal horse could ever have hoped to achieve.

In no time at all, the former Red Rider pulled up in front of them, neither he nor his horse so much as breathing rapidly, although he kept looking over his shoulder is if expecting something unpleasant to be looming there.

"Greetings, brother," Gregori said. "It is good to see you again, Jenna." He gazed at her stomach and his eyes widened the tiniest bit. "You are looking . . . well."

"Did you speak to the Queen?" Day asked. "What did she say?"

"There will be time to discuss such things later," Gregori said, his tone calm but urgent as he turned to look back again. "Might I suggest that you follow me and ride as quickly as possible? It would be in our best interests to find ourselves far away from here."

"But what about the third Key?" Jenna cried. "We've been trying to get it for hours. Days. Maybe even weeks."

Gregori slid a hand inside the red leather pouch hanging at his waist. The hand came out holding a tiny shard of clear crystal on a golden chain. "This is the Key," Gregori said with a slightly smug smile. "I just stole it, and the previous owners are a little unhappy about that. Thus the suggestion to ride away with some haste."

"How the hell did you get to the center of the maze?" Day asked.

"Bribed a maid to tell me the way in," Gregori said with a grin, a rare twinkle glittering in his dark eyes. "And then climbed up the outside of the tower and through a window." He tucked the Key back inside the pouch and dug his heels into his horse's side. It took off at a gallop, followed seconds later by Krasivaya, which caused Jenna to yelp and grab on to the horse's flowing white mane with both hands.

"Oh my God," she shouted at Day over the wind of their passage. "Did he just say he stole that jewel? I can't believe it. He seemed so . . . so . . . mellow and law-abiding."

Day laughed out loud, half from her comment and half from the sheer joy of racing at top speeds again after so long. "The law is a somewhat fluid concept for us Riders," he said. "We are more interested in expediency most of the time. The Baba Yagas are the same, which is perhaps where we get it from. Or possibly the other way around. Besides, Gregori dedicated much of his earlier years to learning many varied forms of martial arts. It wouldn't surprise me if some of that time was spent in the company of ninjas, assassins, and thieves."

He thought about it for a moment as they flew over the grassy ground. "Come to think of it, he would probably make a very good thief, should he turn his mind to it. Perhaps that could be a new career for him, now that he is no longer a Rider." Strangely, saying those words didn't dig quite so deeply into his soul as it had a couple of months ago.

"Maybe you should suggest it to him," Jenna gasped. "As soon as we stop galloping to the far ends of the Earth. Or the Otherworld. Whichever."

Day couldn't believe she wasn't enjoying the ride. "I can't believe you ever want this to stop. It's the best feeling I know." He thought for a moment. "Well, one of them, anyway."

"Maybe that's because you're not a million months pregnant, give or take a month," she said somewhat acerbically. "But if you don't want me to give birth on the back of your horse, I think maybe we should slow down as soon as you and Gregori think it is safe."

Day didn't have the heart to tell her that it had probably been safe some miles past, but he did whistle loudly to signal his brother that it was time to ease up.

After all, he was pretty sure Krasivaya would object to the mess if Jenna meant what she said about going into labor. Nobody was ready for that, least of all him.

\* \* \*

**THEY** finally dismounted under a cluster of weeping willows by the side of a small but elegant creek so they could water the horses and catch their breath. Well, so Jenna could catch her breath; as far as she could tell, neither the men nor their horses seemed at all tired out by their mad dash through the countryside. If anything, they look energized by it all. Gregori may have a potential new career as a cat burglar, but Jenna was pretty sure that she would never cut it as a Rider.

"You've grown since last I saw you," Gregori said, admiring her prominent belly. "How remarkable. The babe is well?"

"She seems to be, although without an obstetrician and an ultrasound, I'm not sure how I can know for certain."

"You carry the child within you," Gregori said in a no-argument tone. "You would know. Especially here."

"Stop staring at her stomach and let's take a look at what you stole," Mick said. "Thanks, by the way. We were just talking about how we were running short on time. It was nice of you to save us some."

His brother shrugged. "I spoke to the neighbors, and it was clear that the owner would never give it up. The Key of Zoroaster is said to bestow great wisdom upon the one who controls it, although from the sound of it, the gem had had no such effect on its current bearer. Either way, it seemed more efficient to simply avoid the argument. Our need is great, after all." He bowed his head in Jenna's direction, and his use of the word *our* spread a sense of warmth through her chest.

"Can I see it?" Jenna asked.

"Of course." Gregori plucked the stolen treasure back out of his pouch. Jenna had to suppress a sigh of disappointment. This Key looked even less impressive than the other two. And it still didn't bear any resemblance to a key of any kind she'd ever seen.

She took the Key of Solomon and the Key of Merlin out of the front of her shirt—she'd been wearing them, since it seemed like the best way not to lose them—and pulled them over her head, holding them out so the others could see them clearly. As Gregori handed her the final Key, a deep chiming sound could be heard, not coming from the gems themselves but seeming almost as though it echoed through the entire Otherworld.

"What the hell?" Mick said, his eyebrows rising.

"I was afraid of that," his brother said.

The sound died away, and nothing else happened. Jenna gingerly put the trio of chains back around her neck. "What do we do now? I have the three Keys that you thought might represent the key mentioned in the riddle. How do I know which one of the three it is, or if it is even any of them?"

Mick shook his head. "A better question might be, 'Afraid of what?'"

"Did you hear that sound?" Gregori said, a hint of grim inevitability in his voice.

"Of course we did," Mick said. "We're not deaf. We heard that chiming noise each time we acquired one of the Keys, although it was never that loud before. I take it you think it is a bad thing?"

"Not exactly. In fact, I suspect it is probably a signal that Jenna is getting close to solving the curse. Unfortunately, it has almost certainly alerted Zilya." Gregori's normally solemn face grew even more shadowed as he handed a scroll to Jenna.

"Before I could appear before the Queen, Zilya approached me and gave me this message to pass on to you," he said. "Presumably, she figured that since Mikhail was helping you, I would be able to contact you."

"That's ironic," Mick muttered, "since before this week we hadn't seen or spoken to each other in months."

"Irony aside, she was quite determined that I get this message into your hands," Gregori said to Jenna. "I very much doubt it says, 'Congratulations and good luck with the rest of the riddle.'"

Jenna unrolled the scroll with some trepidation, and as she read it she went first hot and then cold, a shiver running down the length of her spine. "Shit," she said, and gave the scroll to Mick, who read it out loud.

"If you want your brother to live, come to the house of Larissa and Kelvin the elves at the place where the curve of the Phaedrus River meets the bottom of Farthingale Hill."

"Shit indeed," Gregori agreed. "I take it you have a brother?"

"Had," Jenna said, bitterness filling her mouth. "I had a brother. My mother had to give him up to Zilya because of the curse. It was before I was born, so I never even met him. I have no idea what happened to him after Zilya took him. Presumably, she brought him here to the Otherworld, so it is possible she actually has him in her possession and could kill him if I don't do what she says."

"It is almost certainly a trap," Mick said. "As you said yourself, you have never even met this brother, if in fact she has him at all."

Jenna bit her lip. "I know. But I can't risk it. I lost my brother once already. If there is any chance I could save him now, I have to go."

Gregori's eyes glinted and one corner of his mouth twitched. "Who does she remind you of, my brother? I believe the cosmos is laughing at you."

"If so," Mick said with a glower, "I don't approve of its sense of humor." He turned to her. "Jenna, are you sure we can't talk you out of going? You'll be putting your baby in danger."

Jenna felt as though she was being torn in three different directions at once. How could she go when she knew that she would almost certainly be walking into the clutches of the faery who was determined to steal her child? But how could she not go, when there might be an opportunity to find—perhaps even to save—the brother her parents had given up so many years before? This might be her only chance to see him, and she'd wondered about him for so very long.

She gazed despairingly at the two men. "Tell me—if she

really does have my brother, would she truly kill him if I don't show up?"

They exchanged glances that told her the answer before Gregori even spoke.

"She is very angry and very frustrated. I do not believe there is any predicting what she might or might not do at this point. But she most assuredly does not mean you well, and it is clear she has no intention of abiding by the Queen's ruling."

Day took her hand in one of his larger ones. "What do you want to do, Jenna? Whatever you choose, I will do my best to keep you safe."

"As will I," his brother said with a small bow.

"I have always resented my parents for giving him up," Jenna said softly. "For letting him go without a fight. How can I do the same thing now, no matter the risk?"

"You are a very brave and determined woman," Gregori said, pulling a sword in its sheath from a holder on his saddle and fastening it around his waist. "I have no doubt that you will triumph in this matter."

Jenna thought that Mick didn't look so sure, but he, too, strapped on a sword and placed another impressively large knife on the opposite side of his belt.

"I hope I don't let you down," he said in a voice so quiet she could barely hear it. "I couldn't live with myself if I did."

A chill ran down her spine, almost as if another chime had rung out that only she could hear. What had she set into motion now?

# CHAPTER 23

**DAY** and Gregori were both familiar with the address Zilya mentioned in her note, so they set off at a brisk trot. Farthingale Hill was no more than a half a day's ride from where they were now, nearly on top of the place where Day and Jenna had come through the doorway from the Enchanted Rock. Ironically, they'd come almost full circle, but in some ways, it seemed to Day as though they were no closer to the answers they needed than when they'd first arrived.

At least, not the answers Jenna needed to save her baby. Day had a better idea of what was happening to him physically, although he didn't know why or what on earth he was going to do about it. More questions he couldn't answer.

He ground his teeth, grateful that Jenna was facing forward and couldn't see him. He was certain his expression was not a pleasant one.

Frustration bubbled up like the murky potion the evil Brenna had stirred in her cauldron all those months ago. What good was his strength if he couldn't use it to help the person he'd grown so attached to? He should have stuck to his vow to remain uninvolved and avoid women in need of rescue. Never mind that Jenna didn't expect him to rescue her and was perfectly determined to save her child on her own if necessary. Never mind that he had at least been able to come to her aid a few times. None of it was worth a hill of beans if in the end she lost that which she valued the most.

When had her life become so entwined with his own? Was it when she'd heard his story and looked at him without pity or scorn? Or when he'd felt the kick of little Turnip's tiny yet powerful foot against his hand? Certainly, the two nights they'd spent in each other's arms had opened his heart to the tendrils of fondness that now bound him to her, but it was more than that.

Somehow, without intending to, she had mended his broken spirit. Not completely, no. That journey would be long and probably take the rest of whatever time he had left. But because of her, he rode at his brother's side again. Because of her, he had stopped hiding and returned to the world to discover who and what he was. He had many questions, but she had given him the courage to seek out the answers, just by being the bright light that she was.

Day knew that she could never be his. Despite her insistence that she was no longer afraid of his change into something so blatantly magical, he had no illusions that she would want to raise her child around such a monster, especially if he could not learn how to control it—or even if it *could* be controlled. And as they rode toward this final confrontation, he had to confess (if only to himself) the ground-shaking truth he'd been avoiding for so long.

That this was what he wanted. To be with Jenna, to help raise her baby, to keep them both safe through days filled with sunlight and laughter and nights full of passion. Gods help him, the lonely Rider wanted to be lonely no longer.

Too bad it was impossible.

No, even if they managed to thwart Zilya, Jenna would

return home, where she belonged. Perhaps to the father of her child, if she could find a way to forgive him for his actions. Perhaps to find some normal Human man to share her life and all those glorious nights.

Acid burned down his throat and into his heart as he swallowed hard. Day was nothing if not a realist. Jenna could never be his, nor could she ever know that he had ever wished for such a thing. He couldn't bear it if she finally looked at him with pity in her eyes, all because the White Rider had fallen in love with a dark-haired, light-filled angel who would always be out of his reach. This time with her had been a gift that he would never be allowed to keep. All he asked of the universe now was the chance to do what he had sworn he had no interest in doing—save the only damsel in distress he had ever truly cared about.

If he could triumph in this, perhaps it would in some way redeem his soul from his previous errors. He couldn't undo the past, or the damage done to his brothers, but maybe, just maybe, he could give Jenna the future she deserved. That would be enough for him, no matter the cost.

When they arrived at their destination, they found Zilya waiting for them.

She was perched on top of the hill, overlooking a large, prosperous house with gabled peaks and lots of windows that looked out on a rolling lawn of blue grass dotted with Technicolor wildflowers. In front of the house they could see a boy of about nine or ten playing with a three-headed puppy. The faint sounds of laughter and barking in three-part harmony could be heard floating up the hillside.

It would have been an idyllic scene, if not for the wickedly sharp arrow Zilya held aimed directly at the boy, already nocked in the bow she held in competent-looking hands.

Zilya seemed quite pleased with herself when they came riding up and quietly dismounted a safe distance away from where she stood. Her smile grew even wider when she took in

Jenna's increased size, and Day had to fight the impulse to charge across the space between them and throttle her with his bare hands. Unfortunately, it was clear she would be able to get a shot off before he reached her, so he settled for growling under his breath, until Jenna put a calming hand on his arm.

She was right, of course; now was no time for him to lose control of his internal beast. Mindless violence wouldn't help them out of this one.

"Oh my," Zilya said to Jenna. "You have been busy, you lovely thing. I so appreciate you making this even easier for me. I have never been a patient woman, alas." She gave a mock sigh, still keeping most of her attention on the weapon she held aimed at the boy below.

"What is this all about, Zilya?" Day asked. "You've sent minions to try to claim the baby, and they failed. The Queen has forbidden you to touch Jenna yourself. There is nothing you can do."

Zilya might be impatient, but even she wasn't crazy enough to disobey a direct order from the Queen. Skirt it? Yes. Turn herself into a contortionist to get around it? Certainly. But outright defiance? Even Zilya knew that would be suicide. One didn't live for thousands of years without developing a strong sense of self-preservation. He had no idea what the hell she thought she could achieve here.

"You might think that," Zilya said, her dark crow's eyes gleaming. "But you would be wrong." She laughed softly, a sound that reminded Day of a nest of snakes rustling together. "I am not going to do anything to Jenna. She is going to do it to herself."

Day, Gregori, and Jenna exchanged glances. *What the hell?*

Zilya turned to face Jenna, the bow and arrow rock steady in her slim white hands. "I hope you still have that lovely amulet I sent you. I believe you are going to want it."

Jenna held up the medallion in its protective leather bag. "I have it," she said. "Although, really, it's a little gaudy for my tastes. Next time, perhaps you could send something in a nice sapphire?" While Zilya sputtered, Jenna pulled the three Keys out from underneath her shirt. "I also have the Key from the riddle," she said. "I am ready to solve it and break this curse forever. Give it up, Zilya. You've lost." She spoke so decisively, she almost had Day convinced, and he *knew* that she hadn't actually figured out the last part of the riddle yet. He was so proud of her in that moment, he thought his chest would burst wide open.

But Zilya just chuckled. "I think not," she said with soft menace. "Look down there. I suspect you have always wondered what happened to your brother after your mother was forced to give him up."

"So?" Jenna said. She seemed completely at ease, but Day could see the tension in the way she held her shoulders and the effort it took her not to clench her hands.

"So now you can meet him. If you do as I say. Of course, if you do not, you can watch him die right now."

"You're bluffing," Jenna scoffed. "My brother was born two years before me. He'd be thirty-one now. That child can't be more than ten. He's clearly not my brother, just some innocent little boy who happens to have dark hair and look a bit like me. I'm not falling for your trickery."

Day peered down at the boy with his keen eyes, able to see farther and in greater detail than Jenna's merely Human vision could. For instance, he could make out the shape of the boy's face, whose delicate paleness and determined chin echoed the one he'd been staring at for days. But much harder to duplicate were the eyes; large and that unusual icy blue color Day had only seen on one person before, surrounded by the same long, dusky lashes.

*Damn. Why couldn't anything be simple?*

"Jenna," he said quietly. "Remember the strange way that time can work here in the Otherworld. And take a good look at the boy's features. He's got your eyes."

Gregori nodded impassively. "In truth, Jenna, the child resembles you greatly. Zilya has lied about many things, but I doubt very much that she is lying about this."

Day watched Jenna carefully as her expressive face showed every emotion she was feeling. The confident look slid away to be replaced by hope, then fury, then fear. In the end, it held some feeling he couldn't read at all.

Zilya, watching all the transformations with arrogant satisfaction, nodded her head briskly. "You see? You have no choice." She waggled the bow and arrow, still aimed at the boy, and said to Jenna, "You lost your brother once before. Will you stand by and lose him again when this time you have the power to prevent it? Or will you bow to the inevitable and simply place my claiming amulet around your neck? Once you have done so, I will gladly take you down to meet him."

The faery practically radiated triumph, her white dandelion fluff hair crackling around her head like a storm cloud bringing with it doom and destruction. "You are young," she said in a smooth oily tone. "You can have more children. But you will have only one brother. It is up to you: will he live or will he die?"

Day watched Jenna. Tears sprang into her eyes and she put one hand on her chest, as though she could keep the heart inside from breaking. He knew, better than most, how precious the life of a brother was. Zilya had given Jenna an impossible choice, damn the faery's cold and clever mind. He could see the moment when Jenna began to waver.

"I have let too many people down already," Day said to Gregori, in a voice so quiet no one else could have heard it. "I could not bear it if I let Jenna down too."

Gregori started to speak, but Day just shook his head minutely. "She brought me back to life and gave me back my soul. I will not let her make this sacrifice. She would never be able to live with herself. I will not have her go through one moment of the agony I have suffered in this last year."

Jenna stood frozen for a moment, then slid the medallion out of its pouch and started to lift it, hands shaking uncontrollably, a single tear making a forlorn path down over her pale cheek.

"NO, Jenna!" Day yelled, and raced at Zilya, getting between her and the boy. He heard the snap of the bowstring and saw the flash of the pseudo-sun off the arrow, right before it buried itself deep in his chest. And then there was only pain.

# CHAPTER 24

**JENNA** screamed, barely able to comprehend what she saw. She and Gregori would have rushed to Mick, but Zilya stepped forward and put one booted foot on the feathered end of the arrow where it stuck up out of Mick's chest. He lay still, sprawled awkwardly on his back with his arms spread out as if trying to break his fall. Jenna couldn't even tell if he was breathing, but she could see an ominous trickle of bright red blood sliding from the corner of his mouth.

"You *bitch*!" Jenna said. "Get away from him. He never did anything to you. How could you shoot him?"

Zilya shrugged. "He got in my way. Literally." She looked from Mick, lying at her feet, and then back at Jenna. "So that is how it is," she said with a smirk. "That makes things even simpler. Put that medallion over your head, Jenna, or I will shove this arrow the rest of the way through his chest. Day is not immortal anymore, is he? He can die as quickly as any other mortal, without his magical healing to help him."

She smiled, and it was not a pleasant sight.

"The choice is up to you, Jenna Quinlan. Allow me to claim your unborn child. You can see how happy your brother is; his foster parents have given him a pampered and privileged life where he wants for nothing. Give me the child and Day lives. Or at least, he *might*. Refuse me, and he has no chance at all."

Gregori glared at Zilya. "The Queen will have your head for this."

"Not if you both swear to keep your silence, in return for Day's life. This is the Otherworld, after all. You know such vows have power."

Gregori scowled, but Jenna noticed he didn't argue with her.

They both heard a low groan, coming from where Day was lying. At least he was still alive. For now.

"Why didn't he change into that creature?" Jenna asked Gregori in a whisper. "Why doesn't he change now? Wouldn't that make him stronger?"

Gregori's lips thinned into a straight line. "He has only changed forms when you were in danger, right?" She nodded, not taking her eyes off of Zilya, who was waiting, one foot still poised above Day's wounded body.

"When he charged at Zilya, he was only trying to protect your heart, not your life," Gregori said. "Perhaps it wasn't enough to trigger the transition. And he still can't change at will, as far as I know." His deep eyes were sadder than she'd ever seen them. "I thought that perhaps the solution to his condition lay within the riddle, but since we never solved it completely, there is no way to say for sure."

Jenna brushed away tears, unable to look away from the tableau in front of her. "What should I do?" she asked Gregori in an agonized whisper. It felt as though her heart were being torn in two. It had been a difficult enough decision to make when the choice had been between her unborn child and a boy she'd never met but knew to be her long-lost brother. To choose between the baby she carried and Mick? Impossible.

Gregori gazed at her steadily with grief in his dark eyes. "I cannot tell you what to do. Only you can make this choice, Jenna."

"Don't do it, Jenna." Mick's voice was weak and laced with pain, but she could hear the determination in it even so. "It isn't worth it. I'm not worth it. I forbid it."

"The only one forbidding things here is me," Zilya said with a sneer. She nudged the arrow with her toe, forcing it in another quarter inch. A muffled scream made it out past Mick's tightly clenched teeth, although Jenna could see how hard he tried to stop it.

Next to her, Gregori's hands rolled into fists, and Jenna could tell he held himself still through strength of will alone.

"Make up your mind, Human," Zilya said. "I will not wait much longer."

Jenna caressed her belly. She didn't cry. There were not enough tears in either world for the choice she had to make now.

"I'm so sorry, baby," she said softly. "I've never even met you and already I love you so very much. But this man wouldn't be here if it weren't for me, and he has been brave and strong and kind and true. I love him, too, and I can't let him die. I hope you have a wonderful life with whoever is lucky enough to get to raise you. I'll never stop fighting to get you back. I promise, someday I'll come for you."

She lifted the medallion and put it over her head in one swift motion. As it came down, it brushed the Keys that already lay there and three pure, chiming notes rang out in unison. When the sound finally stopped, the thin chains that held the Key of Merlin, the Key of Solomon, and the Key of Zoroaster had vanished, and the three shining stones they'd held could be seen aligned in a single row across the front of the medallion. The new amulet glowed with a soft green light.

"No!" Zilya screamed, her face twisted with fury. "That is impossible!" Incandescent with rage, she raised her foot to slam it down on the arrow.

Gregori yelled, "Change, Mikhail! You can control it now! Change! Change, dammit!"

Jenna held her breath as across the clearing, Mick's fallen figure shimmered, glowing with the same color as the amulet she wore. A bellow of pain and triumph mixed together echoed through the space, and then the man was gone and a massive green-furred beast reared up off of the ground, pulling the arrow out of its chest with a claw-tipped hand.

It growled at Zilya and she growled back, raising hands that dripped with caustic magic, gathering it into a ball of deadly intent that she aimed directly at his head.

Before she could throw it, Mick sent the arrow, still dripping with his own blood, winging through the air. It hit Zilya so hard, she flew backward and was impaled against a tree, where she hung, cursing bitterly, until the light faded out of her eyes and her head fell forward onto her chest. All that could be seen of the arrow was the feathers at its far end, buried to the hilt in Zilya's breast like some bizarre form of jewelry.

It was over. The faery who had cursed her family was dead.

Jenna couldn't quite take it all in.

What she did take in was the sight of Mick, still bloody but clearly much stronger and already partially healed, changing back into his normal, insanely attractive self and running over to embrace his brother, and then, after a moment's hesitation, Jenna. Who hugged him back so hard it threatened to reopen his wound, to make sure he got the message that she didn't care what form he took, as long as that form was alive and well.

"I don't understand," Jenna said, staring from Mick to Gregori and back again. "What happened?"

Gregori's smile was practically luminous with relief. "You solved the riddle," he said. "It was always all about the last two lines: A magic key to a gift divine. True love must merge when stars align."

"Jenna's riddle was about my new powers?" Day said,

sounding as confused as Jenna felt. She was glad she wasn't the only one. "That doesn't make any sense."

His brother snorted, an unusually undignified sound for him. "It's a fairy-tale riddle, Mikhail. They never make any sense until they've been solved. It was your willingness to sacrifice everything for each other that broke the curse, melding the three magical Keys with the talisman intended to claim the baby for Zilya. Instead, you two claimed each other, and the strength of your love not only ended the curse but also enabled Mikhail to be able to control his transformation."

Jenna shook her head. "Does this mean that if my parents had been willing to stand up to the curse and sacrifice everything to break it, the riddle would have somehow worked out for them too?"

"Who knows," Gregori said. "It is the nature of such things that they work out the way they are supposed to. Perhaps it was always meant to end like this."

Jenna had a sudden longing for the simplicity of the Human world, with all its own insanity. Celebrity marriages and political wrangling somehow seemed almost sane. Okay, not really. But they still made more sense than fairy tales and the Otherworld. "Hey," she said as a thought hit her. "Does this mean that the medallion now has control over Mick? If so, then he should have it."

She held it out to him, but he just shook his head.

"Keep it," Mick said. "I have already trusted you with my heart. I might as well trust you with my body too."

Jenna didn't know how to respond to that. She was distracted for a moment by activity down at the bottom of the hill. The boy's parents had obviously heard the commotion and come out of their house; they stood next to him protectively, staring up at Jenna and the two former Riders up above. Jenna raised one hand hesitantly and the little boy waved back.

She took one step forward and then stopped as a powerful ripple flowed across her belly, almost making her fall. "Oh," she said. "And ow." Another ripple quickly followed the first.

"It might be best to leave family reunions to another day," Gregori suggested, putting one hand on her back. "It would appear that we have more pressing issues."

"But . . ." Jenna looked longingly down at the dark-haired child, then clutched at her abdomen, which suddenly seemed to have dropped two inches. "Holy crap, OW."

"If you want your baby to be born in your own world, you and Mikhail had better make tracks for the door you entered through," Gregori said in a firm tone. He and Mick helped her up on Krasivaya with some difficulty and no small amount of awkwardness, even after the horse bent its forelegs down to make things easier, and Mick swung up behind her.

"What about you, brother?" Mick asked. "Will you come with us?"

"Not right now," Gregori said. "I will go to the Queen and report all this, then join you as soon as I can." He winked at Mick. "After all, family is important."

He strode over to where Zilya's still form hung from the tree and yanked the arrow out with one decisive motion. Then he threw her body over his horse's withers, mounted up, and rode off in the direction of court.

"You know," Jenna said between gasps, "I really like your brother."

"I am quite fond of him myself," Mick said, urging Krasivaya on toward the doorway to the Human world. "I can't wait for you to meet Alexei."

"I think I have someone else to meet first," Jenna said, feeling the contractions gripping her more strongly with every step the horse took. "Do you think we could go faster?"

Then all she could do was deal with the strange sensations that seemed to possess her body until it was no longer hers. In between the rippling contractions, she focused on Mick's strong arms, holding her steady and safe as they moved from the Otherworld into the caves they had entered a lifetime ago. As they rode through the sparkling lights that marked the boundary between the worlds, Jenna found herself sitting atop a Yamaha motorcycle instead of a white horse.

"I'll never get used to this magical stuff," she muttered as they came out into the bright radiance of a Texas day. And then she was too preoccupied with labor pains to care about anything other than the fact that it looked like she was going to give birth to her baby in the middle of an empty road surrounded by rocks and sand and dust. There was no way she could ride any farther on the motorcycle, no matter how tightly Mick held on to her.

Suddenly, something blocked the light and Jenna looked up to see a silver Airstream pulling to a stop in front of them. Barbara hopped out of the driver's seat of the silver truck at its head, with Chudo-Yudo and little Babs following on her heels. Babs looked different: a bit older, with her choppy brown hair grown out enough to be tied up in a lopsided ponytail on one side of her head. Barbara, on the other hand, looked exactly the same, all black leather and toughness, with a cloud of ebony swirling over her shoulders.

Mick helped Jenna get off the bike, although it was more of a slithering *thump* than a graceful dismount, then held her upright as they greeted the others.

"Hello, Day. Hello, Jenna," Babs said gravely, giving Jenna's greatly expanded belly an intrigued examination. "Is that your baby in there? Before I could not see it was there, but now it is much larger. How is it going to come out?"

"With great discomfort and right away," Jenna said through gritted teeth.

Barbara chuckled and put one arm under Jenna's shoulder so that she and Mick could half walk, half carry Jenna into the Airstream.

"Not that I'm not glad to see you, because, great gods, I am," Mick said to Barbara. "But what are you doing here? Your timing is impeccable, even for you."

"Interesting thing, that," Barbara said as they lay Jenna

down on Barbara's bed. "Gregori sent me a message saying that he thought it would be a good idea for me to be here on this date at this time. He said he had a feeling I would be needed."

"Really?" Mick said. "We just left him."

"That's the interesting part," she said. "He sent me the message six months ago, right after you went through to the Otherworld."

Mick's eyebrows rose toward his forehead. "But we hadn't even met up with him yet at that point. How could he have possibly known?"

"That's a damn good question, isn't it?" Barbara gave Mick a not-so-gentle shove toward the door. "I suggest you park your steed where no one will bother it and get back in here. I'd like to get Jenna to the hospital before she gives birth in my trailer. The damned thing is already temperamental enough as it is; I'm pretty sure that playing midwife would only make it crankier."


**AS** the dawn crept sleepily through the hospital window, Day sat in a chair next to the institutional bed and watched Jenna nurse her little girl, who she had named Flora after her grandmother. He thought he had never seen anything so amazing in his entire long, long life.

Jenna's pale face was glazed with exhaustion and incandescent with joy, and the baby was about as perfect a Human being as he had ever seen, plump-cheeked and healthy, with her mother's dark hair and icy blue eyes. The one thing she didn't have was a curse hanging over her head, for which he was eternally grateful.

In truth, he was grateful for so many things; he could have listed them all day and not run out. Not being dead—that was a big one, since it turned out that he had much to live for. The success of their mission, being reunited with Gregori, and finally being free of most of the burden of guilt he had carried for the last year. He still needed to seek out Alexei at some point and clear the air between them.

But mostly he was grateful that a woman like Jenna could actually love him, the man who had charmed many but loved none. That was the greatest miracle of all. Especially since he occasionally turned into a light green Paranormal creature.

But somehow she had come to trust him, just as he trusted her. He'd never given his whole heart to anyone other than his brothers before. It felt strange and a little bit unreal, like a fairy tale come to life. He had thought he was saving Jenna, but in the end, she had saved him from the black hole of despair he'd been wallowing in, and given him back at least one of the brothers he thought he had lost forever. Now he just had to convince her to let him stick around so they could take care of each other, and that beautiful baby, forever.

He'd formulated twenty different ways to suggest such a thing—and discarded them all—when the door to the room swung open and a man burst in, a large bouquet of red roses in one hand and a gigantic teddy bear with the price tag still dangling from it in the other. Day's teeth bared in a growl, but the unruffled expression on Jenna's face told him that whoever this was, he wasn't a threat.

The man's suit was expensive, and his haircut probably had been once, although it was overdue for a trim. Lines of strain curved around his mouth and Day could see a hint of desperation in his eyes, despite the bright smile he aimed at Jenna and the baby.

"Jenna!"

"Hello, Stu," Jenna said in a calm voice. "This is a surprise. How did you know we were here?"

*This is Stu? The Stu?* Day didn't think the man meant Jenna any harm, but he scooted his chair a bit closer to her anyway. She patted his arm softly, signaling the beast to stay quiescent.

Stu took another couple of steps into the room, holding the flowers and the bear carelessly, as if he'd forgotten they were there.

"When you disappeared six months ago, I set up an alert for any woman answering your description who showed up in a hospital to give birth around this time. It was the only way I could think of to find you." He shook his head. "Where the hell have you been, Jenna? I threw all my money and power into tracking you down, but it was as if you'd disappeared off the face of the Earth."

Jenna and Day exchanged glances, and Jenna giggled. Of course, it was the literal truth, but there was no way they were telling Stu that.

"It's not funny," Stu said, the anxiety he'd been trying to hide surfacing more strongly. "When I couldn't find you, my father disowned me. I lost everything. The money, the influence, everything. He thinks I'm an idiot. A failure who can't even keep track of one pregnant woman." His voice cracked. "But now I've finally found you again, and if the baby is mine, maybe taking it to my father will earn me my place back."

"Her," Jenna said gently. "Her name is Flora. And I'm sorry, but that is never going to happen."

"I'll give you whatever you want," Stu said. "When my father reinstates me, I'll be able to buy you and the baby anything you could ever desire."

Jenna shook her head, her long dark hair sliding over one shoulder. "No, Stu. You don't have anything I want." She smiled up at Day, her arms tightening around Flora's swaddled little body. "I already have everything I desire."

"But that's my baby!" Stu protested. "You told me so."

"I was wrong," Jenna said, looking her former lover in the eyes. "At the time I said that, I really did believe it. But I've since discovered that the baby's true father is someone else. I'm very sorry."

She shifted the baby into the crook of her elbow and put out her other hand. Day took it, feeling as though he had been kicked by a mule and given the greatest gift in the world, all at the same time. He thought he'd lost everything, and it turned out that he'd been given a miracle.

Stu's patrician face suddenly turned red and blotchy. "You've ruined my life, you bitch! What am I supposed to do now?"

The sound of a throat clearing came from behind him and Barbara's low voice said, "You might want to consider running away before I kick your ass into the next state." She stood in the doorway, all head-to-toe black leather, scowling at Stu with her arms crossed over her chest.

When Stu didn't move, Day rose from his chair and took one step forward, allowing his eyes to glow and his form to shift subtly so that he somehow took up even more space in the small room.

Stu gave an alarmed squeak, dropped the flowers and the stuffed animal, and left in a hurry, rudely shoving his way past Barbara. She raised one eyebrow and twitched a finger, and from beyond the room Day could hear the sound of someone tripping over what sounded like an entire cart full of hospital breakfast trays. The cursing wafted down the hallway for a minute or two and then stopped.

Barbara ignored the mayhem and stepped into the room, holding one hand out to Day. "I heard," she said, a tiny smile hovering at the corner of her mouth. "Congratulations, Dad."

"I'm not really the baby's father," he protested. "You know that."

"Yes, you are," Jenna said in a firm tone. "A child's father is more than the person who happened to be there at the conception. You were there for all the moments that mattered afterward."

"And I will be there for all the ones that matter in the future," Day said, feeling as though he was going to explode with pride and joy. He sat on the edge of the bed and put an arm around Jenna and Flora.

Barbara patted the baby gently on the head, then touched

the tiny nose in wonder with one finger. "Speaking of the future," she said. "Do you two have any idea what you are going to do now?"

They looked at each other, and Jenna nodded slowly.

"I think that once Jenna and the baby are up to traveling, we are going to go to the deep forests of Russia and see if we can find my mother," Day said. "I don't know if she is still alive or not, but if she is, I think she might like to know she has a grandchild. After all, as Gregori said, family is important."

"Maybe she'll be able to give us some insight into Day's new powers," Jenna added. "Something that will help him to figure out the best way to use them."

"Oh?" Barbara said. "Did you have something in particular in mind?" Mischief glinted in her amber eyes.

"Well," Day said, smiling at Jenna, who nodded as though she had read his mind. "Jenna told me once that just because I wasn't a Rider anymore, that didn't mean I couldn't be useful. It seems to me that the Baba Yagas still might have need, from time to time, of a strong and loyal friend. Even if he isn't technically a Rider."

Barbara gave him one of her rare grins and winked at Jenna. "I think that's a great plan," she said. "After all, Baba Yagas have never been all that good with technicalities anyway. Besides . . ."

"Besides?" he asked.

She chuckled. "Besides, I am going to enjoy watching you fall under someone else's charms for a change." A tiny fist closed around her outstretched finger. "I think you've finally met your match, Mikhail Day. I suspect that nothing in either world is ever going to be the same again."

# EPILOGUE

**WHEN** Flora was a month old, Day and Jenna took her to court.

After all, Jenna had promised the Queen that she would return once the baby was born, and it was never a good idea to break a promise to royalty. Especially that royalty.

For the moment, the three of them were living in a small rental property not far from Barbara's farmhouse while they planned out what they were going to do next and adjusted to their new circumstances. Day figured that eventually they would build a home of their own, but at the moment their hands were full enough tending to a very small, very demanding baby, and working with Barbara to explore the boundaries of his new abilities.

Babs and Liam were always happy to entertain the baby, and Babs in particular was relishing her role as honorary elder cousin, so being close by meant they had not only each other, but an extended family as well. It was more than Day would have ever dreamed of, and he gave thanks every day for the

miracle that was his new life. The fact that it was now limited
in length only made every moment that much more precious.
He supposed that was what it was like to be a Human.

When Jenna decided that Flora was old enough to take
through the doorway, they all dressed up in their best finery—
Flora looking particularly adorable in a frilly pink dress covered with embroidered roses—and passed through the closet
in the Airstream to emerge into a glorious meadow filled with
matching blossoms in every shade from the palest blush to
the darkest crimson. A mossy green path led to the castle,
which could be seen in the distance, but still much closer than
usual, as if to make it easier to reach.

"What?" Jenna exclaimed, turning around in circles as
Flora chortled merrily. "How did she know?"

Barbara shook her head, looking half impressed, half re-
signed. "She is the Queen. She always knows."

Day thought that was a bit of an exaggeration, since they
were all well aware that *certain individuals* whose names were
not to be uttered in court had managed to sneak things past
the Queen from time to time. But it was true, she was almost
always aware of what was happening with her subjects. Apparently, she had decided that Flora fell under that heading.

They strolled slowly down the plush corridor, pointing out
the sights to a fascinated Babs and to Flora, who mostly blew
bubbles and gazed about her with the same wonder she displayed for the world on the other side of the doorway.

Once they arrived at court, a glossy purple lizard wearing
a striped black tuxedo ushered them down to a lake nestled
behind the castle. Its waters were a crystalline blue, edged
with lavender shadows where the shallows met the shore.
Lime green frogs and lemon yellow fish jumped over lily pads
in some complicated game involving musical balls and silver
rackets they held in their mouths as they swam. Courtiers in
silk and velvet crowded the waterline, making bets and cheer-
ing on the competitors. The water's clear, clean smell could

be detected even over the clashing perfumes of the ladies (and some lords) of the Queen's entourage.

Overlooking the water, the Queen and her consort sat in throne-like chairs carved from ebony and decorated with gleaming rubies, emeralds, and citrine. As always, Their Majesties were glorious and resplendent, the Queen attired in a flowing violet gown with actual violets growing across the bottom hem, and the King in a mouse gray tunic and purple breeches with lavender hose. The Queen's white hair was piled high on her head with jeweled pins, and an enormous faceted amethyst drop that matched her eyes exactly swung between her perfect breasts.

"Welcome," she said as the functionary bowed the group in. "We are most pleased that you have come to visit Us at last." She actually rose to meet them, a rare honor Day was quite certain had nothing to do with them and everything to do with the tiny babe in Jenna's arms.

"You are all looking quite well," Her Majesty said, nodding her head regally at Barbara and Liam, and venturing a tiny smile for little Babs. Then she ignored them and turned all of her not-insignificant attention on the new parents and their charge.

"She is so very lovely," the Queen said in a wondering tone, putting out a slim hand to touch the baby's cheek. "Worth all the trouble she caused, one supposes."

"Indeed, Your Majesty," Jenna agreed, curtsying the best she could considering her current burden. "And we are most grateful for all your assistance in the matter."

The Queen waved one white hand languidly through the air. "We did nothing more than give you a small space of time in which to arrive at the solution yourselves," she said, although Day could have sworn he saw her wink at Barbara, almost too fast to see.

"What have you named the child?" the King asked from where he sat. "Not one of those foolish modern appellations your people have become so fond of, One hopes. Apple or Pear or something."

Day grinned at him. "I assure you, Sire, we stuck with the traditional. Although I did vote for Turnip. Her first name is Flora, after Jenna's grandmother, who fought so hard to end her family's curse."

"Ah, lovely," the King said. "So her full name is Flora Quinlan? Or, perhaps, Flora Day?" He returned Day's smile, seemingly confident of what the answer would be.

Jenna gazed at the Queen. "If it pleases Your Majesty, we named her Flora Titania Quinlan Day. Mick told me that Titania was one of the names you were known by, and we wanted to acknowledge her connection to this world."

Day held his breath, since you never knew how the Otherworld's volatile sovereign was going to react, but it appeared that Jenna had chosen well, as the Queen's normally solemn face lit up with unambiguous delight.

"Indeed, it pleases Us greatly," the Queen said. "We are quite honored." She looked unaccustomedly hesitant.

"Would you like to hold her, Your Majesty?" Jenna asked.

The Queen nodded, and Jenna put little Flora gently into her arms. One tiny hand rose up to grab on to the amethyst pendant with a grip like steel. Jenna winced as the priceless jewel was tugged downward toward Flora's rosebud lips, but the Queen just laughed, apparently not at all concerned about drool on her jewelry. The King rose and came to join them, standing tall by his lady's side.

"I had forgotten how small they are," he said softly. "And how fragile." He looked at Day. "Are you not afraid you will drop her, or injure her in some way?"

Day exhaled loudly. "You have no idea, Sire. But apparently babies are tougher than they look." He grinned at Jenna. "Or so I am repeatedly told."

The Queen finally handed Flora back to her mother, and she and the King returned to their seats.

"You must come back to visit Us often," she said in a tone

that made it clear that this was a command and not a suggestion. "Perhaps it will be good to remind our people of the joys of having little ones around." She and her consort exchanged a glance that held longing so intimate and raw, Day had to look away.

"We would be honored," Day said.

"Of course you would," responded the Queen, sounding more like her normal self. "Now that we have met Our namesake, perhaps you would all like to join Us in a picnic." She swept her arm out to indicate the many tables laden with food that surrounded the scattered seats and benches nearby. The aromas that rose from the plates were enough to make any five-star restaurant on the other side jealous, filling the air with the scents of exotic spices and hints of sweet caramel, chocolate, and strawberries.

Day bowed low. "That would be very nice, Your Majesties, but I wondered if first it would be possible to ask a small boon."

The royals smiled at each other, looking the tiniest bit smug. "We believe we have anticipated your requests," the King said. "And are happy to grant them."

Requests, plural? They had only one. Still, it was never good to question the King or Queen. He supposed they'd find out soon enough. Hopefully, their exalted majesties hadn't seen fit to gift tiny Flora with her own dragon, or something else equally unsuitable.

The Queen snapped her fingers and a small page ran off to a canopied tent tucked into a sheltered glade nearby. He came back with three people in tow: an attractive elf couple with delicately pointed ears showing through long straight hair as blond as Day's and fine elegant features. The man wore a dark blue velvet tunic and hose and the woman was dressed in a Grecian-style toga made of white silk and decorated with complicated embroidery.

With them was a dark-haired boy of about nine with striking icy blue eyes. The boy simply looked excited to be at

court, but his parents both wore matching expressions of
anxious apprehension, inadequately hidden behind their polite
formal demeanor.

Next to him, Day could feel the tension vibrate off of Jenna
like a lute being strummed. She'd been afraid the Queen
would refuse to let her meet her brother; neither of them had
considered that her Majesty might have anticipated their request and been prepared to grant it on the spot.

"We introduce to you Larissa and Kelvin, and their adopted son Syrius." The Queen inclined her head toward the
couple, and then back toward Jenna and Day. "Larissa and
Kelvin, you are probably acquainted with the former White
Rider, Mikhail Day; this is his lady, Jenna, and her infant
child, Flora Titania. We believe you have much to discuss."
She sat back on her throne-like chair, looking as satisfied as
a cat with cream on its whiskers at having brought them all
together.

Day and Jenna glanced at each other, not sure what to do
next, when the boy walked up to stand in front of Jenna and
bowed, his innocent face alight with curiosity.

"Is it true?" he asked, gazing up at Jenna's features, so
much like his own. "You are my sister from the other side of
the doorway?"

Jenna handed little Flora to Day and knelt down to be at
the boy's level. "It is," she said. "I wasn't sure if your parents
would have told you about me."

The boy nodded solemnly. "After you and the White Rider
saved me from the faery Zilya, they told me all about the
curse and how our mother was forced to give me up. They
said it must have made her sad, but that having me in their
lives has given them much happiness." He looked back over
his shoulder at them, and Larissa nodded, biting at her lip but
encouraging him to continue.

"It did make our mother sad. More sad than you can imagine," Jenna said. "But she would have been very happy to
know that you had people who loved you and took care of

ou. And now you have a sister, too, and a little niece. I hope
at is okay."

Syrius nodded. "It is a good thing to have a sister. Will I
e going to live with you now? On the other side?" A shadow
rossed his face, wiping away his cheerful manner like a
ponge. "I am not sure I would like it there. I have always
ved here." He looked back at his parents again, lower lip
rembling a little, and they took a few steps forward until they
vere standing behind him, one hand each on his narrow
houlders.

Jenna stood up. Day could see all the emotions crowding
er thoughts, but they had already discussed this moment
nany times, and he knew what she was going to say.

"You love him very much, don't you?" she said to Larissa
nd Kelvin.

Kelvin's visage was grim, like a man facing a fatal blow.
We do. We are sorry for the tragedy that has befallen your
amily, and we know we should have turned away the faery
vhen she came to us all those years ago with an infant in her
rms and lies on her lips, asking for gold and favors in return."
Iis hand tightened on his son's shoulder until the boy let out
muffled squeak of complaint. "But he was so beautiful and
ve wanted a child so much."

A tear trembled on the edge of Larissa's pale lashes. "We
ave raised him from that day onward and given him all a
oy could want. He is well treated and treasured and knows
nly this world and us as his parents. Please, please, don't
ake him away from us, I beg of you. We offer you all that we
ave, knowing it can never be equal to his value. Please do
ot take our son from us."

The Queen leaned forward, her face as calm and unreveal-
ng as the lake behind them. "You have the right, Jenna. He
s your kin, wrongfully stolen from your family. If you choose
o reclaim him, We will not stand in your way."

The courtiers who had been watching the entire scene
nfold all grew so silent, Day could hear the grass growing

under his feet—although admittedly, in the Otherworld, grass grew with greater than usual exuberance. Even the betting stopped, although those in the court tended to wager on anything at all. Immortality could grow boring after a while.

Jenna leaned down and hugged the boy, her brother for whom she had longed her entire life. And then she gave him a gentle shove in the direction of the two who stood behind him.

"I know what it is like to lose someone you love," she said to Kelvin and Larissa in a soft voice. "I fought Zilya so she would not take my child from me; I do not have it in me to do such a thing to another." She gave them a tremulous smile. "He is your son. It is enough for me to know that he is cared for and loved. And perhaps, you will allow me to visit you from time to time, and get to know him better?"

Larissa threw her arms around Jenna's neck and kissed her soundly on both cheeks. "Thank you! Thank you! You are welcome anytime, I assure you." Kelvin was more restrained, but Day could see the relief draining the strength from his limbs as he put arms that trembled around his wife and child.

"We look forward to becoming better acquainted with our new family," he said with hard-won dignity.

The boy beamed from ear to ear. "I get to stay *and* I get a new sister? This is the best day ever!"

"It is a good day, isn't it?" Jenna said, smiling at Day. He was so proud of her strength and her wisdom, but most of all of the huge heart that had attracted him to her in the first place.

"A very good day indeed," the Queen said, her voice ringing like a bell through the clearing. "Well chosen, young Jenna. We are quite pleased with how all has unfolded."

Jenna curtsied, unobtrusively brushing away a few stray tears. "Thank you, Your Majesty. So I have your permission to come from time to time to visit my brother and his parents?"

The Queen gestured to one of her ladies in waiting, who

came forward bearing an indigo velvet cushion with a silver bracelet sitting atop it. The bracelet was wide and gleaming, carved with mysterious runes.

"More than Our permission," the Queen said. "Our blessing. We have had this token created especially for you, so that you may come and go to Our lands at will. We consider you one of Our subjects now, with all the rights and obligations that come with such an honor."

"Oh boy," Barbara muttered from her spot not far from where they stood. "That could get interesting."

Day thought things were quite interesting enough, thank you. "You are most gracious as always, Your Majesty," he said, as the lady-in-waiting presented the bracelet to Jenna. "But we have imposed upon your hospitality long enough. It is time to return to our lives on the other side of the doorway." He glanced down at the droopy-lidded baby in his arms. "I believe your namesake is ready for her nap."

The Queen gave him a slight smile, amethyst eyes glittering. "Ah, but you cannot leave yet, White Rider. We still have another request to grant, do you not recall?"

Jenna and Day exchanged bemused glances. "I don't believe we made a second request, Your Majesty," Jenna said. "Begging Your Majesty's pardon."

"I'm afraid this one is down to me," Barbara said, stepping forward.

Day was completely confused. "What?"

The King smiled at Day. "We have long searched for a gift that would be adequate to thank you for your long service to this kingdom and to the Baba Yagas. It was Barbara who gave Us a suggestion for something you might wish to have. Or should I say, some*one*."

He gestured for Day to turn around.

Behind him there stood a figure he had not seen for more years than he could count—a tall woman of upright posture, with pale green hair in many tiny braids that reached below her waist, wearing a loose tunic and trousers of supple leather dyed in multiple shades of greens and browns so that their wearer would vanish into the forest like a ghost. On her face was a smile so bright, it almost outshone the light of the moons and artificial sun overhead.

"Mother!" he said, so stunned he couldn't move. Jenna plucked the baby out of his arms before he could drop her and gave him a little nudge.

He had sent out inquiries, but had been unable to go out and look for her himself, unwilling to venture into the depths of the Siberian forests until Flora was a little older. Of course, even with her limited access to the other side of the doorway, the Queen had resources well beyond any he could ever have hoped to muster. No doubt she had simply sent out a royal request to all the nymphs and tree sprites who had remained behind, until one of them had been able to search out his mother's hidden retreat.

"My darling Mikhail," the woman said, reaching out both hands and clasping his, before pulling him into a bone-crushing embrace. "It has been too long. I am glad to see you looking so well. When the Queen told me of your ordeal, I was beside myself that I had not been here for you during your long recovery."

"It wasn't your fault, Mother," he said, embracing her in return. He was rocked by the depth of his emotions at this unexpected reunion. "I haven't been very good at keeping in touch."

Barbara gave a cough that sounded suspiciously like "*Understatement*," and he raised his head to glare at her over his mother's shoulder. As one might expect, the Baba Yaga was completely unimpressed.

"Family is important," she said to Day, giving him the full force of her basilisk stare. She gestured at Liam and little Babs, standing next to her, and then at Jenna and the baby, and beyond that to the elf couple and their son. "It can come in all different shapes and sizes, and often isn't at all what we expected, but it is one of the most important things in the world." She smiled up at Liam. "A Human sheriff taught me that, among other things."

Day nodded. "I have been learning that particular lesson myself," he said. "And I hope that you will still allow me to consider you family, for all that I am no longer your White Rider."

Barbara flushed and punched him on the upper arm, her version of a full-body hug. "I would be most unhappy if you did not view yourself as part of my own extended family," she said in a suspiciously gruff voice. "And you will *always* be my White Rider, no matter what."

Jenna interrupted what was threatening to become an embarrassingly emotional moment between two people who hated overt displays of sentiment by taking a step forward to stand next to Day and his mother.

"I'm Jenna," she said. "Your son's fiancée. And this is Flora, your granddaughter." She held the baby up and offered her to Day's mother, who took Flora into her arms with exaggerated care.

"I have a grandchild?" she breathed, joy suffusing her plain features and transmuting them into beauty. "How is that possible?" Her naturally stern expression dissolved into a broad smile as the baby discovered the tiny beads hidden within her many braids and chortled in delight.

Day opened his mouth to explain, but Jenna just shook her head. "It was a miracle, really. A fairy tale with a happy ending for everyone. Now we have you, and our family is complete."

"Not quite," Day said sadly. For him, two people were still missing.

No one had heard from Gregori since he had come to visit Jenna and the new baby in the hospital and then disappeared again.

When Day had returned to the cabin by the lake, it had been deserted. No sign of Gregori, not even his unusually tame salamander. The stove had been as cold as a stone and the blankets were neatly folded at the end of the bed.

Day had left a note for his brother, asking for him to get in touch when he could, and wrapped it around the brightly hued phoenix feather that was all he had to leave as a thank-you for Gregori's help. Alexei was still absent as well, although there had been rumors of a huge man seen brawling in taverns and bars from Alaska to Southern California.

"Ah, We knew there was yet something else," the Queen said, her interest already half returned to the competing fish and frogs below. She was not known for her long attention span, and emotional moments gave her indigestion. "We were given this note to pass on to you on this day." Her regal face looked momentarily bemused. "Although We are still not certain how he would be sure that all would unfold as it has. One suspects there is another interesting story to come."

She handed a scroll to a small page in a silken tunic and trousers, who ran to give it over to Day. It bore flowing black lettering on red paper, written in Gregori's distinctive hand.

*My Dear Brother Mikhail,*

*Congratulations on your new family and on finding your mother. I have no doubt it was a fascinating experience for everyone involved. In fact, you have inspired me; perhaps I will go looking for my own. I have heard it said that she was such a powerful shamaness that she found a way to transcend death and still lives somewhere with her disciples. It is hard to believe such a thing would be possible, after all these years, but stranger things have happened. We are both living proof of that.*

*Whether or not I attempt such a search, I have decided it is time for me to stop hiding in the Otherworld. I am not finding that which I am seeking here anyway. I, too, need to find some means to make peace with my new life and try to discover a path back to my lost inner balance.*

*If such a thing can even be achieved, which I am no longer convinced is true. My faith has deserted me, and*

*I do not know quite how to make my way through the world without it.*

*I wish you all good fortune in your new life. Oh, and you asked me once if I had seen any signs that I might be developing any sort of strange new abilities, such as your shape-changing gift. I am beginning to suspect that the answer to that question is yes.*

*Yours affectionately,*
*Your eldest brother,*
*Gregori Sun*

# CHAPTER 1

**GREGORI** Sun stared at his reflection in the spotty bathroom mirror of a cheap motel: waist-length straight dark hair pulled back in a tail, black eyes set at a slight slant over the flat cheekbones of his Mongolian ancestors, and the Fu Manchu mustache he'd worn since he'd become a man, longer ago than anyone who met him might imagine. The harsh glare of the light fixture glinted off the straight razor in his right hand. It trembled almost imperceptibly, a leftover echo of the debilitating damage he'd taken a year ago at the hands of the deranged and powerful witch who had once been his ally and a trusted friend.

A deep breath and a moment's focused attention banished the tremor and steadied his hand for the task ahead. Sun entertained the wistful thought that it would be nice if all his other remaining issues could be dealt with as easily. But he was not a man who had ever taken the easy way, even if there had been one available, which there was not. Hence this next step.

Before he could change his mind, the razor flashed—once,

twice, three times. Black hair fell into the sink, its darkness a stark contrast against the pitted white porcelain, just as his former life was a stark contrast to his present existence and his future path. The acrid smell of the motel's antiseptic cleaner echoed his mood.

Now the face staring back at him seemed to belong to a stranger. Clean-shaven, with hair barely long enough to be held back by the leather thong he wore, the man in the mirror seemed somehow younger and more vulnerable, although he still wore Sun's habitual aura of impenetrable calm. As with much else in Sun's life these days, it was more semblance than reality.

The Buddhist monastery he was entering didn't require first-year novices to shave their heads, any more than it mandated any formal clothing. Students were only expected to obey the basic rules and follow the regimen of study, practice, and service. Sun had laid aside his traditional red leathers and silks anyway, as another way of putting aside the past, and now wore loose black wool pants and a black cotton turtleneck more suited to the frigid Minnesota winters.

The commitment he was making felt worthy of a symbolic sacrifice, even if no one was aware of it but him.

This was a new beginning in search of a new man; he couldn't go into it looking the same as he had for more than a thousand years. Sun was so changed on the inside, he barely knew who he was anymore. His outside might as well reflect that.


**THE** alley reeked of rancid garbage, burning grease from the Chinese restaurant at the far end, and other pungent odors best not examined too closely, the smell so strong it almost seemed like a solid presence. An abandoned collection of ramshackle cardboard, once the temporary shelter for a home-less person, continued its slow decaying crumble down the brick side of the building to her left, and rats scrabbled over some half-frozen garage in an overturned can to her right.

Ciera Evans ignored them all as she concentrated on her silent pursuit of the man she'd followed for the last six nights. He vanished into the back of a dimly lit building, the door gaping open long enough to reveal a smoky interior and a circle of men sitting around a faded green table playing poker. Drunken laughter spilled out into the night and then cut off with a slam that even the rats ignored. It was that kind of neighborhood.

Not what she was looking for, she thought. Not tonight. But soon.

She backed away, careful not to trip over anything in the alley as she tucked a stray lock of dark curly hair under the hoodie that kept her reasonably warm on this cold Minneapolis night while also masking her distinctive features. The worn brown leather jacket she wore on top of the hoodie fit right into the usual local attire, so she wasn't too worried about being noticed on her way back to the car.

A couple of blocks away, though, Ciera realized she was being stalked in turn. Ironic, really. And a little inconvenient, but she could feel the pulse speed up in her throat and admitted, to herself at least, that she was almost eager to be forced into action after long nights of watching and waiting and doing nothing.

The two men who followed her no doubt thought she was easy prey. They were about to find out just how wrong they were.

"Hand over your money and your phone and nobody needs to get hurt," said the bigger of the two toughs as they closed in on her. His heavy boots clattered on the icy sidewalk, the same sound that had alerted Ciera to her unwanted escort.

"That's what you think," Ciera said, using a low raspy voice to disguise her sex. A twist of her wrists sent her fighting sticks sliding out of her sleeves and into her hands, and she set her feet in a stance that was both rooted and flexible. "Last chance to walk away, boys."

The shorter man, underdressed for the weather in ripped pants and holey sneakers, shook his shaved head. "Not a chance, dude. In case you haven't noticed, there are two of us and only one of you, and you're kind of scrawny. A couple of pieces of wood aren't going to save you." He nodded to his friend and they both moved in closer, scruffy faces wearing matching expressions of stubble-adorned menace.

"Too true," Ciera whispered, lower than they were likely to hear. "But a couple of pieces of wood and years of self-defense classes will go a long way."

She didn't bother to show off—a rookie mistake—attacking instead in a flurry of kicks and hits aimed at vulnerable knees, elbows, and collarbones that left the men lying groaning on the ground behind her. She shoved the fighting sticks back up her sleeves and kept on walking without a backward glance.

A few twists and turns later and she was back at the car she always used for her evening forays. It couldn't be traced to her since it was registered in the name of a woman long dead. A practical vehicle, it also served to remind her of why she did what she did. The dead woman had been her friend. More than her friend—her savior. Now Ciera carried on her mission, because it was the only way she could repay the debt she owed. And because she'd made a promise to the only person in her life who had ever kept their word to her.

Back in her apartment, she stripped off the anonymous hoodie and stared at herself in the bathroom mirror. She wasn't sure she recognized the woman staring back at her. It was hard to say which one was real—the face she showed the world during the day or the one she hid at night. Maybe neither. But if there was another Ciera beyond those two, she wasn't sure *what* that woman would look like. Or if she'd even like her if she ever had a chance to find out.

# CHAPTER 2

**SUN** unpacked his few belongings into the plain pine dresser that was one of only three pieces of furniture in his narrow room at the *Shira-in Shashin* Monastery, the other two being a twin bed covered with a wool blanket and a wooden meditation bench. Once he'd been forced to admit that he was unable to regain his spiritual balance in the solitude of the Otherworld, Gregori had crossed through one of the few doorways between that enchanted place and the more mundane world of Humans, and searched for a likely alternative.

After much thought, he'd decided to become a Buddhist monk, hoping that the peaceful introspective path would finally enable him to find the connection to the spiritual world he'd lost when the crazy Baba Yaga Brenna had tortured him and his half brothers until they were nearly mad and on the brink of death.

In the end, the *true* Baba Yagas, Barbara, Beka, and Bella, had rescued them, with the help of Barbara's dragon-dog Chudo-Yudo and a hefty dose of the magical elixir known as the Water of Life and Death. But even the powerful witches hadn't been able to get to them in time to save their immortality, and now he, Mikhail Day, and Alexei Knight were as mortal as the Humans they had chosen to live among. Mortal and more than a little bit broken.

It was a new experience for Gregori, who had spent most of his very long life in a state of poised, calm control, at one with the natural world and in harmony with the universal energy that surrounded him. He had always supposed that this was in his nature, although nurture had certainly played a part, since his mother had been a powerful Mongolian shamaness. Now that he had lost that connection and balance, he questioned everything he'd ever been. And had no idea of what he would become.

Gregori hoped that embracing the monastic lifestyle would give him back the equilibrium he had always taken for granted. At the very least, it should be quiet; quite the change from the years he and his brothers had spent as the Riders, companions and warriors for the Baba Yagas, who traveled together in between assignments, brawling and drinking and generally enjoying one another's company.

Those days were behind him now, for better or for worse, and the sooner he accepted it, the better off he'd be.

Broken bones eventually mended. Broken spirits were a much more difficult and lengthy matter.

Sun had chosen the *Shira-in Shashin* Monastery for a number of reasons, including its somewhat non-traditional approach, its roots in Yellow Shamanism, which sprang from the same Mongolian soil that he had, and its location in Minneapolis.

Admittedly, the location wouldn't have been a selling point for most people, with its bitterly cold winters and abundant snowfall. But Sun enjoyed the stark beauty of the landscape, which reminded him of the Siberian steppes where he and his long-lost mother had taken long treks with her disciples when he was a child. Its proximity to the Wilson Library, part of the University of Minnesota, was the other basis for his choice, since he thought it was his best chance of actually tracking her down. If she was still alive, which even he realized was unlikely in the extreme, given the many centuries that had passed since last he'd seen her.

Still, as someone who had spent his life in the company of Russian fairy-tale witches and their Chudo-Yudo dragon companions, traversing the boundaries between the Human world and an enchanted land filled with faeries, ogres, and other mystical creatures, Gregori Sun knew better than most that unlikely was not the same thing as impossible.

He had already made the decision to enter a monastery; it was possible that a rare moment of sentimentality had influenced his choice as to which one. Either way, the *Shira-in Shashin* program offered him both discipline and freedom, a vital combination.

The expectations for a layperson living at the monastery were simple; hours spent in meditation and study, following the general rules of the residence (no alcohol, drugs, sex, or violence), and performing some form of community service. Other than that, his time was his own, which would allow him to pursue the knowledge he sought.

It was assumed that most who entered would eventually find the constraints of the spiritual life to be unappealing and leave. Those who did not would be allowed to continue the long path that would lead to becoming a monk.

Sun just hoped to find some kind of peace and perhaps a place to live out the rest of his life. Giving up the temptations of the outside world was no hardship at all. If anything, it would be a relief. There was nothing out there for him anymore.


**CIERA** was doing some research on the computer at her desk when someone cleared his throat gently. She started, dropping the pen she was holding so that it hit the desk's cluttered surface with a muffled thud, rolling from there onto the white tile floor. She prided herself on her ability to be aware of her surroundings at all times; she couldn't remember the last time someone had approached her without her sensing their presence. And yet a man stood in front of her desk, and she hadn't even known he was there.

Of course, now that she saw him, he was impossible to miss.

The dark hair and sharp Asian planes of his face were attractive—maybe even striking—but there was something more than mere handsomeness about him. Some might have thought his expression stern, but Ciera thought he had a kind of poised, self-contained air that made him stand out from most of the people she met, and yet there was a sadness in his black eyes that made her instinctively want to reach out to soothe whatever it was that had caused such pain.

The strength of her reaction caught her by surprise. Men weren't a part of her life, not outside of professional interactions, anyway. She'd made that choice a long time ago and never for one moment regretted it. Until now. She ducked under the desk and scooped up her fallen pen, using the action to get a grip on herself. *It's pheromones or something like that,* she told herself sternly. *A chemical reaction at the back of your brain. Ignore it and it will go away. At least as soon as he does.*

She sat up, back straight as she put the writing implement down with a decisive click, and put one hand up reflexively to make sure that her unruly kinky-curly hair was still firmly tucked into the neat bun she always wore it in at work.

"Good afternoon," she said in a pleasant voice. "Can I help you with something?" *There, see? Nothing but business.*

"I hope so," the man said, his voice smooth and deep and touched with the hint of an accent. Russian, she thought, although from his looks she would have expected maybe Japanese or Chinese.

There were plenty of foreigners who did research at the Wilson Library, with its many special collections covering such esoteric areas as the Ames Library of South Asia and the East Asian Library, both of which were part of her areas of expertise, as was the Bell Library located on the fourth floor, which housed non-circulating rare books, maps, and manuscripts that documented trade and cross-cultural interaction throughout the world prior to around 1800. Maybe he was a professor she hadn't met yet, or some kind of visiting expert. He certainly didn't seem like a student, although these days, you never could tell. She thought he might be in his thirties, or possibly a youthful forty.

"I was told that you might be able to assist me with some research I am doing," he said, bowing slightly with both hands in front of his chest. "I am afraid it is somewhat eclectic in nature, covering a wide range of obscure topics, but I will be happy to do the digging myself if you can simply point me in the right direction."

Ciera tried to ignore the fact that something about the timbre of his voice sent a frisson of heat down her spine in a most disconcerting manner. "Some of our collections are only available by appointment," she said in her best impersonal librarian tone, "but I'm sure we can help you find what you need. Can you give me some idea of the areas you were interested in?"

"I am looking for references to a particular obscure Mongolian shamaness named Iduyan and the sect of worshippers and disciples who followed her, as well as anything on modern shamanism in a fairly widespread area—Mongolia, Russia, and China, to start out with. In addition, I need any information there might be on the legend of Shangri-La or related lost cities."

Ciera blinked. "That *is* a rather strange and eclectic set of search parameters. It might take some time to turn up anything useful, assuming there is anything to be found at all.

Some of the items you are looking for might be in the East Asian collection, I suppose. Either way, most of the books and maps you'll need can't be taken out of the building, so I'm afraid you'll have to do the bulk of your research here. But there are a number of spaces in the library where you can have relative privacy and quiet."

The man nodded politely. "There are many worse places to spend one's time," he said softly. "I have been in most of them. I am certain it will be a pleasure to spend a portion of my days here."

Another shiver fluttered down her spine and she reminded herself again that she wasn't interested in men. Especially not mysterious men who had an aura of danger around them like this one did.

"I'll write down a few books you can start with," she said, pulling a pad out of the top drawer. These days most of the people she dealt with would whip out a tablet or a smartphone to take down the information, but he didn't strike her as the electronics type somehow. "And I'll compile a more detailed list over the next day or two. Can I get your name?"

"Gregori," he said. "Gregori Sun." That hint of an accent made the name seem exotic and foreign, although his English was flawless. Maybe a second-generation immigrant.

"Very good, Mr. Sun. I'm Ciera Evans. If I'm not here when you come back, I'll leave a folder for you at the front desk. I hope you find everything you're looking for." She handed him the list, then turned purposely back to her computer.

She barely heard him when he muttered, more to himself than to her, "I suspect that is very unlikely."

SUN was so focused on his search, he hardly noticed the librarian behind the desk, other than to note that she had seemingly taken the stereotype to heart, complete with drab, modest clothing, square black-rimmed glasses, and hair pulled tightly back into an unflattering bun. A pity, really, since she had the potential to be quite beautiful, but it was just as well, since he couldn't afford distractions, even abstract ones. It was bad enough that he was already splitting his focus between his path to spiritual enlightenment and his search for his mother—which admittedly, was at odds with his goal to detach from the world, but that was the way these things went.

With any luck, he would be spending all of his time at the library with his nose buried in obscure reference books and dusty maps, and any other distractions would be kept to a minimum. Especially oddly intriguing ones wearing glasses.


**IRONICALLY,** Sun probably wouldn't even have recognized her when he saw her later that evening, if it hadn't been for those same glasses. The drab professional attire had been replaced by equally nondescript jeans and a black hoodie, the dark hair was still pulled back, although this time into a tightly woven braid, from which tiny curls escaped at her nape and around the edges of her forehead. Only the glasses and the slightly prickly exterior remained the same.

Plus, of course, he hadn't expected to run into her at the homeless shelter.

He'd been assigned by his teacher at the monastery to do his community service at a soup kitchen in Minneapolis, one attached to a homeless shelter that served many local homeless youths, along with a number of mothers with children. He wasn't sure which population was more heartbreaking. Sun wasn't sure if the volunteer work was intended to test a novice's ability to be compassionate without becoming emotionally involved, but he could see how that would be a challenge for many.

For someone like Sun, who had lived more than a thousand years and watched countless shorter lives come and go, it was a little less challenging. He had had to learn to keep a certain distance long ago.

What he found so fascinating was that someone like this librarian seemed to have learned it too.

He studied her from across the room while listening with half his attention to the head of the shelter explaining how the food kitchen worked, and what Sun's duties would be as a volunteer. Despite what he thought were attempts to blend into her surroundings, almost chameleon-like when he factored in her completely different appearance at the library that afternoon, she stood out like a peony among a field of daisies.

It wasn't just her beauty, although that certainly drew the eye, no matter how much she tried to disguise it with plain clothing and lack of makeup. Wide lips and dark, slightly kinky hair spoke of an African American contribution, while the high cheekbones and fine features suggested some Native roots. The light hazel eyes were probably Caucasian, but that tawny skin was a shade no white person ever achieved. Either way, no matter her origins, she was striking and unusual looking, as though someone had taken the best parts of a varied gene pool and combined them into a rare and gorgeous creation.

One that she clearly made an effort to downplay, Sun thought, based on her attire and attitude. She seemed friendly enough as she dished some unidentified brownish mass onto the plates of those who paraded past her with their trays, and chatted lightly with the people standing beside her on the serving line. A restrained smile flickered over her lips from time to time, and she made a small boy laugh at some joke she'd told him. But Sun's second sight, a dubious and erratic gift most likely left over from his massive dose of the Water of Life and Death, showed him her aura as a subdued dark silver glow that reminded him of nothing so much as a suit of armor. On the surface, she might seem as open as one of the books at her library, but the reality he saw was as closed down and defensive as a castle with its drawbridge up and its moat filled with alligators.

Intriguing.

None of his business, but intriguing nonetheless.

Eventually, the director of the shelter, a soft-spoken man named Philip Roman with the muscular build and battered face of a former boxer, finished up his instructions and brought him over to join the others.

"Gregori, these are a few of our regular volunteers." He pointed at a stocky woman in her fifties with short-cropped iron-gray hair and a tattoo of a broken chain wound around one wrist. "This is Elisabeth. She was one of our clients, once upon a time, went back to school, got her GED, and now she has a steady job and helps out here when she can. It's good to have a success story, to show it can be done, you know."

Elisabeth rolled her eyes, probably tired of being introduced as a shining example, but she gave Sun a cheerful enough grin anyway. "Welcome to the asylum, where most days it is impossible to tell the inmates from the guards. As long as you're not afraid of hard work and the occasional knife fight, you'll do just fine."

Phillip shook his head. "Elisabeth," he scolded, sounding like he was trying not to laugh. "Try not to scare away our new volunteer. You know it is hard enough to find them in the first place." He turned back to Gregori. "Elisabeth is exaggerating. We don't allow weapons or fighting here, and for the most part, to be honest, the folks who come in don't have the energy to waste on making trouble. They just want food and maybe a warm bed for the night."

He indicated the tall, skinny young man standing next to her, whose long straggly ponytail and blond beard made him look like a California hippy who had somehow taken a wrong turn and ended up in chilly Minnesota by mistake. "This is Bryon. He's a student at the University who is studying sociology."

"Extra credit, man," Bryon said with a brisk nod. "Plus, you know, it's cool. Makes me feel a lot better about my crappy dorm room and all." He held out one bony hand for Gregori to shake, wiping it off on the apron he wore first, in case the day's meal was clinging to the plastic glove that enclosed it.

"And this is Ciera," Phillip continued. "She works at the University library."

"I know," Sun said, inclining a tiny bow in her direction. "I actually met Ms. Evans there earlier, when I went to do some research. She was kind enough to help me, although it is an unexpected pleasure to see her twice in one day."

Ciera's expression grew even more shuttered as she stared at him. "It's quite the coincidence, all right." Her full lips pressed together as she turned away to serve a group of teens wearing clothes almost identical to hers, but not as clean.

The odor of unwashed bodies warred temporarily with the aroma of overcooked institutional dinner and stewed vats of coffee, making Gregori long for the sparkling scent of the forests. Or at least, the solitude of his barren room back at the monastery.

Still, this was what he'd signed on for. And at least he had a clean, warm place to go back to, which was more than most of these folks had. Not to mention the freedom to go elsewhere, if he decided he'd made the wrong choice.

"Very nice to meet you all," he said. "I look forward to being of service."

"Excellent," Elisabeth said with another grin, this one wide enough to reveal a missing molar. "There's a mountain of dishes in the kitchen, just waiting for someone brave enough to tackle them." She waggled unkempt brows at him. "Think you're up to the challenge?"

"I would have preferred the knife fight," Gregori said with perfect honesty. "But I am certain I can manage the dishes almost as well."

"A man of many talents," Elisabeth said. "You'll fit in just fine around here." For a moment, Gregori thought he saw a ghostly image echoed behind her—a younger, thinner Elisabeth with the clothes of a well-to-do housewife and the expression of a woman imprisoned by a life that was slowly devouring her soul. Then it was gone, and only the solid, present-day woman remained.

"Indeed," Sun said softly. "But am I one of the inmates or one of the guards?" Then he walked toward the kitchen to do battle with a stack of plates and his own demons.

ALSO FROM BESTSELLING AUTHOR
# DEBORAH BLAKE

# WICKEDLY DANGEROUS

## A BABA YAGA NOVEL

Older than she looks and powerful beyond measure, Barbara Yager no longer has much in common with the mortal life she left behind long ago. Posing as an herbalist and researcher, she travels the country with her faithful (mostly) dragon-turned-dog in an enchanted Airstream, fulfilling her duties as a Baba Yaga and avoiding any possibility of human attachment.

But when she is summoned to find a missing child, Barbara suddenly finds herself caught up in a web of deceit and an unexpected attraction to the charming but frustrating Sheriff Liam McClellan.

Now, as Barbara fights both human enemies and Otherworld creatures to save the lives of three innocent children, she discovers that her most difficult battle may be with her own heart...

"An addicting plot combined with a unique adventure and an intelligent, pragmatic heroine kept me glued to the page. I never had so much fun losing sleep!"

—Maria V. Snyder, *New York Times* bestselling author of the Healer series

deborahblakeauthor.com
penguin.com

M1737T1015